Pra   **s**

"[A] steamy, high-octane thriller. . . . A story full of edge-of-your-seat thrills and unexpected twists, all perfectly underscored by a toe-curling romance."
—*Entertainment Weekly*

"McCarty's first installment in her Lost Platoon series—*Going Dark*—features betrayal, murder, and ecoterrorism. The nonstop action and love story are guaranteed to keep you turning the pages to find out what happens to Dean and Annie."
—*#1 New York Times* bestselling author Catherine Coulter

"A sexy thrill ride from start to finish. Steamy and suspenseful, *Going Dark* is a must read."
—*#1 New York Times* bestselling author Jennifer L. Armentrout

"McCarty's exciting contemporary series launch will not disappoint fans of her historical Highlands romances."
—*Publishers Weekly*

"McCarty's foray into romantic suspense is nonstop action from beginning to end."   —RT Book Reviews

"Readers will find it hard to wait for the next in the series."   —*Booklist* (starred review)

OUT OF TIME

THE LOST PLATOON

Monica McCarty

JOVE
New York

A JOVE BOOK
Published by Berkley
An imprint of Penguin Random House LLC
375 Hudson Street, New York, New York 10014

Copyright © 2018 by Monica McCarty
Excerpt from *Going Dark* copyright © 2017 by Monica McCarty
Penguin Random House supports copyright. Copyright fuels creativity, encourages
diverse voices, promotes free speech, and creates a vibrant culture. Thank you for buying
an authorized edition of this book and for complying with copyright laws by not
reproducing, scanning, or distributing any part of it in any form without permission.
You are supporting writers and allowing Penguin Random House to continue to
publish books for every reader.

A JOVE BOOK, BERKLEY, and the BERKLEY & B colophon
are registered trademarks of Penguin Random House LLC.

ISBN: 9780399587740

First Edition: December 2018

Printed in the United States of America
1   3   5   7   9   10   8   6   4   2

Cover art: *Ranch* by ipkoe / Getty Images;
Storm clouds by Herianus Herianus / EyeEm
Book design by Laura K. Corless

*To my longtime friends and
fellow Hawaii writer retreaters,
Jami, Nyree, and Veronica.
You guys are the best.
Looking forward to a "Four Non Blondes"
repeat next year.*

Prologue

"What are we gonna do now, sir?"

It was Travis Hart who posed the question, but there were five gazes pinned on Scott, waiting for his response. Scott was the officer in charge. The leader. The one who was going to get them out of this shit creek without the proverbial paddle. FUBAR, the age-old military acronym for "fucked up beyond all recognition," was putting it mildly.

They were lucky to be alive. Even if it didn't feel that way. Instinctively, his hand went to the circle of metal in the chest pocket of the high-tech tactical black uniform they wore for clandestine missions. He didn't even know why he'd brought it with him. An engagement ring wasn't exactly something you carried on a mission, like a blowout kit or extra ammo. A good luck charm, maybe? If so, it had worked.

For six of them.

The platoon had been on a highly covert, no-footprint recon mission to Russia in search of doomsday weapons that broke God-knew-how-many laws and treaties. It had seen over half their team killed in a missile strike that would have killed all of them if the girlfriend Scott wasn't supposed to have hadn't warned them of the trap. Six of them had survived the missile strike with little more than the clothes on their backs. Now they had to find their way out of BF Russia without letting anyone know they were alive—good guys or bad—because they didn't know whom to trust.

Just another day at the office for SEAL Team Nine.

After fifteen years in service, Scott should have been ready for something like this. First he'd had four years as a midshipman at the Naval Academy—his last year as brigade commander. That had been followed by twenty-four of the most miserable weeks of his life in BUD/S, three weeks of jump school, and twenty-six more slightly less hellish weeks of SEAL Qualification Training. Add another two years of training, workups, and overseas deployments with Team One as a JG (lieutenant junior grade), six months of sniper school, and finally, after another two-year tour, he'd had the brutal six-month selection process that had gotten him into the tier-one (aka highest level Special Mission Unit) SEAL team.

Scott had jumped from airplanes at high altitudes too many times to count, run until his feet were bloody stumps, swum in icy-cold water until he thought his fingers and other more important appendages might fall off, gone without sleep and food for too many hours to remember, been deployed to more shit hole corners of this world than anyone in their right mind would want to see, and led hundreds of successful missions in the past five years as lieutenant (as of a few months ago as lieutenant commander) of one of America's most elite special operations units. He'd been shot at, stabbed, ambushed—

he'd even gone down in a helicopter once. Along the way he'd picked up two Bronze Stars for valor, a Purple Heart, and enough ribbons and commendation medals to fill out the jacket pocket of his dress blues.

But none of his qualifications or years of training and experience had prepared him for how to get six military-aged men—who even with longer hair and beards weren't going to pass for locals—from an isolated coal-mining city north of the Arctic Circle to safety a few thousand miles away, without travel documents, supplies, or anyone to call for help. Hell, they didn't even have phones to make that call right now. They'd tossed everything electronic they had into the fiery explosion that had killed their eight teammates. Ghosts couldn't leave electronic footprints, and they didn't want anyone to be able to track them.

It was almost axiomatic that SEAL commanders always had a plan. They had backup plans for their backup plans. But possibly being betrayed by someone on the inside wasn't exactly covered in SEAL Officer 101, and Scott was in full-on improvise mode here.

As he was pretty sure "no fucking clue" was not what these guys needed or wanted to hear right now, Scott knew he'd better figure it out fast. He'd gotten them this far, through two days of some of what had to be the most inhospitable, bug-infested countryside known to man. He'd get them through the rest. Challenge was what he excelled at. It was what had drawn him to be a SEAL, and then to the elite echelons of the tier-one Team Nine.

They all had a love of challenge in common—officer and enlisted. These guys could handle anything he threw at them. They were the best. He ought to know. With blood, sweat, and a few tears of pain, he'd honed the operators of Team Nine into the finest unit in all of US Special Operations. They were the president's go-to force when mistakes and failure weren't an option. Even shell-shocked, suffering various levels of injury, hungry, exhausted, and mourning the deaths of their teammates, Scott knew if anyone had what it took to get out of a goat fuck like this, it was Senior Chief Dean Baylor and Special Warfare Operators Michael Ruiz, John Donovan, Steve Spivak, and Travis Hart.

The special warfare operators of Team Nine knew how to do their jobs. And he knew how to do his. He made life-and-death decisions all the time; it came with the job. But losing eight men didn't, and Scott was still reeling. They all were. But right now he had to focus on keeping the rest of his men alive. That meant projecting confidence and acting as if this weren't pretty much worst-possible-scenario, one-wrong-move-and-we're-dead territory.

"We hold tight for the time being," Scott said. They were safe enough in this apartment building. They'd had their pick of abandoned buildings in the old center of town, which was now essentially a ghost town located across the river from the current city center. Although from the looks of it, the new city center wasn't going to be far behind the old. Vorkuta had definitely seen better days. The once-thriving city had dwindled in the past decades from over two hundred thousand people to about seventy thousand.

But in this remote corner of the world, even among seventy thousand, six strangers were going to stick out—especially non-Russian-looking-and-speaking strangers. Well, except for one. Thank God, they had Spivak, whose grandparents were Ukrainian and had passed on their language. Spivak's lineage also gave him a good cover story. He was a Ukrainian sent to Vorkuta to work as a diver on the Nord Stream gas pipeline.

"We'll send Spivak back out for more food and supplies," Scott said. Then cutting off Donovan before he could renew an earlier joking request, he added, "And sushi is off the menu. Keep it simple and preferably cheap, Spivak."

They all carried cash on missions—both US dollars and a small amount of local currency. The latter was a precaution that Scott had insisted upon but they'd never needed. But precaution was another way of saying "damned glad of it" when you did. It was going to save them from having to "borrow" everything.

"Try to make it something I can pronounce, Dolph," Donovan said, using Spivak's call sign. The big blond-haired operator who served as the team's breacher bore a resemblance to the actor Dolph Lundgren, who'd played Sylvester Stallone's Soviet foe in *Rocky IV*. "And I hope fresh clothes are on tonight's menu. Jim Bob here smells like a freaking animal."

"Fuck you, Donovan," Travis responded with his heavy Southern accent. The young sniper was from Mississippi and country through and through. Thus, the Jim Bob call sign. "You aren't exactly smelling like a rose."

"See what you can do," Scott said to Spivak, ignoring the giving-each-other-shit banter between the guys as he normally did. With John Donovan around it was constant. "We're also going to need a phone at some point— and pick up a newspaper."

The other horrible consequence of their failed mission was war. For all they knew, WWIII was already under way.

Spivak nodded. "I saw a couple places that sold phones when I was looking around earlier. But if it seems too iffy, I'll figure out something else."

Meaning he'd pick one up in a way that didn't involve questions. Scott nodded. He didn't need to tell Spivak to be careful. The situation was painfully clear to all of them.

Well, mostly clear. The guys didn't know exactly who had warned Scott and why he trusted her. They just knew that he'd received a text right before the first missile hit that had saved their lives, and they trusted *him*.

But he knew they had questions. Questions that he didn't want to answer. How did he tell his men—men to whom he was supposed to be above reproach—that he'd been hiding something from them? That for the last six months he'd had a girlfriend who worked in the Pentagon. That it was serious. That for the first time he'd met someone who meant as much—more—to him than the job. That he had a ring in his pocket that proved it. That he should have said something to them and command months ago.

Scott had been well aware of the rules of Team Nine when he'd joined. No family, no wives, no girlfriends. No one to wonder where he was or when he'd be back. No one to cause problems if he didn't come back.

He should have come forward when it had gotten serious, even if it meant having to leave Nine. But he'd allowed himself to be talked out of it by Natalie, who was just as worried about losing her own job as he was about losing the team he'd helped build.

Breaking the rules wasn't like him. Even for an officer, he had a reputation for being by the book. Rules. Honor. Integrity. Standards. Discipline. It might be old-fashioned, but those things mattered to him.

None of which explained Natalie Andersson. Although nothing about Natalie had ever made any sense. She'd confused and confounded him from the first moment he'd seen her in that bar in DC. Maybe that was part of her appeal. He couldn't figure her out. On the outside she projected this sophisticated, confident career woman, but beneath the surface he detected a sweet vulnerability that roused protective instincts in him that he'd never experienced before. She was like two sides of a coin that had different faces.

But one thing he did know. Without her warning, he wouldn't be sitting here within spitting distance of Siberia in this run-down, abandoned apartment building that looked more like a cellblock. He'd be dead.

All six of them owed her their lives. They'd been

betrayed, and Natalie's message suggested that it had come from someone on the inside. The text that he'd seen by chance was burned into his memory, though it had chilled him to the bone when he'd first read it.

Leak. Russians know you are coming. No one is supposed to survive. Go dark and don't try to contact me. Both our lives might be at stake. And then the last three words that she'd never said before. *I love you.* A declaration that under normal circumstances would have made him the happiest man in the world. Instead it made him the most terrified.

This wasn't a joke; she was deadly serious. That realization, and the fact that she knew about the mission that only a handful of people were supposed to know about, convinced him to call back the platoon—or half the platoon. Lieutenant White's squad was already inside one of the gulag buildings, and the comms were out. There'd been no way to warn them.

The rock that had been crushing his chest since that moment got a little heavier.

Against his orders, the senior chief and Brian Murphy, their newest teammate, had tried to reach them. Murphy had been killed when the first missile struck, and the senior chief had barely escaped the explosion. Scott didn't know how Baylor had made it across almost seventy miles of hell with his injuries. But the senior chief epitomized the BTF—aka the Big Tough Frogman. You couldn't knock him down. He'd keep popping back up and coming at you.

And Scott knew that as soon as the shock wore off and they were out of this, Baylor was going to have questions for him, and he wasn't going to be content with *We'll talk about it later.*

Feeling the senior chief's questioning gaze on him, Scott pulled out his coated paper map that he was damned glad of right now—another precaution when going to places with likely spotty communications—and started to consider options. There weren't a lot of them. They had to get out of the area as quickly as possible, which basically meant a plane, train, or automobile. Of the three, a train seemed the least risky.

"What are you thinking, Ace?" Ruiz asked, using Scott's call sign.

The guys said Scott always had an ace up his sleeve. Well, he sure as hell hoped they were right. They were going to need a full deck of them.

With Spivak gone, the four remaining men gathered round his position on a metal bed frame and mattress, which had both been left behind for a reason. "I'm thinking a freight train to Moscow." He moved his finger diagonally in a southwest direction. "From there we can connect with lines that go to Europe in the west or the Trans-Siberian line in the east."

"The Trans-Siberian Railway?" Donovan repeated. "You gotta be shitting me? That's on my bucket list, LC."

"Glad to accommodate, Dynomite," Scott replied dryly. "Although you might not like the facilities. This is freight or baggage class only."

Without papers they'd have to stay out of sight.

"It's a week to Beijing," the senior chief pointed out. "Not counting the two days to Moscow."

"Sounds about right," Scott agreed. "Or you can stay on until the end of the line in Russia and cross the Bering Sea to Alaska."

"Isn't that just a little over fifty miles, LC?" Travis asked. "I can practically swim that."

They all laughed. "At its narrowest point," Scott said. "But unfortunately where the train lets off"—he pointed to Vladivostok—"you'll have to find a ship to take you."

"My vote is for London," Donovan said.

"I think what the LC is suggesting," Baylor said,

eyeing Scott, "is that we all head out from Moscow in different directions."

There was a long silence, which Scott confirmed with a nod. If they really were going to go dark, it was safer to separate. "We scatter and lay low until I can figure out what happened out there."

"What did happen out there, LC?" Miggy asked.

Scott answered truthfully. "I don't know, but someone tipped off the Russians, and none of us were supposed to make it out of there alive."

"Someone sent you a warning," the senior chief said. It wasn't a question.

Scott nodded. "But that's all I can say right now."

Baylor held his gaze for a moment. Clearly, the senior chief didn't like Scott's response, but just as clearly the senior chief realized he didn't need to like it. Scott didn't have to tell him anything. Eventually Baylor nodded, but Scott knew that rank and the chain of command wouldn't keep the other man silent for long. Baylor was a pain in his ass, but the senior chief was one of the best operators he'd ever worked with. Scott respected the hell out of him, even if he and the platoon's most senior enlisted SEAL didn't always see eye to eye.

Once Scott found out what the hell had happened out there and made sure Natalie was all right, he would come clean about the girlfriend at the Pentagon who had warned them.

Spivak returned a short while later after securing a phone, some clothing that wasn't going to win them any fashion awards, and most important to all of them right now, a couple of pizzas. Most of the toppings were unrecognizable, but they were so hungry no one cared what they were.

"No salad or Parmesan cheese?" Donovan said. "Shit, Dolph, next time I'm coming with you."

Before Scott could grab a slice, Spivak handed him a newspaper. "You aren't going to believe this."

As Scott couldn't read Russian, all he could see were the picture of the Russian president, Dmitri Ivanov; a map of the eastern side of the Ural Mountains where they'd been reconnoitering the gulag; and a satellite image of a massive explosion.

But that was enough.

He swore. "It's out, then. I can only imagine what Ivanov is saying. A team of Navy SEALs sent in to 'invade' a sovereign nation? He must be calling for blood."

And war. After an American fighter plane accidentally strayed into Russian airspace and was shot down, Ivanov vowed the next incursion—accident or not—would be considered an act of war for which Russia would retaliate.

"That's just it," Spivak said. "He isn't. There isn't a damned thing in here about us. They're claiming the explosion was just a missile test."

The room was dead silent; Scott wasn't the only one taking a few seconds to process what this meant.

"Then we aren't going to war?" Travis asked.

"Not for this," Spivak said. "And there isn't anything in the world news, either."

Which meant that the US hadn't gone public about their missing SEAL platoon.

Retiarius had been effectively ghosted, with neither side wanting to fess up that the platoon had been there.

It made horrible sense. Despite his belligerent threats and big words, Ivanov must have known that he would be seriously outmatched in a war with the US. By not acknowledging their presence, he could save face and avoid a war that no one wanted—not to mention savor the personal satisfaction of wiping out an entire platoon of Navy SEALs without the US being able to retaliate.

There were plenty of hawks in President Clara

Cartwright's administration who were eager for war and the chance to put Ivanov in his place. The most vocal among them was General Thomas Murray, the vice chairman of the Joint Chiefs of Staff, as well as the father of the pilot shot down by the Russians a few months ago. But the president had proved more cautious than her advisors, and Scott knew she would stay quiet to cover up their illegal operation and avoid a war in a situation that was already teetering too close to the edge.

Which made any survivors inconvenient, to say the least—to both sides.

Scott stayed up most of the night planning their exfil and searching for any news from Washington. He didn't need much sleep, and even with the lack of rest the past few days, he slept only a few hours.

By dawn he'd taken over watch from Miggy and was sitting by the window overlooking the footbridge to town, eating a piece of leftover pizza and surfing the web again for anything new. He would kill for a cup of coffee right now. Coffee and this time of day reminded him of Nat. Those lazy mornings when they could sit on her tiny balcony in the early hours while the city was quiet, drinking coffee and talking. . . . He'd never guessed that something so small and seemingly simple could make him so happy. That was how he knew he wanted to grow old with her. God, he missed her. He needed to hear her voice and make sure that she was all right.

Knowing that Russia censored media and the Internet, he was careful about search terms, but none of the big European news agencies or Al Jazeera was reporting anything. He decided to take a chance and try a few US newspapers. He doubted the Russian surveillance was that broad, but he'd be getting rid of the phone soon anyway.

New York Times, nada. *Washington Post*, same. *DC Chronicle* . . . his stomach dropped and all the blood slid from his face.

No . . . oh God, no!

He wanted to turn away and pretend he'd never seen it. If he didn't see it, it couldn't be true.

But there was the headline in cold black-and-white: *DC Staffer Killed in Fiery Car Crash That Shuts Down Freeway for Hours.* The story didn't add much, except the name and what she did: *Natalie Andersson, executive assistant to the deputy secretary of defense, was killed in a car crash last night when her car careened into the cement underpass of the Southeast Freeway on 4th Street SE in the Capitol Hill neighborhood where she lived. Excessive speed is believed to have caused her car to explode. Ms. Andersson was killed instantly.*

Scott put down the phone, unable to breathe. His chest was on fire. His eyes burned. The ring that he'd had in his pocket for the past month because he hadn't found the "right" time to give it to her, felt like an unbearable weight dragging him under. After losing eight men, he thought he was numb, but the pain eviscerated him with excruciating savagery.

Oh God, Natalie, baby. I'm so sorry. I'm so fucking sorry. Her words rang in his head. *Both our lives . . .*

He had no doubt she'd been killed because of him. Because she'd warned him.

And he'd never even told her he loved her. He didn't even know why.

That wasn't true. He hadn't told her because he wasn't sure she felt the same way. And now . . . now it was too late to hear her tell him that she did.

For the first time in his life, Scott wanted to put his face in his hands and bawl like a baby. But he wasn't going to do that. He was going to get his men the hell out of here and find whoever was responsible for this. There wasn't a place they could hide where he wouldn't hunt them down.

And then he'd make them pay.

One

AUGUST 17

He'd been honey-trapped.

Scott sat at his recently acknowledged sister's dining room table, feeling as if he had the word "sucker" tattooed across his forehead. No one was saying it, but he knew that was what they were all thinking.

Kate, the aforementioned sister, was looking at him worryingly; her ex-husband and his ex-chief, Colt Wesson, wouldn't meet his eye (although Colt was probably grappling with his own demons right now); the recently arrived senior chief Dean Baylor was looking pissed off (which admittedly wasn't unusual); and the always-ready-with-a-wisecrack John Donovan had fallen into a rare contemplative silence. Brittany Blake, after being kidnapped and nearly killed, was resting in one of Kate's guest rooms, or she'd likely be thinking it as well.

How could they not? It was true. Scott had just had it confirmed from her compatriot's—or should he say *comrade's*—mouth right before he'd been killed. His girlfriend, Natalie Andersson, aka Natalya Petrova, had been a Russian spy who'd passed on the information that had gotten eight of Scott's men killed. For almost three months he'd been mourning her and thinking of her as their savior, and all along she'd been the one responsible for their mission being compromised.

It didn't matter that she'd warned him and been killed. She'd been lying to him. Using him. *Fucking* him for information.

Shit, that hurt. Betrayal curdled in his gut like acid, eating away at him mercilessly.

He'd had no clue. She'd deceived him and betrayed him in the worst possible way, and he'd been ready to put a ring on her finger. A ring that would have taken him away from the team that had been his life. If Scott had that damned ring with him right now, he'd throw it as far as he could into the Potomac, which ran outside Kate's swanky town house.

When he thought of how he'd held on to it like some sort of precious talisman, refusing to sell the Easter egg–sized diamond even when he desperately needed cash as he made his way out of Russia . . . it made him want to slam his fist through the table and turn the fine mahogany into kindling. Scott was an expert at controlling his emotions, but right now they'd been pulled too close to the surface and stretched taut to the snapping point. His pride hurt worse than the patched-up shoulder where he'd taken a bullet a few hours ago.

For the first time in his life a woman had made a fool of him, and Scott didn't know how to handle it. It was a bitter pill for any guy to swallow. For a SEAL officer whose job it was to see things like this coming a mile away, who was supposed to be smarter and savvier than everyone else, it was the worst kind of humiliation.

Kate had tried to warn him, but Scott hadn't wanted

to believe it. He'd defended Natalie, even when the coincidences piled up. Russian birth and adoption that she'd kept secret? So what? There were thousands of kids adopted from Russia—were all of them suddenly suspected spies? Phone contact with the same guy who'd targeted the reporter writing stories about "The Lost Platoon," and who also happened to be born in Russia and came to America via the same adoption agency as Natalie? Not enough.

But when that same guy, Mikhail "Mick" Evans, kidnapped Brittany in an attempt to capture and kill John Donovan, all Scott's doubts had been put to rest. Brutally.

He could still hear the bastard's taunts as Scott tried to question him. "She played you like a fool. How long did it take for her to get in your bed? A few hours? And you never suspected a thing. Man, it was almost too easy."

Scott had wanted to kill him. But Donovan had done it for him after Scott had been shot, and Mick had turned a gun on Kate.

For almost three months, Scott had been busting his ass trying to figure out what had happened out there and how their mission had been compromised, while his men had been forced to scatter across the globe and go dark. He'd looked into everyone who could have known about the mission, followed leads that went nowhere, and searched for motive or anything suspicious that could lead him to figuring out who was responsible for the deaths of eight of his men and the woman he'd loved.

But the person responsible for feeding the information to Russia about their mission had been right there in front of him the whole time. One of their own hadn't betrayed them; the leak had come from a Russian mole. His Natalie. No, *Natalya*—and definitely not his.

Maybe he should be relieved. He had an answer. The

Russians were responsible. There wasn't anyone on the inside waiting to take them out. His men could come out of hiding.

But nothing could lessen the bitter sting of betrayal that filled him with anger and shame.

Sucker.

"If you won't go to the hospital, at least let me call my doctor," Kate said. "I'm sure he will be discreet." She paused, staring at him in earnest. "You don't look good, Scott."

Not surprising since he felt like shit. But the pain from the gunshot wound was the least of it.

He and Kate had known they were brother and sister for almost three years, but it was still strange having someone worry about him. Scott had been alone for a long time. His parents had been killed in a boating accident when he was in his first year at the Naval Academy. Actually his father had survived for a few days, which was how Scott had learned that he wasn't his biological father. He'd needed blood and their blood types had been incompatible.

Scott's seemingly idyllic family and happy childhood had been built on a bed of lies. The man whom Scott had loved and admired more than anyone in the world— who'd left Scott the family fortune—hadn't been his biological father. The discovery had devastated him. Scott had been angry at everyone—at everything—but especially at his recently deceased mother. How could she have betrayed his father, her husband, like that?

He'd never given much thought to the man she'd cheated on his father with or the fact that Scott might have half siblings somewhere. He never would have known if Kate's ex-husband's jealousy hadn't led them to the truth.

"I'm fine," Scott assured her. "This isn't the first time Colt has had to patch me up."

Rather than reassure her, the mention of her ex-husband's doctoring made Kate look even more upset. But she didn't need to worry about Colt using his old corpsman's skills for bad. Whatever reason Colt might have had to want to kill Scott was gone. The only person Colt looked like he wanted to kill right now was himself. Which was good. After what he'd done to Kate, the bastard deserved to suffer.

Colt had thought Scott and Kate's unusual closeness was because they were having an affair, and he'd only just learned that they were actually brother and sister. For years Colt had hated Scott—blaming him for the destruction of his marriage—but now Colt was facing the truth. There was only one man responsible for the mess Colt had made of their lives, and it wasn't Scott.

"What now, LC?" Baylor looked at him, asking the question that was foremost on all of their minds.

The six survivors had been in hiding since their mission had gone bad, and Scott knew how anxious the guys were to get back to the land of the living and the frogman work that they all loved.

"Now that we know where the leak came from and who was behind it"—i.e., Russia and not someone inside—"we don't have to play dead. I will contact command and explain what happened. They can decide how they want to handle our sudden reappearance."

In an attempt to quiet the public interest roused by Brittany's "Lost Platoon" articles, equating the missing platoon of Navy SEALs from a secret team with the famous Lost Legion of Rome, the navy had recently announced that a platoon of SEALs had been killed in a training exercise.

Baylor and Donovan looked relieved by Scott's pronouncement.

Colt not so much.

"You sure that's a good idea, Ace?" Colt asked with

that lazy drawl that belied the savvy operator whose mind was always working every angle. Colt wasn't a part of their team anymore, but he still worked for the military in some kind of clandestine unit that Scott didn't know much about—didn't want to know much about, as he was sure it was of questionable legality.

It was the first time Colt had used Scott's call sign in over three years. But if his former friend thought Scott was going to forgive and forget all that had passed between them, he was out of his mind.

Colt had been the senior enlisted man in Team Nine when Scott had joined as a young lieutenant. Colt had showed him the ropes and taught Scott everything he knew about being a SEAL. To most people their friendship didn't make any sense. Scott was by the book and believed in rules. Colt didn't. But somehow they'd jelled. Scott had looked up to him as an older brother, which made Colt's accusations and turning on him even more unforgivable. How could Colt think he would ever do that to a teammate and a friend?

Scott and Kate hadn't betrayed Colt; Colt had betrayed them.

"We don't have a choice," Scott said. "Technically we've been AWOL since the explosion. Without a good reason to not come forward, we could have a hard time explaining ourselves."

Or defending themselves against a court-martial.

"I wouldn't be so ready to make a reappearance," Colt said. "Not until you learn the extent of the damage done by Mick and Natalie. We don't know what Mick was able to pass on to his superiors before he was killed. We also don't know the extent of their cell here in Washington. I suspect it was a small one since the guys Mick had with him when he took Brittany were more hired thugs than professionals. But that isn't to say there isn't someone else out there. Who else knows there were survivors? Mick found out about Donovan, but what about the rest of you? You guys are safer dead than alive."

"You think they might come after us again?" Donovan asked.

Colt shrugged. "I don't know. I just think it will be easier to find out why they went after you in the first place if you all stay dead."

"They went after him to shut him up," Baylor said. "The Russians don't want any survivors showing up to ruin their nice little story about what happened out there. Ivanov won't want to appear to be avoiding the war that he vowed to start if there were any more 'incursions.'"

But if that was true, coming out would be the safest thing for them.

Scott watched Colt's face. His expression didn't give anything away, but Scott could guess what he was thinking. "You think there's more to it?"

Colt met his gaze for the first time since learning that he was Kate's brother. "I think it's worth not jumping to any conclusions too quickly. Not until we know all the facts."

Ironic advice coming from Colt, given his conclusions about Kate and Scott.

"Which could be easier to find out with help from the inside," Scott pointed out. He was close to his direct superior in the chain of command, the commander of SEAL Team Nine, Mark Ryan. Scott wasn't looking forward to explaining why they hadn't come to him right away.

Colt guessed the direction of his thoughts. He didn't have much regard for the brass in general. "Ryan might be your friend, but he's an officer first, and he'll do his duty even if he doesn't like it."

The same thing could be said about Scott. Once. But

look at him now: scruffy, AWOL, and definitely not by
the book, unless it was called *How to Look Like a Low-
life*. He didn't even recognize himself.

"What are you getting at, Colt?" Kate asked.

"The government is going to be looking for someone
to blame, and right now that's Taylor. They'll want to
know exactly what and how much he told her."

Scott felt his spine go ramrod stiff and his shoulders
turn just as rigid. Blood surged through his veins at a
boil. "It sounds as if you are accusing me of something,
Wesson." Colt didn't shy away from Scott's fury. Scott
looked around the table at the other blank faces staring
at him. "Is that what you all think?" He swore. "I didn't
tell her a damned thing!"

The sound of his voice reverberated in the oval room,
shaking the floor-to-ceiling windows, which were there
to take advantage of the river view.

Suddenly memories came back to him. Images. Snip-
pets of conversation and clumsy questions when they
were lying naked and twisted in the sheets after she'd just
brought him to his knees for the God-knew-how-many-
eth time.

When he was at his weakest.

"I heard there is trouble brewing in Syria again. . . ."

When all of his defenses had been shattered.

*"You'll tell me when you have to leave . . . and when
you'll be back?"*

When she'd fucked every ounce of sense from his
head—both of them. The one he was supposed to think
with, and the one that had been at her mercy from the
first moment he'd seen her at that Capitol Hill bar.

Unlike most Teamguys, bars weren't stomping
grounds for him. He didn't do drunken hookups or one-
night stands.

But he'd made an exception that night. An accidental
bump—at least he'd thought it was accidental—that led

to a drink, a flirty conversation that had gotten closer and closer until somehow their lips were touching, and a scorching kiss that had lit his blood on fire. They'd barely made it out of the cab and into his hotel room before her legs were wrapped around his waist, and he was sinking into her for the first time. The first of many times that night.

His face heated with some of that pounding blood. How could he have been so stupid? How could he not have seen it?

He'd been too damned bewitched by tilted green cat eyes, long fluttery lashes, pouty red lips, high, sharp cheekbones, long, tousled blond hair, and a body that could have sold sexy lingerie to a Mennonite.

But it hadn't just been her beauty that had attracted him. She was smart and knew it. She'd walked into the bar with the cool confidence of a woman who knew she could handle anyone in the room—man or woman—and that had been freaking irresistible.

Which, of course, was the point. She'd been chosen to deceive and entrance. And like a damned glutton he'd taken a dive right into the honey.

Over and over. He hadn't been able to get enough of her. He'd been utterly captivated, out of his mind with lust, and, for the first time in his life, head over heels in love.

As much as he hated to admit any of that, it was the damned truth. And he'd own it, even if it made him the world's biggest sucker.

But he wasn't a complete fool. He'd never forgotten his job or what that meant. He hadn't told her a damned thing about what he did or where he went. He'd never told her anything that could be considered confidential or secret. His job was everything to him; he'd be damned if he'd let her take that from him, too.

Whatever information she'd passed on, it hadn't come

from him, and he dared anyone at the table to suggest otherwise.

Colt didn't seem inclined to argue—a rarity for him. Instead he shrugged. "They won't believe you even if it is true, and you'll spend the next few weeks in some small room trying to convince them otherwise."

Scott cursed; Colt was right. Scott would be the scapegoat, and proving that he hadn't told her anything would take some time. Assuming he could persuade them, that is.

"Wesson is right," the senior chief agreed. "The way it looks now, they'll hang you from the nearest rafter first and worry about right or wrong later."

"Maybe," Scott admitted. "But I'm not going to let you and the rest of the team face AWOL or desertion charges just to save my own skin."

"I never try to second-guess better minds than mine," Donovan said sarcastically, referring to command, "but I'd wager that charges against the rest of us will be the last thing on their mind. There's going to be all kinds of spin going on, but trying to punish us for not coming out right away, given everything that happened?" He shook his head. "No way."

"Dynomite is right," Baylor said. "They won't be looking at us when they have a nice fat target to aim at." Aka Scott. "We're safe. But if you want to avoid time in that small room, you're better off getting your facts lined up first. Besides," the grim-faced Texan reminded him, "we're a team. We do this together, and you aren't going to be much help to us if you are locked up somewhere or spending all your time defending yourself."

"What difference is a few days going to make?" Colt pointed out.

But Scott still wasn't convinced. They might be right, but he had a duty as an officer not only to come forward but also to protect his men.

It was Kate who came up with the solution.

"How about a compromise?" she said. "My godfather is already involved. We could go to him and get his take. You'll have technically reported in to someone in the chain of command"—Kate's godfather, General Thomas Murray, was the vice chairman of the Joint Chiefs of Staff and was one of the handful of people who'd been in the loop about their mission—"but we minimize who knows for a little longer."

It was a great suggestion. Two birds with one stone. Scott looked around the table, and the three men nodded their approval.

Kate made the call.

She returned a short time later. "He was shocked, but when I explained everything, he agreed with Colt." She said it in a way that suggested that didn't happen often. "He thinks you should lay low a little longer. Your survival is miraculous but inconvenient as it makes a delicate political situation with Russia even more precarious. The US is already on the brink of war, and if this comes out it will only get worse. You aren't going to be popular with those in the administration who don't want war. Some in the White House will wish that you'd just stayed buried, and the secret of your mission along with you."

They all knew that, but somehow hearing it from someone in the general's position made it much more sobering. Nothing like having your life be an inconvenience.

"He offered to help in any way he can," Kate added apologetically, understanding the downer cast by her relayed message. "I told him I would keep him in the loop."

Scott nodded. He might take the general up on it. He was determined to do whatever he needed to do to clear his name. He might have fallen in love with the wrong woman, but he hadn't betrayed his country or his men.

He stood up.

"Where are you going?" Colt asked.

"To make some calls. I need to tell Spivak, Miggy, and Travis to hang tight."

But not for much longer. One way or another this was going to end soon.

Scott had no intention of letting Natalie rest in peace. He could kill her for what she'd done. Too bad someone else had gotten to her first.

Two

This wasn't good for her paranoia, which admittedly was running on all cylinders already.

Natalie—no, *Jennifer*, she reminded herself—pulled the old Yankees ball cap down lower over her brow. But she couldn't hide completely from the curious glances cast in her direction as she moved around the town center doing her errands.

She'd known this would happen, which is why she had so many things to do. She'd put off coming to town for as long as she could, but she'd needed supplies from the hardware store, fresh food, and, more imperatively, almond milk for her coffee.

Done in by millennial taste buds. Wouldn't that be the height of ridiculousness after everything that had happened the past few months? But Natalie couldn't hide out at the farm forever, and the stuff in a jar just wasn't cutting it. Her morning coffee was one of the few small pleasures she had left in life. She was miserable enough without suffering powdered creamer.

If there was ever a made-for-TV movie about her life—and it certainly cried out for one—she could just see it now:

Why did you leave the safety of the farm to go into town?

I needed almond milk for my coffee.

And the wisecracking handsome detective—they were always handsome—would of course add with just the right hint of sarcasm: *And did you pick up avocado for your toast as well?*

Ugh. She'd probably be played by some airhead reality TV blonde, despite the fact that Natalie's hair was more golden brown now.

Well, she'd worry about that injustice later. Right now she needed to focus on not doing anything to draw attention to herself. Check that. *More* attention to herself.

She'd grown up in a small farming community like this one so she understood the interest. New blood always drew attention. But attention was the one thing she couldn't afford right now. She needed to keep her head down and blend in until it was time to move on to the next town. This was her fourth in three months, and she wanted it to last longer than a few weeks.

Natalie finished paying for her groceries, holding her breath as she did every time when the credit card went into the machine. But a few minutes later, she exhaled as the approval came through.

You are safe. No one is looking for you.

But three months wasn't long enough to reassure her that she'd gotten away with it. That she'd gotten away at all.

She left the store, bags in hand, and sighed with relief. It was amazing how a few errands could feel like a major accomplishment. But they did, and now she could return to her rented farmhouse and avoid the prying, questioning gazes until the next time she needed milk. She'd been able to order most of her supplies online, but fresh grocery delivery hadn't made its way to this part of Vermont yet.

Natalie crossed the street to where she'd parked. The market was located in the town's main shopping mall, which, like many malls in rural communities, had seen better days about thirty years ago. Along with a grocery store and pharmacy (Kensington wasn't big enough to have a Walmart), there were a couple of restaurants—the ubiquitous pizza place and what appeared to be a Chinese buffet—a gym, and a duty-free shop as the town border to the north was Canada—Quebec, to be specific. The only evidence of the town's dairy farming base was the small ice-cream shop, boasting "made from local Kensington cows." Maple and apples, the town's other traditional industries, had been left off the poster.

The mall was situated right off Main Street, where she'd found the hardware store and, interestingly, a craft brewery and a small coffee shop that roasted its own beans. These last two businesses hinted at the small organic-and-sustainability-focused businesses that were moving into many of Vermont's traditional farm communities. Some people disparagingly called the young people who ran them "hipsters," but she thought that was unfair. Probably because a business along those lines had always been her dream.

One day, she told herself. In a town just like this. When she was sure no one was looking for her, and she had an identity that no one could connect to Natalie Andersson.

Rounding out Main Street were the post office and the town's municipal building, which presumably served as the headquarters for the local government. There wasn't a police station in town—a bonus, as far as she was concerned—but the volunteer firehouse was at the end of the block.

Natalie had just finished putting her grocery bags in the trunk of Jennifer's ten-year-old BMW convertible that she'd retrieved from New Jersey—a car Natalie never would have purchased even if she lived in California, and in Vermont it was just plain silly—when she heard the first notes of a Tchaikovsky waltz that would stop her in her tracks anywhere. It reminded her of her childhood. Her *Minnesota* childhood. Although Natalie knew now that it probably went deeper than that. Blood deep.

Not long after she and her sister had come to live in America, her adoptive father had taken her to see *The Nutcracker* in the city. Not Mankato, which was the biggest city close to where they lived, but to the *real* big city: Minneapolis.

Her father had worn his Sunday best and had even put on a tie for the occasion. She'd had a new plaid dress that her adoptive mother had had to coax her into putting on. She'd never had anything so beautiful before, and she couldn't believe it was for her. The white tights and black patent leather shoes made her feel like a princess.

But the real magic had begun when she'd heard those first few notes of the overture. When the ballerinas had twirled onto the stage, she'd been absolutely transfixed.

Only years later did she understand why.

She'd been just five at the time, but the memory stuck with her because it was the first time she could remember being happy. She'd had so many good memories afterward, but that had been the first. It had seemed to be a demarcation; a line separating the sad past that she wanted to forget and the happy future that she could look forward to. And it *had* been happy. Perfectly boring, normal, and wonderful. Until four years ago, when another demarcation had sent her life into a tailspin.

She shook off the memory and let the music take her back. She and her father went to Minneapolis to see the ballet every December until a few years ago when his prior heart attack and worsening diabetes had put an end to car trips. When her sister, Lana, was old enough she and their mother sometimes joined them, too, but the tradition had always been with her father, and they'd never thought of going without him.

Her heart squeezed as she thought of her family. God, how she missed them. She wondered how Lana was doing. They'd never been apart for this long. But this was how it had to be. She was keeping them safe the only way she could. By being dead.

Moving toward the source of the music, Natalie realized there was a small glass-front studio a couple of doors down from the hardware store. She smiled, watching the half dozen or so young dancers, ranging in age from about five to sixteen, execute the ballet steps in their classic pink tights and black leotards.

Their dance teacher was young but obviously a traditionalist. The diminutive brunette with her hair in a bun and also wearing dance clothes barked out corrections with the authority of an old general as the girls moved around the room with varying levels of success.

The teacher looked at the door impatiently and caught Natalie's gaze, causing her to start.

Frowning, the teacher headed toward her at the same moment as Natalie turned to leave, realizing what she was doing. Staring at young girls through a window was probably not the best way for a stranger to go unnoticed.

Natalie took one step toward her car when she heard a door slam and a car drive off. A moment later, she saw a flash of pink and black as a young girl who was obviously late for class came racing around the corner toward her. She took the curb with a graceful, well-executed leap that was only ruined when she landed on a wet pack of leaves (it rained a lot in Vermont, with August being the wettest month) and her ballet slipper–clad feet slid out from under her.

The girl would have landed hard on her backside if Natalie hadn't reacted quickly. She heard a cry that she assumed came from the teacher as Natalie lurched forward and caught the girl in her arms. Or mostly caught the girl in her arms as Natalie came down hard herself on the sidewalk.

"Oh my God," the teacher said, helping the girl off her. "Are you okay?"

Natalie peeled her skinned forearms and knees off the sidewalk and came to her feet with only a slight wobble. "I'm fine."

Mostly. The scrapes on her arms and knees—of course she had to be wearing shorts (in addition to rainy, August was also warm)—weren't going to feel too good later. But they weren't bleeding too heavily. Just lots of rocks and dirt with a few spiderweb lines of red.

"Samantha, apologize to this poor woman!"

The girl who was slight and older than Natalie initially thought at about eleven or twelve if the braces were any indication, turned to her with wide eyes. She looked stunned and on the verge of tears. "I'm sorry. I was practicing my dance in my head and didn't see the leaves."

"You should have been practicing the dance in the studio," the teacher said sternly. "You are late again. What did I warn you about last week?"

The glimmer of tears in the girl's big brown eyes grew thicker. "But it wasn't my fault. My dad got a call on the way and we had to stop and check on Miss Mabel's barn. The lock she put on it was cut off, and she found beer cans again."

"Partying teenagers is a job for the county sheriff? If this were the first time, it would be one thing, but you've been late to class the past three weeks in a row."

"My dad is busy," the girl protested.

"But it isn't always your dad, is it?" the teacher said more kindly. "Didn't you say you forgot what day it was last time you were late?"

With obvious reluctance, the girl nodded.

"I thought you wanted this part?" the teacher asked in a gentle voice that showed she was not immune to the burgeoning crocodile tears.

"I do, I do!" the girl protested. "The Sugar Plum Fairy has the best dance. Please, I promise to get to class on time next week."

The teacher nodded and the girl ran off before she could change her mind. But right as she got to the door, the young girl stopped and flashed Natalie with a brilliant smile that gave no hint of the tears looming a few moments ago. "Thank you again for catching me. I would have broken my butt."

Natalie laughed and smiled. "No problem."

When Samantha was gone, the teacher turned to Natalie with a sigh. "Thank you from me as well. Sammie's mother died when she was young, and she's been raised by her father. She's our best dancer. A real natural talent. But she doesn't take it very seriously. I think she prefers hockey over ballet," she added with a dramatic shiver.

Feeling the same way about hockey herself, Natalie could commiserate. "She's young. Maybe she'll change her mind."

The teacher shrugged as if she didn't think that very likely. "You're new around here?"

Natalie tensed defensively, the instinct to cut the conversation short with the question—even an innocuous one—strong. But she knew that in a small town like this it would only provoke more comment if she appeared to be hiding something.

She'd grown up in a town about this size where

everyone knew everything about everyone else. Although they hadn't known everything about her. How could they? Not even *she* had known everything.

It was common knowledge that she and Lana had been adopted from Russia, but who could have imagined that they were the daughters of Soviet "traitors," who had been put in some sort of secret program as punishment for their parents' sins.

Her parents had been ballet dancers in the old USSR who'd tried to defect to the West after a performance but had been forced to abandon their plans when the woman who was watching Natalie and her sister fell asleep in front of the TV and failed to bring the girls backstage after the show as she was supposed to have. Natalie's parents had been arrested and thrown into a Russian prison to die, and the lives of their two children had been destroyed because of a boring TV show.

Ironically, the Soviet Union dissolved later that same year. But it was too late for her parents, and the former KGB members who emerged in the new government as SVR (Foreign Intelligence Service of the Russian Federation) agents had not forgotten the children of the former traitors. They were unknowing and unwitting "sleepers," sent to America as children via an adoption program and ready to be "awakened" if the relations between Russia and the US were to chill again.

If it sounded like something that could happen only in a book or movie, that is exactly what Natalie had thought, too. Until hockey player Mick Evans walked into her perfectly wonderful, boring, and normal life four years ago and made her believe it.

She'd never been able to watch hockey again without a shudder, which, coming from Minnesota—or the USSR for that matter—was something akin to sacrilege.

Mick can't find you, she reminded herself. *Relax.*

Natalie forced herself to return the broad smile of the

other woman, who she could see was just being friendly; the ballet teacher wasn't a hit man sent to kill her. Again.

"I am new to town," Natalie said. "I'm renting the old Lewis farm and moved in a couple weeks ago."

The other woman's brows shot up. "I'm surprised that place is habitable. It hasn't been lived in full-time since Mrs. Lewis died a few years back."

More like five. And she was right. The place was horribly run-down. But Natalie had agreed to fix it up in exchange for a minuscule rent. The four children who'd inherited it had no desire to be farmers, but they hadn't been able to sell it. They were just happy to have someone living in it so its value didn't depreciate further.

Natalie's chest squeezed. She loved the place. It was perfect—or would be if she had the chance to do everything she wanted. But she knew she probably wouldn't have the opportunity. She couldn't stay long. She had to keep moving.

But maybe one day she would find a place just like it to continue the artisanal cheese business that she'd just been getting started when her father had been forced to sell the family farm. That was when she'd made the fateful decision to go to Washington and the nightmare had begun.

If only she could go back. She would be safe and secure in her nice boring and ordinary life, instead of feeling as if she'd woken up in some sort of bad James Bond movie.

And the man she loved would still be alive. They might never have met, but at least he would be alive. The squeezing in her heart turned to the familiar ache that she suspected she would carry with her forever.

Realizing the other woman was waiting for her reply, she said, "I'm doing some work on it—fixing it up a little."

"A little? I'm surprised the place even has water."

Natalie smiled, which felt odd from disuse. She hadn't

had much to smile about in months. "It was a little rusty at first, but once I got the water heater going again, I've even been able to manage hot showers."

"Wow! You know how to fix a water heater? I'm impressed. But you might not want to let Joe Randall hear you say that. He's the town's plumber, and he's protective of his territory." The woman smiled again, her eyes crinkling. She was older than Natalie had thought—probably a few years past Natalie's twenty-nine—but her diminutive figure and tidy build coupled with delicate, dark features made her appear much younger. "I'm sorry. I haven't introduced myself." She held out her hand. "I'm Becky Randall." Her grin deepened at Natalie's reaction to the last name. "Yep, the plumber's daughter who can't even fix a leaky toilet."

In the face of such overt friendliness, there was nothing else Natalie could do but return the shake. "Jennifer," she said. "Jennifer Wilson."

"Welcome to Kensington," Becky said. "Are you a dancer or just a ballet fan?"

Natalie tried not to startle, but the question hit too close to home. "Uh," she stumbled awkwardly, "just a fan."

"Too bad. I'm looking for help with our annual Christmas *Nutcracker* production." Natalie wanted to bite but forced herself not to say anything. "Well, if you are looking for work, the diner needs a new waitress, the hotel a bookkeeper, and the middle school a new psychologist."

Natalie gave a sharp bark of relieved laughter. "Are you the town's job recruiter?"

Becky grinned back at her. "Nope, just its manager."

Natalie couldn't hide her shock. She took in the pink tights, black leotard, toe shoes, and the thin, short black dancer's sweater that crossed in the front. "You're the mayor?"

"Town manager in these parts, but the job is essentially the same. You aren't the only one who is surprised. I didn't sign up for it, but no one else would agree to step up after our previous manager was caught dipping into the community fund to take his girlfriend on fancy vacations. They moved to the city before anyone figured it out."

Natalie assumed she meant Burlington, which was Vermont's most populous city at forty-five thousand. Tiny by most American comparisons, but big compared to the six thousand in Kensington. Burlington was about forty miles to the south from Kensington, which was on the Vermont-Canada border. Her picking a town so close to the border hadn't been a coincidence.

"What do you do?" the other woman asked. "Other than fix water heaters and put my inheritance in jeopardy?"

Natalie laughed. It felt good. Unfamiliar, but good. Despite her initial reserve, she found herself liking the ballet teacher/mayor—manager, she corrected herself— and responded truthfully. "I guess you could say I get things done." My Girl Friday. That was what the deputy secretary had called her. The wistful smile fell from her face. Her handle-everything reliability had been her downfall. If she'd been less sure of herself, less the starry-eyed millennial who thought she could change the world, maybe they would have left her alone.

She shook off the what-ifs that didn't help and explained, "I was a legal assistant for a law office in New Jersey the past five years."

It wasn't a complete lie. That's what Jennifer had been doing before . . .

Natalie forced away the memory of her best friend before the tears in her throat rose to her eyes.

Becky's eyes gleamed as if she'd just won the lottery. "I could use exactly that kind of help if you're interested. You should see the mess the former manager left of the files."

Natalie's defenses were up again. A friendly conversation on the street was one thing, but she sensed it would be hard to keep her barriers up against someone as easy to talk to as Becky Randall. Ballet teacher, town manager, and plumber's daughter.

"I'm pretty busy at the farm right now, but I will keep it in mind. Thanks for thinking of me." Natalie glanced at the window, glad to see the girls were standing there staring at them. "I think they're waiting for you, and I better get back to the farm. I still have some work to do before dark."

The afternoon had gotten away from her.

"You okay out there by yourself? It's pretty remote. I can call the county sheriff—Samantha's dad—and have him check in on you if you'd like. I have to talk to him anyway." She didn't seem to relish the conversation.

Those flared instincts turned into full-on alarm bells. Natalie should have cut and run earlier. "No, please," she said with what she hoped was not as much panic in her voice as she felt. "Don't trouble him. I like the quiet, and I'm used to being alone."

"In New Jersey?" Becky said with a healthy dose of skepticism.

This was turning out to be a disaster. Natalie had never been very good at lying, which was ironic given what she'd had to do the past few years. "I grew up on a farm." Before she could ask where, Natalie added, "I better go. See you around."

She got into her car as fast as she dared, waving when she saw that Becky was still standing there looking at her.

So much for not acting suspicious. Natalie's hands were shaking as she started the five-mile drive down long county roads to her farm. No, not her farm. She couldn't think of it like that. Her temporary place to live.

Her eyes kept darting to the rearview mirror, half expecting someone to be following her.

She had to calm down and stop imagining Russian hit men behind every corner.

The early-evening skies had darkened with clouds by the time she turned onto the long driveway, and even the shadows were making her jumpy.

Anxious to get inside, she pulled around back into the barn that served as a garage and pulled the groceries out of the trunk. She'd get the rest of the stuff in the morning.

She was about to turn around when a shadow fell across her from behind. The tall, powerfully built shadow of a man.

Her heart jumped to her throat as panic and fear turned every drop of blood inside her to ice. Oh God, they'd found her!

Three

Where the hell was he?

Scott put down his phone after leaving another message for Travis Hart. It was his fourth or fifth in the past week, and he didn't like it. The survivors had scattered to all corners of the globe after they'd reached Moscow, but the guys were always supposed to let Scott know where they were, give him a way to reach them, as well as a heads-up if they were going to be out of touch for any length of time. In the past few months that they'd been in hiding, there were times when it had taken one of the guys a day or two to get back to him, but it had never been this long.

For operational security reasons Scott was the only one who knew where they were all located. Travis was in Alaska working as a deckhand on a fishing boat. The boat was only a day-tripper, meaning he would put out one morning and return the next evening—usually working thirty-six hours straight—but they didn't go out to sea for weeks or even months like some of the bigger commercial ships.

Travis should have gotten back to him by now.

"He's still not answering?" Kate asked, knowing how worried he was getting.

Scott shook his head. "He better have a damned good excuse for going incommunicado."

They were at Kate's town house, using her well-equipped office and computers—having a sister who worked for the CIA had its benefits—to go over every inch of Natalya Petrova's life, just as they'd been doing for every day of the past week. And what did they have to show for it? Plenty, if the goal was to show Scott how little he'd known her. But if he'd hoped to find anything helpful to lead them to learning more about the cell or how she'd operated . . . nada.

He hadn't even known she'd had a sister, which he'd discovered courtesy of a deactivated Facebook account that they'd uncovered. There were only a couple of pictures. The most recent was from Christmas three years ago with Natalie and a slightly younger-looking version of her with glasses standing in the snow in front of a big outdoor Christmas tree. Though she deflected questions about her family, which took on a new significance now, Scott knew she was originally from Minnesota so he assumed the picture was taken on a trip home for the holidays.

Both women were bundled up from head to toe, with heavy wool coats, scarves, and matching pink mittens and knit stocking hats with pompoms. All you could see were strands of long blond hair, identical big, wide-set baby-doll eyes, pink cheeks, and big, happy smiles.

Scott must have stared at the picture for hours, as if looking for a clue. Looking for something he had missed.

But it didn't even look like the same person. He couldn't put this sweet-looking Midwestern girl with her arm protectively around her sister in fuzzy pink mittens—mittens, for Christ's sake—together with the coolly confident and sophisticated Washington staffer, or the covert Russian spy who'd been responsible for the deaths of eight of his men.

It was as if she were a chameleon, changing appearances based on her surroundings.

But he'd never been able to figure her out. It had been part of the attraction. Now he realized it should have alerted him that something wasn't right. Instead of asking questions, he'd been too busy counting the moments until he could get her naked again.

From the first time he'd seen her, he'd wanted to take her to bed, and that had never changed. He'd expected the relationship and the fiery passion to burn out quickly. Natalie hadn't been his type. Sleek, polished, and sophisticated, she was nothing like the wholesome, girl-next-door type that he usually gravitated toward.

When they'd first met, he'd assumed she was like all the other power-hungry political brokers in Washington who were interested only in what he could do for her. Which was why it was so surprising when he told her he was a navy seaman on temporary leave visiting a friend at Walter Reed—which also happened to be true—that she seemed almost relieved. Her claim to be "an assistant" didn't seem out of line with his first impressions, and he assumed she worked for someone on the Hill.

But after forty-eight hours of virtually nonstop sex, he realized how wrong he had been when he walked into op brief at the Pentagon and the woman he'd left tousled and limp from lovemaking in bed that morning was sitting next to the deputy secretary of defense.

She didn't hide her shock as well as he did—or her anger—on learning that her "seaman" visiting a friend at the hospital was actually lieutenant commander of the president's favorite secret SEAL team.

Later, when he cornered her after the meeting as she came out of the ladies' room, she had accused him of lying to her and told him she never wanted to see him again. Oddly, she'd seemed almost frightened.

He'd wanted to argue but knew she was right. Anything between them was impossible. Guys on Team Nine weren't supposed to have girlfriends, let alone one who was so highly connected in the Pentagon. A relationship between them would have gone over about as well as a turd in the punch bowl, as Travis liked to say. The government didn't like when high security clearances mixed.

Scott had thought she'd meant it until she turned up at his hotel room later that night with something else clearly in mind. He knew he should back away, but with that sleek, sexy body pressed up against his, he found himself pushing her forward . . . onto the bed.

He'd returned to Honolulu the next day, but he'd come back to DC a few weeks later. He told himself it was to check in on Kate, who had recently gotten engaged—an engagement that had ended recently, not long after Colt had reappeared in her life—but when Natalie walked into the bar where they first met, he realized how much he'd been lying to himself.

That had been almost nine months ago. He hadn't been able to get enough of her for the next six months—until he'd deployed for the Russia mission. And the knowledge of how easily he'd slid into her trap still infuriated him.

"What are you going to do?" Kate asked, referring to the subject at hand, that of his uncommunicative operator.

Scott had been thinking about that the past couple of days. "I'm going to see if Colt can track Travis down. Have you heard from him?"

Kate tried to hide it, but Scott could see her muscles tense. "Why would I have heard from Colt? He and I have nothing left to say to one another."

Scott doubted that Kate believed that any more than he did. "I thought he might have tried to apologize."

"Apologize?" she scoffed. "You know him better than that. Colt doesn't apologize; he attacks. He's been doing it since he was a kid. What's that adage they use in football? The best defense is a good offense."

It was a military adage as well, known as the strategic offensive principle of war, and it summed up Colt to a T.

Scott looked at the tired face that was so like his own and tried to think of what to say. In retrospect, it was amazing that it had taken them so long to figure out that they were related. The resemblance between them was pronounced. His hair was a darker shade of blond, maybe, but they had the same color blue eyes, straight noses, and similarly shaped mouths.

But despite their parents' knowing each other when they were younger, it had never occurred to him that her father could have been the man his mother had the affair with until Colt had angrily referred to them as "Ken and Barbie Country Club Edition." Suddenly Scott had seen what he'd never noticed before. The odd nonsexual closeness he'd felt instantly with her suddenly made sense. A later blood test had confirmed what by then he already guessed: Kate was his half sister.

Scott wished he could say something to make it better for her, but Kate and Colt were going to have to figure it out on their own.

If they figured it out at all.

"Do you know where I can reach him?" Scott asked.

"I have a number, but you'll probably get ahold of him faster if you go to McNally's. My guess is he's been spending the past week with his head in a bottle and listening to Patsy Cline's 'Crazy' on the jukebox, which is the only song that ever seems to be playing there."

She was probably right but Scott left a message for him anyway, telling him to call him back and that it was important.

He was going to call it a night but decided to finish

going through the various social media accounts of the dozens of Facebook friends on Natalie's account. He was lucky it wasn't hundreds. The account had been active for only about a month before she'd apparently decided better of it.

He wasn't surprised. No social media was Spy 101. Operators in Team Nine weren't supposed to have any— even accounts under false names or aliases. Ghosts couldn't leave a footprint.

About an hour later, Kate pushed back from her chair. "You almost done? You might not need it, but some of us actually have to sleep a few hours a night."

They had been burning the midnight oil. "Almost." He'd gone through the names alphabetically and was almost finished. "I just have a few more names."

Kate rolled her eyes, as if she'd heard that one before. "I'm going to get some coffee. But we're shutting it down in an hour. Your shoulder needs rest even if you don't."

His wound was healing just fine, but he knew better than to argue with her. Last time that had forced him to sit through her changing the dressing—again. Which, as she didn't have much nursing skill and insisted on following instructions off the Internet, was a prolonged experience.

He was on the last name of his list when she came back in the room. A few minutes later, he jolted up in his chair. "Bingo!"

Kate looked over. "I take it you found something?"

Scott turned the screen that he'd been working on toward her.

Kate had shared the office in the town house with her former fiancé, Sir Percival Edwards, and there were two desks built into an L shape that each housed top-of-the-line computers and multiple screens. His desk had two; Kate's had three.

"Look at this," he said, indicating the picture he'd found on Jennifer Wilson's Instagram account.

Kate looked back and forth between the two smiling faces. It was the same smile Natalya had with her sister in the Minnesota picture. With stilettos and a slinky black silk dress replacing the hat, scarf, and fuzzy pink mittens. "Which one is she?"

Even though Kate had seen a picture of Natalie, he wasn't surprised she'd asked. The two women looked enough alike to be sisters. They were both knockouts, although Jennifer was curvier, shorter, and had more brown in her dirty blond hair. "The one on the left," he said.

Kate squinted at the photo. "Where was that taken? It looks familiar."

"You've probably been there. It's the Treasury Bar on the Hill."

That was one of the reasons he'd jolted. He'd recognized it right away, too. It was the same bar where he and Natalie had first met.

Kate nodded. "This Jennifer Wilson could be a good lead."

"More than that. Look at the date the picture was posted."

He zoomed in so she could see it easier. A moment later she gasped. "May the twenty-fourth!"

He nodded. "The night before our mission, and a couple days before Natalie was killed."

Jennifer Wilson might have been one of the last people to see her alive.

"And look at this." He scrolled through the pictures. "It's the last picture she posted, and before that she posted almost daily."

Kate looked at him. "You think she knows something?"

"I'm going to find out."

He'd planned to go to Minnesota to talk to Natalya's

family, but tracking down Jennifer Wilson had just become priority number one.

Natalie wanted to scream, but it was another primitive instinct that took over. The urge to survive. To avoid death. To fight.

She turned and tossed the bag toward the man who'd come up behind her. She knew he'd reflexively try to catch it, and she intended to use the moment of surprise to her advantage with a swift kick to an area that would give her the moment she needed to get past him.

He caught the bag with a surprised "oof" and she was about to proceed to part two of her escape plan when she noticed the uniform.

The color slid from her face. The man who'd snuck up behind her wasn't Mick or a Russian hit man; he was a policeman. Noticing the badge, she corrected herself. Not a policeman, the sheriff, who happened to be a dead ringer for Tom Selleck circa *Magnum, P.I.* He even had a mustache, although his wasn't 1980s bushy but trimmed much shorter.

She was relieved, but only for a moment. When you were on the run, hiding for your life and the lives of everyone you loved, with only a fake ID to protect you, a policeman was almost as bad as a hit man. What did he want?

He realized he must have frightened her by coming up behind her. "I'm sorry for scaring you. I was parked around front when I saw the car pulling into the garage."

Natalie took a deep breath, trying to recover her composure. *Act normal. Don't panic just because a cop showed up out of nowhere.*

She smiled as if embarrassed. "You startled me, that's all. What can I do for you?"

She held out her hand for the grocery bag that she'd

tossed to him, but he shook it off. "I'll carry it for you. I'm Brock Brouchard—the county sheriff. We had some reports from neighbors of lights on in the old farmhouse and assumed it was teenagers or squatters. I was in the area so I thought I'd check it out."

The sheriff smiled. He didn't have the Magnum dimples, but even without them, he was a good-looking man in the rugged outdoorsman kind of way. Her mom would say he looked like the Marlboro Man, which was basically how she referred to every ruggedly handsome man.

"Not a squatter or a teenager," she said. "Just a renter."

"Do you mind if I see proof of that?"

She knew he had no right to see it, but she also knew that it would get rid of him faster if she just did as he asked. But her heart was pounding like a drum. "No problem. The paperwork is inside."

They carried the groceries into the house and she told him to put the bag down on the counter in the kitchen while she went to fetch the lease. When she returned, she could see him, with his observant lawman's gaze, taking in every inch and detail of the work that she'd done.

It gave her a moment of hesitation—and caused her heart to beat even faster—when she handed him the lease and driver's license. The likeness was good—really good—but there were subtle differences if you looked. Most people only glanced at the picture.

The sheriff was not one of them. He studied the license for a long time before handing it back to her. "You look different."

Her racing heart stopped beating with a hard jolt. The words were threatening but the tone was not. She replied in the same offhanded manner as his comment, "Yeah. That picture was a few pounds ago."

He looked embarrassed, which had been her intention. If there was one thing a man knew was off-limits in conversations with women, it was weight. "And grew a couple inches," he said. "It says you are five-five, but I'd put you at five-seven."

Way too observant. "That was a typo that I never got around to correcting."

He nodded. He seemed to believe her, but his poker face was better than her mind-reading skills. "You can do it when you apply for a new license. That one is about to expire."

She didn't say anything, but a powerful weight of sadness passed over her. She knew that. Jennifer's birthday was in December. December first, to be precise.

"So you are from New Jersey?" he asked conversationally.

But she didn't want to start a conversation; she just wanted him to leave. The last thing she needed was to draw the attention of the local sheriff, and there was something about the way that he was looking at her that made her think he might be interested in other ways. "*Was* from New Jersey," she corrected.

"And now you're fixing up the old Lewis farm?" He looked around. "You've done a lot of work. All by yourself?"

She'd been right. Despite the innocuous question, she knew what he was getting at: was there someone else in the picture?

"Yes, and it's been exhausting." Before he could follow up with some other personal question, she added, "It was nice to meet you, Sheriff Brouchard, but I need to put these groceries away and get cleaned up."

He nodded. "I noticed the scratches on your arms and knees."

Of course he did. She thought about mentioning that it was probably his daughter that she'd saved from a spill, but then thought better of it. It would just prolong the conversation that she wanted to end. "I fell."

She could see he was curious, but he took the hint and

walked to the door. "Nice meeting you, Ms. Wilson. Hope to see you around."

She smiled but not wanting to encourage further contact simply replied, "It was nice to meet you, too, Sheriff."

She held her breath until the car turned onto the highway. The cold sweat on her brow and the frantic beating of her heart, however, remained.

She slunk against the door. That had been terrifying. Not for the first time in the past few months she felt as if she'd dodged a bullet. But that had been the biggest one yet. A sheriff. God in heaven. What if his observations about the license had been more? What if he'd guessed that it wasn't her? How long would it have taken the people who had tried to kill her to learn that she was alive?

She was tempted to pack up her car and leave, but she talked herself off the ledge. The ID had worked. She couldn't panic every time someone asked her questions or a man looked at her. She had to live somewhere, and this place was perfect.

She liked it here, and she was tired of running. Besides, she held up the ID that she'd shown him. Even if he ran a check on her, he would see that she was telling the truth.

Her eyes filled with tears. Jennifer Wilson had been a real person. She'd been Natalie's best friend. And she'd been killed when the person trying to kill Natalie mistook Jennifer for her.

Four

Natalie was correct in her initial estimation of Becky Randall. The town manager was a hard person to refuse—or dislike. It had taken Becky less than two days and three phone calls to get Natalie to agree to help her out.

Becky was trying to prepare for a big meeting with developers who hoped to purchase a large parcel of land as part of the town's redevelopment plan, and the files were a mess. The previous town manager had purposefully left them that way to help cover his questionable business expense tracks. By the end of the first workday, however, Natalie had already begun to make significant inroads in the files and had just finished organizing the information and research related to the meeting. She'd also handed Becky an additional list of sources and articles she might want to look at. Natalie had seen firsthand what could happen to small farming communities when developers moved in.

Becky shook her head. "You are a miracle worker. Are you sure you can only work two days a week? I could use you every day for the next month—at least."

Natalie smiled, more pleased than she wanted to admit. It was nice to feel that sense of accomplishment again. Of making order out of chaos. She'd been enjoying her renovation work on the farmhouse, but she missed the intellectual challenge of her job at the Pentagon. It was a job she'd never wanted but had grown to love.

Becky skimmed over the list of resources and notes that Natalie had made in hopes of conveying to Becky the need to proceed with caution in her upcoming meeting with the developers. But the town's coffers were dry, and from a few things Becky had mentioned, it was clear she was under a lot of pressure from some of the ranking members of the community to back the sale to the developers quickly.

But quick money came with a cost. A development like that would change the character of the town forever. Natalie had heard a statistic when her father was battling to keep their farm that the US was losing two acres of farmland a minute to developers.

"Did you ever consider going to law school yourself?" Becky asked. "This almost looks like a legal brief."

The question hit home with surprising force. Trying to prevent what happened to her town and her family's livelihood was exactly why Natalie had gone to Washington. What was that old movie . . . *Mr. Smith Goes to Washington*? That was her. A naive, idealistic Jimmy Stewart, millennial style.

She'd accepted the internship with their local representative to fight from the inside for farming communities and after working in Washington awhile had wondered if maybe law school might be for her.

Instead she'd caught the attention of Mick Evans and the powerful men in Russia that he'd worked for. If she'd stayed in Minnesota and hadn't accepted that internship, maybe none of this would have happened.

"I think my father would have disowned me," she said

with a laugh, although it was true. "A legal assistant"—or in her case a politician, which was just as bad in his eyes—"is close enough to the enemy. You can't imagine how many times I heard that adage about lying down with dogs and waking up with fleas."

Becky laughed. "I take it your father didn't care much for lawyers."

"That is putting it mildly," Natalie said dryly. "He thinks they are all lying, untrustworthy snakes who use the law to make money for rich people and trick honest, hardworking folk who didn't go to college and learn how to talk fast."

"A not completely inaccurate portrayal of some lawyers I know." Becky smiled. "I should like to meet your father. He sounds like he would get along great with mine."

Natalie immediately sobered, a wave of sadness pouring over her. She missed her family desperately. One of the hardest things she'd ever done was letting them think she had been killed. But she knew it was the only way to keep them safe. She hadn't been able to save Scott, but she wasn't going to let them take her family from her, too.

Instead of answering directly, she said, "I'm looking forward to meeting your father soon. There's a leaky pipe in the upstairs tub and replacing it is above my pay grade. I have it turned off for now, but when I get around to it, I'll be calling."

Becky grinned. "You may get back in his good graces yet."

The two women were walking out of the municipal building together when Natalie saw the man heading up the stairs toward them and nearly stumbled. She bit back a curse, recognizing the sheriff.

Unfortunately it was too late to turn around or run and hide as he'd already seen them. Although from the look of annoyance that crossed his face, he might have been considering the same thing. His mouth tightened as his gaze lingered on Becky for an instant before shifting to Natalie, where it lightened considerably.

She didn't need to be a detective to figure out that the sheriff didn't much like the town's manager-cum-ballet-teacher.

"Miz Wilson," he drawled, with a tip of his flat brown sheriff's hat that was only a brim-adjustment away from making the image of cowboy complete. His voice was considerably sharper when he turned to her new friend. "Ms. Randall."

"Sheriff Brouchard," Natalie said.

Becky rolled her eyes a little before adding an amused, "Brock." He didn't seem to appreciate the lack of formality, which Becky explained to Natalie. "We went to high school together. Brock played football with my older brother—although Brock went on to play at college as well."

Natalie nodded, not surprised. The sheriff was built like an athlete. "Nice to see you again," she said to the sheriff. "I'll see you on Thursday, Becky."

She tried to move off, but the sheriff stopped her. "I'm glad to run into you again. It seems I owe you my thanks. Rebecca told me you saved Sammie from a nasty spill. Those were the scrapes I saw on your knees and arms."

It wasn't a question, but Natalie nodded. "It was nothing. I should get going—"

He didn't let her finish. "Sammie said she didn't get a chance to really thank you. She was late to class." He shot a sharp glare in Becky's direction, which Natalie suspected explained his current attitude toward her teacher. Becky must have given him an earful. "We're going to pizza on Friday. Why don't you join us?"

Was he asking her out? Natalie wasn't sure, and neither apparently was Becky. But even if she hadn't just noticed the slight flicker of hurt in her new friend's gaze before she started studying the ground, the last thing Natalie wanted to do was go on a maybe-a-date with the county sheriff. "I'm afraid I can't," she said. "I already have plans."

She glanced across the street, hoping to make a quick getaway to where her car was parked when she suddenly froze—and gasped as she caught a glimpse of a man staring at her from behind the wheel of a black sedan stopped at the light. But it was only for an instant. The light turned, and he drove off before she could react.

But it was as if she'd seen a ghost.

She swayed from the force of the shock. Her knees buckled. She gave a strangled cry of "Scott!" right before everything went black.

I must be dreaming.

It had seemed like a dream the night Scott Taylor walked into Natalie's life.

She hadn't felt that kind of excitement—that kind of teenage lust—since she was, well, a teenager.

Maybe not even then.

She hadn't been the one to see him first. Her friend Hannah, whose engagement they were celebrating, had noticed him the moment he walked into the Capitol Hill bar with two also nice-looking and clean-cut companions.

Hannah leaned over and whispered in her ear, "Serious eye candy at six o'clock." She let out an exaggerated dreamy sigh. "If I wasn't engaged, I'd go for it myself, but that guy is exactly what you need to make you forget about Todd. Six months is too long to mourn a breakup, Nat."

Her breakup with Todd wasn't what had been bugging her. Todd had been great: kind, solid, steady, understanding, and wonderfully uncomplicated. In other words, exactly what Natalie needed after Mick.

They'd dated for over two years, but Todd wanted *really* long-term—as in marriage—and she didn't. How could anyone in her life be long-term?

But Natalie didn't object to Hannah's premise. It was easier to let her friend think that she was nursing a broken heart than explain about Mick.

Mikhail "Mick" Evans was a dark cloud looming over Natalie's life that she couldn't escape. But God, how she wished she could. Even if just to forget for a little while.

She turned and did just that, forgetting everything in the space of one very hard slam of her heart against her ribs. She forgot that her life was a mess, that she was probably going to end up in prison—for espionage or for murder if she could figure out a way to get rid of Mick—and that she wasn't a normal twenty-eight-year-old woman who was free to do what she wanted.

There was no question who her friend was talking about. That dreamy sigh of Hannah's hadn't been exaggerated. The guy—the man—commanded attention. He stood out, and not just because of his golden-ticket good looks—although they certainly didn't hurt.

Eye candy was putting it mildly. He was gorgeous. Tall and incredibly fit—she hadn't missed the muscular arms below the short-sleeved edge of his polo shirt or the flat stomach where his shirt was tucked into nicely tailored flat-front khakis—his face was tanned and chiseled masculine perfection. Wide brow, straight nose, sensually curved mouth, and slightly squared jaw. His dark blond hair was short but impeccably groomed. Everything about him was impeccable. There didn't seem to be one thing out of place. He was seriously put together. She did a surreptitious scan of his body again. In *every* way.

She shouldn't have been able to tell the color of his eyes from this far away, but she'd bet her favorite broken-in pair of jeans that they were a riveting blue.

And she was completely, 100 percent riveted.

He gave off this aura of confidence bordering on arrogance that was almost hypnotic. Actually not almost. It took Natalie a moment, and a nudge by her friend, to realize she was staring. Gaping. All right, inwardly drooling.

Nonetheless, Natalie turned back to her friend and said with a chagrined smile, "I don't think so."

"Why not?"

Natalie shrugged. How could she explain that she didn't need any more complications in her life, and a guy like that practically screamed serious complications?

But it didn't take long to change her mind.

A short while later, as she fought her way through the crowded hallway from the bathroom, she'd accidentally bumped into him and spilled his beer. Embarrassed, she'd tried to buy him another one, but he'd insisted on buying her a drink instead.

One drink had led to two, and somehow they'd ended up talking in a mostly secluded corner of the room. It had been dark and noisy but undeniably intimate. When he leaned in to listen to her responses, the heady scent of his spicy aftershave had sent her pheromones into overdrive.

Actually her pheromones had been in overdrive pretty much since her breast had come into contact with his arm and knocked the beer out of his hand. The hot flush that had flooded her body hadn't just been embarrassment; it had also been attraction. Instant, very hot, and very kinetic attraction. She could practically feel the sparks flying between them.

She wanted to kiss him, and every time he leaned in her breath hitched and her pulse raced with anticipation.

It was hard to remember that he was a complete stranger. Except that he didn't feel that way anymore. She'd been cautious at first with the getting-the-basics-out-of-the-way introductions. He was one of those guys who walked into a room and took command. The natural-born leader type. A guy like him was probably a high-up somewhere and important men were off-limits. Natalie wouldn't make Mick's job that easy for him.

When Scott—Taylor, as he'd introduced himself—told her that he was a navy seaman on leave visiting an injured friend at Walter Reed she was more than a little surprised. He looked more like a successful lawyer or lobbyist who'd just stepped out of *GQ* magazine. But the military certainly explained his neat, put-together appearance.

It also made her hesitate. Getting involved with someone in the military was asking for trouble—even if he was just an enlisted sailor—if Mick ever found out.

She probably should walk away, but she was wedged into the corner and those broad shoulders were kind of blocking her way. It was hard to look—or think—past them.

She was also having trouble looking away from his deep blue eyes—she'd guessed correctly on the color—the dazzling white grin, and the faint shadow of whiskers that were beginning to show through his clean-shaven jaw.

She kept thinking naughty thoughts about those whiskers grazing against her flushed and very sensitive skin, thoughts that were proving distracting. Especially for someone who didn't have those kind of thoughts.

But for the first time in a long time, she felt perfectly—wonderfully—*normal*. Like a girl at a bar who'd met a guy who she wanted to hook up with.

That Natalie had never done anything like that even before Mick came into her life didn't seem to matter. She felt like that girl now, and it felt pretty darn amazing. Standing in that corner with this guy who didn't know anything about her, except her name and that she worked on the Hill as an "assistant," Natalie felt free. What was that thing that Amish kids did in their teens? Rumspringa! That was what it felt like.

"How long will you be in DC?" she asked, standing on her toes so that her mouth was in line with his ear and he could hear her.

She wobbled—and it wasn't from the wine. It was from the heat radiating from him and the nearly overwhelming urge to put her hands on his chest and see if it was as hard and solid as it looked.

His hand circled her arm to steady her, but not before their bodies touched for an instant. Touched in all the right places that made her heart leap right through her throat and her nerve endings flare with awareness. Redhot, "I want to kiss you right here to heck with PDA" awareness.

"Not long," he said in his rich, dark voice. She liked how he talked. Short and to the point. There wasn't a lot of messing around with him. "Only a few days."

Her body was still humming from the brief moment of contact and from the hand that was around her arm so it took her a moment for her synapses to connect again.

Under normal circumstances she might have been disappointed by his response. Actually, even under these extraordinary circumstances, she felt a twinge of it, knowing that he would be leaving soon and she wouldn't be able to get to know him better.

But then, she realized that "a few days" might just be the answer—or excuse—that she needed. If Scott wasn't around, Mick wouldn't be able to find out about him, and she wouldn't have a reason to put the brakes on where this was heading. And she didn't need to be a mind reader to figure out exactly where this was heading.

His eyes were dropping just as often to her mouth as hers were to his, he was getting into the close talking just as much as she was, and his hand didn't seem to be too eager to release her arm. Actually it was sliding down and doing a little caressing.

But she had to make sure. He'd said he was on leave, right? "Then it's back on the ship?" she asked.

His mouth curved in a wry smile that revealed a dimple in his left cheek, which made her heart skip a few beats.

God, this guy was almost too much to take. "Dreamy" was putting it mildly. Despite his interest in her, he'd been a little reserved at first. But as they'd talked he'd relaxed considerably.

"Something like that," he said.

"You guys are at sea for months at a time, right?"

"Can be." He stopped the movement of his hand over the bare skin of her arm that was turning her knees to mush and frowned. "Do you have a boyfriend or something?"

"No," she said, surprised. "Why?"

"You seem kind of eager to get rid of me."

Her cheeks heated, which she hoped he took as embarrassment, not guilt. "No. Just trying to get the lay of the land."

He held her gaze for a moment. She wished she knew what he was thinking, but she got the sense that this guy would be very hard to read if he didn't want you to.

"Fair enough." He took a final sip of his beer and set it down on the bar. "You want to get out of here?"

Her heart slammed against her chest. It was the moment of truth. Now she understood what that look was about. He'd been trying to see whether they were on the same page. The same one-night-stand, casual-hookup page.

Were they?

Natalie's heart pounded. She didn't know. Could chemistry really be this good? Could she really do this?

There was one way to find out. She closed the narrow

gap between them with more of a sway than a step so that their bodies were touching.

The reaction was instantaneous. It was like walking into an oven. She was drenched with heat. Her skin tightened and tingled.

All over.

It was amazing. Literally amazing. This was a whole new world of desire for her—before and after what had happened with Mick. But what she'd experienced with Todd had been . . . nice. This wasn't nice. It was raw and fierce and intense. It was mind-blowing terrain.

Scott guessed her intention and took the lead. His arm looped easily around her waist and drew her in even tighter as their lips touched for the first time.

Good God. It was like a shock of sensation going off inside her. She dissolved into the heat of his mouth, consumed by the raw energy of the passion firing between them.

His lips were soft and firm at the same time as they moved over hers skillfully and possessively. This man knew how to kiss and how to take charge.

And he did so fantastically. Perfectly. Incredibly. Nothing had ever felt more natural. It was almost too easy. It was hard to think. Hard to be rational when something felt this good. This right.

He was also a man used to getting what he wanted, and she'd just jumped to number one on the list.

She opened her mouth, wanting to taste him deeper, and he was already there. The sensation of his tongue stroking and sliding against hers sent her stomach right to the floor. The strokes grew deeper and deeper. Hotter. Wetter. More frantic. It was too much to take. She rode up against him, needing to feel the hard press of his desire. She wasn't disappointed. The thick slab made her stomach drop again. Her moan mixed with his groan as a pool of heat flooded between her legs.

She had her answer. Yes, chemistry could be this good, and yes, she could *definitely* do this.

But unless they were going to put on a show for the rest of the bar, which they kind of were already, it was time to make a decision. She wasn't romantic enough to call it fate, but whatever the sexual equivalent was, this was it. It was something that she might never have a chance to experience again. An opportunity to put what had happened with Mick behind her for good.

Mick had stolen her life from her, but she wasn't going to let him take this from her. She felt normal. Free to do what she wanted. She wanted this for herself.

She'd like to have said it was a moment of recklessness that made her pull back and say, "Yes. Let's get out of here."

But it wasn't. She knew exactly what she was doing.

It took his eyes a moment to clear the haze and focus. "I have a room at a hotel nearby."

He gave her the name of a well-known, upscale hotel a few blocks away.

Her brows lifted. "The navy must pay you well."

He looked mildly embarrassed. "Not really. I used points."

She nodded and let him lead her out of the bar, but not before saying good-bye to Hannah and making sure she knew exactly where she was going and with whom.

Natalie wasn't oblivious to the danger of leaving a bar with a guy, but neither was she going to let it stop her. She was going to trust her instincts—something else she wasn't going to let Mick take from her. And every bone in her body was screaming that Scott Taylor was a good guy. Safe. A man worthy of her trust.

Even if she wasn't of his.

Her friend couldn't contain her glee. "Did I call it or what?" she whispered. "You naughty girl."

Natalie blushed, not disagreeing. She did feel naughty—but in a good way. In an exciting way.

In a way that was rewarded a few minutes after he opened the door to his hotel room. She barely even glanced at the fancy suite before he pulled her into his arms and started up right where the kiss at the bar had lcft off.

From there it went fast—very fast—as in up-against-the-door fast. One minute she was melting into his erotic kiss, and the next she was melting into him.

The door behind her had become her support as her body turned to molten lava. Boneless. Fluid. Hot.

She didn't know how to describe it other than their bodies just came together. First their mouths, then their tongues, then her breasts to his steely hard chest, and then her hips to his even harder erection.

She was grabbing at his shoulders, sliding her hands under the shirt that she'd tugged from his waist to spread her hands over the fevered skin of his stomach and chest, needing all the contact she could get. Her fingers were clenching, trying to dig into the hard slabs of muscle as she fought to hold on.

Faster.

He had one hand under a leg that she'd somehow looped around his waist and the other on her breast. Cupping . . . squeezing . . . kneading as their hips bumped and grinded to the ever-increasing frenzy of pleasure.

And that's what it was. A wild, wicked frenzy of pleasure that washed over her and transported her into a different world. A mindless world. A world where the only thing that mattered was him being inside her.

A stroke of his hand between her legs, the hurried biting off the top of a condom wrapper, the lifting of her skirt, the unfastening of his pants, and her prayers were answered with a hard, body-jarring, heart-stopping thrust.

She cried out at the possession. At the relief. At the feel of him deep and hard inside her—filling her.

Good God, was he filling her. The size of the erection she'd felt was no joke.

Their eyes met for one brief instant and something equally as fierce and possessive passed between them.

"You okay?" he asked through gritted teeth. His handsome face was taut with the effort that it was taking to stop—to hold back at the freight train of need that was barreling down on them both. It wasn't going to stop, and she didn't want it to.

She was better than okay. She was fantastic. She was free. The black cloud was gone. If only for this brief moment.

It had to be a dream.

She met the concern in his gaze with a smile that reached from somewhere deep inside her. Somewhere that hadn't been touched in a long time. "I'm perfect."

At least she thought she was until a few minutes later when he showed her exactly what perfection was. What it felt like to reach the highest peak of pleasure while looking into the eyes of the man who had possessed her so completely.

She had no idea how completely. But over the next two days, locked together in that hotel room and barely coming up for air, she would find out.

Scott Taylor was everything she'd dreamed of and she just wanted to hold on to him for a little while. Was that so wrong?

Natalie blinked, recoiling from the light that set off an explosion of pain in her head as she slowly came back to consciousness.

It *had* been a dream. If only she could keep her eyes closed and never remember what had come next.

She opened her eyes and saw two worried faces leaning over her.

"How do you feel?" Becky asked.

Natalie lifted her head only to feel a fresh explosion of pain that made her put her head back down on the hard ground behind her.

"Easy," the sheriff said, putting his hand on her arm. "You hit your head pretty hard on the pavement when you fainted. You've been out of it for a couple minutes. I was about to call an ambulance."

Natalie winced as she reached around behind her head and felt the bump, which confirmed what he'd said. Fainted? Suddenly the memory came back to her in a hot rush. For one incredible, horrible moment she thought she'd seen the man she'd loved. Incredible because he was dead, and horrible because even in death she knew how much he must hate her.

Her chest squeezed with a fresh wave of pain. For the hundredth time, she wished she could go back and change things.

But what would she change? Meeting him at that bar and going to bed with him? Having Mick find out about him before she could get Scott away from her? Or falling in love with him when she was supposed to be spying on him? If she needed any more proof of her self-imposed Worst Spy Ever title—which she didn't—that was it. What kind of "honey" falls in love with her trap? A foolish one who was courting heartbreak and misery. Most of all she wished she could change the message that hadn't reached him in time to save his life.

"I fainted?" she repeated, and then frowned. "I never faint."

Becky smiled. "Well, you gave a good impression. One minute you were standing there, the next you were white as a sheet and flat on the ground."

Feeling silly, Natalie started to sit up. But the world

started to swim so horribly she had to stop for a minute so she didn't throw up.

"Not so fast," the sheriff said. "Maybe I should call that ambulance."

"No ambulance, please," Natalie said. "I'm fine."

But clearly neither the sheriff nor Becky believed her.

"Okay," the sheriff said. "But we're taking you to urgent care. It's just down the block."

Natalie was feeling bad enough not to argue—even if she thought it would have done her any good. They helped her up and started to lead her down the block, supporting her on each side.

"You said a name," the sheriff said, eyeing her sideways. "It sounded like 'Scott.' "

Natalie hoped he would attribute the sudden loss of blood in her face to her injury. She shook her head—which was a mistake as she would have stumbled if they hadn't been holding her.

When she found her equilibrium again, she was ready with an explanation. She hadn't seen him, and she wasn't going to say anything to make them curious. Scott was dead. Mick had been only so happy to tell her that her attempt to call off the mission hadn't worked. The entire platoon had been killed in the missile blast.

"I said 'shoot.' I didn't eat much today and low blood sugar must have caught up with me when I tried to move too fast." She smiled at Becky. "Next time I'll have some of that sandwich you offered me."

"Or she could let you take a break for lunch," the sheriff said with a reproachful glance at Becky. "All some people think about are their jobs."

The diminutive brunette seemed to grow a few inches taller in outrage. She obviously didn't appreciate the implication. "That's rich, coming from you."

Natalie rushed to Becky's defense, even if she didn't need it, as it looked as if an argument was brewing.

"Becky tried to get me to take a lunch break, but I was in the middle of something and didn't want to stop. I guess I learned my lesson."

Fortunately, the conversation didn't go any further as they arrived at the urgent care facility and Natalie spent the next hour in a number of medical rooms being poked, prodded, and scanned.

The sheriff and Becky were checking on her while she waited for the doctor in the final room where they'd wheeled her in after the scan. Dr. Peters, as he introduced himself, was probably in his mid-fifties, slightly paunchy, with thick wavy gray hair that was long enough to suggest he took pride in it, and a kind face.

He stood right beside the bed, looking down at her. "How are you feeling?"

Natalie's mouth curved in a wry grin. "A little silly to have caused all this trouble. I didn't have much to eat all day, and I guess it caught up with me."

He didn't argue with her explanation, but began a few tests with her vision, hearing, reflexes, and memory.

When he was done, he looked pleased. "You have a nasty bump on the head, but it seems you were lucky—or have a hard head."

She laughed. "Probably the latter."

"Well, in this case that is good. The CT scan didn't pick up anything, either."

"Does that mean I can go home?" Natalie asked hopefully.

"I'd like you to stay overnight for observation."

She heard the operative word: "like." "But I don't have to."

He frowned but admitted, "No. I can't hold you if you don't want to stay here. Do you have someone who can stay with you?"

Guessing what Becky and the sheriff were going to say, she nodded and lied, "I can call someone."

"Good," the doctor said. "But you shouldn't drive."

"That's okay," the sheriff said. "I'll drive her home. I have to head out that way to pick up Sammie from hockey practice later anyway." Before she could object, he added to her, "You can call me in the next day or two when you need a ride back into town to pick up your car."

"Or me," Becky offered.

"That's fine," the doctor said. "I have some paperwork for Ms. Wilson to fill out, but if you two wouldn't mind waiting outside there is something I would like to discuss with her in private."

Both Brock and Becky looked curious but did as Dr. Peters asked.

Natalie gripped the sheets in her fists, her heart pounding in her chest. She felt like a cornered animal about to be asked a question she didn't want to acknowledge, let alone answer.

She suspected what the doctor was going to say. From the bandage on the inside of her arm, she figured that along with the head scan they'd taken her blood.

"Are you aware, Ms. Wilson, that you are . . . ?" He paused uncomfortably.

"Pregnant," Natalie finished for him. "Yes."

He looked relieved to not be the one breaking the news to her.

Her pregnancy was the reason she was alive and Jen was dead. Natalie had been violently ill and Jen had gone to the drugstore for her. Jen had come down from New York on the train for a long weekend visit so she'd taken Natalie's car. The men who'd killed Jen thought it was Natalie who'd crashed into that freeway underpass.

As had everyone else. There had been no reason to think otherwise. It had been her car, her keys, and her wallet had any of it remained after the fire that had burned almost everything beyond recognition. Including Jennifer. Ironically, Natalie had insisted Jennifer take her wallet to pay for what she bought at the drugstore. She never dreamed that less than an hour later that insistence would enable her to take over Jennifer's identity.

A wave of sadness hit her. The horror of her friend's death was never far from her mind.

Even Natalie's mother hadn't realized who it was. She'd been the one to identify the body as it was too difficult on her father to travel. She didn't want to think about what her death had done to him. To any of them: her dad, her mom, or her sister. The sister who needed her. She never could have cut herself off from Lana—Svetlana—if she wasn't convinced it was the only way.

Identification mistakes in accidents weren't unheard of. There was that big case a number of years back involving two Indiana college students in a car crash. One of the girls had been killed and the other so horribly injured no one—not even the parents—realized their IDs had been mixed up by an officer on the scene until the surviving girl woke from her coma five weeks later and wrote her name.

They, too, had looked close enough to pass for sisters.

In college Natalie and Jennifer used to joke about their resemblance. Jennifer had even used Natalie's driver's license as a fake ID for the couple of months before she turned twenty-one.

But now her friend was dead because Natalie had been too sick to drive herself to the store. Natalie had thought her sickness was from the news of Scott's death, but Jennifer had guessed the truth: she was pregnant with the child of the man who she never should have fallen in love with.

She didn't know what to think about it so she didn't think about it. It was called denial. Big-time denial.

Instinctively—almost protectively—her hands went to her stomach. She hadn't wanted a baby, didn't know if she was ready to be a mother, and had no idea what she was going to do when the baby came in about twenty-three weeks. But she'd never thought about not having it.

This baby was all she had left of Scott, and she could never give that up—no matter what the difficulty.

"Have you seen a doctor?" Dr. Peters asked.

She nodded. "A couple months ago." Anticipating the lecture, she added, "I've been moving around a lot the past few months. But I'm taking my vitamins."

"You should make an appointment with one of my colleagues." He wrote down a name and handed her a card.

Natalie promised to do so in the next few days, and he left, telling her he'd be back to check on her again before she was discharged.

The doctor wasn't kidding about paperwork. It took her an hour to fill out all the insurance forms—along with identity theft she was now committing insurance fraud—but about two hours later after instructions from Dr. Peters, she was discharged into the sheriff's care.

Becky walked with them back to his squad car before giving Natalie a hug good-bye and telling her not to come in on Thursday if she didn't feel well.

The sheriff didn't attempt to make much small talk during the short drive, which she was grateful for. Being forced to confront the child she was carrying had left her in a contemplative mood. She had to start making plans. She couldn't pretend this was going to go away. She would be showing soon. Already, she could feel a small bump in her stomach. She needed a story . . . a father.

For about the hundredth time, she said a silent prayer to Scott, begging for his forgiveness.

But she knew he wouldn't give it to her. She'd betrayed and deceived him. She knew he'd thought he cared for her. But the woman he'd fallen for was an illusion—a fabrication and fantasy. Natalie had been pretending to be someone she wasn't. Someone confident and savvy and worldly. Someone who weighed fifteen pounds less, whose hair was the perfect shade of California blond, and who loved wearing four-inch stilettos and tight suits.

But that wasn't her. It was the glossy mask Mick had insisted upon. The real her was much more boring and not at all glamorous. She wore jeans and T-shirts and sneakers and liked her hair in a ponytail. She also liked dessert.

Brock pulled up to the farmhouse a short while later. It was after eight, but thanks to being so far north, it wasn't completely dark yet.

"Thanks for the ride," she said to the sheriff as she got out of the car.

He nodded. "You sure you have someone you can call to come stay with you this late?"

"I'm sure." It was hard enough as it was keeping track of her lies. She'd learned not to offer information unless someone asked. It was a valuable tool.

Fortunately, he didn't ask, although she could tell he wanted to.

The sheriff waited until she went inside to turn the lights on. She waved from the doorway as he drove off. Only when the taillights had disappeared from the highway did she heave a heavy sigh and close the door.

The sigh didn't last.

A scream tore from her throat when someone grabbed her from behind, but a swift hand over her mouth snuffed out the sound. Not that it would have done much good. There was no one to hear. Suddenly she was brutally aware of how alone she was out here. The quiet and privacy she'd been seeking could turn out to be her doom.

Instinct took over. She stomped on his foot and heard the welcome groan. Taking advantage of his surprise, she slammed her elbow straight back into his gut and whipped around ready to use the flat of her palm to shove his nose up to his brains.

But his moment of shock was gone. He easily blocked her blow, caught her wrist, and twisted her arm around—hard—to bring her tight against him. She'd been well taught, but he was in a different league. He made her efforts seem like child's play. It took only an instant for her to realize why.

The contact and the heat of his body stunned her. Confused her. It was almost . . .

Muscle memory.

The instinct to fight died. She knew even before she looked up and saw his face. The man in the car hadn't been a ghost. Scott wasn't dead.

Euphoria rose up inside her. "You're alive!" she burst out, the tears not far behind. "Thank God, you're alive!"

"Save it," he said sharply, pricking her happiness as if it were a balloon. *Pop.* Clearly, he wasn't feeling the same happiness and relief at seeing her aboveground and not six feet under. His face was an icy mask of rage. Even his eyes—normally deep blue—had turned as wintry as slate.

He looked so different from the man she'd come to know that she was surprised she'd recognized him at all. Scott was the quintessential naval officer. Though most SEALs adopted the "relaxed grooming standards" of secret special operations units, Scott wasn't the relaxing type—about anything. He was by-the-book regulation, and rarely had she ever seen him not shaved and impeccably groomed.

Now was one of those times. His face hadn't seen a razor in at least a week and his hair was both darker (she suspected dyed) and longer than she'd ever seen it. Maybe even a little past his ears. And wavy.

She'd had no idea.

Even the clothes he was wearing were standard, off-the-rack cargo shorts and a long-sleeve T-shirt. The very first night they'd met she'd been struck by his well-put-together appearance. Later she learned why. Scott had been raised with incredible wealth—that old East Coast family kind of wealth—and his clothes reflected that. Not that he was flashy. It was actually the opposite. Everything was just *nice*: the fit, the fabric, and very understated. She'd never met anyone who had bespoke suits from London—she'd actually never even heard that word before she'd questioned him about why his suits looked as if they'd been made for him. They had.

Only the flexed jaw and small white lines around his mouth were vaguely familiar. But this wasn't the un-yielding, tough-as-nails, but always controlled SEAL commander that she'd seen once or twice in a meeting. This was the dangerous special ops commando who looked as if he could take down anything in his way. His fierce expression and scruffy appearance coupled with eyes that were bloodshot from lack of sleep gave him a feral, menacing edge that she'd never seen before.

"You work fast, Natalya. I see you found another poor sucker to get information out of. What state secrets does the county sheriff have?"

She barely heard the last two sentences. She was too stuck on the first. *Natalya.* Dread fell through her like a rock. He'd used her birth name.

He knew.

Five

Colt Wesson stood outside his ex-wife's front door and experienced a rare moment of indecision. He probably should turn around, get back in his car, and head straight to the airport like he'd originally planned. But he'd been driving by her exit and decided impulsively to make a detour.

He'd stayed away from Kate for ten days. After having the rug pulled out from under him twice on the same day—not only learning that some of the guys that he'd thought were dead for months, guys who were like brothers to him, were alive, but also that his now ex-wife hadn't had an affair with one of his best friends when they were married, they were actually brother and sister—he hadn't trusted himself to talk to her. How could she have kept that kind of information from him? How could she have let him think the worst?

But after returning Scott's message last night—two days after it had been left—and agreeing to go to Alaska to track down Travis Hart, Colt had broached the subject with his former friend, teammate, and unknown ex-brother-in-law.

"Why didn't you tell me?" he'd asked Taylor before they'd hung up.

There had been a long moment of silence on the other end. Colt didn't need to explain. Taylor knew what he was asking: if Colt had known Kate and Taylor were related, he never would have . . .

Shit. Colt wasn't sure he wanted to go down that path. Everything would have been different. His marriage. His job. His stomach knifed. The miscarriage and baby he'd thought wasn't his. A baby he hadn't wanted then but now couldn't stop thinking about. He'd had a *daughter*.

Why the fuck hadn't they told him the truth?

"If you have questions, you should ask Kate." Scott paused before adding, "Better yet, you should have done that three years ago."

Colt didn't miss the censure in Taylor's voice and it pissed him off. Colt had tried, damn it. But what the hell was he supposed to think? He and Kate had been having problems in their four-year-long marriage. Big problems. He knew he'd been pushing her away. But he'd never expected her to turn to Taylor.

It seemed as if every time Colt turned around, his wife was talking to his friend. There were texts. E-mails. Obviously private conversations that Colt felt as if he was interrupting when she came to see him in Honolulu. Taylor sat on Colt's living room couch more than he did. At first he'd attributed it to rich people bonding. Their parents had known one another, which didn't surprise him in the close-knit circles of the East Coast elite. But when he discovered that Taylor had been in DC for weeks where Kate lived and worked while Colt had been training with the team in Arizona, he'd finally confronted her.

She'd denied it, of course, but she'd never said they were *related*. No, he was just supposed to take her word for it that they weren't sleeping together, when she had to have known how it looked.

So that's why Colt was here. Three years too late maybe, but he deserved a fucking answer. It was the "fucking answer" part, however, that made him hesitate. It never went well when he was angry like this. He tended to say things he didn't mean. Things that couldn't be taken back. All that SEAL discipline couldn't control his caustic tongue.

He turned around to leave. He'd talk to her when he got back from Alaska. Maybe by then he would have cooled down and the betrayal eating away in his gut wouldn't taste like battery acid.

The door opened behind him. "Running away again, Colt? You are good at that."

Her voice stopped him in his tracks. He turned around, seeing his ex-wife—his sexy-as-hell ex-wife—standing in the doorway in her running clothes. What there were of them. He'd obviously caught her on her way out for her morning run.

Kate was a beautiful woman whether in her usual suit and pearls or in spandex and a ponytail. She had that patrician Grace Kelly WASPy look going that screamed old money and privilege. He'd assumed she was a bitch the first time he met her—which admittedly hadn't been in the best of circumstances, when she'd overheard him call her "CIA Barbie" to the rest of the guys on a mission briefing.

For a poor kid born on the proverbial wrong side of the tracks, Colt could admit that the rich-girl thing might have been part of her appeal initially. But he'd quickly learned that the woman who looked like an ice princess on the outside had a heart of gold. Worse, she'd seen through his belligerent-asshole schtick—which admittedly wasn't always a schtick—with alarming speed.

Having grown up in foster homes of incrementally varying degrees of bleak and horrible, no one had ever given a shit about him, and Colt couldn't believe that someone like Kate wanted him for anything more than a good fuck.

Although "good" was putting it mildly. It had never been just good between them; it had been hot, wild, and off-the-charts incredible. She might look prim and proper on the outside, but in bed she liked it rough and a little dirty. Which was definitely in his wheelhouse. But the fierce, almost primitive attraction between them had never been the problem. It was sorting out all the emotions that had come along with it.

Initially he'd thought it was the "slumming it" novelty of fucking the bad boy that she wanted. That was why rich women like her wanted men like him. But she'd convinced him otherwise. At one time, she'd loved him with every inch of her soul. He just hadn't known what to do with it.

He'd been so sure that something would fuck it up like it always did that he'd pushed her away and ensured it. He'd started hanging out with the guys longer on the base after work. Instead of one beer after a long day, he'd have three or four. He'd find himself at a bar flirting with some woman he didn't give a shit about. He'd stopped talking to her—really talking to her. When he came home angry or upset after a bad mission or difficult deployment, and she asked him what was wrong, he shut down—and her out.

He knew he was doing it, but he just couldn't seem to stop himself. Maybe in his perverse mind it had been some kind of fucked-up test. Some kind of way of proving that she *really* loved him. But the test had backfired big-time when he thought she'd cheated on him with the man who was like a brother to him. Colt had been destroyed. Shattered. He'd lashed out cruelly—unforgivably—and then sunk into a hole so deep he still hadn't pulled himself out.

For three years he'd been living half a life. His job in CAD—the nickname (aka Control-Alt-Delete) for Task Force Tier One, the secret unit where he was an operative—was all that mattered. He'd lost everything else that mattered to him. His marriage. His team. His fucking *soul*.

It was hard to stand here and not blame her when with one word she could have stopped it. Yeah, definitely not a good idea to be here.

He let the "running away" comment slide, although he was sure she knew how much that pissed him off. He'd never run away from a fight in his life. "We need to talk, but not right now."

She lifted one perfectly arched and waxed brow in that haughty, "I care so little about you that just this tiny part of my body is affected" way that drove him nuts. This woman who used to love him with every part of her body and soul now looked at him with as much interest as a bug under her heel. "You and I don't have anything to say to one another."

So much for his good intentions. You could almost hear him snap. He moved so quickly up the stairs, she gasped when he pushed her back into the hall and closed the door behind him. He resisted the urge to back her up against the wall, but his body was definitely leaning in. He could feel the heat of anger radiating from her lean body, drawing him in like a magnet.

"Is that right?" he asked. "I think you have a hell of a lot to say. How about a goddamned explanation for why you never told me Scott was your brother? Or for how you not only let me think that all my former teammates were dead, but how you lied to me and led me on a fucking goose chase the past month to keep me from finding out the truth?"

It had stung when he'd figured out that the only reason she'd been spending time with him was to keep him busy and prevent him from learning that some of the guys had survived. She'd known how much they meant to him, and she'd let him think they were all dead.

And here he'd been thinking how much he liked

working with her again. How much it felt like old times. The worst part was that he'd known she was lying to him about something. But he'd followed her to a hotel, saw her with a man, and assumed . . .

Shit. "It was Scott, wasn't it? He was the man you met at the hotel that night?"

"You mean the man you accused me of cheating on my fiancé with?"

He'd done more than accuse. Colt had been so out of his mind with jealousy that he'd cornered her in an elevator and kissed her. They'd been a few seconds away from doing a lot more before she'd pushed him away, apparently coming to her senses. But was there more to it? Had she kissed him back just to keep him off the trail?

His gut wasn't the only part of his body twisting as she took a step toward him and met his anger full force. She'd never backed down from him. Never. He'd always loved that about her. The bigger problem now was that she was wearing a tight tank top and her breasts were one deep breath from brushing his chest. Heat pooled in his groin. *Not the time to get a hard-on*. But his body wasn't exactly listening to him.

"I don't owe you a damned thing, Colt. Get the hell out of here. Go back to whatever dive bar you've probably been hiding in the past week."

He wanted to deny it, but she knew him too well. He drank and played pool when he was angry. It made him feel better. Usually. There was something else that always made him feel better, but he hadn't taken any of the offers thrown in his direction the past week. Month. And that pissed him off even more. Kate didn't care whom he fucked; why should he?

Because the only woman he wanted to fuck was her. It had been like that since the first time he'd met her. Sex before he'd met her had always been satisfying. But after . . . he knew what he was missing.

Damn her to hell.

He wanted to touch her but he didn't dare. Not when she was so close to him, and not the way he was feeling like this. He was likely to explode. In more ways than one.

He stepped back and took a deep breath, trying to ratchet down the anger—and the heat. "You knew how much I cared about those guys, and you let me think they were all dead. How could you do that? Do you hate me that much?"

Her cheeks were still flushed, but when she looked away, he knew he'd gotten to her. "Scott didn't want anyone else to know. He thought it was too dangerous."

"You should have trusted me."

Her gaze lifted back to his, but there was nothing in her expression to give her thoughts away. He used to be able to read her. But she'd changed. Hardened.

God, had he done that to her?

"My trust and loyalty belong to my brother. You lost them a long time ago, Colt."

"Is that why you didn't tell me you were related? Did he ask you to keep it secret so there wouldn't be any problems with the team?"

"Scott wanted to say something. It was me who asked him to keep it a secret. I didn't want to hurt my mother. I don't think she knew my father cheated on her."

He'd heard that Kate's mother had died last year.

Despite the explanation, he felt his temper firing again. "Didn't you think I deserved to know that my wife wasn't sleeping with my best friend?"

"I told you that I wasn't. More than once. You just didn't want to hear it."

"I would have listened if you'd said he was your god-damned *brother*!"

Her cheeks flushed with bright pink spots of anger high on her cheekbones. "When was I supposed to voice my suspicions—suspicions that were only confirmed right before my accident, by the way? When I came to see you in Honolulu at the bar and you had another woman on your lap or when you told me that you wished the drunk driver had killed me along with our baby?"

She might as well have slapped him. The truth of the accusation brought him harshly back to reality. The reality where all his anger and resentment were just a front, an excuse to prevent him from having to think about his own actions. About the accusations he'd made and the cruel things he'd said. Words that he hadn't meant but that could never be taken back. About how he'd left his injured wife in a hospital to mourn the death of their unborn child alone because he'd been half-crazed with jealousy and hurt.

Kate had always been good at forcing him to confront what he didn't want to acknowledge, and just like that, his anger disintegrated. He wanted to be ill. Could someone throw up from shame?

The destruction of their marriage was his fault. *He* was the one responsible, not her.

Hurricane Colt. That was what she called him. Destroying everything in his wake.

She was right.

He didn't know what to say. Everything was going to sound like excuses—which they were—but he tried anyway. "I've never been so scared in my life as I was on that airplane. The message I'd received was that you had been in a bad car accident, and I thought I'd lost you. When I arrived, the nurse at the desk told me you'd been pregnant and had lost the baby, and that the father was in there with you now. I looked in the room and saw Scott lying next to you in bed, holding you, and something inside me just snapped. I knew I'd lost you to him, and I was so jealous and angry I couldn't see straight."

He couldn't see what was right before his eyes. That his wife loved him—had always loved him—and only him. As little sense as that made to him even now. What the fuck had she seen in him?

"He was comforting me. Scott was my friend. I'd just been told I'd lost our baby, which I know you didn't want, but I did. I was devastated. You weren't there, and I didn't know if you'd bother to show up." Her gaze held his unrelentingly, not letting him off the hook. "You hadn't been there for me in years."

He didn't know what to say. What could he say? It was the damned truth.

"I don't know what the hell was wrong with me. I was just so fucking scared of losing you."

Their eyes held for a moment longer, but then she released them—him. "Well, you did."

Her tone was matter-of-fact and left no room for argument. Did he want to argue? Fucking hell, he did. "I'm so sorry, Kate. I'm so damned sorry. I'd give anything if I could go back and change what I did."

She took a deep breath and shook her head. "It wasn't just your fault. I expected too much. I knew you didn't want a wife—or a child. I just thought I could change your mind." The wry smile she gave him tore through his black, shriveled, and scarred heart. It was the smile of someone who had gotten over a painful event and put it in the past. Her words confirmed that. "It doesn't matter anymore. We've been divorced for three years, and we have both moved on." She looked up at him and said the words that cut him to the quick. "You need to let it go, Colt."

He knew what she really meant. *You need to let me go.*

She was right, but only now as the magnitude of what he'd done—and what he'd lost—became clear, he wasn't sure that he could.

Six

Scott had experienced a number of devastating shocks in his life. The first was when he'd learned the man he'd idolized wasn't his biological father. The second was when he'd read about Natalie's death in a car crash. The third was a week and a half ago when he'd learned that the woman he'd thought had been killed for warning him had also been betraying him. And the most recent was a few hours ago when he sat at the stoplight and happened to glance over at the woman coming out of the city's municipal building. It had brought him up with all the subtlety of a two-by-four slammed against his forehead.

At first he thought the woman was Jennifer Wilson—the person he was on his way to see at the rented farm he'd spent the last couple of days tracking her to. He'd known he was on to something as soon as he learned that Jennifer had broken a lease for a new apartment in New York and never showed up for the job that went along with it.

Jennifer Wilson was running. And the three towns he'd tracked her credit card receipts to since only made him more certain of it.

But then he felt a buzz up his spine. The woman was wearing glasses, her hair was slightly darker, and she was a little curvier, but that buzz exploded with recognition.

Was it . . . ?

Could it be . . . ?

For one unthinking moment his chest filled with relief and joy, before he caught himself. When the car behind him honked, and she turned to look at him he knew the truth. It was her.

Natalya had fooled them all. She wasn't dead. She was alive and posing as her friend.

He'd turned away quickly before she could recognize him and drove to her farm to wait for her. It had taken her so long to get here that he'd begun to wonder if she'd made him and ran, when the sheriff's car turned down the driveway.

Now that she was standing right in front of him, it was hard to rank all those shocks, but after three hours of festering, he was putting this one right up there.

For the first time in his life, Scott didn't trust himself. His grip tightened as rage boiled inside him. When he thought of the men—his friends—who'd lost their lives, he could kill her.

He was holding her so close, so tight, the temptation should be strong. But that wasn't the temptation he was feeling. The familiar sensations of overwhelming heat and fierce, almost animalistic attraction had taken hold. He caught the scent of her shampoo and the urge to bury his nose in the silky strands and inhale was so strong he hated himself for it—which only intensified that feeling of uncontrollable anger.

His muscles tightened, and he drew her in infinitesimally closer. But only for an instant. Seething and with a harsh curse, he pushed her away and forced himself to take a step back.

She looked up at him pleadingly, her green eyes round and huge behind horn-rimmed glasses that were giving him all kinds of sexy librarian fantasies—

He stopped. *You have to be fucking kidding me. Is anything about her real?* "Your eyes are brown! Or is that another disguise?"

He didn't bother hiding the disgust in his voice; he wanted her to know what he thought of her.

If she thought it was strange that after all that had happened, the first thing he'd asked her about was her eye color, she didn't show it. "It isn't a disguise. My eyes are brown. You have to understand it wasn't my idea—none of it was my idea. I never wanted to deceive you. But thank God, my warning reached you in time."

"It didn't."

"But you are alive."

"But over half my men aren't."

Just saying the words was like a stab in the gut—or maybe he should say *back*. She'd completely blindsided him.

Her face crumpled. She looked horrified—or rather he should say she was doing a damned fine job of *acting* horrified. "Oh God, Scott, I'm so sorry. I never meant any of this to happen."

"What—spying or getting caught?" She slunk down, avoiding his gaze, which was so unlike her it made him angrier. Where was the denial? The outrage? The lies? He reached out and grabbed her by the arm to force her to look at him. "What the fuck did you think would happen when you passed on information to Russia about secret operations—about *my* secret operations?"

He'd never sworn at her—at any woman—before, and she seemed to realize it, flinching at the word. He might have felt bad if he hadn't just had his nose almost flattened. The wounded doe-eyed crap was another act. She'd had training and knew how to defend herself. She was an operative—*an operative*, damn it. And the probably reopened wound on his shoulder proved it.

"It wasn't like that," she pleaded, tears filling her eyes. "Please, you have to understand. I didn't have a choice. Not about any of it. And I didn't know that what I was doing had anything to do with you or Team Nine."

Scott pushed her away from him, so filled with hatred and disgust he didn't want to look at her. He didn't know what he'd expected. Some kind of excuse? Some kind of denial? Even if it was a lie shouldn't she try to say something to give him a reason not to hate her? He sure as hell hadn't expected this instant capitulation. This "I'm sorry," "I didn't know," fall-on-his-mercy crap. He didn't have any mercy. Not where she was concerned.

"Well, it did—it had everything to do with me. And you did have a choice, Natalya. You just chose fucking wrong. Now get your shit together. We're getting out of here before your new boyfriend gets back."

She had the gall to look affronted. "The sheriff? He's not my new boyfriend. I barely know him. Where are you taking me?"

"Where do you think? I'm taking you in—back to DC. There are a lot of people who want to talk to you. You can tell them your sob story and make damned clear while you are at it that I didn't tell you anything."

She took a step back, clearly afraid. "You can't do that. They'll kill me if they find out that I'm alive."

"Is that supposed to be a deterrent? It's no more than you deserve and probably what will happen to you anyway when they convict you of treason. But if by 'they' you mean your comrade Mikhail, you don't have to worry about him." He paused and gave her a hard look. "He's dead."

Natalie reeled back at Scott's pronouncement. She covered the gasp from her mouth with her hand. "Dead?" she repeated dumbly, too stunned to let herself dare to believe it and shout for joy.

But Scott—this Scott who hated her and looked at her as if he didn't know her—mistook her reaction from one of relief to something else. But could she blame him? She'd made them strangers by lying to him from the start.

This whole thing had taken on the feeling of the surreal. How could she just be standing here with him and not in his arms? She'd mourned and missed him every day since learning that he'd been killed, and now that he was here all she wanted to do was plaster herself against that big, safe warrior's body, let him hold her and make her feel better, and weep with happiness. But she couldn't. Everything had changed because he knew the truth. There wouldn't be any happy reunions for them. Hatred was her new normal.

She'd feared this moment in her worst dreams, but it was far worse than she could have imagined. It felt as if her heart had been ripped to shreds and stomped on, leaving her with a longing so strong it threatened to cut off her breath. She wanted what had been so desperately, it was hard to accept this new reality.

"Sorry to break the bad news," Scott said—clearly not sorry. "But one of my teammates shot your comrade when the bastard tried to kill my sister." His gaze sharpened as he appeared to have just thought of something. "Let me guess: there was more than just a love of treason and Russia between you and Mikhail."

Natalie knew Scott had every right to his sarcasm and every right to be angry and hate her, but she wasn't going to take that—not about Mick.

She looked him straight in the eye and spoke in a firm voice. "You are wrong. I barely remember Russia, and I'm glad he is dead. There was never anything between us. I despised Mick. He was the one who forced me into this."

Literally.

But her words fell on deaf ears and an indifferent shrug of shoulders. "What makes you think I give a shit?" He picked up her purse, which she'd dropped in their scuffle, and tried to hand it to her. "You have three minutes to get you stuff together, and then we're leaving." He gave her a warning look. "Don't try anything. I won't go gentle on you next time."

She flushed, both angry and embarrassed. She hated how easily he'd evaded her defensive maneuvers. But that was the problem. Her training was defensive—meant to give her time to get away. She didn't have the kind of training that would enable her to go head-to-head with him.

There probably wasn't any training she could do to do that.

She knew every inch of his body. He was ripped. A physical specimen whose muscles weren't just for show, they were for a purpose. They'd been built to help make him one of the most elite warriors in the world. His strength and skill were on a different level—i.e., not her level. Not 99.9 percent of the population's level, either, for that matter. Even a small glimpse of his skill had proved that what she'd heard and read about tier-one SEAL operators was true.

Although she probably shouldn't be thinking about his body right now. Or have her head filled with visions of resting her cheek on that bare chest she was just imagining with his powerful arms wrapped around her after they'd . . . what? Made love? Had sex? Screwed like bunny rabbits?

What meant one thing then was now confused. Tainted. It had been real for her, but in a fantasy world that was now gone.

His body and what they'd once shared were off-limits. She needed to keep her head clear if she was going to get through to him. Somehow she had to convince him not to take her in. It wasn't just about her; she had to protect her family and the child she was carrying. The only way to keep them safe was for her to stay dead.

She ignored the purse he was holding out to her. "Please, Scott. I'm begging you just to hear me out. I know you have no reason to trust me—"

He made a sharp sound. "Christ, if that isn't the understatement of the year."

She ignored the sarcasm. "But if Mick's superiors find out I'm alive, they won't just go after me; they'll go after my family. They know I betrayed them. I never meant to pass on anything important. I didn't intentionally pass on information about your mission—it was a mistake. As soon as I found out about it, I tried to stop it and warn you. But then they tried to have me killed. I think they wanted someone to take the fall."

She could tell he was furious by how hard he tossed her bag on the sofa. "So let me get this straight. Your defense is that you didn't intend to be a good spy, but when you actually gave them something worthwhile by 'mistake' that I should give you points because you tried to warn me?" His voice was reaching dangerous levels of anger and that well-bred facade was definitely looking a little volatile. Had she really wanted to see him lose control just once? *Be careful what you wish for.* "And now I should feel sorry for you because they decided to make you their patsy?" He laughed harshly and looked at her as if she were an idiot—which is about how she was feeling. "Tough luck, *Natalya.* That's the chance you take when you get into the treason and spy business. But I'm

not going to let you take me down with you. You are going back."

She had never hated her birth name as much as when
he said it. It was worse than the grade-school teasing
she'd endured that had precipitated the change to Natalie.
Apparently, he was done listening to her. He grabbed her
arm and started dragging her toward the door with one
hand, and with the other grabbed her coat and threw it
at her.

"Wait! I need my—"

"Too late." He opened the door and tried to shove her
through it in front of him. "Your three minutes are up."

But she stopped in her tracks, refusing to budge.
"Stop, Scott!" she repeated. "You can't do this."

"The hell I can't. I'm taking you back if I have to tie
you up and drag you."

He was about to physically force her forward and
close the door behind him—with her purse and keys
inside—when she blurted, "I'm pregnant!"

His forward momentum came to a chillingly cold
stop. But it was nothing compared to the icy glare he
leveled at her. It was a look as sharp and eviscerating as
the edge of a razor. "What did you just say?"

She swallowed uneasily, having never been the re-
cipient of that much raw hostility directed at her, especially by a man who'd once looked at her with such
tenderness. "I . . . I'm pregnant."

Her wobbly, uncertain voice apparently didn't help her
credibility any.

He still had her arm and hauled her up to meet his
gaze. "You're lying."

The hatred emanating from him made her want to
shiver. And cry. Most of all cry over what she'd lost. But
maybe she'd never really had it. Whatever feelings he'd
had for her had been predicated on a lie.

But not all of it had been a lie. She had to try to find a way to convince him.

"I'm n-not. It's the truth, I swear." Suddenly she thought of something. "I can prove it to you tomorrow morning."

"Why not right now? I'm sure we can find a store with a pregnancy test. Or didn't they teach you how to fake a pregnancy test in spy school?"

Her cheeks flooded with heat, but she didn't rise to the bait or let him distract her. This was about the baby. *Their* baby. He might hate her, but he couldn't change the fact that they were going to have a child together. "I fainted after I thought I saw you—or rather, did see you—at the light in town earlier and hit my head. The sheriff and town manager took me to the urgent care. The doctor drew blood and discovered the pregnancy. You can ask him. The drugstore in town is closed. There's a Walmart about twenty miles away. It might be open—or you can wait until morning when the doctor is back and ask him."

Natalie could tell from his stony expression that he didn't believe her—or didn't want to believe her. But there was just enough uncertainty for her to add, "It's your child, Scott. I'm pregnant with our baby."

If she hoped that her words might bring a drop of softness to his gaze, those hopes were quickly dashed. If anything, it only seemed to make him angrier. His expression grew fiercer and the icy barrier in his gaze more remote.

"How convenient for you."

She jutted her chin up, responding to the snideness in his voice. "No, it isn't, as a matter of fact."

Did he have any idea of how hard this had been on her? Pregnant and alone, trying to protect not only herself but the baby she had no idea how she was going to provide for and keep safe? Did he think she'd planned this as some sort of elaborate scheme if he miraculously returned from the dead to exact sympathy from him? He'd read too many bad spy novels.

He held her gaze for so long she felt like squirming. But she didn't. She forced herself not to look away. She was telling the truth.

About the pregnancy, at least.

Seven

*P*regnant.

Even just thinking the word made Scott feel sick. It couldn't be true.

He had no reason to believe her, and she had every reason to lie. It was one of the oldest tricks in the book, wasn't it? An attempt to play the one card that would guarantee his sympathy and stay his hand with caution.

Scott should call her bluff and take her back to DC right now. It was his duty, not just to the SEAL badge or the bars on his uniform but to his men, and she'd already compromised his job enough. The job that he'd built his life around. He needed to stay on track. To not let her distract him with pregnancy tests and doctors.

She made a fool of you. . . .

But what if she wasn't lying? If there was even a small chance that she could be telling the truth, he had to know.

Damn it, a baby?

His stomach turned again, but he stepped to the side to let her walk back into the house. "If you are lying about this, Natalya, I swear I'll kill you myself."

How someone who had betrayed him so horribly

and committed treacherous and treasonous deeds that led to the death of eight men could manage to look so affronted—as if *he* was the one in the wrong—he didn't know. But her acting skills were Oscar-freaking-caliber.

"I'm not," she said, brushing by him.

It wasn't just her nose-in-the-air, "how dare you question my honor?" attitude that pissed him off—although it did—it was the brushing part that really made him angry. Or rather, his reaction to it. How could he feel anything after what she'd done?

But he felt it, all right. He felt the same blast of heat and firing off of every nerve ending—including the major one—that he had when she'd accidentally brushed by him on the way to the bathroom at the bar that first night they'd met. He'd never felt anything like it. It had almost been like the zap of an electrical current of attraction. Instantaneous, shocking, and sparking with all kinds of intense impulses.

She was a knockout, but he'd known a lot of beautiful women. This had been different. It had been elemental. Bone-deep. Chemical. Whatever you wanted to call it. Whatever had caused him to leave the bar with her and spend the next forty-eight hours in bed with her.

But instant attraction like that was one thing that couldn't be faked. He didn't know whether to be glad about that or not. Did the fact that some of it had been real make up for the fact that the rest of it hadn't?

No. And he sure as hell wasn't going to let it get in his way now. His dick might not have gotten the message, but he sure as hell had.

He shut the door behind her. She crossed the foyer and started heading up the staircase. "Where the hell do you think you are going?" he asked.

She turned around and glared at him. "To take a shower and then go to bed."

"At 2030 hours?"

She held his gaze in a silent challenge. "It's been a long day."

Did she take him for a fool? Better not ask that. It would just piss him off. But he wasn't going to let her out of his sight. "I don't think so," he said. "Not without me."

She arched an eyebrow in the way that she did when she was about to tease him. "You want to shower with me?"

The naughty twinkle in her eye was so familiar it made the black hole in his chest squeeze. It was hard not to respond, but he tightened the steel vise around his emotions and ignored it. She needed to know that they were never going back to the way it had been. "If you want to shower, you can do so with the door open—after I make sure there aren't any windows you can climb out of."

Her cheeks flushed as if the insinuation had offended her. Too bad. He didn't trust her not to run the moment his back was turned.

What he should do was drag her back to the urgent care and demand to see her records right now—whether the doctor was there or not.

But that could attract more attention than he wanted. Like her, Scott was in hiding and supposed to be dead. Besides, he was almost certain she was lying about the pregnancy and would try to use the time to escape. He wasn't going to show his face around here or anywhere else if he didn't need to.

But as sound as his reasoning was, he knew that wasn't all of it. She looked wiped out. Fall-on-the-pillow-and-sleep-for-hours wiped out. He'd thought it was just exhaustion from a long day of work, but when she'd told him about fainting and hitting her head, he knew there could be a more serious explanation.

If she wasn't lying to him about that, too, that is.

"I'm surprised the doctor let you leave if you hit your head when you fainted."

She stood on the stairs looking down at him for a few moments before responding, understanding exactly what he was getting at. "He advised that I stay the night. I wish I'd listened to him."

Her meaning was clear: because of Scott being here waiting for her. "I would have caught up with you eventually."

She shrugged as if it didn't matter any longer—which it didn't. "I'm supposed to have someone wake me up every few hours. I guess you get to play nursemaid."

He looked around; a thought suddenly occurring to him. "Is there someone else living here with you?"

Someone like the sheriff?

He felt a blast of something angry and irrational that he didn't want to acknowledge.

"No. I told the doctor I would call someone." He waited until she added, "I lied."

Not for the first time.

She sighed as if she knew exactly what he was thinking. "Can I go upstairs now? Or do you want to check me for weapons first?'

"Good idea." He should have thought of it himself. It was the first thing you did once you'd secured enemy combatants. A mistake like that could get him killed. He didn't need another bullet in his shoulder. Which hurt like hell right now, by the way, after their scuffle.

She gasped as he crossed the distance between them and started to pat her down. It wasn't anything he hadn't done countless times with suspects or prisoners in numerous places around the globe. But no matter how hard he steeled his mind, he couldn't separate the body he was feeling beneath the T-shirt and denim shorts from the naked one he'd caressed only a few months ago with his hands and mouth. He knew every inch of her. It had been consigned so deeply to his memory that even if he wanted to forget, he didn't think he could. She was fuller—softer—but it was all there in scorching-hot XXX detail.

No amount of steeling could prevent the rush of heat that surged through his blood from standing so close to her. She didn't need a shower. She smelled incredible. The familiar citrusy scent of her girly shampoo and lotion filled his nose as the air between them grew thick with tension and memory.

There was nothing sensual in the cold, impersonal slide of his hands over her chest, hips, and legs, but when his hand skidded over her breast and her nipple tightened reflexively, he felt a tug in his groin that was so hard that he stopped for just an instant and had to clench his teeth against the urge to rub his thumb over the tip.

It was hard not to think about different times and circumstances. Times and circumstances where he would have let his hands linger. Where he would have pinched that beaded nipple between his fingers and then between his teeth. Where the slide of his hand up between her legs would have been much slower and with an entirely different purpose. To lead him to the sweet juncture between her thighs that was so soft and warm. She was always so wet for him. So slick and ready. She would tremble in his arms when he touched her. He could almost hear her soft little moan. A few strokes of his finger and she would go off like a . . .

Shit. Not what he should be thinking about.

He stopped and took a step back. But the feel of her still lingered on his hands and his body still swelled with heat.

"Finished?" she challenged, the high flush on her cheeks a hint that maybe he hadn't been alone in his thoughts. "Are you sure you don't want to look closer? I might have a stiletto built into my bra or a wire noose spun in my watch."

Her sarcasm and his anger at his own thoughts brought

him up sharply. What the hell was he doing? How could he have forgotten even for a moment? "This isn't a James Bond movie, Natalya. Eight of my men were killed because of what you did."

She immediately sobered, the Academy Award–winning portrayal of heartfelt sorrow back in her eyes. "I'm so sorry, Scott. You have to believe me. I never meant for any of this to happen. I know you don't want to hear it right now, but I lov—"

"You're right," he said before she could get the word out, every muscle in his body taut with anger. "I don't want to hear it. Ever."

How could she say that to him now? Before he'd gone on that damned mission, it would have made him the happiest man in the world. But not now. Now it just brought home how much of a lie it had all been.

None of that mattered anymore, and he had to focus on what did: getting her back to DC to clear his name and face her punishment. She could explain herself to a court. He didn't care about her feelings or her reasons. This supposed baby was just a temporary hiccup.

And if God forbid by some hideous twist of fate she actually was pregnant?

He wouldn't even think about it. She wasn't. But he'd give her the night to prove it.

Natalie feared her plan wasn't going to work. She'd gone to bed without a shower, unable to bear the idea of undressing near him even with the half-closed door partially blocking his view.

Considering how fast he'd divested her of her clothes that first night, it would have been funny if it wasn't so painful.

Due to the nice, oversized window in the bathroom, he'd refused to let her close the door even to pee. She'd forced him to take her to the downstairs half bath—without a window—to do that. Some indignities were too much to bear without objection.

He'd waited for her in the kitchen, blocking the exit to the back door, and helped himself to one of the blueberry muffins she'd made the day before.

"Hungry?" she'd asked. "I can make you some more with some nice almond flavoring."

His mouth twitched. He'd almost smiled before catching himself. "I think I prefer them arsenic-free."

She gave a small, indifferent shrug of her shoulders. "Let me know if you change your mind. I could also make you an omelet—without the poison. I'm assuming you didn't have dinner."

"The muffin is fine." He took another bite. "These are really good. You made them?"

"You don't need to sound so surprised."

"You never cooked for me."

She shrugged again. "It didn't fit the ambitious, hardworking-businesswoman-by-day, sex-siren-by-night image you wanted to believe."

"You mean that you wanted me to believe."

"Don't blame me for your unrealistic fantasies. Do you think women like that really exist other than in porn movies?"

He tossed the rest of the muffin in the sink. His gaze was as hard as onyx. "You faked it well. You could make millions on the Internet when you get out."

She flushed, ignoring the jab at prison—and at porn. Of course he missed the point. "That wasn't what I was faking."

No one could fake that kind of passion. But just thinking about what they'd had—what they'd shared—made her feel like crying. The cold, professional way he'd touched her earlier had been horrible. It reminded her of all that she'd lost.

Her cheeks still heated when she thought of the humiliating way her body had responded. He was patting her down like a prisoner, but she was so desperate for his touch that her body had jumped into full sex mode.

She'd gotten Scott back, but he wasn't her Scott. He was essentially a stranger. A stranger who didn't smile, joke, or look at her lovingly. A stranger with ice-cold eyes and an unyielding, granite-hard expression. A stranger who hated her.

Ironically, it wasn't until she'd seen the hatred that she realized how much he must have cared for her. Scott was so good at hiding his emotions—at keeping his thoughts to himself—that she'd never been sure.

Their eyes held for one long heartbeat. She thought he wanted to say something, but he let the subject go.

She was too exhausted to try to press. It was clear he wasn't going to believe anything she said. She knew it would be like this, but it still hurt.

She fell asleep almost as soon as her head hit the pillow with him sitting in the chair opposite her bed, watching her like a hawk. A giant hawk who filled the whole room with his presence.

Scott's size had been something she'd had to get used to. She didn't like overwhelming men, and he certainly fit the bill—big-time. He was six feet three inches of solid muscle. Broad shoulders, washboard stomach, powerful arms. Basically the type of physically imposing guy she avoided.

But rather than threaten her there was something about his size and strength that made her feel safe and protected. He'd become her rock in a world that had been turned upside down by Mick. A world that had become dark, tumultuous, and scary. Scott was something solid and steady to hold on to. When they were together it felt as if nothing could harm her. Lying on his chest and wrapped in his arms, she could forget Mick and the nightmare her life had become.

And after months of running, having him here watching over her—even in these horrible circumstances—allowed her to relax enough to sleep solidly for the first time since Jennifer had been killed.

She'd let him wake her up twice before putting her plan into action. She was counting on the glass of water he had next to him to do its job.

After he'd woken her up the second time, she didn't go back to sleep. She only pretended to while she waited. And waited. While trying to ignore the pressure in her head that seemed to be getting worse.

She'd almost given up hope. Had he changed biorhythms in three months and gone earlier while she'd been sleeping? He always got up to go to the bathroom when the sun came up.

It was just after dawn when her patience and faking-asleep abilities were rewarded. He quietly stood from the chair and slipped out of the room into the hallway. She waited until the light went on in the bathroom to make her move.

If she'd ever held out any hope that she could turn to him, she didn't anymore. From the first moment she'd seen his face, she'd known that leaving was her only option. Any feelings he'd once had for her were gone. She'd betrayed him, and he wasn't going to forgive, forget, or even try to understand. He didn't even want to hear her explanation—or that she loved him.

None of which surprised her. It was why she hadn't gone to him for help in the first place. She knew him too well. Scott held himself and those around him to a very strict code. It was one of the things that made him such a good leader, and one of the reasons she loved him so much. His moral compass only went in one direction. He wouldn't understand her betrayal no matter how well motivated. To Scott, honor and integrity would always win out over treachery.

Doing the right thing always seemed so easy for him. Scott pushed himself and those around him to be their best, like the old army "be all you can be" slogan. Rules, honor, personal integrity, discipline, loyalty . . . as long as you adhered to those principles you were fine, but he had no use for people who didn't. For proof of that, all she needed to do was think about his biological father.

Ironically, Natalie had been thinking about confiding in Scott until he told her about his fathers—both the man who'd raised him and the man he'd refused to meet even though he was dying of cancer. Scott was intractable on the subject, no matter how much prodding from her or his sister, Kate, whom he'd confided in her about. He had no use for cheaters, and he would never forgive the man who'd cuckolded the man whom he admired above all others.

As overjoyed and relieved as Natalie was to learn that Scott was alive—and having some of her prayers answered—his finding her had put everything she'd done to protect her family in jeopardy. She couldn't let him take her in. If anyone learned that she was alive, they would come after her again, or worse, punish her by going after her family.

Her love for him had to take a backseat. She had to get away and disappear—this time for good. Staying here and taking her chances with him was not an option. Not when the stakes were so high. Natalie wasn't going to gamble with her parents' and sister's lives, and the only way to keep them safe was for her to stay dead.

Scott wasn't going to let her do that. Her pregnancy may have made him hesitate, but he believed in the system. He'd take her in and assume he could protect them. But she couldn't take that chance. Not with her life. Not with their child's life. And not with her family's lives.

A tear slipped passed the reins she held on her emotions, and she hastily wiped it away. The raw ache in her chest was not so easily dismissed. It ripped her heart out to leave him, but what other choice did she have? If she'd felt alone before, it was nothing to how she felt now. The worst part was that she couldn't blame him. He had every right to turn away from her. They were never going to be a happy family, no matter how much she dreamed about it.

Scott hadn't closed the bedroom or bathroom doors completely so she knew she would have to be silent and quick. Fighting a moment of dizziness and a blast of pain, she slid from the bed. She didn't bother to put on shoes and went straight for the window, which was partially open due to the heat.

She lifted it a few more inches to slip outside onto the porch roof. She hoped Scott would think she'd gone down the stairs and out the front door.

How much time did she have? Minutes? Seconds? Did she imagine the flush of the toilet and running of the water? There was so much ringing in her ears it was hard to tell.

She tried not to think about how much her head hurt or the long slide down the roof onto the ground if she lost her balance, and carefully crept along the rough asphalt shingles to a corner at the far side of the front porch.

Now came the hard part: getting off the roof. It was a good fifteen feet to the ground. She peered into the semidarkness below and the ground seemed to sway. Or maybe that was her. The dizziness was getting worse, and she was fighting to keep the meager contents of her stomach where it belonged. Taking a deep breath, she used the vines of a long-dead plant that were wrapped round a gutter and the wooden slats of the house to work her way down.

As she didn't have a car, her plan was to hide in the

cellar—the house had the kind that could be accessed from the outside—until Scott left. She'd then retrieve her purse and keys before making her way back into the town through the countryside.

It all hinged on Scott assuming that she'd run into the fields or to the road and going after her.

Somehow she made it to the bottom. Or what she thought was the bottom. The dirt ground was dark below her feet and she misjudged the distance when she jumped the last couple of feet.

Her body jolted with the unexpected pressure of the extra distance, turning her legs into jelly. Under normal circumstances she might have been able to keep her balance, but her equilibrium was off and she fell on her backside.

The force of it took the wind from her lungs—and her sails. What was she doing? She wasn't Spider-Woman or a trained operative; she was a farm girl from Minnesota. She was lucky she hadn't killed herself with her little jaunt across the roof.

Her head was pounding, and she could barely see straight. She didn't need to be a doctor to realize that she must have a concussion.

Where did she think she was going to go anyway? Relentlessness was in the Navy SEAL DNA. Scott was just going to keep coming after her. He was one of the most highly trained warriors in the world, skilled not just in physical strength and toughness but in intelligence, tactics, escape, survival, and clandestine operations. She was a reluctant spy thrown into a situation way over her head who only knew the basics of self-defense. How long did she think she could stay ahead of him?

She hadn't had a chance of escape since the first moment he'd seen her.

She wanted to put her face in her hands and cry with frustration, but she was suddenly jerked to her feet.

Scott didn't think he was still capable of being disappointed, but he clearly had a stupid chip when it came to Natalie.

She'd seemed so dazed and groggy the couple of times he'd woken her up that he'd just about convinced himself that she was telling the truth. When he got back from taking a piss, he'd half expected her to be lying there still asleep.

He knew immediately where she'd gone, as the broom from the hall that he'd propped strategically in the bedroom doorjamb hadn't moved. However, the window—or more precisely the curtain that he'd left tucked in it—had.

He'd been standing on the porch waiting for her as she made her way off the roof and nearly broke her leg by the fall into the dead flower bed. Obviously the Russians had neglected the escape-from-second-floor-of-a-building training. She sure as hell wasn't going to win any Spy of the Year prizes.

Still, something about the fall pissed him off. Not just that she'd run from him at the first opportunity, or that she could have killed herself on that roof, which from the look of it, didn't seem all that sturdy. But that she was willing to go to such lengths to get away from him seemed to reinforce just how far apart they were now. The woman he'd thought he loved and had wanted to marry was now climbing out of second-floor windows to get away from him.

It was like a bad dream. Except it wasn't. It was painfully real.

Her attempt at escape also told him something else. He took her by the arm and hauled her up. "I knew you were lying."

She blinked, looking a little dazed and confused. "Lying?"

"About the baby." How the hell could she lie about something like that?

She seemed taken aback. "I'm not lying."

"Yeah, right. Then why the hell else are you running? And I don't know a lot of pregnant women stupid enough to climb out of a window when a fall like that could make you lose the baby."

Suddenly she blanched. "Oh my God," she said, with wide eyes. "I didn't think. Do you think . . . ?" Her eyes filled with tears as her hand covered her stomach. "I didn't mean to hurt it; I was just scared."

Now he was really angry. She was taking this way too far. "Stop it," he said. "Just stop it. Enough with the baby . . . oh, shit."

She swooned in his arms and lost consciousness. If he hadn't been holding her by the shoulders she would have crumpled to the ground like a rag doll. He knew she wasn't faking it; she was utterly deadweight in his arms.

At first he thought it was something he'd done. He'd been holding her. But he hadn't shaken her . . . had he? But then his hand reached around to cradle her head and he felt it—the huge knot at the back of her head.

She hadn't been lying—not about the fall at least. Why hadn't she said anything?

She had, he realized. He just hadn't believed her.

His heart was pounding hard in his chest. He told himself it didn't mean anything. He wasn't worried—or panicked. But her face was so still and colorless that for one gut-dropping moment he thought she was dead.

He felt his chest tighten as he gazed down at the pale, lifeless features that had tormented him for months. First in mourning and then in rage.

She was so damned beautiful. The blackness in his chest tightened again. Her delicate features seemed frozen in a waxen, doll-like mask. Her warm velvety ivory skin was as thin and glass-like as alabaster. And the red lips that he'd kissed so passionately—that had enticed him in so many ways—were nearly colorless. But the tiny nose, the high cheeks, the delicately pointed chin, and softly arched brows were all the same. He'd traced them all so many times with his fingers, he would know her even if he were blind.

He had been blind. So blind.

How could such fragile beauty hide such treachery? He should want her dead. But the fear that gripped him told him otherwise, and he couldn't hide the sigh of relief as she fluttered her eyes open as he carried her toward the car he'd hidden behind the barn.

"What happened?" she asked.

"You lost consciousness."

"I think I have a concussion."

He gave her an incredulous look. "You think?" he bit back rhetorically. "God damn it, Natalie, what were you thinking? You could have killed yourself up there."

It made him furious just to think about it. It seemed only more proof of her guilt. She was so determined to escape that she'd rather go out a window with a concussion and risk a fall than face him.

He put her down gently as he fished around in his pocket for the key fob to unlock the door.

"Where are we going?" she asked.

"Back to the hospital."

"Urgent care," she corrected. "And they can't do anything for a concussion."

He knew that. He'd treated enough men concussed by explosions to be well versed in concussions. But this was different. This wasn't one of his guys, it was . . . damn it!

His jaw hardened. "You lost consciousness," he said, stating the obvious.

In other words, they weren't talking about this. She seemed to understand his tone and got into the car without any argument.

She directed him back into town to the urgent care—which wasn't far from where he'd seen her—and a short while later, after a little heated insistence on his part that might have involved a growl or two, she was admitted for another CT scan.

Fortunately there didn't appear to be any swelling so the doctor who came in the room afterward prescribed rest and acetaminophen for the pain as necessary.

"You should watch her closely for the rest of the day, Mr. Wilson," the doctor, a woman who couldn't have been much older than twenty-five, instructed him. If Natalie was surprised that he'd adopted her false identification—or that he'd posed as her husband—she didn't show it. It had seemed simpler when he was trying to get someone to help them. "Don't let her sleep longer than an hour or two. You'll want to assess her consciousness every time you wake her."

Scott nodded. "I'm familiar with the AVPU code." The acronym stood for alertness, response to a voice, assessment of pain, and making sure they weren't unresponsive to any of the tests. In the Teams they used something similar but more detailed called MACE when someone had their cage rattled.

The doctor nodded, eyeing him a little closer and clearly trying to size him up. "Good. And don't hesitate to bring her back in if the symptoms worsen or don't improve in a day or two."

Natalie had been unusually quiet, but she finally broke her silence. "Is my baby okay?" She looked as if she was going to cry. "I fell."

Scott froze.

The doctor smiled down at her kindly. "It wasn't a body scan, but I saw from your chart that you are pregnant. Your husband mentioned the fall, but I didn't see anything to concern me. You aren't bleeding?"

Natalie shook her head, not correcting her on the wrong assumption of their marital status.

"I'm sure the baby is fine," the doctor assured her. "They have a nice soft landing in there. But try to take it easy for the next few days, all right?"

Natalie nodded.

Scott was reeling. He sat, glad there was a chair behind him to catch him. Natalie hadn't been lying. She *was* pregnant.

"Are you all right?" the doctor asked him with a frown. "You look a little shell-shocked—like you were the one with the lump on your head."

Scott was having trouble finding words.

Natalie filled in for him. "He didn't know," she said. "I was going to surprise him." She turned to look at him. "Surprise, sweetheart. You're going to be a father."

Eight

Father? Scott still didn't want to believe it. He stared at the door long after the doctor went out.

She's pregnant. Pregnant, damn it!

But as soon as the shock began to fade, another thought stole through his head. A possibility that he didn't want to believe but that he couldn't ignore. "Even if you are pregnant, how do I know it's mine? For all I know the baby could be the hockey player's."

She flinched as if the accusation had physically struck her, which seemed odd. Her gaze pinned him as if to say, *How could you ask that?* But could she blame him? She'd lied to him from the first moment they'd met. Why should this be any different?

"I told you before that I despised Mick." The truth of her words was punctuated by the fierceness of her expression. She was angry, but there was something more. Something raw and intense. Something that came close to revulsion and was too reactive to be feigned. "It's your baby, Scott. I haven't been with any other man since I met you."

Her gaze didn't falter from his. Either she was telling

the truth or she was one of the most accomplished liars he'd ever met.

The fact that he didn't know which one pissed him off. Detecting bullshit was his job. For a SEAL commander, not being able to trust his judgment could be deadly.

"How the hell did this happen?" he said with an angry drag of his fingers through the long hair that he wasn't used to.

He didn't expect an answer, but she gave him one. "I think you know exactly how it happened. Or should I remind you?"

She didn't need to. He remembered. He remembered that night only too well. It was what had given him that niggle of doubt from the beginning. They'd had sex without a condom. Once. But once was all it took, as every mother everywhere told their teenagers.

Scott was the one to look away first. He raked his fingers through his hair again and moved to the window, staring absently through the blinds into the parking lot.

What a mess. Just when he thought things couldn't get any more fucked up. He should have known better. Things could always get more fucked up. But he didn't have a backup plan for this.

Was it possible? Could the baby be his? And if it was, where the hell did that leave him? He had to take her in to clear his name and see justice done for his men, but what would happen to her and the baby after? She would probably be imprisoned. Could he do that to his unborn child?

It wasn't even a question. As she must know. She had played him perfectly.

He turned back to face her, furious at her and at his own stupidity—he wasn't a teenager, and he knew better than to have sex without protection. But that night . . . he'd needed her.

"I want a blood test."

She held his gaze for a moment before letting her eyes drop as if she didn't want him to see how his words had hurt her.

Scott felt something akin to shame twisting in his chest. But he told himself he had every right to do this. He had no reason to trust her about this or anything else. And he knew firsthand how devastating it was to find out you had the wrong DNA running through your veins.

"Of course," she said with just enough disappointment to make him feel like a world-class asshole. "Whatever you want, Scott."

She looked so wronged and innocent lying there in the bed that it pissed him off. He wasn't the bad guy in this. No matter how much she played the wounded dove. "Jesus Christ, Nat, can you blame me?"

The errant slip of the nickname was proof of just how pushed to the edge he was by all this. She had him twisted up in knots. Confused and angry. He didn't know what was a lie and what was the truth anymore. She'd betrayed him every way that mattered; what to think and how to feel should be crystal fucking clear.

She held his gaze, maybe understanding his confusion. "No. I guess I can't."

If the doctor was surprised by the request for a blood test, she was too professional to show it. She drew the blood from Natalie and collected the cheek swab from Scott for the NIPP test.

NIPP apparently stood for non-invasive prenatal paternity test. Not surprisingly, as this was Natalie's first time being pregnant or being accused of lying about the father, she hadn't heard of it before. But thanks to advances in medical science and DNA testing, paternity could now be established without the risk of miscarriage that used to come from amniocentesis or CVS testing.

Natalie knew she had no right to be hurt by Scott's request for proof. She'd lied to him in so many ways, why should he believe her about this? But could he honestly think she could be sleeping with someone else when they were sharing that kind of passion and intimacy?

What they'd had was special. She knew that, and part of her wanted him to know that, too. To believe in her—in them—just a little. To see the real her. Not some Russian Mata Hari but the woman forced to do something against her will. If he had truly cared about her, shouldn't he believe her just a little? Shouldn't he wonder why? Shouldn't he have questions and not be so ready to rush to judgment?

Maybe it was foolish and unrealistic. Rationally she knew it was too much to expect, but the tightness squeezing her chest told her that her heart just wasn't getting it.

And Scott had no idea how wrong he was about Mick.

She knew why Scott suspected him. Mick had been gorgeous. The type of guy women flocked to. When she first met him, Mick had still been playing hockey, and she'd been over the moon, not to mention the envy of all her friends, when the tall, muscular, bronzed god had come up to her in the Georgetown restaurant where they were celebrating her coworker's twenty-fourth birthday to ask her out.

She'd refused at first. She didn't go out with strange guys—even ones as good-looking as Mick. He'd persisted, however, and told her she could check him out—that he played professional hockey and wasn't a psycho.

The first part had proved correct. She'd foolishly taken Google for a reference and accepted the date. But their "date" was all a pretense, as she would learn when he came to pick her up.

He didn't even bother to take her to dinner before telling her what he wanted. That job at the Pentagon that she interviewed for, but didn't want? She was going to take it. And the freshman fifteen that she'd put on in college and hadn't taken off almost seven years later? Lose them. He wanted her ready when and if she was called upon.

Ready for what? she'd asked, totally discombobulated. To—get this—*spy* on the only country she'd ever known for Russia, the country that had imprisoned and killed her parents and left her and her sister in an orphanage. He had to be crazy. She'd actually laughed in his face.

Which was a mistake she never made again. Mick had shown her exactly how serious he was by trying to take her power away. He'd held her down right there in her apartment and raped her.

But it hadn't broken her, maybe because of what she'd been through at the orphanage as a child. She knew bleakness and suffering, and she knew she would recover. She wouldn't let his physical strength make her cower.

Even after the rape, she'd refused to do what he asked until he'd made threats that she couldn't ignore. It was the kind of leverage that governments used on "assets" all the time, albeit more deadly.

It wasn't ideology that had turned her into a spy; he'd threatened her family. First he'd started with her birth parents in Russia, insisting they were still alive and would suffer if she refused. Not believing him and knowing in her heart that they were dead as the orphanage had told her, she'd demanded proof. When he showed her a picture, she'd known he was lying. The dour woman in the photo was not her mother. Natalie might not be able to remember her face, but she'd known it on a bone-deep level.

But it hadn't taken him long to find a threat that could make her jump. *"I hear your father is in bad health."* Her breath had frozen in her lungs. The thought of him targeting the loving parents who'd adopted the two scarred and scared children and brought them into their home . . . how could she let that happen?

And then, just in case there was any doubt, he uttered the coup de grâce that would assure her agreement. *"You have a younger sister, don't you?"* he'd asked, looking her up and down. There was no mistaking the gleam in his eyes. He would hurt her sister the way he had her. Just the thought of it had made her sick. She would do anything to protect her sister. Anything. Natalie had failed Lana once; she would never do so again.

Natalie had accepted the job, lost weight, dyed her hair a lighter blond, wore the stupid colored contacts, and dressed in the sexy heels and suits he told her to. She learned to act cool and confident, even when she wanted to just curl into a ball and cry.

It hadn't been so bad at first. Natalie had kept her head down and did her job as quietly and efficiently as she could. Which turned out to be a mistake, when her efficiency—not, ironically, the sexy silk blouses—caught the eye of the deputy secretary of defense. Mick forced her to take the new job. Fortunately for her, however, the deputy secretary was happily married to a wife he adored. Natalie was thus spared the horrible "request" from Mick to sleep with her boss for information.

That was the man Scott thought had fathered her child. An opportunistic, rapist thug who sold out the country that had offered him a home, not for idealistic or sentimental reasons but for money.

But she'd learned that many years later. As she had learned why she'd been targeted.

"It will take about a week."

The doctor's words brought Natalie back to reality. Mick was dead. The only bad thing about that was that she had not been the one to pull the trigger.

How many times had she dreamed of it? Only knowing that the men he worked for would retaliate had stayed her hand. But although killing Mick might not have ended her nightmare, it definitely would have been personally satisfying.

"A week?" Scott repeated, clearly finding that unacceptable. His expression was what she imagined his men saw when he needed something done. The flexed jaw. The steely gaze. The confidence and unwavering authority that was hard to argue with. "I can't wait that long."

The doctor was young but had already learned the skill of dealing with difficult patients—or, apparently, difficult authoritative SEAL commanders. She was equally firm and unyielding as she responded, "I'm afraid that's our standard turnaround time."

Scott seemed to realize he'd overplayed his hand so he changed tactics to one Natalie had never seen him use before.

"Can it be expedited? I don't care what it costs. I'll pay whatever it takes if you can have it sped up."

Natalie knew all about Scott's blue-blood background, but he rarely flaunted or even discussed his wealth. She'd certainly never seen him use it to get what he wanted. His father had left him millions, but Scott told her he'd put it in a trust. She knew he felt guilty about inheriting money from a man who had been duped into claiming another man's son.

His wealth and perceived influence due to his family connections had been part of the reason Mick had forced her to target Scott—not to mention his role as a SEAL. She'd never forget her shock at walking into a meeting at the Pentagon and seeing the man she'd just had forty-eight hours of almost nonstop sex with in a hotel room seated at the table. Worse was discovering that her "sailor" was actually the OIC (officer in charge) of one of the platoons of the president's personal secret SEAL team. Natalie still didn't know how Mick had found out about him so quickly.

But neither she nor Mick could have guessed how fruitless her efforts would be. Scott was closemouthed about his work and not interested in using family connections, and she was the worst spy ever who stupidly fell in love with her target.

But recalling Scott's background put another spin on his request for the paternity test, and Natalie felt the ache in her chest ease a little. It wasn't just about not trusting her. Her pregnancy had unwittingly struck a still-raw wound. One that he tried to pretend didn't matter to him.

The doctor frowned. "I'm not sure. No one has ever requested that before."

Scott wasn't used to acting like a rich asshole, and Natalie could see he was uncomfortable with how his request had come out. "I'd really appreciate it if you could check into it. There are extenuating circumstances that I'm not at liberty to discuss."

He smiled, and even though Natalie knew it wasn't meant to be charming it definitely was. Scott was usually so serious and no-nonsense that the appearance of a smile had always made Natalie feel as if she was basking in a special glow—a side of him that was rarely revealed. It had been that way the first night they'd met in the bar and his guard was down. She wondered whether she would have fallen for him so quickly if their first meeting had been the mission briefing where he'd been 100 percent "don't try to stand in my way" SEAL commander.

Probably. She looked at him. Definitely. There was something supremely sexy about a man confident in his own skin. A man who knew he was one of the best and commanded authority wherever he went. Scott was the guy whom everyone would turn to when things went south—to use SEAL parlance—and he shouldered that burden with an ease that seemed effortless.

And then there were his looks.

Put it all together and she hadn't had a chance. The

dull ache in her chest told her that she still didn't. She would love him until the day she died. Which, admittedly, might not be that long from now.

Maybe the doctor wasn't quite as skilled at hiding her reactions as Natalie thought—or having all that masculine perfection beaming on her was too much for any woman to resist. Natalie thought she detected a slight blush in the doctor's cheeks as she smiled back at him. "I'll see what I can do."

Scott thanked her and the doctor left.

"Do you always get what you want?" Natalie asked.

She'd meant it wryly, but his reply was deadly serious. "No. Sometimes I'm completely disappointed."

It was hard to misinterpret that. She turned away, unable to bear the condemnation in his eyes or the burning in her chest.

Nine

It was late afternoon by time they returned to the farm-house from urgent care. Scott left Natalie in bed to rest and went downstairs to make the phone call to his sister that he'd been putting off. He wasn't ready to talk about Natalie—or what the hell he was going to do with her—even to Kate. Not until he knew whether the baby was his. He was relieved when she didn't answer. He left her a message not to worry, but he was going dark for a day or two.

Glad for the respite, he turned off his phone and went into the kitchen to see what he could find to make for dinner. He wasn't much of a cook, but he could boil water for pasta or throw potatoes in the oven to bake.

He'd noticed an old grill outside, but as Natalie ate mostly rabbit food, he wasn't holding out much hope for meat to put on it. The sandwich that he'd picked up at the market to have for lunch hadn't been enough to put a dent in his hunger after the two missed meals that had come before.

It was strange how when he was downrange on missions he could go for days subsisting on MREs or whatever other almost-inedible food the military thought to provide them, but as soon as he was stateside he was starving if he missed a meal.

He caught sight of the plate of muffins and helped himself to one of the two that remained. They really were good, and as he wiped the remnants of the crumble topping from his mouth with a napkin, he still found it hard to believe that she baked. He didn't know why. It wasn't as if it was unusual, but the domesticity of it seemed so incongruous with the sophisticated, high-powered DC insider that he'd known.

His mouth fell in a hard line. That was just it. He hadn't really known her. She'd confounded him from the start.

When she'd introduced herself as an "assistant" that first night in the bar, he'd assumed she worked for a lob-byist or someone on the Hill—sure as hell *not* the second-highest-ranking official in the DoD. It was well known in the Pentagon that if you wanted to get Deputy Secretary of Defense Richard Waters to do something, you needed to appeal to his assistant.

She was known as being smart, a tough negotiator, extremely protective of her boss, and hot as hell. But her cool, confident exterior scared a lot of guys off. She definitely had that Eastern European sexy, but hard "don't fuck around with me" thing working for her. Ironically, he'd thought she might be Russian or Czech and had asked about it one time. She'd paled, and only now did he realize the significance.

Given that he usually dated the girl next door, he'd been surprised by that initial attraction. But not by what had come after. He'd never forget the first time he'd looked down at her in bed—when they'd finally made it to the bed—and he'd seen that soft, tousled, well-sated look of a woman who'd been well pleasured.

Knowing that he'd done that to her. That he'd been the

one to make her look like that . . . it was satisfying as hell. It had made him feel powerful—as if he was revealing a different side of her that no one else could see.

That two-sides-of-the-coin thing had sucked him in. Hard. It was still doing it.

Scott opened the refrigerator and he had this very fact brought home to him again. He was stunned to see a variety of leftovers that included not only chicken and steak but *bacon*—a food she'd turned away from every time he'd offered it to her. His herbivore was apparently a hard-core carnivore.

Was there anything about her that had been real?

It was hard to believe that the woman he'd shared so much with—whom he'd fallen in love with—had deceived him so completely. Their relationship might have started on the X-rated side, with forty-eight hours of pretty much nonstop sex, but it had never been just about that. Over the next six months every moment that he wasn't working he'd spent with her, making up every ridiculous excuse in the book to get to DC. He'd been drawn to her in a way that he'd never been drawn to another woman. When they were together, he could put the stress of his job behind him and relax. He'd told her things—personal things—that he'd never shared with anyone else. He'd always been too focused on his job to get serious with anyone.

How the hell could he have gotten it so wrong?

He pulled out the plate of roasted chicken and mashed potatoes and sat down at the table to eat. He didn't bother heating it in the microwave; it looked too damned good. It tasted better.

Natalya Petrova wasn't just a spy, she was also a hell of a cook.

He was so busy devouring the food that he didn't hear her come up behind him. "Hey. I was going to have that for dinner."

He frowned when he saw her. "You should be resting."

She was pregnant. *Pregnant.* It was still hard to accept or know how to react. A few months ago, he would have been shouting from the rooftops. He would have jumped up and pulled out a chair for her and made her put her feet up. Hell, he probably would have swung her into his arms and carried her back to bed. But now . . . now it wasn't his place. Even if the baby was his, he couldn't pretend the happy-family thing. He could hate her all over again for what this would do to their baby—if it was his baby.

She still wore the clothes she'd put on to go to the hospital. A pair of old jeans and a Yankees sweatshirt that belonged in the trash—and not just because it was ratty. He was a dyed-in-the-wool Red Sox fan. Apparently she'd been holding out on him in that arena, too.

"I couldn't sleep." She handed him a piece of paper. "Here."

He glanced down at it long enough to see that it was a handwritten list of some kind. "What's this?"

"Read it."

Reluctantly, he put down the fork, wiped his mouth with a napkin, and began to read. It didn't take him long. When he was done, he looked up and met her gaze.

"That's it," she said. "That's everything I told Mick."

He'd figured that much out. But in between things like recommendations regarding the military health system, the budget for special operations in Afghanistan, the results of a review on whether there should be a new chief management officer in the DoD, ways of getting costs down for replacing Air Force One, and various other classified but not overly sensitive information, he saw only a few things that might have interested Russia. But they weren't anything critical. What was missing was any information to do with technology, defense systems, or operational plans, including Special Forces operations such as Team Nine.

He put it down and looked up at her. "I think you are missing something."

She shook her head. "I'm not. I told you, I didn't intentionally tell him anything about your mission. I didn't know anything about your operation until Mick told me."

Scott stood up and opened the refrigerator again. He'd been focused on food before, but he'd noticed something else that he figured would help for this conversation. He pulled out a Bud Light, twisted off the cap, took a swig, and sat down. He preferred Coors Light, as most of the guys did on the Teams, but as she'd drunk only wine when they were together before, he couldn't exactly complain. At least it wasn't vodka.

Putting the bottle down in front of him, he leaned back and crossed his arms. "All right. Tell me."

Obviously relieved to have her chance to explain, she took a seat opposite him and folded her hands on the table in front of her.

Her eyes rested on his arms for a moment before turning back to his face. But from the soft pink blush in her cheeks he knew exactly what she'd been thinking, and the knowledge of how his unintentionally flexed arms had turned her on wasn't without effect.

Pissed at the heat rushing to his groin, he let his arms drop and flexed his jaw instead. But he'd never been able to control his desire for her. Why should it be any different now?

"Where should I start?" she asked tentatively.

"At the beginning."

He could tell she was nervous because she reached for the bottle. Not to drink, but to do something with her hands. She fiddled with the label by peeling the edges back with her short nails. Her short, unpolished, and unmanicured nails. It seemed as if everything had been stripped away. From the tips of her fingernails to her fancy clothes and well-made-up facade. The fact that this natural Natalie appealed to him just as much wasn't something he wanted to think about.

Scott listened as calmly and open-mindedly as possible, but ready for lies and inconsistencies, as she told him how Mick had targeted her at a bar four years ago and asked her out on a date. She'd been flattered to be singled out by the good-looking hockey player and had agreed, but that had changed the moment Mick picked her up at her apartment and told her what he really wanted from her.

"I thought he was nuts, but when I realized he wasn't . . . I refused at first. But he . . . uh, threatened me, and when that didn't change my mind, he threatened my family." She told him how Mick had targeted her Russian parents first, but when his proof hadn't convinced her that they hadn't died as the orphanage had told her, he'd moved on to her family in Minnesota.

She paused to look back up at Scott, her eyes bright with fear—as if Mick were threatening them all over again. "He said he'd kill my parents—the only parents I've ever known—if I didn't do what he asked. They are good people, Scott. Whatever you think of me, know that. They brought two troubled children into their home and showered them with love and patience. They gave me happiness, security, and a life I never could have dreamed of in the orphanage."

He wanted to ask about the orphanage, but now was not the time. He suspected that whatever memories she had weren't good, and he didn't want to feel sorry for her. He needed to stay cold and objective.

Was that what he was?

"He didn't stop with my parents. He also threatened my sister. He said he would . . ." Her voice fell off as if she couldn't bear to repeat what he said. When she looked back at him, her eyes had turned dark with anger and a kind of raw hatred that made him almost certain she was telling the truth. Whatever else she'd lied about it wasn't her family. She loved them with a fierceness that was impossible to deny. "He threatened to rape her and then send her back to Russia to be sold as a sex slave."

"And you believed him?"

A dark emotion crossed her face, and she hardened her jaw. "I did."

There was something she wasn't telling him—something she was holding back.

"Why?" he asked. "Some strange guy comes to your apartment to recruit you as a spy for a country you haven't lived in since you were a child, and you just go along with it? You didn't go to anyone? Confide in anyone—even your parents or sister?"

He caught the flicker of the shadow in her eyes again before she lashed back at his tone, which was absolute disbelief. "You don't understand. I knew he would do it, and I couldn't take that chance. My parents . . . my sister . . . things are difficult for them, and I couldn't burden them with this. My father's health isn't good. But of course I just didn't jump right into happily committing treason. I only pretended to go along with it at first. I tried to sabotage my job at the Pentagon, but Mick found out about it, and . . ."

Tears filled her eyes. Her gaze turned imploring, as if she was begging him to believe her.

"And what?" Scott said evenly, not letting himself be swayed by her obvious despair. But it wasn't easy.

Her eyes met his. He could see the stark horror that still lingered there. "He sent me a picture of him with my sister. It was taken back home at the place where she works a few hours a week."

Even now, the panic in her voice was still almost

visceral. It was hard to remain unmoved. "Did you warn her to stay away from him?"

"Of course I did," she snapped. "But you don't know Lana. She doesn't understand. She's sweet and innocent, and she can't protect herself."

He knew there was something she wasn't saying so he waited. The label was almost completely peeled off by now. "She's special, okay. Something happened to her in the orphanage, and she will never be able to live a normal life."

Natalie wasn't looking at him as she said it, but from her reticence he sensed that it was true.

Crap. He hadn't been expecting that. He felt a wave of compassion but forced it back and steeled his emotions. Maybe he could understand her protectiveness of her family, but that didn't make what she'd done okay.

He had to think about her betrayal.

"At first they didn't ask for that much," she continued. "I think they just wanted me in place and were waiting."

"Waiting for what?"

"I don't know. Relations to worsen with Russia? Me to be in a position of authority?" She looked at him. "You."

"They had you target me in the bar?"

It made him sick to think about. Christ, how many guys had she gone back to hotel rooms with to get information?

Her brows jumped together. "What? No. Our meeting was an accident. What happened wasn't planned—any of it. I had no idea who you were until I walked into that mission brief at the Pentagon and saw you. Much to my horror, since I knew what it would mean if Mick learned about it. I tried to break it off with you, but somehow Mick found out about you and sent me back to your hotel room. I don't know how he did it, but it seemed as if he was always one step ahead of me."

Scott remembered their argument after the meeting

and how adamant she'd been about not seeing him again—and how scared.

"That's when everything got worse," she said.

He gave her a look, and she blushed. "I didn't mean in the hotel room, I meant the pressure got worse. It was about the time that Russia shot down our fighter plane and people were screaming for retaliation and war. I tried to string Mick along with insignificant information, but he wanted to know about your missions. He wasn't happy when you wouldn't tell me anything. I tried to hide it, but I think Mick guessed how I felt about you and thought I was holding back so he gave me incentive not to lie to him."

Scott wasn't sure he wanted to hear this, but he asked anyway. "What did he do?"

"He had my father's insulin switched at the pharmacy with something that would have killed him had he not warned me ahead of time."

"So it's my fault for not telling you anything? That's your excuse for doing what you did?"

She gave him a look of pure frustration. "Of course not! I'm just trying to explain to you how it was and how I felt as if I didn't have any choice. I knew only too well from personal experience that Mick had the morals of an adder, and he showed me how easy it was for him to get to my family. But things were spinning out of control, and I wasn't going to be able to hold on much longer. I think Mick sensed it, too. That was when he came to me with one last 'request.' He promised it was the last time. I was so relieved. I thought it was going to finally be over."

Scott's mouth tightened. "The Russia mission."

It wasn't a question but she nodded. "But as I said, I didn't know about the specifics. Mick said that they'd heard rumors of something big going down. He wanted me to find out what it was, but my boss was keeping me out of the loop. All I was able to find out was that there was a meeting coming up in the Tank"—a slang term for the Joint Chiefs of Staff's Sensitive Compartmented Information Facility (SCIF) at the Pentagon—"which I typically had security clearance for. But this meeting was different and unusual in that no staff were being admitted."

Without the beer bottle label to play with, she started to twist her hands. She was clearly anxious for him to believe her.

He didn't know what to think. But he wanted to hear her out first. All of it.

"So how did you get admitted?" he asked.

"I didn't. I was so relieved, thinking that would get me out of it, but I should have known better. Mick gave me a spyware program to download on the deputy secretary's computer that would enable them to hear everything." Before Scott could ask, she added, "He claimed it wouldn't be able to be picked up by the countersurveillance technologies like Tempest that were in place."

Scott's mouth drew in a tight line. "Fine. So you didn't tell them yourself; you just enabled them to find out. Big fucking difference, Natalya. Treason is treason, and my guys were killed because of it."

He couldn't believe he'd actually been listening to this sob story and feeling sorry for her.

She flushed angrily. "No. You didn't let me finish. I loaded the program, but once Mick confirmed that it was working, I deleted it."

"Then how did they find out? Maybe you screwed up and thought you removed it."

"I removed it," she said adamantly. "I don't know how they found out, but it wasn't through that program. Just to make sure I messed with his Wi-Fi password so it wouldn't connect in the Tank. I was shocked when Mick bragged about what they'd discovered in the meeting,

and that I wouldn't have to spy on my boyfriend anymore."

His face was stony. "You expect me to believe this?"

She jutted up her chin defiantly. "It's the truth."

She didn't know the meaning of the word.

As if she could read his mind, she added, "Why else
would I risk everything to try to call off the mission and
send you that text?"

"You tried to call off the mission?"

"I sent an e-mail to my boss before I sent you the text.
I warned him that there had been a leak and that people
knew about the mission."

He lifted a brow. If that was true, she could have been
putting her spy-hood in jeopardy. "And what did he say?"

She shook her head. "Nothing. Mick intercepted the
message—I should have realized they were keeping tabs
on me—and informed me that it was too late. That you
and the rest of the team had been killed in the explosion.
Thank God he didn't know about the sat phone text. That
night he tried to kill me and ended up killing my friend
instead, and I ran." She looked up at him, holding his
gaze. "I loved you, Scott. I was out of my mind with grief
when Mick told me you were all dead. I never wanted to
hurt you. I did everything I could not to betray you, but
I was scared and trying to balance two horrible evils.
Mick would have done what he promised to my family."
Her gaze hardened. "You didn't know him like I did."

Scott didn't say anything. He was still trying to take
it all in. But once again, he had the feeling he was missing something.

It was so obvious, he wondered how he didn't see it at
first. He knew why she'd been ready to believe Mick.
Personal experience. He leaned forward across the table,
his fingers white as they clenched the edge of the table.
"What did he do to you?"

Natalie clenched her jaw and looked away, avoiding his gaze. But she knew he'd guessed. "Nothing."

He reached over and took her chin in his hand, forcing her eyes back to his. "Bullshit. Tell me the truth, Nat. What did he do to you?"

Nat. Despite the inadvertent use of his nickname, she could hear the simmering rage in his voice and something about it set her teeth on edge. What right did he have to be angry? Didn't he despise her now? She was the one who'd been raped. This was about her, not about him. He didn't get to sweep in and be the protector when it was convenient. Nor was she going to have him feeling sorry for her. She wasn't damaged or vulnerable or in need of his man-outrage.

Her eyes narrowed with fury. "What do you think he did, Scott? What do weak men do to assert their control over women who resist them? They use their physical strength and force them."

Scott had paled, but his expression was still fierce and taut just like the rest of him. But it was a brittle tautness—one that seemed ready to crack. "He raped you."

It wasn't a question, but she responded anyway. "Yes, Scott, he raped me. He was a weak misogynist pig who thought it made him strong to brutalize women. Unfortunately it's not that uncommon. It was horrible and not something I'd ever want to go through again, but it's behind me. *Behind* me—as in *in the past.* I got over it, and I don't need you dredging it up and playing psychoanalyst or feeling sorry for me. But if it helps you understand why I believed he would hurt my sister and parents, then fine. I didn't care about him hurting me, and he knew that—which is probably why he never tried it again." Her smile was definitely on the malevolent side. "That and because I learned how to defend myself. I carried a small knife with me. If he'd tried again, I would have happily killed him."

He accepted her proclamation to commit murder as if it was the most natural thing in the world. "And I would have helped you bury the body."

He sounded serious. But Natalie knew Scott. He was too honorable for murder—no matter what the circumstances. He might have come close if given the chance, but in the end he would have given Mick over to the authorities just as he would have done with her.

But behind his grim expression, Natalie could see the conflicting emotions that he was struggling to contain. Rage. Compassion. Helplessness. For a warrior like Scott, for a man who had to make life-and-death decisions almost every time he went to work and relished the role, she suspected the last was the hardest to accept. He wanted to *do* something but was realizing that there wasn't anything he could do.

She knew he wanted to say something to try to comfort her, but whether it was her warning not to try or the fact that he hated her, his lips were firmly pressed together.

But he was too good of a guy—too inherently decent— not to say something. "I'm sorry."

She sensed he meant it and accepted the sentiment with her own nod. What he felt shouldn't matter, but somehow it did.

Realizing she'd peeled the label completely off the bottle of beer, she put it back down on the table. "Does beer go bad? I'm not sure how long it's been in there."

But Scott wasn't paying any attention to the beer; all his attention was focused on her.

Natalie knew better than to try to discern his thoughts, but she tried anyway. It was an exercise in futility, but she suspected that given their conversation, he was trying to process what she'd told him.

Had hearing her explanation moved him? She doubted it. His gaze was as hard and unyielding as it had been when they sat down. He was always hard and unyielding when it came to things like this. It wasn't stubbornness as much as principles. There was right and there was wrong. To Scott there wasn't a lot in between.

Whatever her motivations, it didn't change the fact that she'd lied to him and betrayed him every time she asked him a question—no matter how insignificant.

She knew how his mind worked so she expected what came next. What to him would be the fatal flaw in her argument.

"Even if what you say is true, you did have another choice. You could have come to me."

Natalie could feel the frustration bubble up inside her. He made it sound so simple. "Don't you think I wanted to? I *loved* you, Scott." His jaw clenched a little, but he didn't otherwise react. "But I know you: Lieutenant Commander 'By the Book' Taylor? You have too much integrity to hide something like this. You would have gone right to the authorities, and I couldn't take that chance. Not with my family's lives at stake. You have far more trust in the system than I do. Although maybe you've seen the light on that."

"What is that supposed to mean?"

Her gaze met his. "If you trust the system so much, why did you let everyone think you were killed, and—if the dark hair, stubble, and 'Mr. Wilson' are any indication—why are you still in hiding?"

His jaw was clenched so tight that his lips were white. She could see he wanted to argue but also recognized that there was some truth to what she said.

"You should have trusted me more than that, Nat. I would have protected you."

"Would you? I wasn't sure that you wouldn't lock me up yourself."

He drew back as if stung by the accusation. "How can you say that? You know I cared about you."

"I thought you did, but you never told me as much. You never told me you loved me."

She looked at his steely expression, but if she hoped he would say anything now, she was crazy.

Maybe she should have been more sure, but what if she was wrong?

She sighed heavily. Wearily. She was tired and this wasn't an easy conversation. But it needed to be had. "I thought about confiding in you, but after you refused Kate's request to visit her dying father—your biological father—I changed my mind."

His expression turned icy with irritation. The way it did every time the subject came up. "What the hell does he have to do with anything?"

"You don't exactly have a forgiving nature when it comes to people who don't hold themselves to the same high standards as you do, Scott. I was lying to you—betraying you—far more than your biological father ever did. How could I trust that you would understand?" She gave him a wry smile. "The only reason I'm probably not in jail right now is because I'm pregnant."

She might be right, but that was because in the interim men had been killed. If she'd told him before the mission, he would have been pissed—okay, more than pissed—but he would have listened.

He would have. But he wasn't going to tell her that he'd been stupid enough to fall in love with her and would have done anything to keep her safe, including setting aside those supposed "principles" and risking the job and career that meant so much to him.

Damn it, even now, he found himself being affected by her story more than he wanted to be. How could he believe anything out of her mouth? Was he going to let her make a fool of him again?

But Scott had never seen her scared before as she had been when talking about her parents. Natalie had always seemed so cool and collected. The only times he'd ever seen a crack of vulnerability in that facade was when she'd cuddle up against him after making love and seemed to hold on a little too tightly or when he'd wanted to come out to command about their relationship. She'd freaked out, begging him not to. She'd said she couldn't lose her job.

At the time he hadn't understood her panic, but in retrospect, it made sense. She'd thought Mick would blame her and was scared what he would do to her family.

Mick. Scott's fists tightened as his teeth clenched. The bastard was lucky he was dead. Scott would have taken him apart limb by limb if he'd known about the rape.

Whatever else she might have been lying about, Scott believed her about that. Not only because that was what thugs like Mick did but also because of her "butt out of it, I don't want to talk about it" reaction. It was the opposite of the vulnerable card she could have played if she'd wanted to make him feel sorry for her.

Just thinking about what the bastard had done to her made Scott want to be sick, punch the wall, and hold her in his arms all at the same time.

It was the latter that bothered him the most.

He couldn't let her get to him. But just looking at her was getting to him. She might not have wanted to play the vulnerable card, but there was something about the woman seated across from him that was bringing out his Galahad instincts. And it wasn't just the jeans, T-shirt, and ponytail instead of glamorous DC power broker high heels, carefully made-up face, and tight-just-to-the-edge-of-sexy business suits. The mask she'd taken off went much deeper than that. The woman seated before him seemed much less sure of herself and more fragile than the one he'd known before.

Just how much of a part had she been playing? Or was she playing a part now?

Who was the real Natalie?

Neither, he realized. Her name was Natalya, and he'd better remember it. Even if he believed that she'd tried to remove the spyware program, it obviously hadn't worked. Mick had learned about the mission, and eight of Scott's teammates had died because of it. Not to mention that she'd spied on him for months.

What difference did her reasons make to the eight men who had never come home?

She'd been scared—he got that—but it didn't change the facts or the repercussions. There were always choices, and giving in to blackmail to commit treason was never the right one.

She should have come to him. She should have trusted him more. There was a big difference between her and his biological father: he'd loved her.

But she hadn't known that, had she?

He pushed the errant thought away and steeled himself against that vulnerable, *I'm so alone* thing she was giving off.

She hadn't been alone.

But whether she should have told him no longer mattered. She hadn't, and that was the reality they would both have to deal with.

A reality that apparently included a baby. "When did you find out you were pregnant?"

It was the wrong question to ask for someone who was trying to resist the silent *help me* expression on her face. Her composure crumbled and tears sprang to her eyes. Big brown eyes that were even softer and more expressive than the green contacts he'd spent months looking into.

If the eyes were the window to the soul then the barrier had been removed.

"It was right after Mick told me what happened. I'd been nauseous off and on for a couple days, but that was when I started getting sick. Really sick. I thought it was because of everything that was going on and the news Mick had told me about your death, but my best friend from childhood was visiting for the weekend before taking a new job in New York, and she suspected something else. I'd told Jennifer about you."

"But you never told me about her."

Natalie looked down, clearly ashamed. He saw her shoulders tremble a little before she took a deep breath and looked back up at him.

How the fuck could someone he knew was strong appear so fragile? The past few months had obviously broken her down. Or maybe it was the relief of not having to lie anymore. The urge to reach for her was so natural that he had to physically squeeze his muscles tight not to do so.

"I didn't want you to learn anything about me, Scott. I thought it would protect me."

"From what? Me finding out about your being adopted or that you had family and friends you cared about?"

"I thought that if I didn't let you in I would be able to keep you at a safe distance. But it didn't work."

His muscles tightened even more. He reached for the now label-less beer and took a long drink, not caring if it was stale. Beer was beer. But Bud Light wasn't going to take the edge off the demons wrestling in him right now. He'd need something far stronger for that. A bottle of whiskey would be a good start.

"So your friend Jennifer figured it out," he said, prompting her to continue and get back to the story.

She nodded, eyes still big and dominating her pale

face. "I didn't take the possibility well. I'd just found out you'd died and I was panicked at the idea of a baby. I told her I couldn't be, but I got it in my head to go to the drugstore to get a test. I didn't make it to the door before I was sick again. Jennifer told me to lie down and she'd go get me something and a test. She didn't have a car so she took mine." It was getting more and more difficult for her to talk as the emotion in her voice crept up higher and higher. She tried to take a deep breath, but it came out unevenly. "Jennifer called a little while later and said she thought someone was following her." Natalie looked up at him pleadingly, tears rolling down her cheeks. "She was so scared, Scott. It was horrible. I could hear the terror in her voice. I knew it was Mick. I tried to warn her, but she screamed, there was a loud crashing sound, and then the line went dead."

She let out a sob and buried her face in her hands as the tears really started to flow. His hand was halfway to her shoulder before he forcefully pulled it back.

What the hell was the matter with him? Damn it, he didn't want to feel sorry for her or see her side of anything. He didn't want any gray messing up his black-and-white.

He sat there, his insides twisting in torturous knots, as she cried. Good thing for him it didn't last long. He didn't know how much longer he could sit there playing stony.

She sniffled and used a napkin from the wooden holder on the table to wipe her eyes and nose. After a moment, she regained her composure and continued. "I heard the sirens a minute or two later and suspected what happened. I didn't know what to do. I posted anonymously on our social media neighborhood group and a bunch of people in the area posted within a few minutes that a car had exploded under the freeway overpass, and the driver had been killed." Who needed police blotters anymore? She shuddered as if the news were still fresh.

"I knew I had to get out of there. Either Mick would realize he'd killed the wrong person and come after me, or the police would be showing up with questions that I didn't want to answer. I took my purse, Jennifer's things, and a few things I couldn't bear to leave behind and ran. I lived in fear that the police would realize what had happened, especially since it took me a couple days to remember to destroy the SIM card in my phone, but they never did. Jennifer had my car and my keys, and her purse must have burned up in the fire. Not even my mother realized," she said in a whisper.

"She identified the body?"

Natalie nodded. "Jennifer and I looked a lot alike, and I'm sure there was . . . uh, trauma." The body would have been badly burned. "I watched my mom go into the coroner's building, but I couldn't watch her come back out. I wanted to tell her so badly, but I knew it was safer for my family if they thought I was dead, too."

"You were there?"

"I had to be. I couldn't let her go through that alone."

He didn't know what to say to that. She obviously loved her mother a lot to risk returning to DC. "The police didn't do an investigation?"

She shook her head. "I assume there wasn't a reason to. Everything was cut-and-dry."

Not so cut-and-dry because here she was. But it wasn't all that surprising. City police stations didn't have CSI budgets, and with an identification they wouldn't go to the trouble of obtaining dental records.

Scott watched the emotions play across her face and knew what she was thinking. He'd steeled himself long enough, damn it. He might want to be made out of stone, but he wasn't. "It wasn't your fault, Natalie."

"Of course it was. It should have been me. Jennifer should never have been in that car. If I hadn't been freaking out—"

"That's bullshit. She was your friend, Natalie. You were upset and sick. That's what friends do. You have a lot of other things you can take the blame for, but that isn't one of them."

He was glad she didn't ask him what things. Truth be told, he didn't know. He didn't know anything right now.

He stood to leave while he still could. "Get some sleep. I'll take the couch tonight."

He saw the look of surprise in her eyes but didn't react. It wasn't because he trusted her. He just didn't think she was going to be trying to climb out of any more windows while pregnant.

Turned out that it wasn't a window he needed to worry about. Her opportunity to escape arrived a few minutes later.

Ten

Scott took a seat on the couch while Natalie went upstairs to get him a pillow and blanket to use later. It was still too early for him to crash, but a couple of more stale beers and the Sox game, and he should be able to eke out a few hours.

He had a lot to digest.

"Here you go," Natalie said, putting the stack of bedding on the seat beside him. "Let me know if you need anything else."

He didn't, but with the situation in limbo for the next few days until the test results came back, he figured he better set down some ground rules before she headed back up. First and foremost, he needed to make sure she wasn't communicating with anyone. He wanted her phone, computer, and . . .

A knock on the door startled them both. Natalie's gaze shot to his, obviously looking for direction.

But one glance out the big living room window and he knew that it was too late for instructions. He swore, seeing the sheriff's car parked along the driveway.

His operational awareness had obviously gone to hell.

The TV was on, and the car was parked away from the house, but Scott should have heard the footsteps up the weathered and creaky front porch stairs. Whatever work had been going on inside of the house hadn't moved to the outside yet.

Realizing that the sheriff had probably already seen him, Scott knew the jig was up.

"Why is he here?" Scott whispered angrily. "Did you call him?"

She gave him an *are you out of your mind?* glare. "Of course not. I told you I barely know him. What do you want me to do?"

"Get rid of him—fast." He caught her gaze with a hard look. "And don't try anything. There's a lot at stake, Natalie. Other lives, not just mine, okay?"

She nodded, but he cursed inwardly, knowing the balance of power had shifted. He just hoped to hell she didn't realize it.

But of course she did. Natalie was too smart not to recognize the opportunity that the sheriff's unexpected— Scott hoped unexpected—arrival gave her. She could get away. He could see the indecision on her face as she paused at the door and glanced back at him. Their eyes met for a long heartbeat. She seemed to be searching for something.

He didn't know whether she found it, but he gave her an encouraging nod, acting more confident than he felt. "Go ahead. Open it."

He resisted the urge to stand, knowing that he had to appear as relaxed and unthreatening as he could.

As soon as the door opened, Scott knew his instincts had been dead-on. The sheriff *had* seen him. Beneath the wide brim of his felt hat, the lawman's sharp-eyed gaze shot directly to Scott, taking in every detail of his scruffy, hard-edged, living-off-the-grid appearance. Scott knew he looked more like a hired hit man than a highly decorated

SEAL officer. He'd taken "low vis," as they called it on the Teams, to heart the past couple of months.

Natalie stepped in front of the door, trying to block the sheriff's view, and asked, "Is there something I can help you with, Sheriff Brouchard?"

She was trying to appear casual and friendly, but her acting skills had apparently gone the way of his operational awareness skills, and her voice was shaking. Of course, if it had been intentional and she was trying to alert the sheriff, Scott was in trouble. From the way the sheriff's gaze narrowed, he definitely hadn't missed her nervousness, either.

"I was in the area so I thought I'd check up on you to see how you were doing. I saw your car was still in town, and I was worried about you being stranded out here." Scott didn't like the way the sheriff was looking at her—it wasn't just neighborly concern in his gaze—and something hot and possessive surged through his veins. His muscles tensed and his posture probably wasn't quite so relaxed and nonthreatening anymore. The sheriff hadn't missed the movement, and his gaze shifted to Scott on the couch. "But I see that you have company."

There was an unspoken challenge in his gaze that Scott wasn't going to ignore—even if he should. "She does," he said. "And she's being well taken care of."

In other words, fuck you and the horse you rode in on, buddy.

"Who are you?"

Scott smiled; he knew the law. He didn't have to answer that. "Not sure that's any of your business unless you got some kind of warrant there that I can't see?"

The friendly tone didn't mask the underlying words. Another fuck-you.

Not surprisingly, the sheriff's suspicion turned to anger. The last thing Scott should be doing was provoking him, but this guy set him on edge. He was sure it didn't have anything to do with the fact that the sheriff was his size—maybe even a little bigger—looked like a TV star, and was clearly interested in Natalie.

Natalie hadn't missed the dangerous undercurrent between the two men and tried to turn the sheriff's attention back to her. "Thank you so much, Sheriff. I really appreciate your stopping by. I'll make sure to pick up my car in the morning."

The overbrightness of her reply made her anxiousness all the more obvious. If she wasn't trying to make the sheriff suspicious, she really needed to reconsider the whole spy thing. She might as well be wearing a flashing red sign that read SOMETHING WRONG HERE.

The sheriff looked intently back and forth between them. "You sure everything is all right?" he asked her.

Scott hadn't missed that the other man's hand had moved toward his holster, as if he was just waiting for her to say the word.

But would she?

Her gaze flicked to Scott's for just the barest of an instant. He could see her temptation. All she had to do was say "yes" and Magnum would jump at the chance to take him in. Scott—or Rob Preston, as his ID stated— would be out in a few hours, but that would be more than enough time for her to get away. And despite what he'd told her about finding her, he suspected she wouldn't be as easy to track down the next time.

Natalie could make it even harder on him if she told the sheriff who he really was: an AWOL Navy SEAL who everyone thought was dead. It wouldn't tie him up for just a few hours.

Hell, Scott couldn't even say he'd blame her if she did it. Were he in her position, he just might do it.

She turned back to the sheriff.

Scott waited, feeling as if a hammer were pounding in his chest, for what seemed like the longest pause ever for her to answer.

"I'm fine. He's my ex, that's all." She hurried to add, so there wasn't any mistake, "Ex-boyfriend—not husband."

Scott felt the tension dissipate into relief. He relaxed his posture—and the flare of muscle. He even decided to be a little more magnanimous and throw the dog a bone. "Rob," he filled in his name for the sheriff. "And I'm working on the ex part."

All right, so maybe not so magnanimous.

Clearly the sheriff didn't like that part of the answer. He also knew that something was off, but as there wasn't anything else he could do, he tipped his hat to Natalie. "I'll be going then, ma'am. But you have my number if you need anything."

Natalie nodded, thanked him, and closed the door. A few minutes later—after looking back a few times at the house—the sheriff got in his car and drove off.

Natalie watched out of the window, not breathing, until the sheriff's car disappeared. Only then did she turn on Scott, who was sitting calmly on the couch apparently enraptured by the baseball game on TV. She marched over and stood in front of it.

"You're blocking the screen."

She ignored him, demanding angrily, "What was that all about?"

"All what?"

Apparently she'd found the one thing that Mr. Lieutenant Commander of America's Top SEAL Team didn't do well: play dumb.

But she knew male posturing when she saw it. "I'm surprised you didn't break out rulers."

His gaze went to hers, piercing her with its intensity—and something else. "I didn't need one."

Natalie felt her cheeks and other parts of her body flush, not with embarrassment but with the heat of awareness and memories. He was right. He didn't. Nor should she be thinking about how much she'd enjoyed that fact.

God, she almost let out a groan. Dick size didn't matter. Yeah, right. She'd thought that until she met Scott.

If he'd meant to fluster her, he had. "You know what I mean."

He shrugged, returning his interest to his beer and to the parts of the screen he could still see. "I didn't like the way he was looking at you."

She wanted to stomp with frustration and get him to pay attention to her. "You are seeing things then because he was looking at me like a concerned neighbor."

"A concerned neighbor who wants to get in your pants," he said, muffling the last with a sip of his beer.

But she'd heard it. "Why do men always assume other men are thinking about sex?"

"Uh, because they are," he stated as if it was the most obvious thing in the world.

Natalie rolled her eyes, refusing to be baited about something so ridiculous. "Even if you are right, why do you care?"

Something angry flashed in his eyes, but she wasn't sure whether it was directed at her or himself. He put his beer down with a hard slam. Now she had his attention. "I don't. I just don't want him sniffing around while I'm here."

"Well, if that was your goal you picked an odd way of going about it. The friendly route might have made him less suspicious."

"He was already suspicious. You weren't exactly making your nervousness unclear. What happened to the cool, confident woman who deceived everyone around her, including me, for the past few years?"

"I don't know. Maybe I just got tired of being that person." She didn't even know who she was anymore. Not the young idealist who'd gone to Washington thinking she could save the world, but not the Stepford Washington insider, either. Natalie's shoulders sagged. "Maybe I'm just tired."

And she was. It was as if the weight of the past few years had finally caught up with her, and she just couldn't pretend anymore. Why should she? The cat was out of the proverbial bag. She was amazed that she'd gotten away with it for so long—especially given who Scott was. He was trained to see deception everywhere. But maybe she was so bad, she'd actually been good. She hadn't deceived him because her feelings had been authentic. She'd truly loved him.

She still did.

She moved out of his view and headed for the stairs. But he stopped her, standing from the couch to block her path. There were a couple of feet between them, but that didn't stop her body from reacting. From feeling as if his shadow had somehow enveloped her in heat. From smelling the warm spiciness of his soap and shampoo. He always smelled incredible. He might look scruffy and disheveled, but his aroma hadn't changed.

"Why didn't you say anything? Why didn't you try to run?"

Natalie wasn't sure. She'd thought about it. She gazed up at the man she'd thought she'd never see again. To the man she'd wronged so terribly. She knew every detail of that handsome face, but she couldn't stop her eyes from roaming over it freely—gluttonously—as if still unable to believe that he was alive.

The strong jaw, the navy blue eyes framed by thick golden brown lashes, the straight, patrician nose, the small scar on his left cheek, and the tiny crow's-feet lines etched in his skin from the months—years—spent in the harsh Middle Eastern sun. Only the darkened hair, stubbly beard, and fierce expression reminded her that she couldn't reach out and touch him. He wasn't hers anymore.

"I didn't want to put you in danger," she said.

"It's a little late for that."

"Any *more* danger," she qualified. "I figured you are in hiding for a reason."

She wasn't surprised when he didn't take her up on the chance to enlighten her.

She took a deep breath. "And maybe I thought I should try to give you the trust that I didn't give you before. I don't want to be looking over my shoulder the rest of my life, and I don't want that for the baby, either. Even if you don't want to protect me, I know you will protect our child."

His eyes blazed and his expression grew even more fierce. "Assuming it is 'ours.'"

"Right," she said, a spark of anger firing her own gaze. "Assuming I didn't plan all this by finding some random guy to sleep with so I could pass his baby off as yours in case you came back from the dead. That makes a lot of sense as opposed to me getting pregnant on the night we didn't use a condom." She brushed up against him seductively, using a soft, sultry voice that belonged in the bedroom. "Or maybe you want me to remind you what happened that night."

She was so close now, her breasts were grazing his chest. It wasn't enough. She leaned in closer, sliding her body up his with a movement that wasn't at all suggestive. It was explicit. Obvious. It told him exactly what she wanted him to remember.

Them. Together. In bed. Their bodies sliding together as he thrust inside of her.

He'd been out of control that night. He'd taken her roughly. Desperately. As if he needed something from her. It was a wild, uncivilized, stripped-to-the-core version of her always-in-control, buttoned-up-tight SEAL commander that she'd never seen before. Later, she found out that something had gone wrong on a mission, and he'd lost one of his guys. But after that night, something had changed between them. He'd showed her a side of him that she suspected few if any people had ever seen. It had brought them closer, fusing their connection even tighter. She'd almost convinced herself that he might love her.

Except that hadn't been her. If he'd cared about her then, it was the version of her that Mick had created. She wasn't fancy or sophisticated. Far from it.

She could see from the way his eyes blazed that he got the less-than-subtle message. But she didn't know whether the heat was anger or arousal. Maybe it was both.

"It wasn't my idea, Scott," she taunted him. "*You* were the one who forgot to put on the condom. I even reminded you. But do you remember what you said?"

She gave him a hint, nudging her hips provocatively against the part of him that answered her question about arousal. He was hard as a rock. She felt a rush of heat and pleasure that spread over her in a warm glow. He wasn't immune to her. Not completely. He might hate her, but he still wanted her. It was something she could hold on to. One connection that wasn't fake and hadn't been severed.

"I remember," he bit out angrily.

But she ignored him, heady with the rush of feminine power. "You said that you didn't care. You said that you didn't want anything between us."

Scott grabbed her shoulders and for one heart-leaping, stomach-dropping moment she thought he was going to kiss her. The air between them seemed to crackle with fire.

His fingers dug into her arms, and he lifted her ever so slightly closer. Every muscle in his body was taut and he seemed pulled as tight as a bow, radiating a raw primal energy that made her knees weak and turned her insides to liquid. His angry, lust-filled eyes dropped to her mouth.

Natalie's heart pounded, and her lips parted with a soft gasp of anticipation.

The sound seemed to startle him. Remind him. He let out a sharp curse, and instead of taking her in his arms, he set her harshly away from him.

She could practically see the blood pounding through his body. He was furious. The taut clench of his jaw made all the more ominous by the ticcing muscle below.

"Pretty damned ironic, don't you think, with all the lies that were between us?"

He was right, and just like that Natalie felt the anger that had been lit by his suggestion that the baby wasn't his die as quickly as it had caught fire.

She was left feeling embarrassed—maybe even ashamed—for taunting him. But he'd provoked her, damn it.

Still, the femme fatale thing wasn't her, and she'd never played the seductress before with anyone. All she'd probably succeeded in doing was reinforcing every horrible thought he had about her.

"You're right," she said. "And maybe I deserve that. You have a right to be angry. But I'm not going to let you beat me up forever. I hate what I did to you, but whether you agree or not, I didn't think I had any choice. You don't have any idea what it is like to have someone controlling every facet of your life—how could you? *Look* at you! Well, I'm not six feet three of solid muscle with good looks, wealth, and connections, nor am I a highly trained SEAL officer with the weight of the US military behind me. I didn't think I had anyone I could turn to and protect my family at the same time. I did the best I could with the horrible choices I had. I did everything in my power not to hurt you or put you at risk. I *loved* you, Scott, whether you want to believe it or not."

They stared at each other for a long moment. He didn't say anything. Whether her words had penetrated, she didn't know. As always his expression revealed none of his thoughts.

But enough had been said for tonight. Without another word, Natalie moved around him and headed upstairs to bed.

Eleven

Scott woke to the sound of a shattering crash above him. He jumped from the couch, grabbed the Glock 19 that he'd stashed under the cushion, and raced up the stairs, taking them two or three at a time.

Had someone broken in? Had she fallen? All kinds of horrible scenarios raced through his mind in the space of a few seconds. His adrenaline had shot from zero to a hundred. But it was the pounding in his heart that he didn't want to think about.

"Jesus, Nat, are you o—"

He stopped midsentence and lowered the gun. The panic—for that was what he had to acknowledge it was—came crashing down. She was fine. She was bent over in the hallway picking up the small metal stepladder that he'd noticed the other night.

She glanced over at him with an apologetic wince that included a gnawing of her lower lip. A very lush, very red lower lip that was sexy as hell and made him think of all kinds of really inappropriate things. Things that wouldn't have been inappropriate a few short months ago. Things that she'd been really good at.

Shit, blood rush.

"Sorry," she said. "I was trying not to wake you. But I put the ladder down to lean it against the wall while I opened the window and it fell."

Scott nodded and started to tuck the pistol into the back waistband of his shorts but realized at the same time she did—if the widening of her eyes and pink flush on her cheeks meant anything—that he wasn't wearing his shorts. Or a shirt for that matter. Only his boxer briefs, which were tight and had space for just one gun.

A gun that was going to be primed and ready to shoot if she didn't stop looking at him like that.

The way she'd looked at his body had always turned him on. She'd never hidden the appreciation she had for the results—in this case benefits—of his constant physical training, especially when it came to his arms and abs. She used to lie in bed curled against his chest and trace the bands of stomach muscle with her fingers, counting. Not all guys could get an eight-pack, but she'd been fascinated by his.

Fortunately, his body didn't have time to betray him. The look in her eyes changed. She gasped and stood upright, her eyes pinned to his shoulder. "What happened?"

He glanced down, seeing the bandage stained with the now-dried blood from where the wound had opened yesterday. He'd forgotten about it and hadn't cleaned it up.

"Nothing."

She glanced up, mouth flat and eyes narrowed. "That isn't nothing." She marched over to him, closing the distance in a handful of steps. "Tell me what happened."

"I took a bullet—"

"My God, you were shot!" Her eyes widened again and worse, she put her hands on him. One on his bare chest and the other on his arm near the bandage—which was two hands too many. His reaction was instantaneous.

Every nerve ending flared and blood rushed to all corners of his body—including key extremities. "Why didn't you say anything?" The obvious distress in her voice made his chest feel too tight. "Let me see it. . . ."

He grabbed the hand by the wrist that started to move toward the bandage. Not because he didn't want her to see the wound but because the feel of her hands on him was leaving very little to the imagination. "It's fine. I just need to change the bandage."

"I can help you."

"No," he said more harshly than he intended. But the thought of her standing near him like this in a small bathroom, where the citrus scent of her shampoo—seemingly designed to make him want to bury his head in it—would be even more pungent, putting her hands on him . . . no thanks. He was already jumping out of his skin. But seeing the wounded look in her eyes, he added, "Thanks, but it isn't necessary. Really, Nat." He stared intently into her eyes. "It's almost healed."

She held his gaze for a long moment and nodded, but then a look of pure horror came over her. "Did Mick do it?"

He shook his head. "It was one of the men he hired."

She bit her lip again, the distress returning. "Will you tell me what happened?"

He nodded. "But let me get some clothes on and clean up a little, all right?" Suddenly it was his turn to frown, taking note of the open window. "What are you doing up here? I thought you weren't going to climb out of any more windows."

She blushed. "I'm not. I'm just getting ready to sand before painting."

"*You've* been fixing up the place?" He'd seen all the tools and equipment lying around, but he'd thought they'd belonged to workers.

She put her hands on her hips, with an expression on

her face that made him think about minefields and being careful where to step next. "And why do you sound so surprised? Don't tell me you are one of *those* guys."

He hesitated to ask. "What guys?"

"The kind that thinks that just because I don't have a Y chromosome I can't hold a hammer."

He caught himself from saying something about her holding his hammer anytime. That was something he would have said in the old days. Not now.

But it was getting harder and harder to keep his mind from slipping back into the way it used to be. To keep the distance and the wall he'd put up between them. To remind himself that she'd betrayed him in a way that was unforgivable.

Their conversation from last night had kept him up most of the night. He didn't want to believe anything she told him. But he did. If not all of it then most of it. Some of it was too implausible not to be true. And the rest of it was consistent with what he knew.

But if she wasn't lying then he'd have to concede that she *might* have been in a horrible catch-22 situation where what to do might not be as straightforward as he wanted to make it. Her accusation last night had struck a chord. She wasn't in his position and hadn't had his resources. Could he fault her for not trusting others to protect her and those she cared about, when he was doing the same thing right now with the team?

He also couldn't ignore that she'd risked her life—and her friend had lost hers—to warn him. That warning had saved him and five of his men.

He didn't know what to think, which was part of the problem. Scott always knew what to do. It was his greatest strength and why he had been put in charge of America's most elite special operations unit. Spies went to prison. It should be as simple as that. But her guilt no longer seemed so clear-cut, and Scott was having a hard time invoking the anger and hatred that gave him the emotional detachment and headspace to think straight.

His feelings for her had blinded him once. He wouldn't let that happen again.

But instead of commenting about the hammer, he said, "I think I'll take the Fifth on that."

"Smart guy."

"I'll get changed and give you some help."

She arched one brow. "Lots of manual labor experience from those long summers playing golf at the country club?"

He'd always loved how she teased him about his wealth as if it didn't matter to her. It honestly seemed *not* to matter to her. Unfortunately, in this case, the teasing was kind of true. He didn't have much renovation experience. Okay, any. "Yeah, well, I'm a quick study."

Over the next two days, while they waited for the doctor to call with the blood test results, Natalie put Scott to work, challenging that assessment. He was definitely out of his element with stripping wallpaper, sanding, cutting trim, fixing loose floorboards, and painting, but she was right at home. He couldn't believe how handy she was—or that she'd already tackled much of the plumbing work.

He was glad of something to do to keep busy, but he hadn't anticipated the difficulty of close daily contact. Nor of the intimacy of working side by side. It was stretching his control to the limit. The sexual attraction between them had always been red-hot and trying to tamp that down wasn't easy.

He was just as attracted to her as he'd ever been. Maybe even more so. DIY, cutoff shorts, and ponytail Natalie was just as erotic as sexy, businesswoman Natalie—maybe more so. He felt like he'd been dropped into a home show porno. Who knew sanding could be sexy? He'd forced her off the ladder not just because of the baby but because it put the soft curve of her butt cheek beneath the edge of her shorts perfectly in view, and it was driving him crazy not to touch that soft velvety skin.

In addition to sexual frustration, the forced proximity was taking a sledgehammer to the wall he was trying to keep between them. More than once he'd found himself lapsing back into their old pattern. Into the easy— sometimes teasing—conversations that had made him realize early on that what was between them wasn't just incredible sex.

Except now the conversations weren't so one-sided. With the truth out, her wall had come down, and she seemed eager—almost anxious—to share her background with him. Subjects that had been so deftly turned in the past that he hadn't even realized she'd done so were now wide-open. It was hard holding back his curiosity, and although he knew he shouldn't if he wanted to keep thinking of her as the coldhearted Russian spy who'd betrayed him, he found himself asking questions.

Yesterday, while they'd been picking up her car, she'd told him how she'd ended up in DC. He was surprised to hear that Mick had nothing to do with it. He hadn't appeared on the scene until a couple of years later. She'd explained how when Big Dairy moved into their town her family lost their dairy farm, including the burgeoning artisanal cheese business she'd started with her sister to make the farm more profitable. It was hard enough to picture her growing up on a farm let alone starting a cheese business. But reading between the lines, he realized she'd done it just as much for her sister as for herself. "It's so hard for special-needs adults to find jobs, and something like this was perfect for her. She loved it. It gave her such a sense of pride."

His heart would have really had to have been made of stone not to feel a pinch at that. The Russian spy with the heart of gold—great.

Later he learned how she'd gone to Washington to work for a congressman who shared her interest in sustainability and was trying to protect small farms. Scott never would have guessed that beneath the polished, glossy exterior beat the heart of a crusader. But maybe with what he'd seen here so far it made sense. She had a strong sense of service and wasn't the type to walk away from a problem.

Which were both things he could get behind.

She'd thought about law school and had applied for the job at the Pentagon to save money to go, when Mick came into her life.

The reminder of Mick was enough to stop his questions for the day. But today he found himself handing her tools as she took apart a toilet to try to fix a slow leak, and couldn't resist asking, "How did you learn so much about fixing toilets?"

She'd tried the rubber flapper first, but when that hadn't worked she'd had to replace the entire fill valve. He wasn't sure he'd ever removed the top part of the toilet—the tank lid, she'd called it—before, let alone tried to fix one.

She blew a wisp of hair that had come loose from her ponytail out of her face as she leaned down to finish screwing something in place before answering. "My dad was handy, and I liked to follow him around to help when I was little." She looked over at him and smiled. He tried to ignore the sudden tightness in his chest, but how could someone fixing a toilet look so freaking adorable? "I pretty much did what you are doing. Sitting there and handing him tools and watching. Eventually he started to let me really help."

Scott lifted one eyebrow. "Are you suggesting that I'm not really helping?"

She laughed. "Pretty much. But you are good at lifting heavy stuff—and you're pretty mean with a hammer."

"Good to know I'm not completely useless," he said dryly.

Nothing like having the holes in his skill set pointed out. It had been a long time since he'd been humbled.

Well, maybe he wasn't Mr. Fixit, but he could take out terrorist cells, rescue hostages, and lead cover operations deep behind enemy lines with some of the most highly trained operators in the world. Shouldn't that count for something?

She grinned as if she knew exactly what he was thinking—she probably did. Not many people could read him as well as Natalie could. Apparently he wasn't as opaque as the guys on the team thought.

She shrugged unrepentantly. "We didn't have a lot of money and my father didn't believe in picking up the phone to pay someone for something you could do yourself."

"I like to think of it as adding to the economy."

She laughed, knowing he was joking. "You don't know Herb Andersson."

No, Scott didn't. But he wished he did. From what Natalie had said the past couple of days, her father sounded like a tough, hardworking family man who loved his wife and adopted daughters more than anything in the world. "Any other hidden talents I should know about? Like fixing carburetors?"

"I'm not as good with cars as my father is, but I can fix farm equipment."

Jesus. "I was joking."

She grinned. "I know."

"But you weren't?"

She just smiled and went back to the toilet.

Something had changed. It wasn't like the way it had been before, but it wasn't like a few days ago when Scott had first showed up, either. The wariness and distance was still there, but the biting layer of ice had cracked.

Natalie knew not to put much hope in the temporary lull while they waited for the doctor to call, but it was hard not to think that Scott had softened toward her. He wasn't looking at her as if he hated her anymore, which was definitely an improvement. Once or twice she'd actually caught him looking at her with something else entirely in his gaze. Lust . . . desire . . . *I want to rip your clothes off and push you up against the closest door—* whatever you wanted to call it. He was trying to hide it, but it was clear that Scott still wanted her.

It was a crack, but not one she wanted to press. No matter how difficult it was not to respond to those heated looks. There never had been a lot of holding back between them; it was hard to get used to not touching him when she wanted to. All the time.

She was tempted to put in air-conditioning with how hot all this working-together time was making her. The rooms in this house were generously proportioned, but he made it feel like a dollhouse. He dominated the space and sucked up all the air. Every time she moved around she seemed to be bumping into that big, too-hard-and-muscular body. And not much had changed since that first time at the bar. Her nerve endings still flared with awareness. *Heated* awareness that was worse because she knew exactly how incredible it was to make love with him.

Yes, she was tempted. Very tempted to press her one advantage. But she didn't want to be accused of trying to seduce him and reinforcing every negative Mata Hari stereotype that he probably thought about her. Whatever he might think, sex had never been her weapon, and she wasn't going to make it one.

Besides, she didn't think it would be effective. Even if she could get him back into bed, she knew better than to think that would translate to anything more. Scott was too compartmentalized. He would never let his personal feelings or emotions impact his duty or what he thought was the right thing. That was why trying to spy on him had been so useless. And why she hadn't gone to him for help the first time around.

No, if he was going to help her this time, it wouldn't be because she gave great head. Although he did love it when she got on her knees. . . .

Not what she should be thinking about when he was sitting on the edge of the tub and she was on her knees next to the toilet to access the base (the entire assembly unit needed to be replaced). It would be so easy to move around in front of him and . . .

She shook her head in an attempt to clear the thought. But she could still feel the heat on her cheeks from the erotic images. That eroticism where he was concerned still surprised her. It had never been that way for her even before Mick. "Can you pass the new locknut?"

Her cheeks fired even hotter at the unfortunate terminology, but thankfully he didn't seem to notice. "The white plastic thing," she clarified.

"I'm not a total idiot," he said. "I know what a nut looks like. It screws on the bolt."

She was clearly going off the deep end because everything was turning dirty in her mind. Instead she put an exaggerated impressed look on her face. "You'll be fixing toilets around the compound before you know it."

He shot her a look. "You know very well that I don't live on a compound."

"Anymore," she qualified. He had a condo in Honolulu and a loft in DC. But to her knowledge he hadn't sold the place where he'd grown up in upstate New York not far from the Rockefeller estate.

He shot her a glare. "It isn't a compound."

She gave him an exaggerated sigh. "Scott, anything that has a main house, a guesthouse, a gatehouse, a playhouse—with a bowling alley—and a boat shed is a compound."

"I should never have told you about that."

She rolled her eyes. "You didn't tell me. I saw the pictures and pried it out of you."

She regretted her words instantly. Their eyes held and she knew they were both thinking about other information she'd tried—with much less enthusiasm—to pry out of him.

She felt her chest pinch uncomfortably and wanted to say she was sorry. But she'd already said that. Instead she asked him for the bucket and went back to changing the valve.

Once the excess water had drained from the tank, she pulled out the old assembly and asked him to hand her the new unit, adjusting the height to fit the tank before putting it in. Less than five minutes later, the new valve was in place. She flushed the toilet, replaced the tank lid, and sat on the lowered seat. "Good as new," she said with a smile. "Without the one-hundred-and-fifty-dollar repair bill."

"A hundred and fifty? I've been ripped off. Last time I had to call in a plumber it was over three hundred bucks."

"My father would have had a heart attack," she said with a laugh.

But she quickly sobered. Her father *had* had a heart attack. The stress of losing the farm had been too much for him. Between that and the worsening diabetes, he could barely get up from his favorite recliner anymore.

She was so worried about him. The news of her death would have been horrible for him. She'd give anything to hear his voice.

She sighed and started to get up.

But Scott stopped her.

The need to touch her had been instinctive. But the moment Scott's hand closed around her wrist he knew it was a mistake. They were sitting too close and it would be too easy to pull her onto his lap and comfort her. Traitor or not, he couldn't stand seeing her in pain.

Scott knew he should drop her wrist and let her go. It was getting late, and no matter how much he'd been putting it off, he needed to check in with Kate. He'd turned his phone back on a little while ago for the first time since yesterday when Natalie had insisted on calling the town manager—who she apparently worked for—to prevent her from showing up, and the message light was on. Colt had probably caught up with Travis by now so she might have news.

Scott stood from his seat on the edge of the tub. Having every intention of letting her go and walking away. Natalie's emotional pain wasn't his problem. He needed to keep a clear head and not cloud it up with sympathy.

But when it came to Natalie, knowing what to do and actually doing it were two different things—which was better than saying that he was an idiot.

She'd come to her feet as well, so all his plans to leave had done was to bring them closer together. His hand was still wrapped around her wrist, the soft beat of her pulse reverberating through him like a drum. There was something mesmerizing about it—almost primal in the connection. It had always been like that between them, even with something so small.

"You're thinking about your father?" he said.

She nodded.

"You said he was in poor health?"

She nodded again. "He had a heart attack about seven years ago after he lost the farm and never really recovered. He also has ongoing complications from diabetes." She looked up at him, tears heavy in her eyes. "I just wish I knew that he was okay. The news of my death would have been horrible for him—for all of them. But I feared that if I confided in them, Mick would find out. I thought it was the only way to keep them safe."

She was obviously second-guessing herself and looking to him for reassurance.

"I would have done the same thing in your position."

He meant it. It also made him realize just how desperate she'd been and how much she feared for her family if letting her sick father think she was dead was her best choice.

She attempted to smile, but it wobbled. "Thanks. That means a lot."

She was standing too close. Their bodies were almost brushing. He could feel her warmth. Smell the faint feminine scent. And when she looked up at him, those big sad brown eyes cut off his breath. Everything in his chest seemed to come to a sudden halt. He had that itchy feeling. That feeling that he would do just about anything to make it better.

So much so that he found himself saying, "I could have Kate make a few inquiries. She's good. She won't leave a footprint if anyone is still watching. And it might help you put your mind at ease about your father until this is all, uh, sorted out."

In other words, until he decided what the fuck to do.

She sucked in her breath. The erotic sound was bad enough, but it also made her lips part invitingly. Enticingly. He could almost taste the sweetness on his tongue.

She betrayed you. She lied. She put the job that meant

*everything to you—that you've dedicated the last fifteen
years of your life to—in jeopardy.*

But the reminders didn't seem to be packing the same
wallop. They barely penetrated the haze that was descending on him like a lead curtain.

"You would do that?" she asked sweetly, having no
clue what she was doing to him.

He nodded, unable to breathe. The rein on his control
was taking everything he had to handle it. The temptation to lower his mouth, to cover the lips of the woman
who had haunted him for months . . .

"Oh, Scott! Thank you!" She threw her arms around
his neck and pressed her body to his in an innocent,
grateful hug.

Almost instantly she pulled back in shock, realizing
what she'd done, and realizing, no doubt, that every muscle in his body was pulled as tight as a bowstring. "I'm
sorry," she said, trying to back away. "I didn't mean
to—"

She didn't get the word out. With a sharp growl—or
maybe it was a curse—he dragged her into his arms and
did what he'd been wanting to do since the first moment
he saw her on the town steps.

His mouth covered hers in a deep groan. The intensity
of the sensation—of the relief—overwhelming. His
heart slammed hard against his rib cage just as it had
done the first time he'd felt the incredible softness . . . the
warmth . . . the honey-sweet taste.

He felt her surprise and then her almost instant response. Her almost instant surrender as her body melted
into his. Her arms went around his neck and the soft
weight of her dragged him down a black hole of an indescribable need—of a craving that seemed to pull from
his very soul.

His tongue was in her mouth, wrapped against hers,
stroking deeper and deeper. His hands were in her hair,

on her breasts, on that curvy ass that had been driving him crazy.

And her hands were on him. On his arms. His chest. His back. Pressing. Clenching. Digging. Trying to bring him closer.

The subtle press of her hips against his already throbbing erection was too much to take. He spun around, leaning back on the sink to wrap her leg around his hips and lifting her up on him so she was right where he wanted her. He circled, pressed, and slid up and down, mimicking a thrust as he let her feel the long thick length of him.

She responded with a gasp of pleasure that went right to the tip of his cock and a press of her own hips that increased the friction. The madness. The desperation.

It felt so damned good, and knowing that he was going to be inside her in the space of a couple of buttons and she would be riding him for real was pushing him over the edge. Fast.

They'd never been much on foreplay for the first time of the night. And almost four months of built-up pressure seemed to have only made it more explosive.

He was right there. And if the increasingly demanding sounds coming from her were any indication, so was she.

The kiss was out of control. They were devouring each other. Her moans mixed with his groans in a firestorm of passion. The frenzy egged him on. It was as if they both wanted to get there before something—

A buzz in his shorts jolted him. His phone was vibrating. For a moment, he kept kissing her. But it was too much reality to ignore. With a curse, he released her leg and broke the kiss. She was still plastered against him, but slowly he stood and let her find her feet as he fumbled around to dig his phone out of his shorts, the effort hampered by the size of his erection making them about two sizes too tight.

He glanced at the number before answering, seeing that it was Kate.

His heart was still hammering, his blood was still pounding, and other parts of him were still protesting as he bit out a terse "What's up?"

"Thank God," she said. "I've been trying to get ahold of you. Didn't you get my message?"

He could tell right away that something was wrong. "I hadn't had a chance to listen to it yet." He'd been too busy nearly having sex with the woman he was supposed to be bringing in to clear his name. "What is it?"

"Colt found Travis." There was a pause where he could guess what she was going to say before the words were out. His stomach dropped. "He's dead, Scott. Travis is dead!"

Twelve

Scott felt as if he'd taken another bullet—this one in the gut. He'd thought that Travis might have run into some kind of problem, but dead? The news Kate had just imparted cut his legs out from under him.

What the hell had happened?

Aware of Natalie's gaze on him, Scott turned and walked out of the bathroom into the hall. The heat and the passion of a few minutes ago had turned numb and cold.

"Scott, are you there?" Kate asked.

"I'm here." He paused, his voice tight. "How? When?"

"A bar fight in Alaska two weeks ago. Colt said there was a verbal argument over a pool game—some guy accused Travis of pool-sharking—that spilled out into the parking lot later. Colt got someone to pull the security tapes for him, and they showed two guys jumping Travis just after one in the morning when he was heading back to his car. One of the guys hit Travis over the head with a bottle, breaking it, and then the jagged glass ended up in his jugular when the second guy struck him and he fell back."

Scott wished he could believe that it was a coincidence, but there were two things wrong with the story: Travis sucked at pool, and he was a SEAL. A tier-one, best-of-the-best SEAL. Two guys—two normal guys—wouldn't have been able to get the jump on him or do that kind of damage. He didn't need to see the tape to know that they had to have been trained.

Scott could tell from Kate's voice that she didn't believe it, either. "Let me guess," he said. "The two guys weren't local, no one had ever seen them before, they've disappeared, and the police have nothing."

"Yep, they checked into a hotel two days before and seem to have left that night. They didn't check out."

"Fake ID and cash to rent the room?"

"How did you guess?"

"Photos?"

"Nothing clear on any of the bar security cameras. Colt is having someone pull the street, ATM, and nearby building cameras."

"Descriptions?"

"A couple. Travis was with one of the guys he worked with, and the guy was pretty shaken up, but he got a good look at one of the guys. He had some pretty elaborate neck tattoos that might give us a lead."

But Scott already knew where it would lead: back to the Russians. Mick must have been able to pass on the information about other survivors before he was killed—the timing was right—and the Russians were hunting them down, picking them off one by one.

It wasn't over.

A wall of conflicting emotions hit him at the same time: denial, rage, sadness, frustration, and guilt. Travis's death was on him. Keeping the survivors safe was his responsibility. If they'd come out earlier maybe . . . *don't go there.*

It wasn't often that Scott lost his cool, but he was struggling with it now.

"How the hell did they find him?" he asked. They'd taken precautions, and his guys knew how to disappear.

"I've been looking into that," Kate said. "Remember the payoff to the young woman who claimed to be pregnant with Travis's child that we thought was from the government?"

"The five thousand dollars Colt told you about?"

"Yes. I've done a little digging, and I don't think it came from the government. I think it might have come from Travis."

Scott cursed, not wanting to believe it. "Travis wouldn't be that stupid. He knows better."

He'd been trained better, damn it. And Travis knew the stakes; the eight teammates who'd never left the gulag were proof enough of what could happen.

"If the baby really was his, I wouldn't be so sure," Kate said. "I've seen a lot of smart people do stupid things when a child is involved."

Kate had no idea how well her point had been aimed. She could have been talking to him.

"Have you talked to this woman to see what she knows?" he asked.

"I tried to call her a little while ago, but she hung up on me as soon as I mentioned Travis's name. She's in Vicksburg now so I'm catching a flight to Jackson"— Vicksburg, Mississippi was Travis's hometown—"this afternoon to track her down in person."

"Not by yourself." Scott spoke without thinking. He would have put it more delicately—less like an order—if his brotherly protective instincts hadn't been kicking in hard. Before she could get mad at him, he added, "It could be dangerous. Take Colt with you."

"You do realize I work for the CIA, right, *little* brother?"

In other words, *I don't take orders from you.* He got it. But Travis's death had rocked him, and if anything happened to her, he would never forgive himself. Fourteen months younger or not. "I don't want you anywhere near this, Kate. I never should have brought you into it, although God knows what we would have done without you. But you're an analyst, remember—not a field agent. I'll have Colt go and talk to her."

She made a sharp sound. "You're kidding, right? Have you seen my ex-husband lately? He looks like an ax murderer. She'll probably take one look at him and run away screaming. And unless he's prepared to lean on a pregnant woman—which I suspect may be too low even for Colt—his less-than-charming bedside manner isn't likely to get us any information." She took a deep breath, probably realizing that Scott's poorly chosen words had come from a place of concern and love. "Look, I know you are worried, but I'll be careful. I know how to take care of myself. I may not be a field agent, but I have had training. And I was married to Colt for almost five years."

He sighed. "I know you can take care of yourself, but Travis had training, too—a hell of a lot more than you."

There was silence on the other end so he knew he'd made his point.

"Call Colt," he urged. Another long silence. He could almost hear her resistance and anger. Both of which he understood. He had plenty of reasons not to want any contact with his old teammate and former friend, either. But no matter what had happened between the three of them, Scott could trust Colt to keep her safe. "I'd go with you myself, but I'm a little tied up."

Understatement.

"Does this have something to do with Jennifer? Is she why you are in Kensington, Vermont?"

He swore again. "How the hell did you . . . ?" His

voice dropped off. "You're tracking me? God damn it, Kate—"

She didn't let him finish and clearly didn't have any intention of apologizing. "The general wanted an update, and I was worried when I got your message and said you were turning off your phone. That isn't like you."

He swore again, knowing she was right. He just hadn't been ready to face the music, so to speak.

"Next time tell me what's going on." She paused. "What *is* going on?"

He got ready to drop his bombshell, knowing there was going to be blowback. Lots of blowback. "It wasn't Natalie in the car crash. It was her friend Jennifer."

Shocked silence followed. "Natalie is alive?"

"And pretending not to be. Yep."

It didn't take long for Kate to process the ramifications and pummel him with the questions he'd been trying to avoid thinking about, let alone answer. "But why haven't you brought her in? She could have all the information we need to clean up this mess."

"I promise to explain everything, Kate, but it's more complicated than I realized."

He could sense her skepticism through the phone. "What do you mean, 'complicated,' Scott? She's a spy! She betrayed you and leaked information that got your guys killed."

Scott felt his anger rise and couldn't hold it back even though he knew it was grounded in defensiveness. "I know exactly what she did, Kate. You don't need to tell me." Remind me. "But it isn't that straightforward."

"She was a spy or she wasn't."

He gritted his teeth, trying not to take his anger out on her for saying what he'd thought himself. "She had her reasons, okay? I'll explain everything when I get back."

"When will that be?"

"I'm not sure. I, uh, need a few days." She didn't say anything. But he knew what she was thinking. *Idiot.* The thought had crossed his mind more than once.

"Are you sure you are looking at this objectively, Scott? I know you cared about her. But she could destroy your career."

If she hadn't already done so. He knew that well enough. And his objectivity had definitely taken a beating—he couldn't believe he'd lost control like that and kissed her.

But objective or not, he didn't have a choice. He dropped the second bombshell, knowing this one would be far more painful for Kate. He alone knew how desperately she'd mourned the loss of her unborn child. "She's pregnant, okay? Natalie is pregnant and I'm waiting for the blood test to confirm the baby is mine."

The hope that Natalie felt after the explosive kiss in the bathroom died a quick death when Scott hung up the phone and turned around and saw her watching him.

Whatever softening there might have been in his attitude was gone. His face was a cold mask of rage, his gaze every bit as fierce and accusing as it had been that first day he'd showed up at the farm. "Did you get everything you need?"

She flushed at the unspoken accusation. "I wasn't listening." At least that hadn't been the reason she'd been waiting in the hall. "I was worried. I could tell something was wrong, and I wanted to make sure everything was okay."

She took a few cautious steps toward him as if approaching a lion on a chain of unknown length. She didn't want to be in range if—when—he decided to pounce.

His eyes narrowed. "How exactly do you plan to do that?"

Her flush deepened at the suggestiveness in his voice.

It was obvious what he meant. "I didn't kiss you, Scott. You kissed me."

A look of self-disgust penetrated the anger. "Yeah, well, that was a mistake that won't happen again."

The steel in his voice made her heart pinch. It sounded like the jaw of a bear trap snapping shut. It was clear he meant it. Whatever that phone call had been about, it had brought them back to square one. Or maybe she should say square negative a million and one. The divide between them had grown so wide she'd need a rocket launcher to span it.

"Was it your sister?" she asked.

Something about her question set him off. His expression turned even more furious and he closed the distance between them in a few long strides. He took her arm to haul her up to meet his gaze. "Did you tell them about Kate?" He shook her. "Did you fucking tell Mick she was my sister?"

"What?" She blinked off the shock of his rage. "No. Of course not."

"There is no 'of course' about it. You lied to me about everything else, why should I believe you about this?"

Natalie felt the tears in her throat, knowing that he was right. Trust wasn't something that could be given out piecemeal. You either had it or you didn't, and she'd lost his the moment she allowed Mick to force her into spying on him.

If only Scott could look into her heart and see the truth. She loved him and had done everything in her power to minimize her deception. But it hadn't been enough. "I don't know, but I swear I'm telling you the truth. I would never have betrayed your confidence like that. I never gave any personal information. . . ."

She stopped, biting her lip guiltily.

"What?" He shook her again. "What did you tell him?"

"Only what I had to. Mick wanted to take advantage

of your wealth and connections, but I told him that you'd cut yourself off from your family." Before he could ask, she added, "I didn't tell him why. I didn't tell him anything about your mom and Kate's father. Or about Kate." His gaze penetrated hers as if probing the depths of her conscience for the truth. "I swear to you, Scott, on the life of the child that I am carrying, that I did not tell Mick anything about Kate. If he knew about her, it was not from me."

The anger and tension radiating from him was burning her up. He was scaring her, and that was something she'd never thought she'd say. He never lost his cool—or he never used to lose his cool. Where was that well-bred facade when she needed it?

But after a moment, he released her. "If anything happens to her, and I find out you lied to me . . ."

He didn't need to finish the sentence.

Natalie knew it was silly and that she had no right, but Scott's fierce protectiveness for his sister made her sad and maybe even a little jealous. She wanted that for herself.

Even if she didn't deserve it.

"Kate is lucky to have a brother like you looking after her," she said softly.

Maybe he'd heard something in her voice. His fury seemed marginally less intense. "You don't know Kate. She doesn't need anyone looking after her."

"Maybe not, but it must be nice to know someone is."

He didn't say anything, but just stood there staring at her, seeing far more than she wanted him to.

She straightened her back and lifted her chin. She didn't want him feeling sorry for her. She was strong, too. She didn't need anyone watching her "six" as Scott called it. She'd done the best she could with the nightmare she'd found herself living in. All by herself.

But it would have been nice to have someone to turn to.

After a moment, he finally broke the silence. "One of my men was killed."

Her eyes widened and she covered her mouth with a gasp. "Oh my God, how horrible." No wonder he was so upset. She remembered what he'd told her about less than half his men making it out of there. "It was one of the guys who survived the missile attack?"

He nodded, his expression hard again. "In case you are keeping score: your team nine, mine five."

She flinched. In other words, he was laying one more death at her feet.

She understood his lashing out, but it didn't make it any easier to take. "I'm so sorry, Scott."

It was the most natural thing in the world to put her hand on his chest as she looked up at him. She'd moved closer without even realizing it.

All she'd meant to do was comfort him. She wasn't trying to seduce him or get him to kiss her again.

But Scott was too angry, too upset by the loss of his teammate, and too ready to blame her to give her the benefit of the doubt.

He jerked her hand away. "Don't fucking touch me, Natalya." She didn't miss the reemergence of her birth name. The lines had been redrawn. "I told you I'm not going to make that mistake again. You can stop looking at me with those big bedroom eyes because I'm not going to fuck you."

The harshness of his words seemed to startle them both. She sucked in her breath and jerked back as if stung. Scott was always—unfailingly—a gentleman. He'd never spoken to her so crudely. She'd wager he'd never spoken to any woman so crudely, and it seemed to sum up just how low his opinion of her was.

The unfairness of his accusation struck a flare inside her. She lifted her chin and met his gaze with anger of her own. "Go to hell, Scott."

She started to walk away, but then thought better of it. She turned around with a smile that was decidedly wicked and let her gaze move slowly down his body to come to rest on the big bulge in his shorts. She swept her tongue over her lips thoughtfully—suggestively—and when she saw his fists clench, she looked back up at him with a very sultry haze in her eyes. "But if I wanted you to fuck me, you can be sure I would do a hell of a lot more than put a hand on your chest."

She had the pleasure of seeing the shock on his face before she turned and walked away. Mic drop that!

Thirteen

Colt made it to the gate right as it was closing. He suspected the agent let him through because she felt sorry for him. He looked—and felt—like hell.

He could tell himself that it was from flying back and forth across the country—his flight from Alaska had just landed when Taylor got ahold of him—the two to three hours of sleep he'd averaged in the past two weeks, or investigating the death of the kid he'd recruited for Team Nine before he'd left, or the overindulgence in his drink of choice (whiskey), but he knew it was more than that. He was being eaten up from the inside out by guilt and regret. He'd fucked up royally and it showed in every line, every pore, every fiber of his body.

He saw Kate right away as he came on the plane. She was seated in the third row looking out the window. Making note of his late arrival, the flight attendant joked, "I guess it's your lucky day. Maybe you should buy a lottery ticket."

He wanted to tell her that he'd already won the lottery and had thrown it away, but she wouldn't understand. No surprise since he didn't understand himself.

"Yeah, I'll do that," he said instead.

What were the chances of hitting the lottery twice? If the look in his ex-wife's gaze was any indication when she looked up at the sound of his voice, they weren't good.

Her eyes flashed and her mouth tightened to white before she gave him the cold—no, *arctic*—shoulder and turned her attention back to looking out the window.

Scott had warned him that she wouldn't be happy to see him. But Colt didn't give a shit. She wasn't the only one pissed off. She could hate him all she wanted, but she didn't get to be stupid about her safety. He didn't want her anywhere near this. Travis's murder had shaken him. This thing wasn't over and he wasn't going to let her get caught in the cross fire.

The seat next to her was occupied, but he'd paid through the nose for another first-class seat and the old lady next to her was happy to switch places when he explained the situation.

He thought Kate would drop the "ex" into the conversation when he referred to her as his wife, but she just pressed her lips tighter.

That was one good thing about all that breeding, he thought. Kate still didn't like to make scenes, and she must have realized that he would have made one.

She waited until he'd taken his seat and the flight attendant started the announcements before commenting, "I didn't realize you could be charming." She was apparently referring to his conversation with the old woman. He wasn't sure a forced smile or two qualified, but maybe in comparison. "But next time you might want to add a razor and some eye drops in the mix. You look like you haven't slept in days."

Fourteen to be precise—since the day he'd found out the truth about her and Scott—but who was counting? "I would have if I hadn't received a call from your *brother* that you were being stubborn and stupid."

She ignored his emphasis and drew up her shoulders, early affronted. "Scott didn't say that."

"Maybe not in so many words, but it's true. What the ıck were you thinking, Kate? You should have called ıe. No matter what you think of me, you know I can ɛep you safe."

She brushed away his anger with a lift of her chin. "I ıought you were on your way back from Alaska."

He gritted his teeth so he wouldn't yell. "I was. I got ıe call when I landed. But you could have waited for me ɔ get back."

Her gaze met his. "I didn't want to wait."

That was fucking obvious. He stared at her angrily ntil she turned away.

Except she didn't turn away. He did. He didn't want to ght with her. He wanted to . . .

Fuck if he knew.

He didn't know what to say, so he got angry. That was hat he always did. It was easier than dealing with emo- ons that he didn't know how to handle.

Colt let her go back to looking out the window. What id you say to the woman who'd given you her heart and ɔu'd thrown it back in her face?

No, he'd *ripped* it apart, set it on fire, and then thrown back in her face. That was his MO. Scorched earth. eave nothing behind but destruction, desolation, and ash.

He should have cherished her. Kate had been the only ɔod thing to happen to him other than being a SEAL. ıt instead of giving everything like he had with the am, he'd held back the love he had for her, pushed her vay, and refused to give her the one thing she really anted but would never ask for: a baby.

Why? Because he was a fucking coward.

He'd feared that he wasn't good enough. That he ould screw up a kid the way he was screwing up his ıarriage. He feared losing her every day they were

married. But that fear was infinitely better than the real
ity of actually doing so.

Ironically, he'd thought loving her would take him
away from the team, but it had been their divorce tha
had done that. Being around Taylor . . . Colt hadn'
trusted himself. He'd wanted to kill him, and Colt was
too good at doing that to chance sticking around.

He'd taken a job with CAD and had slipped deepe
and deeper into the black hole he'd made of his life
He was good at his job—even liked the challenge
sometimes—but without his teammates or Kate there
wasn't any light to balance the dark.

He hadn't realized what a difference she'd made—
how much he needed her—until she was gone. He felt a
if he were living in a one-dimensional, black-and-white
slide show that moved from op to op with nothing in
between. The job wasn't enough anymore.

He'd never gotten over her, and he never would. He
loved her. Had always loved her even when he though
she'd betrayed him. If only he'd realized it before he'
made her hate him.

She had to hate him, didn't she?

If she didn't, she should. He could be a mean bastar
when he wanted to be. He knew how to inflict pain. How
to make someone hurt. It was the law of the jungle where
he'd grown up—when someone hurts you, you hurt bac
harder so they never do it again.

It was a real fucking talent.

With everything he'd said to her—everything he'
done—he had no right to think she could ever forgiv
him, let alone care about him again.

But she still wanted him. He knew that from the kiss
It was a crack. Something to work with.

For the past three days, he'd been thinking about wha
she said. *"Let it go."* Let *her* go. Maybe that was the righ

hing to do, but he couldn't. It might make him a selfish
sshole, but if there was any chance left for them, he was
oing to take it.

He knew he didn't deserve her. He never had. But at
ne time she'd thought he was good enough and maybe
hat was all that mattered.

First he had to stop lashing out—stop being angry all
he time—and start owning up to his mistakes.

"I fucked up," he said, not knowing what else to say.
Ie'd apologized before, but she needed to hear it again. She
urned to meet his gaze. "I'm sorry. For everything. For
ushing you away, for not trusting you, for saying all those
orrible things in the hospital"—he drew a deep breath, the
ark, twisting knot in his chest burning again—"for leav-
ng you alone to mourn our daughter."

He barely managed to get the word out, his throat was
o thick.

He saw the surprise and the flicker of pain—raw pain
hat cut right through him—before she looked away. It
vas the first time he'd acknowledged the baby they'd lost.

He didn't think she was going to respond. But maybe
he was only giving herself a moment to collect herself.
Vhen she turned back, her expression was calm and se-
ene, with no sign of emotion.

"Don't beat yourself up, Colt. What happened with
cott and the baby probably only hastened the inevitable."

He didn't let her reflective, "it's in the past" tone dis-
ourage him, which wasn't easy. "What do you mean?"

She shrugged. "In therapy I realized that I'd pushed
ou into marriage and family even though it wasn't
omething you'd ever wanted." She shrugged, the wistful
mile tearing him to shreds. "Some people just aren't cut
ut for tricycles and picket fences."

It was the truth, so why did it make him feel shittier
 hear her say it? He'd never wanted any of that. Never

thought it was right for him. Until he'd met her, and she'd made him change his mind. She'd made him think that he could make her happy.

But he'd never believed it—not really.

Maybe that had been the problem. But he swore if she gave him another chance he would make it his life's mission to prove her right. He'd do whatever it took to make her happy. Colt didn't have any right to ask for that second chance, but he was going to do it anyway.

He took a deep breath, knowing she had every right to laugh in his face for what he was about to say. "What if I want to be that guy?"

She didn't laugh. She just gave him a long look as if trying to figure out whether he was serious. Apparently she must have realized he was. She shook her head. "It's too late for any of that."

The sadness and bitterness in her voice made him realize that she wasn't just talking about him. When their marriage had been destroyed, she'd lost picket fences and tricycles in more ways than one. Complications from the miscarriage had resulted in Kate's not being able to have children. He didn't even want to think about what he'd said when she told him.

"Karma."

"God, Kate, I'm so sorry. I wish I'd been there for you."

She must have realized he meant it. Her eyes filled with tears, making his chest feel as if he'd just swallowed a bottle of acid. "Me, too."

He would have given anything to put his arms around her, tell her he loved her, and try to take her pain away, but he knew she didn't want that from him. She didn't want anything from him.

But he intended to change that. He couldn't go back in time and change what happened, he could only go forward. He would have to prove to her that it could be different. That *he* was different.

He'd fought his whole life with the odds stacked against him; he would do it again. Except that nothing had ever mattered more. Not getting out of those foster homes, not becoming a SEAL, not Nine, not anything.

This was one fight he had no intention of losing. He would do whatever it took to get her back. Even if it meant that he had to fight dirty.

Good thing he was good at that.

For the first time in a long time, the darkness that followed him felt a little lighter.

Kate got angrier and angrier as the flight went on. Colt didn't get to do this. He didn't get to waltz back into her life when she'd finally picked up the pieces and say he was "sorry." *Sorry* wasn't enough. It wasn't nearly enough. And he sure as hell didn't get to play on her heartstrings by offering up false fantasies. *"What if I want to be that guy?"* He'd had a chance, and as he said, he'd fucked up. There weren't any do-overs for the suffering and heartache he'd put her through.

What were they supposed to do? Try again and pretend none of it ever happened?

What had really changed other than now he knew she hadn't been lying about an affair? He was still ready to believe the worst of her. Just a couple of weeks ago he'd seen her go into a hotel room and accused her of cheating on her then fiancé.

She didn't want to think about how that had ended up. She'd been doing far too much thinking about that kiss as it was.

But the sexual attraction between them had never been the problem. Clearly. Even now just sitting next to him—when he looked like hell—she could feel the quickening of her heart, the rush of blood through her limbs, the prickle of her nerve endings on suddenly

sensitive skin, and the feeling that her senses were tuned
to every small sound, movement, or shift in the air between them. The heat that radiated from his body didn't
help. He was crowding her. His shoulders were too
broad—they kept touching her—and he was sucking up
all the air!

She'd been shocked when she'd looked up and seen
him talking to the flight attendant. She'd never seen him
look so ragged—even after a long op in whatever not-so-
lovely part of the world they'd sent Team Nine to. He
looked like a man being eaten away by guilt and cheap
whiskey.

Three years ago, after he'd said all those horrible
things and left her in the hospital, she might have enjoyed
it. She'd hated him then. Or thought she had. But now . .

Now she just felt sorry for him. He'd sabotaged his
happiness because he thought that was his lot in life. Her
problem had been not understanding that, and letting her
happiness get caught up along with his.

Colt had been dealt a bad hand, and he was determined to play it out that way. No matter how much she'd
loved him.

Love*d*. In the past, she reminded herself. The past
month of having him in her life again had been difficult, wreaking havoc on her objectivity and hard-won
recovery.

That kiss in the elevator was proof of just how much
havoc. Undeniably, no one had ever made her as hot as
her ex-husband, and maybe no one ever would. She could
accept that. But it wasn't a substitute for love, respect,
and trust. Without those, all she had was a spectacular—
really spectacular—climax and lots of misery.

No thanks. Been there, done that.

She wasn't going to let him push his way back into her
life and do it all over again. *"What if I want to be that
guy?"*

Every time she heard his voice in her head, and she felt the accompanying tug in her chest—no matter how small—it made her even more furious. She wanted to scream, yell, and rail at him like a madwoman. He didn't get to be that guy. He'd has his chance. He'd done this to them, not her.

Keeping that anger contained during the flight took up every bit of the good and proper manners that had been drummed into her since childhood. By the time they'd landed, picked up the car, and driven to the address she'd connected with Travis's ex-girlfriend, Kate was close to violence. *She*, who'd never struck anyone in her life, wanted to sink her fist hard into that perfect washboard stomach—what almost-forty-year-old guy had a body like that anyway?—and return the sucker punch that he'd just given her.

That guy . . . Her fists clenched. That guy wasn't him and it never would be.

She got out of the car and slammed the door, maybe a little harder than she intended. She just wanted to get this over with. The sooner they talked to Joelle—Travis's ex—the sooner she could get rid of her unwanted bodyguard.

"Wait here," she said. "I'll let you know if I need you."

His eyes narrowed to green—piercing green—slits. Those stupid nerve endings were buzzing again. "Not a chance. And you need me whether you like it or not."

There was something in his voice that made her think he wasn't talking about his defensive—or offensive, in his case—skills, but she pretended not to hear it. Her eyes raked over him. "Have you looked in the mirror lately? You'll terrify her."

"Not up for negotiation, sweetheart."

She bristled at the endearment, but she wasn't going to let him get under her skin. That was exactly what he was trying to do. "Fine. But stand to the side and let me do the talking." She looked him up and down. "And try to smile or something. Don't be so threatening."

"I'm not doing anything."

"You don't need to do anything. Just standing there you look dangerous. It's your superpower."

He smiled, which made her immediately regret asking for him to do so. Colt's smiles were so rare they always made her heart do silly things.

The smile came with a knowing look. "That isn't my superpower."

She was about to ask what was and snapped her mouth shut. If the way that look was making her body heat was any indication, she didn't want to know.

She did know.

Damn him! She turned and started—stomped—up the path. The address belonged to an apartment building in what might be nicely called a "transitional" neighborhood. Joelle was in number twelve, which was on the second floor.

Kate knocked, but no one answered. As it was almost nine o'clock, she had hoped to find her home. That was why she'd traveled tonight rather than waiting until morning.

"What now?" Colt said. "You want to wait her out?"

Kate didn't get a chance to reply. A door opened next door and a head popped out. It belonged to a heavyset woman in her early to mid-forties with pale, freckled skin and dyed red hair who looked as if she'd just woken up. "What's all this racket out here?"

"We're sorry to disturb you," Kate said, coming around to stand in front of Colt. Although from the way the woman was eyeing him appreciatively, she probably hadn't needed to worry. Apparently, she wasn't the only one in the place with a looks-like-a-gunslinger attraction problem. "We're looking for Joelle."

"She ain't here."

Kate tried to hide her disappointment. "Do you know when she'll be back?"

The woman hesitated.

"It's important," Colt said. "We'd really appreciate it."

It wasn't flirtatious . . . exactly. But it didn't need to be. Kate had been on the receiving end of enough of those dark, penetrating stares to know the raw, masculine magnetism that went along with them.

The woman looked at Colt and her gaze went back to Kate, taking in the heels, silk blouse, skirt, and pearls. Kate didn't need to be a mind reader to know what she was thinking. They didn't go together. They never had. If only she'd accepted it sooner.

"She's at the hospital," the woman finally said. "The ambulance took her away earlier."

Colt swore. "What happened?"

The woman shrugged. "Dunno. I was trying to sleep. I work nights."

Kate and Colt looked at each other, obviously both fearing the same thing. Had the men who'd killed Travis gotten to her, too?

Kate's fear turned out to be unwarranted. It wasn't the guys who'd killed Travis who were responsible for putting Joelle in the hospital; it was her pregnancy.

They'd arrived at the hospital after visiting hours, but Kate's CIA badge got them the access they needed. As this wasn't exactly a sanctioned operation, using her credentials was a risk, but the woman barely glanced at it before waving them toward Joelle's room. A glance at Joelle's chart showed that she'd been admitted for early contractions. The doctors had given her terbutaline and the contractions appeared to be under control. Joelle was scheduled to be discharged tomorrow.

She was sleeping when they came in. There was

another bed, but Colt looked around the curtain to check and shook his head. No one was there.

Kate's first impressions were that Joelle looked young and vulnerable. Except for the big bulge of her stomach there wasn't much to her. She was slight of figure and of features, with wispy, dirty blond hair, pale skin, and a small turned-up nose. She couldn't be more than an inch or two above five feet.

Her eyes when she opened them were green and definitely her best feature. They were striking.

Fortunately Colt was out of eyesight when Joelle woke—she was startled enough by Kate. But she took in her businesslike appearance and relaxed. Until she saw Colt.

She tensed, her knuckles white as she gripped the sheets. Her eyes widened with fear. "Who are you? What are you doing in my room?"

Kate moved to calm her down, putting a gentle hand on the foot of her bed. "I'm Kate. This is my . . . uh . . ." She settled on what she thought would relax the other woman. "Husband, Colt."

Joelle couldn't hide her surprise. "You two are married?" She looked back and forth between them. "For real?"

It wasn't the first time their being married had provoked that reaction.

Colt appeared to be taking Kate's "try not to be threatening" advice because he sat down in a chair. "Believe me. I don't know what she ever saw in me, either."

He said it with a wry smile that was directed at Joelle, but his eyes were all for Kate.

She felt a fresh stab in her chest and pushed it away. Damn him. She wasn't going to let him do this to her.

But he always did this to her.

Turning back to Joelle, Kate could see from the conspiratorial lift of her brows that she knew exactly what

Kate had seen in him. Even looking like hell, Colt was hot. Bad boy, "I'm going to break your heart" hot, but undeniably hot. Six foot four, two-twenty—95 percent of that heavily stacked muscle—dark hair, green eyes, with a face that belonged on a movie screen, there wasn't a lot not to like.

Except the attitude. *Remember the attitude.*

"Whaddaya two want then?" Joelle asked with a Mississippi accent that was every bit as heavy as Travis's had been.

Kate had met the young SEAL only a few times, but he'd been a good kid with simple but strong values: God, country, family. In that order.

She inched a little closer to Joelle and rested her hand on the bed rail. "We wanted to talk to you about Travis Hart."

Any friendliness in Joelle's expression was immediately replaced by wariness and defensiveness. "It was you! You're the one who called me!" Tears filled her pretty eyes. "You're going to tell me he's dead, aren't you? That's why you're here?"

The girl—for Kate was guessing she couldn't be much older than twenty—was instantly distressed. Kate tried to calm her, glancing anxiously at the monitors. She wasn't sure how to read them, but she knew the jump in activity and beeping couldn't be good. "Relax," Kate said. "Breathe deeply. We aren't here to upset you—or your baby."

Was that what had landed her in here in the first place? Kate hoped it hadn't been her phone call, but she suspected it was.

She felt a twist of guilt and was relieved when the sounds and activity on the monitors started to abate.

Joelle was crying and gripping Kate's hand something fierce, but the deep, even breaths were helping.

"He's really dead, isn't he?" She was watching Kate

when her gaze flicked to Colt. "I heard about the training accident, but it sounded like some kind of government cover-up so I was hoping that . . ." Her voice lowered to a whisper. "But I knew. He would have called me back if he was alive. He swore he'd take care of me if I went through with it."

Colt gave Kate a nod, but she would have told Joelle anyway. This girl and her baby deserved an answer, and she wasn't going to lie to her and give her false hope. Kate nodded. "I'm sorry."

Surprisingly, the news seemed to calm the girl. The tears were still flowing down her cheeks, but her grip on Kate's hand relaxed. "I knew it. Travis was a good guy. He would never have left me high and dry like this. He would have kept his word. What happened?" She glanced back at Colt. "You worked with him, didn't you? You are a SEAL, too."

Kate was surprised the girl had made the connection, but maybe she shouldn't have been. There was a look to guys like Colt, and if you'd been around it, you would recognize it. Maybe it wasn't all bad that he was here with her. Joelle seemed to trust him.

Colt nodded. "I worked with him a few years back for a little while. He was killed in a bar fight in Alaska."

"Bar fight? That doesn't sound like Travis. Are you sure it wasn't on a mission?"

"It wasn't," Kate assured her. "Can you tell me the last time you heard from him?"

"It was a few months ago. He said he would be out of contact for a while, but he would send me more money when he got back."

"For the baby?" Colt asked.

She nodded.

"Were you and he planning to raise the child together?" Kate asked.

"Raise it?" Joelle repeated the words as if they terrified her. "No way! I didn't want the baby. Travis and I used to go out in high school a little, but we just messed around one night when he was visiting a friend and . . ." Her voice dropped off. "Who gets pregnant when on birth control?"

Kate felt a twisting stab low in her gut but pushed it aside. *Me.*

The girl didn't wait for anyone to answer. "When I told Travis that I was pregnant it was to tell him that I was going to get an abortion." Neither Kate nor Colt gave any reaction—nor would Kate have judged—but Joelle became defensive. "I know it makes me sound horrible, but you don't understand. I have to get out of this place. I worked two jobs to go to community college, and I'd just found out that I'd been accepted to Ole Miss on a scholarship when I found out about the baby."

"How old are you?" Colt asked.

"Twenty-one," Joelle said. "Travis was a senior when I was a sophomore," she added, explaining the age discrepancy.

"But you decided to keep the baby?" Kate asked.

Joelle shook her head. "Travis convinced me not to put it up for adoption. I put my scholarship on hold for a semester, and he agreed to pay for all my living and medical costs to have the baby. I had some problems a few months ago—high blood pressure—and had to be hospitalized. I called him and left a message but he never got back to me. I knew he had to be dead. But no one would tell me anything." She looked at Colt as if he'd said something. "I know I wasn't supposed to tell anyone about him being a SEAL and everything, but I called the base in Honolulu and they wouldn't tell me anything. I was getting desperate. When the money showed up, I thought maybe I was wrong about Travis being dead and all. But I should have known it wasn't Travis. He was too decent to pay me off. He would have called."

Kate exchanged a look with Colt. They didn't need to tell the girl that it indeed had been Travis, and it was his decency in sending the money that had gotten him killed.

"What can you tell us about the money?" Colt asked.

"Nothing. It just showed up in my bank account one day. But the text said if I wanted more, I needed to stop talking to the press."

"There was a text?" Kate asked.

Joelle nodded.

"Can I look at your phone?"

She nodded again and motioned to the stack of clothes in the bathroom. "It's in my jeans."

While Kate went through the phone log, Joelle turned to Colt. "What am I going to do? How am I going to pay for all this? I'll have to get a job, and I'll lose my scholarship. We had a deal!"

Kate looked up when she heard the sound on the monitor. The girl was obviously getting agitated again. She would have gone to her, but surprisingly Colt had already done so. He'd taken Kate's place by her bed—and her hand. Something about that hand made Kate's insides burn. It was a small gesture, easily given.

To a pregnant woman.

It should have been me.

"You don't need to worry about anything," he said. "You and your baby will be fine. Travis had some savings. I'm sure the baby will have some claim to that. I'll see that you get whatever you need until it can be all worked out."

"You will?" Joelle asked.

She seemed surprised, but Kate wasn't. Colt always took care of his guys.

It was his wife he'd neglected.

By the time they left Joelle, she was looking at Colt as if he hung the moon, and Kate had what she needed from the phone. The text had come from the burner that Travis had been using. But it was the resentment that she was struggling not to show.

It wasn't fair. First Scott's maybe-baby news, and now this young girl was having a baby she didn't want, when Kate had wanted her baby more than anything in the world. She would give anything to change places with the twenty-one-year-old.

And Colt! Where had all that compassion been when she needed it? Her ex-husband had just shown this young girl—this stranger—more kindness and understanding than he had his wife. His wife who'd almost died, who'd just lost their baby, and who had loved him with every inch of her being.

Her eyes blurred as the heat rose up in her throat. Where was the justice in that? Where was the justice in any of this?

And what made her think she deserved justice?

Fourteen

Scott heard the back door slam and thought about going after her. But he glanced out the bedroom window and saw the light go on in the barn. A moment later he heard the music through the cracked open window. Blasting angry-chick music wasn't very subtle.

Natalie was pissed. So was he. Although he wasn't sure who at more—her or himself.

Still, Scott hadn't taken her for an Alanis Morissette fan. Rock was more his thing. She'd always had the radio on some kind of pop station. Katy Perry, Taylor Swift, that kind of stuff—i.e., not his favorite.

Figuring she was sanding down the doors that he'd helped her move out there yesterday—and that they both needed time to cool off—Scott sat down to make some calls.

It took a while to get ahold of Colt, but he touched base with the rest of the guys in between attempts and gave them the difficult news about Travis.

It didn't get any easier with retelling. Like him, Baylor, Donovan, Spivak, and Ruiz were devastated and shaken up by the loss. To have escaped the missile attack

and then to be killed in their own backyard—alone—
was a bitter pill to swallow. Next to Scott, Baylor took
Travis's death the worst. Tex—Baylor's call sign—might
not be a commissioned officer, but as senior chief, he had
the same sense of responsibility and duty toward the
team.

But, as Scott told him, if the kid's death was on anyone, it was on him. Scott was the one who'd made the
decision for them to scatter and go dark. When you were
an officer, you were responsible. You had to learn to deal
with that or you wouldn't be around long. But this one
was different. The six survivors had shared a special
bond and losing one of them . . . it hurt. Badly.

Scott didn't want to think that the kid had disobeyed
his orders and contacted his ex-girlfriend, but given how
things had been going for the rest of them—Baylor, Donovan, and himself—he knew that it wasn't as easy as it
sounded to stay in the dark where women were concerned.

In between calls to Donovan and Spivak, Scott
reached Colt, who had just gotten back to DC from
Alaska. It was still strange to talk to his former friend
after three years of being hated for something he didn't
do. But maybe as a guy, Scott could understand Colt's
side of things a little better than Kate did. What Colt had
seen between Scott and Kate had been innocent, but he
could see how it might not have looked like it. He'd
wanted to tell Colt the truth, but Kate had been adamant.
It wasn't just about her mom finding out. Kate had wanted
Colt to trust her on his own. But trust for a hardened,
jaded guy like Colt didn't come blind. No matter how
much she might want it to.

But strange to talk to him or not, when it came to
Kate, he and Colt were of one mind. Scott didn't need to
ask; Colt volunteered to go with her on his own. Although "volunteered" was a nice way of summarizing

the "what the fuck does she think she is doing?" response Colt had had.

Confident that Colt would track Kate down and that she would be in good hands, Scott finished up his calls and glanced out the window. The lights were still on and the music was blaring—Natalie had moved on to Gwen Stefani and No Doubt. Still pissed. Apparently, she needed more time. He decided to jump in the shower before talking to her.

He'd cooled down, but a cold shower would take care of any lingering . . . hot spots.

He wished that his other issues could be so easily washed away.

When Natalie had put her hand on his chest, he'd looked down and his chest had filled with such longing, it had nearly made him forget everything else—including her part in all of this.

He'd wanted her comfort. He'd wanted to hold her in his arms and love her again. And the intensity of that desire had taken him aback. Which was a nice way of saying it had scared the shit out of him.

He'd been angry at her for making him feel this way and at himself for his weakness. Especially after the blow he'd just taken. Travis's death seemed a brutal reminder of what she'd done. He was mad at himself for kissing her and even madder at himself for the feelings that had come after. So he'd lashed out.

Wrongly, he admitted.

She hadn't been trying to seduce him. But with Natalie somehow it got all twisted together.

How could he still want someone who had lied to him? Spied on him? Betrayed him and had probably been responsible—intentional or not—for leaking the information about their mission to the Russians that had seen eight—now nine—of his men killed?

He wanted to stay angry. But he couldn't ignore her

intentions or that she'd tried to stop it, saving lives—his life—at the risk to her own.

That had to count for something.

If they were going to get out of this, Scott knew that he had to start using his head. Where was the that infamous cool under pressure that made him one of the best at what he did? The levelheaded thinking and judgment that made him always know what to do? He had to tamp down the anger—and the lust. But when it came to Natalie that was easier said than done. He'd never been cool or rational about her. Nothing about his feelings for her had ever made any sense.

He dried his hair before putting on his clothes. He probably should apologize.

After tying his shoes, he looked out the window again and then headed down the stairs. She'd been out there a long time. He glanced at his watch, surprised to see that it was almost 2100 hours.

She must be starving—he was. Maybe he'd make her a sandwich as a peace offering. Although with his culinary skills, he'd probably be better off taking her some of her own leftovers.

He flipped on the light in the kitchen and suddenly everything went dark.

He swore. The power must have gone out. He guessed it shouldn't be much of a surprise. As run-down as this place was, faulty wiring was pretty much a given. But it was still a pain in the ass, especially as he hadn't noticed where the breaker box was.

He hadn't noticed candles or a flashlight, either. It was also a moonless night and dark as hell out here in nowhere land.

As his burner phone wasn't equipped with a flashlight, he retraced his steps to the living room—there was a little more light in there from the big windows (or maybe his eyes were getting adjusted)—and located the gear

bag that he'd left in the hallway. He found the small flashlight but wished his NVGs weren't at the bottom of a
Russian river. Instinctively he also grabbed his Glock.

It was a good instinct.

He'd just finished tucking the gun into the back waistband of his shorts when he caught a flash in the hall
mirror that sent him diving to the floor right as the living
room window shattered behind him.

That cold rationality that he'd been looking for? Scott
found it, thanks to the person who'd just tried to put
a bullet in the back of his head. Instantly Scott was in
full-on battle mode as he low-crawled across the floor,
ignoring the glass and the bullets as whoever was shooting at him sprayed the building with gunfire.

Which was actually a positive. It meant the shooter
was impatient and undisciplined. Scott would rather have
one overanxious blast-'em-up shooter with an automatic
weapon than a well-trained, patient sniper.

The rapid gunfire also told him the general direction
of where the gunman must be. Scott put him at somewhere in the fields to the right of the driveway.

But that cold rationality that he depended on in battle
went out the window as soon as he heard the scream. Not
just any scream. *Natalie's* scream of what sounded like
his name. It turned his blood to ice and all his SEAL
discipline went out the window. The only thing he could
think about was reaching her.

He wouldn't let himself think that it was too late, or
that these guys clearly meant business, or that he hadn't
heard her scream again.

Heedless of the guy still Butch Cassidying the crap
out of the living room, Scott got to his feet and raced in
a low crouch through the kitchen and out the back door.

He didn't stop even as a second shooter, who must

have been covering the back, started firing. Unfortunately this guy was more patient and precise. He sent one bullet whizzing close enough to Scott's ear for him to feel the rush of air as it passed by.

Scott was pretty much a fish in a barrel, but he didn't care. Instead of a plan, he was relying on instinct that had been honed by years of experience.

Ace. He sure as hell hoped he had something up his sleeve. It wasn't his first time being pinned down, although the stakes had never made him feel so . . . vulnerable. Christ, his pulse was racing and his heart was hammering with something he hadn't felt since he was a kid watching a scary movie or going through a haunted house.

The guy who'd kept his cool in any number of hairy situations—including when his gun had jammed just as he'd entered a cave that happened to be occupied by about a dozen ISIS militants, when he'd gotten stuck in barbed wire dumped on the seabed while doing an underwater recon of a Somalian pirate ship holding an American hostage in Eyl, Puntland, with his tank out of oxygen, and even when he'd come face-to-face with a great white in the Pacific ocean during BUD/S (for the record, punching a shark in the nose was a hell of a lot easier said than done)—was pretty much scared out of his fucking mind. The guys would never believe it.

Scott didn't have time to stop, go through his mental checklist, assess, mitigate, and come up with a plan. Whoever was after them wasn't stopping to ask questions. They were shooting to kill. If Scott didn't get to her, Natalie was dead.

If she wasn't already.

Fuck. He wouldn't let himself think that. But the barn that was only fifty yards or so from the house felt miles away.

It had to be the Russians. But how the hell had they

found them? The only explanation was one he didn't like. Had she been right to fear them finding her? Had Scott led them to her?

He cursed again. Not just at himself, but at the appearance of three shadowy figures all in black tactical gear and all heavily armed rounding the darkened but still blaring-with-music barn and heading toward the open doors. Operatives, he realized. More professional than he'd hoped, given the guy blowing away everything in the front. Crap.

Despite the precariousness of his situation—and the second bullet that would have given him a third eye if he hadn't zigged his direction at that instant—Scott felt a swell of relief. Those guys heading into the barn meant that Natalie was probably still alive.

Outmanned and seriously outgunned, Scott knew their chances of getting out of this weren't looking very good. But he attempted to better their odds by one, getting off a decent-enough shot at the third Tango as he entered the barn. Figuring they were probably wearing body armor, Scott aimed for the head. He didn't waste the bullet: the guy dropped.

Scott prayed that Natalie was hiding and that his presence was enough to distract at least one if not both of the guys who'd gone into the barn for long enough to stop them from finding her.

He reached the barn and pressed his back to the wall on the side of the building perpendicular to the entrance. His heart was pounding so loud that it took him a minute to realize that the cacophony of bullet spray in the front of the house had stopped.

Which wasn't good. The guy must be repositioning. Scott didn't have much time to figure out how to get in that barn. But there wasn't much of a play here. With one guy in front of him and another behind him probably closing in, and two in the barn waiting to take him out as soon as he appeared in that entryway, Scott needed some kind of distraction or surprise. Some old rusted farm equipment through the loft opening might work or—

The sound of a police siren tore through the still-blasting music. It sounded close and was moving toward them.

Hallefuckinglujah! Scott had never been so glad to hear anything in his life. Talk about timing! A second later the two guys came back out of the barn shooting, presumably at Scott. He peered around the corner and fired back. He thought he might have clipped one of the guys but they'd disappeared into the darkness of the overgrown fields.

Under normal circumstances, Scott would have gone after them. But these weren't normal circumstances. He didn't think his heart beat or his lungs took in any air for the terrifying few seconds that it took him to get into that barn, having no idea what he'd find.

He couldn't recall ever praying on a mission before, but he thought he might have uttered a few words to God as he came into that dark building. He located the old-fashioned battery-operated boom box and switched off the CD player.

The dead silence that followed was hope crushing.

"Nat," he said. He didn't sound like himself; his voice was so ragged and tentative.

There as an awful pause where he didn't think she was going to respond, before he heard a sound of movement coming from one of the stalls in the back.

"Scott?"

The sound of her voice gave him such a rush of emotion, he almost couldn't speak. *She's alive. Thank God, she's alive.* "It's okay, baby. It's me. You're safe."

She appeared from behind one of the stalls and a second later, she was catapulting into his arms.

Scott grabbed on tightly and buried his nose in her

hair, inhaling the scent of citrus and hay. The feeling of her warm and safe in his arms was overwhelming. He'd lost her once, and the thought of losing her a second time had cut him to the bone. The swell of emotion filled his chest and squeezed his throat. He'd forgotten how slight she was. How soft. How vulnerable. She melted into him, her body giving over in complete surrender and relief. In trust that made something deep inside him warm.

When he thought of what could have happened to her . . .

He actually shuddered. He couldn't go there. Not again.

He might not have the answer, but he couldn't deny this.

"I was so scared," she said, sobbing into his chest. Her fingers were digging into his arms and shoulders like a terrified kitten who wasn't going to let go. Which was fine by him.

"I know. I was, too," he murmured soothingly, not sure whom he was trying to calm: her or himself. His heart was still pounding like a damned freight train. He was sweating, for Christ's sake. The ice in his veins had clearly melted.

She pulled back and looked up at him. The look in her eyes . . . the emotion . . . the fear. He couldn't have stopped himself if he wanted to, and he sure as hell didn't want to. He needed this just as much as she did. Needed the connection. Needed to know she was all right.

He lowered his mouth to hers and kissed her. Gently. Tenderly. Telling her what he couldn't put into words—even to himself.

Natalie felt as if her chest were going to burst. The sweet, tender poignancy of his kiss almost hurt. For the first time there was nothing between them. No lies, no pretense, only emotion. Raw emotion stripped of everything—even lust—by fear.

Those men had been moments away from killing her, and they both knew it. Her hiding place in the back of one of the stalls under a pile of hay wouldn't have lasted long. If Scott hadn't come when he did and delayed them . . .

She didn't want to think about it. Not now. Not when he was holding her and kissing her like this. Telling her with each tender caress of his lips and tongue what she'd never dared hope. He still cared for her. He might not want to, but a man didn't kiss a woman like this if he didn't care about her. Gently. Reverently. As if she meant everything in the world to him.

It was the way he'd kissed her the last time she'd seen him. When he told her he had something important he wanted to talk to her about when he got back from his mission. She hadn't let herself wonder about it, alternately fearing that it would be or wouldn't be what she thought it was. Now, given what she'd done, the idea of a proposal was laughable, but his kiss still made her heart squeeze with longing and possibility.

Those men had done what she might never have been able to do: broken through the wall of distrust and lies that had separated them. The initial anger at his accusation that had sent her to the stables to work had turned to a feeling of defeat and hopelessness. She'd wondered whether she'd made a mistake in not escaping when she had the chance. But now she knew she'd been right to put her trust in him. He still cared for her. She could feel it in every brush, every stroke, every movement of his mouth over hers.

She wished she could hold on to the moment forever. But all too soon, he pulled back.

He stroked the side of her face with callused fingers,

looking into her eyes with an expression that made her heart tighten all over again.

"I need to check and make sure they are gone."

She nodded. He pulled back enough for her to notice the spots of blood on his T-shirt. "Wait, you're hurt!"

He looked down, barely glancing at the blood. "It's nothing." He lifted his arms and flicked out a couple of pieces of glass. "But I'm afraid you're going to have to replace your living room window."

If the number of bullets she'd heard earlier was any indication, she suspected there was a lot more damage than one window. But he hadn't been shot—again. That was what mattered.

Natalie thought about following Scott outside, but she took a few steps and froze. The black-clad, masked, prone figure of a man was partially blocking the doorway. She looked away, feeling suddenly queasy. Scott must have shot one of the hit men.

The *Russian* hit men.

It wasn't until that moment that she'd had a chance to think about it. What blood had returned to her body, promptly rushed back out. They'd found her. Dear God, they'd found her.

Her hand immediately went to her stomach as she sank onto the chair that held the boom box. She felt it pressing into her backside but didn't care. Her legs had suddenly turned to jelly.

What was she going to do? Her baby? Her family? And now Scott?

She didn't have time to think about it as Scott walked back into the barn; he wasn't alone. Natalie had heard the siren, but she was still taken aback to see the sheriff with him. Her gaze shot to Scott's with fresh worry, but he shook his head. She understood. At this point, there wasn't anything they could do to avoid Brock's inevitable questions.

"Are they gone?" she asked, standing up.

Both men's expressions were grim as they nodded.

"I went after them on foot," Brock said. "But I had to turn around when they reached their car. They parked just off the county road and came in from behind the tree line. I called in an APB on the car."

Natalie could hear the "but" in his voice. "But you think they are already long gone?"

"These guys were professionals. They'll have some kind of contingency plan," Scott explained. "They probably have another vehicle ready to go somewhere close and will disappear at the nearest junction."

"I'll alert CBSA just in case," the sheriff said.

Scott translated for her. "Canada Border Services Agency."

Natalie nodded, but it was clear from both men's expressions that they weren't holding out much hope of apprehending the remaining shooters. She turned to the sheriff. "Thank God you arrived when you did. Did one of the neighbors hear the gunfire and call?"

"Not exactly," the sheriff said. "I doubt any neighbors are close enough to hear. You are pretty remote out here."

Yes, she'd already realized that double-edged sword. "Then how did you get here so quickly?"

Scott moved in front of her protectively, apparently anticipating the answer. "He was watching the house."

Brock nodded. "When I saw the perp firing at the front, I tried to come up behind him on foot. But as soon as the other three appeared from around the barn, I realized I wasn't going to have time. I went back to my car and hit the siren."

"After calling in for backup?" Scott asked.

The sheriff looked at him. "I was trying to avoid that."

Natalie looked back and forth between the two men, who were clearly in some kind of silent standoff. "Why?" she eventually asked.

"I figured the lieutenant commander here would rather I didn't."

Scott gave no reaction—his jaw was already clenched tight—but Natalie couldn't hide her gasp of surprise. How had he known?

Brock answered the unspoken question. "I knew something wasn't right." His gaze landed on Scott. "Despite the belligerent attitude, you didn't act like a criminal. From the way you moved, I figured some kind of military or spook. But it wasn't until I got home last night that I put it together." He looked back to Scott. "The hair and the beard were a nice touch, but I never forget a face—especially a dead SEAL. My little brother lost his life in Afghanistan three years ago. DEVGRU," he explained.

Aka SEAL Team Six, Natalie knew.

Scott finally broke face with a curse, giving up the pretense. "Dale Brouchard. We crossed paths a couple of times. He was a good operator."

Brock accepted the compliment with a nod. "I pay attention to every SEAL who makes the ultimate sacrifice—even in 'training exercises.'"

Scott dragged his fingers through his hair. "Which was damned lucky for us. I was severely outmanned." He straightened, facing the other man with much less wariness. "I should have thanked you before."

Brock shrugged. "I've seen you guys operate. You would have thought of something. Who were they?"

"I'm not sure," Scott said, and then motioned to the body in the doorway. "I doubt he'll be much help. I suspect most of his gear is unattributable, and he won't have an ID. But I'll take a picture and see if anything pops up."

The sheriff nodded and then turned to her. "I assume from the number of men who went into the barn that they were after you?"

Natalie nodded. "I was outside when I heard the shots

and saw them coming. One of them yelled 'There she is' before he took a shot at me as I ran back inside."

Scott swore, realizing how lucky she'd been. There were so many ways this could have gone down and most of them weren't with them walking out of there.

"Someone must really want you dead," Brock said. "That's a lot of firepower for one person. You're lucky your boyfriend was here."

Natalie thought about correcting him but realized it didn't matter. "I'm lucky both of you were here."

Brock turned back to Scott. "I assume there is a good reason why the military says you are dead?"

Scott nodded grimly. "Thanks for not calling it in right away."

"I'm going to have to do it now. They'll wonder about the APB."

Scott returned the nod.

"I'll look around a little to see what I can find while I wait for them to arrive," the sheriff said. "If you want to wait in here, I'll have someone come in to take your statement later."

"Thanks," Scott said, extending him his hand. "I appreciate it."

The two men shook and Natalie realized what was happening. The sheriff was giving them time to get away.

Brock turned to her and gave her a nod. "Miz Wilson."

But Natalie couldn't let it go at that. She rushed forward and gave him a hug. A hug, which after an initial stiffening of surprise, was returned with warmth.

"Thank you," she said, not understanding the rush of emotion and tears. But maybe it had been a long time since someone had done something so nice for her—although she suspected it was more for Scott, the opportunity to get away was still more than she could have hoped for.

"Keep her safe," the sheriff said to Scott, who must have moved up behind her. He sounded amused when he looked down to meet her gaze, holding on to her as she started to pull back to add, "And I still owe you dinner next time you are in town."

Natalie grinned. "You're on."

The sheriff stepped back, tipped his hat, and left the barn. A moment later, she and Scott followed after him.

Fifteen

Scott gave Natalie about two minutes to gather her belongings from the farmhouse. They'd just turned onto the main road in the car that he'd stashed behind one of the farm outbuildings when the stream of flashing lights and sirens appeared ahead of them.

He didn't think either of them breathed until the lights and sounds had disappeared into the distance in the rearview mirror. But his pulse didn't come back to a normal pace until they hit the interstate that would take them south. Only then did his fingers lighten their death grip on the steering wheel.

Scott hadn't said much since they left. It wasn't just the concentrating on driving and trying to get away.

Dinner? Over his dead body.

He knew it was stupid and he had no right, but he was pissed. He hadn't liked seeing Natalie in another man's arms—no matter how grateful she was or how in debt they were to him.

She'd been surprised that someone would do something like that for her, which made it worse. Scott suspected that the sheriff was just as by the book as he was, yet he'd put that aside and let them go. In other words, Brouchard had done what she'd thought Scott wouldn't— look the other way—and he was keenly aware that she might have had good cause for that doubt. Scott should have been the one she could turn to.

Was he too rigid? Too uncompromising? He had to concede that maybe the qualities that made him a good SEAL officer weren't necessarily good for a boyfriend. Or a son. His teeth gritted, his mouth in a tight angry line, not wanting to think about that.

He didn't want to think about any of it, but after what had happened, he could no longer pretend that he didn't care. He still had feelings for her. Intense feelings. *Possessive* feelings.

He knew the sheriff had seen just how much that hug bothered him and not only understood why but also enjoyed Scott's reaction. He'd been jealous. Which, as he'd admitted, was stupid. But it didn't stop the feeling.

From the way Natalie was eyeing him warily, he figured she'd guessed his mood if not the source.

He sighed and forced himself to relax. It wasn't her fault he was a caveman. "You okay?"

She nodded, looking far from okay. She looked scared and close to tears. "I can't believe they found me. I thought . . ." Her voice broke. "I thought I'd found a way out of it. But even with Mick dead there is no way out of this nightmare. They're never going to leave me alone, are they?"

Scott's mouth tightened with anger. He wished he wasn't driving so he could hold her. She sounded so fucking alone.

But she wasn't. He didn't know what it meant, but he wanted her to count on him. Even if it meant he had to move his line in the sand a little and compromise on his beliefs, he was going to help her. His goal to clear his name hadn't changed, but he wasn't going to throw her to the wolves to do it.

He reached over and covered her hand with his. It was like ice under his palm. "I'm not going to let them get to you, Nat," he said with a squeeze of reassurance. He'd been caught unprepared, but he wouldn't be again. "Damn it, it's probably my fault. I must have led them to you somehow."

The timing was too much of a coincidence for him not to be responsible.

"You think they followed you?" she asked.

He shook his head. The men wouldn't have waited three days. "I don't think so. But something in my investigation must have alerted them and enabled them to track me to you."

"Who knows you were looking for me?"

"I wasn't looking for you; I was looking for Jennifer. And the only people who knew about that are the people who know I'm alive—and that isn't very many."

As far as he was aware there were the five—now four—other survivors, Annie Henderson (Baylor's fiancé), Brittany Blake, Kate, Colt, and the general. Mick could have warned someone before he'd been killed that some of the SEALs had survived the blast, but whoever he worked for wouldn't have known about Scott specifically.

"And no one knows you found me?"

He shifted his gaze from the road for a moment to look at her. "I told my sister and her ex-husband."

Her eyes widened. Scott forgot that she knew about Colt.

"The same ex-husband who hates you and threatened to kill you?"

"Yeah, that's him," Scott admitted. "But Colt has changed his tune a little since he found out the truth. My

former teammate is, uh"—how to sum up Colt?—
"complicated. It's hard to explain, but even before he
found out Kate and I were related I would have trusted
him with my life—and yours. He would never betray a
fellow SEAL."

The team had been Colt's family; his loyalty to it—to
them—was unwavering. Scott would have been dead
otherwise.

She seemed puzzled but willing to take his word for
it. "Then how did they find me?"

"I don't know, but I intend to find out."

But he was going to have to be a hell of a lot more
careful, especially if, as he suspected, someone had been
monitoring Kate's computers. Did the Russians have
moles that deep? How else could they have tracked him?

He didn't know, but clearly someone wanted Natalie
dead—and maybe him, too. The question was why. The
Russians knew Natalie's role as a spy had been compromised. She was no use to them anymore and already
dead and quiet so why go to all the trouble to kill her
again and risk exposure? Mick, her only contact, was
dead. It could be punishment for betraying them or was
there another reason? Did Natalie know something that
she wasn't telling him? Something she wasn't supposed
to know?

Whatever it was, Scott was beginning to think that
there was more to this than there seemed. Travis's
death—like the attempt on Natalie's life—proved that
the Russians weren't going to quietly let it go. They were
eliminating anyone who knew the truth. So what else
was he missing?

"What aren't you telling me, Nat?"

He was watching her out of the corner of his eye and
saw her stiffen. "What do you mean?"

"They sent five professional hit men after you. Why
do they want you dead so badly?"

She looked at him as if he was accusing her of something. Maybe he was, although he wasn't sure what.

"I thought . . ." Her voice dropped off and she turned away, staring out the black windows.

"You thought what?"

She didn't say anything for a moment before looking back at him. Her eyes were big, luminous, and filled with disappointment and unshed tears in the semidarkness of the car's interior. "I thought you believed me."

"I want to," Scott said, steeling himself against the misery in her voice. "I do. But you have to tell me everything."

"I am," she cried out in frustration and obvious distress. "I have told you everything I can think of. I have no idea why they want me dead so badly. And frankly right now I don't care! All I can think about are my parents and sister." The tears that had been threatening started to slide down her cheeks. "If the people Mick was working for know I'm alive, that means my family isn't safe anymore. They could go after them to punish me." Her eyes widened and she covered the gasp that came from her mouth with her hand. "Oh my God, what if they are after them now? What if they decide to kill my family because they couldn't kill me?" He didn't need to glance over to see her escalating panic; he could hear it in her voice. She sat up and put a hand on his arm. "Please, Scott, I have to warn them. I have to do something to try to protect them. If anything happens to them . . ." Her voice broke and her hand squeezed. "Please."

Scott would have truly had to have had ice in his veins not to be moved by her pleas and terror for her family. He didn't think they were in danger, but he wasn't going to take the chance and be wrong. He was going to do what he could to help her, and protecting her family was a big part of it. He held the wheel with one hand and pulled his phone out of his pocket with the other.

The number he wanted was programmed into the first speed dial slot. Scott and Dean Baylor might butt heads every now and then—or most of the time—but Scott knew he could count on his senior chief for anything. "It's me," Scott said when Baylor answered. "I need you to do something for me."

Natalie's emotions were all over the place. She'd gone back and forth between terror and relief too many times tonight. But the panic over her family gradually subsided as she listened to Scott's calm, authoritative, take-command-of-the-situation conversation with—she assumed—one of his men. She had to fill in information a few times, such as names and addresses, but it was clear, he was sending in a team to watch over them.

He was helping her. She'd been right to put her trust in him.

When he hung up, she didn't know what to say. "Thank you" in no way captured the enormity of the gratitude she felt for him right now. He believed her. At least enough to help her protect her family, and that was all that mattered. It mattered a lot.

It might not be enough, but she gave him her thanks anyway.

He glanced over at her and accepted it with a nod. "There will be a team in place within a few hours, and they will stay there as long as we need them."

Natalie hadn't been expecting something so quick. Whatever residual panic she'd been feeling slipped away and her emotions seemed a little less frazzled. "Do you have a private jet you didn't tell me about?"

He shot her a sideways glance, obviously not sure whether she was joking. She wasn't sure, either. With Mr. Understated, Never Talk about Money, you never knew.

"No, but one of my men's soon-to-be father-in-law is the head of one of the biggest private security contractors in the US. He has the jets and the ability to mobilize an army in a couple hours. His men are mostly former Team-guys so they are used to operating on a short string." She knew Scott had operated on a four-hour string, meaning he would be ready to go on a mission in four hours. His eyes held hers. "They'll be safe, Nat. But you probably should give your parents a heads-up about what's happening." He nodded to the phone that he'd put in the tray between the two seats. "You can use it when you are ready."

She swallowed, feeling the emotion catching in her throat again. "What do I say?"

He seemed to understand that she wasn't just talking about the team who would be descending on her parents and sister. How did you tell the parents who'd loved you and welcomed you into their home that you'd betrayed them by spying on the country that had taken you in? She'd had a good reason and didn't think she had a choice, but that didn't prevent all the shame.

Her parents were as red, white, and blue, apple pie, proud Americans from the heartland as there came.

"Don't worry about that right now," Scott said. "You can explain everything later. Right now, I think they'll just be happy to hear that you are alive."

He was right.

Natalie's hand shook as she picked up the phone and dialed the number. It rang five times before her mother picked up.

The burning in Natalie's throat had built and built with every ring so that when she finally heard the famil-iar voice—her mother's voice—she could barely get the words out before the sobs racked her. "Mom, it's me. It's Natalie. I'm okay."

And strangely for the first time in a long time—since Mick had walked into that bar—she was.

She had Scott to thank for that. They might by speeding south down the interstate, fleeing the hit team that was after them, but by protecting her family, Scott had given her the sense of peace and security she'd never thought to have again.

She couldn't help but wonder how long it would last.

I f Natalie was still lying to him, it wasn't about her family. The emotions Scott heard in her side of the conversation with her mother were too deep and raw to be feigned—Oscar-caliber acting or not.

But he was beginning to realize Natalie wasn't much of an actor at all. Maybe that was what had made her so effective. Even behind the glossy mask that Mick had created, the genuine woman had shown through. That was why he'd trusted her and hadn't guessed what she was up to.

It was also why he'd never been able to figure her out. She really was two sides of a coin, and that was what made her so fascinating. Confident and driven enough to leave the family that she loved to go to Washington to fight an injustice, strong enough to stand up to and defy the man who'd raped her, smart enough to become the right hand of one of the most powerful men in the US government, and yet not too sophisticated or glamorous to know her way around a kitchen, power tools, and a toilet valve or to start an artisanal cheese business to save the family farm and create a job for her special-needs sister.

Natalie might have tried, but she hadn't been able to hide from him. Not completely. Especially when they were in bed or enjoying a leisurely Sunday morning with coffee and a paper—a real paper—on the balcony of his loft. That was when he'd seen the soft, vulnerable side of her that had never made sense.

It made sense now.

He listened to her sobs of relief and joy as she gave a truncated, tearful explanation of how she'd been blackmailed into doing something horrible, how Jennifer had been caught in the cross fire, and how she thought the only way out was to let them think she was dead, but that now the men were after her again.

Scott didn't need to hear the other side of the conversation to know that her mother was taking her to task for not telling them, but ultimately understanding and—as Scott had predicted—just beyond happy and grateful to know that her daughter was alive.

Natalie explained how there would be some men arriving to keep them safe until this was over. Apparently her mother tried to protest, but Natalie was insistent. "It is necessary. These men mean business, Mom. They killed Jen, and they sent five men with assault rifles to try to do the same to me. Dad's shotgun isn't going to be enough. And what about Lana?"

Scott sensed her mother's capitulation. Apparently Natalie wasn't the only one who was fiercely protective of her sister.

There was silence on the phone for a moment. Natalie's gaze flickered to him uneasily. "Yes, he's with me." Another pause, where she seemed to be fighting a smile through the shimmer of tears. "Yes, he still knows how to handle a weapon, Mom. He doesn't sit behind a desk all the time."

Scott shot her a sharp frown. Not because she'd obviously told her mother that he was in the military and an officer but because she'd let her think he wasn't a ground pounder. He sat behind a desk when rotations demanded that he had to, but he was still operational, still deployed with his team, and still went on every op he could.

He wouldn't be ready to sit behind a desk permanently for a long time.

A *very* long time.

Natalie and her mother talked for a few more minutes, and although he got the feeling they were still talking about him, from Natalie's "uh-huh's" and "okay's" he couldn't figure out what they were saying.

Just before she hung up, Natalie said, "I'll call Lana and Dad later, once you have a chance to prepare them, okay?" and then the tearful "I love you, too," that made him grip the wheel tighter and put all his focus on the road ahead of him.

He didn't trust himself to look at her. Hearing those words fall so easily from her mouth . . . it made his chest squeeze with a fierce sense of longing that he didn't want to acknowledge.

Natalie was quiet for a while and found some tissues in her bag to wipe her red-rimmed, swollen eyes. She flipped down the mirror, presumably to repair her eye makeup, but it wasn't necessary—the makeup or the repair job. She was beautiful no matter what she did. The soft skin, the pouty red lips, the long wavy hair, the big baby-doll Slavic eyes . . .

He cursed, feeling the heat stirring certain parts of his body—hard.

Focus on the road.

The focus didn't last long. He could feel her eyes on him.

"Thanks," she said. "You were right; she didn't care. At least not right now." She paused, and when she continued her voice was thicker. "It was so good to hear her voice."

Scott could imagine. There wasn't a day that went by that he didn't miss his parents. He'd been furious at his mom when she'd died, but that didn't mean he'd stopped loving her. Moms were . . . special.

He glanced over at Natalie, and it was as if it suddenly hit him for the first time. She was going to be a mom. Not just any mom, his child's mom. The bump was barely visibly, but it was there.

She might not have wanted the baby, but Scott knew she would love it with the same fierceness that she did her sister and adoptive parents, and that knowledge somehow humbled him.

Suddenly he was ashamed. He'd been so caught up in his own anger that he'd lost sight of the fact that not only was she defending herself to him and trying to evade the men intent on killing her, she was doing so pregnant. A little over four months pregnant if he was counting right.

"Are you feeling okay?" he asked.

She looked at him questioningly.

"The baby," he explained. "Do you need anything? We can stop for food if you are hungry. You haven't eaten anything since lunch, which can't be good."

She looked confused, which didn't make him feel any better. He hated that she thought he didn't care.

"I'm fine. The baby's fine. I grabbed a protein bar before we left. I can eat that if I get hungry."

His frown deepened. "A protein bar isn't enough. We'll stop as soon as I see something that doesn't have arches or a crown."

She smiled, knowing his thoughts on fast food. He didn't train as hard as he did to poison his body with that crap.

"I think I can survive one hamburger or taco," she said.

He gave her a glare that said it all: *no fucking way*.

"Where are we going?" she asked.

He wasn't sure yet. He needed to talk to Kate. "South. I want to get off the main roads soon to avoid cameras. So see if you can pull up a map on the phone."

She sobered, seeming almost upset by his response, but he didn't have a chance to follow up because at that moment he caught sight of something in the rearview mirror that made his heart pound again. A highway patrol car was coming up on him fast.

He moved over into the slow lane and heaved a heavy sigh of relief when the car sped by.

Natalie had managed to pull up a map on the small phone and directed him to a smaller highway that he should see the signs for in a few miles.

Once they were safely on the old highway, he relaxed. "You told your mom about me?"

She nodded, with an uneasy glance that told him she thought he was angry about it. "We're close. She guessed that I was seeing someone. I didn't tell her anything specific about what you did—just that you were a naval officer."

"I'm not mad, just surprised."

"If you knew my mother you wouldn't be. I swear she can tell whether I'm happy or sad from how I answer the phone." She shrugged. "She knew I was happy, and I told her the reason why."

Their eyes held for a long heartbeat. He wanted to probe deeper but wasn't sure he was ready to hear what she had to say.

Instead he turned back to the road. When he saw the billboard ahead of them, he asked, "How does Annie's Country Kitchen sound? It's open twenty-four hours, and I could use some coffee."

He had a long night of driving ahead of him, and he could make his call.

She smiled. "I'm not sure Vermont qualifies as country, but I never turn down chicken-fried steak or biscuits and gravy." He didn't say anything, but she caught herself. "Not anymore at least."

The smile fell from her face, and Scott knew she was remembering Mick.

He hated the power of those memories and swore to himself that he would put that smile back on her face and do everything he could to keep it there.

Sixteen

Kate didn't say much on the drive from the hospital to the hotel. As it was too late to fly back to DC that night, she'd arranged a room for herself at the airport hotel. Colt's suggestion that they share the room, while not exactly a joke but presented as one, had been met with an icy glare that would have frozen his nuts off if she hadn't turned away.

He got the message and booked a second room.

Figuring she was probably still angry about what he'd said earlier about him wanting to give it another shot, when she said she was tired and was just going to go back to her room to order room service, he didn't argue.

He'd given her enough to think about, and he didn't want to press. He could be patient.

For one night.

But it was hard when he was so . . . well, hard. It wasn't easy being around someone you wanted for hours and not being able to do what you knew would make both of you feel a hell of a lot better.

The hotel bar was the typical upscale chain trying too hard to look like it was in downtown Manhattan with mood lighting, a few discreetly placed flat-screen TVs, sleek wood surfaces, and chairs that were more for looks than comfort. It was filled with middle-management types—mostly men—and an odd couple or two. The waitresses were all under twenty-five and attractive.

Colt found a secluded corner where he could see the room—habit—and ordered his eight-dollar Coors Light from one of the waitresses. He hoped to hell the can was gold and not silver at that price. But he was done with whiskey for a while. The waitress tried to chat him up when she brought the beer back, but he made it clear he just wanted the drink and took out one of his burner phones to start checking on a few things.

Colt was very careful with his electronic fingerprint and used only burners. Most people would be terrified of the amount of information they unwittingly gave off with their devices and how easy it was to find out that information.

He checked one of his Dark Web e-mail accounts (even those weren't fail-safe) to see that one of his contacts had gotten back to him. It had taken a circuitous route, but as he and Kate had suspected and the text on Joelle's phone seemed to confirm, the deposit in the girl's account had come from a Western Union in Alaska about twenty miles from where Travis had been staying.

Colt's contact hadn't been able to pull the additional cameras Colt wanted near the bar, which was a little unusual, but he hoped Kate would be able to get them. He'd meant to ask her about it, and thought about knocking on her door as he made his way to his own room, but decided that as excuses went to disturb her, it wasn't a very good one.

A better one came a few minutes after he entered his room and one of his other burners buzzed.

Recognizing the number as Taylor's and assuming he was calling to be filled in on what had happened with

Joelle, Colt was surprised by what he had to say. Apparently Taylor and the Russian spy were on the move after having narrowly escaped a hit team who'd tracked them to the farm in Vermont.

Colt had to admit he'd been shocked when Taylor initially told him he'd found Natalya Petrova (aka Natalie Andersson) and that he wasn't taking her in right away. Breaking the rules was something Colt did. Taylor had always been such a pain in the ass about it when Colt did something that wasn't exactly kosher; it was nice to know the kid had it in him. Although, he supposed the "kid" wasn't much of a kid anymore. But he'd probably always think of him that way, as Scott had been just out of SEAL Qualification Training when they'd first met almost ten years ago, ironically before he'd met Kate.

Scott didn't need to explain the implications. Colt understood that if the Russians had found Natalie, it probably had been by tracking him. Scott said he'd tried to call Kate to warn her to be careful, but she wasn't answering her phone. He'd thought he might find her with Colt.

Colt heard the unspoken question and the warning but didn't bite. As he had every intention of being back in his ex-wife's bed soon, he sure as hell wasn't going to let her little brother warn him off. Even if her little brother happened to be an officer in the most elite SEAL unit in America. Colt might be pushing forty, but he could hold his own with any of his former teammates. Except maybe Spivak. That guy was a beast. But Colt fought dirty, so who knew?

Colt told Scott that Kate had been tired and had probably just turned her ringer off to sleep. He'd go knock on her door and have her call him.

Glad of the excuse to check on her, Colt headed down the hallway. Kate's room was on the same floor about a dozen doors away.

He knocked and when she didn't answer right away, he knocked louder.

He saw the movement of light behind the peephole. She knew better than to make that kind of rookie mistake. "Open up, Kate. I know you are in there."

He heard a muffled "Go away."

There was something about her voice that bothered him. "I have a message for you—from Scott."

She opened the door and the reason her voice had sounded funny was immediately clear. One look at her ravaged face told him that she'd been crying. Hard, and for some time.

It felt as if there were a hole in his heart that everything suddenly drained out of. Had he done this to her? The emptiness in his chest started to burn.

He pushed his way into the room and closed the door behind him. "Jesus, Kate. What's wrong?"

He wanted to reach out and cup her tearstained cheek in his hand. He'd never seen her look so absolutely eviscerated—as if she'd been torn apart and ripped to shreds.

He took that back. He *had* seen her like this once. In the hospital. But he'd been so crazed with jealousy he'd steeled himself against recognizing it. But there was nothing to steel him now, and seeing her like this made *him* feel eviscerated. Kate was strong. She was tough. She shouldn't look vulnerable. He didn't know what to do; he'd never felt so damned helpless.

It only got worse when she looked up at him with those big blue eyes so filled with pain, it made me feel as if he were wearing a shirt that was two sizes too small and lined with nails.

"It's not fair. She doesn't even want . . . and I . . ."

The words were caught between choking sobs, but Colt could fill in the blanks. Travis's girlfriend was pregnant with a baby she didn't want, while Kate wanted nothing more and couldn't conceive.

He cursed himself for not realizing how difficult that meeting at the hospital must have been for her. He should have guessed how she would be feeling. But Kate kept her thoughts so well hidden behind that patrician blond ice-queen exterior that it was hard to remember how deeply she felt.

He was an insensitive bastard.

"And Scott, too," she cried.

Now he was confused. "What?"

"The spy is p-r-regnant." She could barely get the word out before bursting into a fresh wave of tears.

Christ. Well, that explained Taylor's uncharacteristic deviation from the officer playbook.

Poor Kate. It must have seemed like a double whammy. First the news of her brother's unexpected—and presumably unwanted—impending fatherhood, and then the pregnant Joelle, who clearly had no interest in motherhood right now. Both must have seemed like horrible injustices to someone who wanted a child so desperately.

The world wasn't fair—they all knew that—but some injustices were crueler than others.

Colt didn't know what to say. He'd never been much good with words—not in saying how he felt. But he was good with action.

He opened his arms. Before he had a chance to draw her in, she walked right into them as if it was the most natural thing in the world for her to look to him for comfort. As if three years of separation and an ugly divorce were not standing between them.

The feel of her collapsing against him, melting into his chest and arms, letting him support her . . . it was overwhelming. It was the kind of trust that he'd never thought to have from her again. He felt a rush of fierce and intense emotion that made him want to take on the universe for her.

He'd do anything to make her pain go away and make her happy again.

Anything.

He held her in his arms, keeping her upright as she sobbed against him. He murmured soothing words against the warm, baby-soft silk of her hair, telling her that it was all right. That he was here. That he was sorry. So fucking sorry.

He stroked her hair. Her back. The slender curve of her hip. All the while savoring the feeling of her weight in his arms, her face buried into his chest, and her hands gripping him as if he were her only lifeline in a torrential storm.

She needed him, and the physical manifestation of just how much gave him more pleasure than it probably should.

It might be primitive, but he was a man. Men liked to feel needed, and Kate had always seemed so strong and self-possessed; the confident, independent woman who would be fine on her own.

She *had* been fine on her own. He'd left her alone enough to know. Sometimes he thought she got so used to him being deployed that it was harder on her when he came home.

It probably had been, given his propensity for dark moods and shutting down. He cursed himself again, wondering that she'd put up with him for as long as she had. She should have kicked his ass to the curb well before five years.

"I'm so sorry," he said again, apologizing for all of it. For all the things he couldn't take back but vowed to change if she gave him the chance he didn't deserve.

The sobs had ceased enough for her to look up at him.

Maybe it was something in his voice, but her eyes scanned his face as if looking for confirmation that he meant it.

He did. If only she would let him show her how much.

Suddenly he was aware of the heat flaring between them. Not just the heat of two bodies pressed together, but the heat of two bodies that knew each other intimately pressed together. He was hard, and she was achingly soft, and together . . . God, it was good. It had always been good.

The best.

He reached down and gently swept away a strand of hair that had been caught in the dampness of her lashes. How anyone with such blond hair could have lashes that dark and thick, he didn't know. They looked fake, but they weren't.

"Let me make you feel better, Katie." His voice was thick and husky, as his finger skimmed the velvety soft pillow of her plump bottom lip. Her mouth had always driven him crazy. It was the only trashy-looking thing about her. He could feel the catch of her breath, and it egged him on. His eyes dropped to her mouth as his hand skimmed lower.

Her nipple was already taut when the pad of his thumb slid over it. He sucked in his breath and swore. His cock jerked a little harder.

But this wasn't about him. It was all about her. He was going to make her feel good and show her exactly how he felt.

Action, not words that he could screw up.

He covered her mouth with his and took her answering moan as a "yes."

Rather than devour as the flames leaping in his body demanded, he kissed her gently. With tenderness he didn't even know he possessed. He let his lips linger, soften, caress.

He'd kissed Kate hundreds—thousands—of times,

but in many ways it felt like the first time. It was different not because the lust wasn't there—it was—or because he was holding it back—which he wasn't used to doing—but because *he* was different.

He wasn't turning away from the closeness and intimacy as he'd always done before; he was embracing it. He was letting himself feel, and maybe even more important, letting himself express those feelings.

He'd always kept a little bit of himself apart. A little bit of himself protected from disappointment. But look where that had gotten him. Divorced and alone.

This time he wanted her to know how much he cared about her.

How much he loved her.

So he held nothing back. He worshipped her with his mouth, prostrated himself with his tongue. He told her with every touch and every caress just how much she meant to him.

Everything.

She was so soft. So sweet. So cautious yet eager in her response that he felt the first stirrings of hope.

Without breaking the kiss, Colt swept her up in his arms and carried her to the bed. A few minutes later they were both naked.

He knelt over her, his breath catching at the display of feminine perfection beneath him: the slender, toned limbs, the flat stomach, the small round breasts with dusky pink tips, the miles and miles of flawless baby-soft skin.

For a moment, he didn't want to touch her. It was as if she were a delicate piece of china that he could break or a pristine canvass of freshly fallen snow that he would somehow sully.

But he couldn't do that anymore. He couldn't put her on that kind of pedestal. He would be good enough for her. He swore it.

Just give me a chance.

He touched her then. He let his hands roam all over that flawless canvas. She didn't break; she shattered.

He watched her face as his fingers slid up her thighs, as he swept his fingers across her dampness, as she shuddered under his touch.

"Please, Colt."

He heard the agony in her voice and knew what she wanted, but he wouldn't give it to her. She wanted it hard and fast. She didn't want to hear what he was telling her.

But he wouldn't hide behind lust, and he wouldn't let her hide, either.

He kept his eyes on her face the whole time as he brought her to the very peak. He reveled in the power, in the gift of her response.

And then he took her with his mouth and made her come again. Slowly and deliberately. He dragged out her pleasure, not giving either of them the release they craved. No matter how much she begged. Or how hard she fought to make him lose control.

She was good at that. She'd always been good at that. But he wouldn't let the feel of her hands on him, the grip of her body, or the lifting of her hips distract him from his purpose.

By the time he was finally sinking into her, his body was a taut, raging inferno of need. It was like trying to hold back a steam engine, but he did. He sank into her inch by inch, never letting his gaze fall from the flushed cheeks, the half-lidded gaze, or the softly parted lips.

"Why are you doing this to me?" The pleasure on her face belied the tortured sound of her voice.

"You know why."

Their eyes met and held. Three years of disappointment and heartbreak seemed to pass between them before she looked away.

But he wouldn't let her turn from him. He forced her gaze back to him with each small thrust of possession.

Feel this. Feel how good it is. We belong together.

When he was finally seated fully inside her . . . the feeling was indescribable. His chest pounded, not just with lust, but also with something far more important.

"I love you," he said.

And then he proved it.

How could he do this to her? How could he be so gentle and tender?

This was *Colt*, for God's sake. Her hardened, angry ex-husband who'd slept with her for months before giving her any clue that she was more to him than the flavor of the week. She could count on one hand the number of times he'd said he'd loved her, and it had never been like this.

She almost hated him.

Almost.

But that stupid, weak part of her that would always love him was too busy basking in—savoring—every touch, every caress, and every heart-tugging look in his eyes as he thrust slow and deep—achingly slow and deep—inside her.

The pain was almost unbearable. Not in her body—although she'd forgotten that feeling of stretching—but in her squeezing chest.

Her heart wanted to remain indifferent, but under the weight of such a fierce onslaught, it was yearning—longing—to reach for the brass ring that he offered. To let him take away the pain. To let him love her. To let him fill the cold emptiness inside her even if just for a moment.

And with him on top of her, holding her, filling her body so completely with his, that brass ring seemed hers for the taking.

He was tearing down her resistance with every tender,

poignant stroke. With sweetness. With gentleness. With emotion.

With the feeling of his body sliding into hers.

"I love you."

She didn't want his love, damn it. She wanted to come. She wanted him to take her hard and fast in a blaze of fiery passion. She wanted to pretend it didn't mean anything. That none of this meant anything. That he wasn't giving her everything she'd longed for for almost five years.

But he wouldn't let her. No matter how hard she fought. No matter how she touched him, what naughty things she whispered in his ear, or how hard she gripped the rock-hard ass that she'd always loved to urge him to go harder and faster.

It didn't matter what she did. He wouldn't fuck her the way she wanted.

He fought off her attempts with unrelenting purpose that left her nowhere to hide.

For the first time, Colt made love to her. Thoroughly and completely. And when they finally came together, he broke her.

Looking into his eyes as the emotion inside her built to the point of no return, she felt her heart open. She let him in. For one incredible moment she let him fill her with everything he wanted to give her, and she cried out with the joy and pleasure of it.

But when she came down, she came down hard. She hit the ground in a free fall of regret and anger. It jarred her. It made her body, still warm in the afterglow and heat of his embrace, cold.

Reality set in, and the horror of what she'd done—what she'd let herself feel—hit her full force like a slap in the face.

Did she enjoy pain? Was she some kind of masochist? She pushed him off her and tried to roll away, which was easier said than done with six feet four inches of heavily muscled operator on top of her.

"You have to go," she said, her voice sounding panicky even to her own ears. "I can't do this, Colt."

She was too weak. Too vulnerable. Too stripped to the core from her uncharacteristic loss of control earlier.

She tried to scoot out of bed—or maybe she was pushing him out—but he held her down with one arm and lifted up on the other elbow to look down at her.

God, he was sexy. His big, perfectly muscled body leaning over her like that. Perfectly muscled *naked* body. She didn't want to look—*liar!*—but it was hard to miss. His shoulders, arms, chest, stomach . . . lower . . . were all in peak condition and top operational form. In other words, he looked like one of those guys in a fitness magazine but with more scars and without the baby oil. He didn't need oil to emphasize his muscles. Although the sweat was kind of doing the same thing.

She turned her gaze away harshly.

He tried to bring her back with a tender brush of her hair from her face. "I know you're scared to trust this."

She jerked away and sat up to grab her shirt. She felt naked—exposed—in more ways than one. "I'm not scared, but you are right. I don't trust *this* anymore than I trust you."

"I love you, Kate. I've never stopped loving you."

She didn't know whether she was angrier with him for tempting her with false promises or with herself for wanting to believe them. "If that is true, then you and I have very different definitions of love."

Rather than get angry, he accepted the criticism and the sarcasm. "You're right. You don't treat people you love the way I did. But I wasn't like you, Kate. I didn't have any good examples to follow when I was growing up. But I'm trying to change. I'm not going to make the same mistake twice. I can't promise to be perfect, but I can promise to be better. I know I fucked up, and if you need to punish me for the rest of my life, I'll take it. I'll take whatever crumbs you want to dole out. Just give me another chance."

"Give me another chance." "That guy."

Her stupid heart tugged with treacherous force, even as her temper exploded. She jumped out of bed and turned on him, not caring that her silk blouse barely covered the part of her that was still wet with his semen. They hadn't used a condom. Not that it mattered—with pregnancy anyway.

"Are you crazy? After everything that we went through, do you think I can just forgive and forget? No one changes *that* much, Colt. How can I ever trust you again or believe you would ever trust me? What's going to happen the next time I have to work with a good-looking guy?"

His mouth tightened just enough. "I'll trust you and deal with it."

Kate went to her tote bag and pulled out her phone and a file. She held the phone out to him first. "Have you seen the new head of my section? His name is Dan and we've been working closely and long into the night on a couple of things." She smiled, seeing his mouth tighten even more. "Ah, it looks like you recognize him. He was Delta back in the day, wasn't he?"

"That asshole was a dog with women," Colt gritted out between clenched teeth.

"Same could be said of you before—and after—we married."

She didn't say anything for a minute. She didn't need to. It was clear he was festering enough on his own. But he gritted his teeth even harder and said, "I wouldn't like it, but I said I trusted you and I meant it. If you have naked hot-tub parties together and you tell me nothing is going on, I'll trust you."

She quirked a brow at that. Naked hot-tub parties? Right. She didn't believe that, but it was clear he was going to be stubborn.

She'd expected that. That was what the file was for. He'd sat up in bed—naked—so when the file landed in his lap it was only partly by chance. That part of him that made her stupid.

"What's this?"

"Read it."

He opened the file and as he flipped through the documents, Kate had the satisfaction of seeing him get pale.

Except the stab in her heart told her it wasn't really satisfaction. Because part of her—maybe a bigger part of her than she wanted to acknowledge—had wanted to believe him more than she realized.

He might have changed but not enough.

By the time he put the folder down, he wasn't just pale; he was looking ill. "You've filled out adoption papers?"

She nodded, and maybe she was a coward, but she couldn't look at him. She couldn't bear to see the rejection in his eyes even if she knew it was there. "I don't know how long it will take, but I want to be a mother, Colt."

As much as she'd wanted to be his wife. But she knew the futility of putting those two things together.

Did she expect him to say something? What was there to say? Out of the corner of her not-watching-him eye she saw him get up and start to put on his clothes.

That was that, then.

She hated him for the disappointment burning in her chest, in her eyes. How could she let him do this to her all over again? How could she let him give her hope only to have it pulled out from under her like Charlie Brown's football?

She'd quickly tugged on her underwear and skirt and sat on the edge of the bed while he finished. He was moving slowly. It was obvious he was trying to find the right thing to say.

But that was the problem. There wasn't anything to say—right or wrong. They were at an impasse. She wanted a child and he didn't. She'd put that aside for him once—or tried to put it aside—but she wasn't going to do it again.

He finally came to stand before her. She couldn't not look up.

"You deserve to be a mom, Kate. If that's what you want. But . . ."

He turned away, dragging his fingers through his hair uncomfortably.

"But you don't want to be a father," she finished.

He looked back at her angrily. "God, Kate, what kind of father would I be? No kid deserves to have someone like me for a dad."

He didn't see it. He would never see it. But Kate had always known in her heart that once he held their child in his arms, he would love it just as much as she did.

He would have been a great father to their daughter. But now that could never be.

Because of her. Maybe this was her punishment.

She looked up at him. "You've never been curious how I got pregnant? I was on birth control."

He frowned, obviously surprised by the change of direction in the topic. "I assumed it was an accident."

"Right. Everyone knows birth control isn't one hundred percent effective, but I had an IUD and that is pretty darn close."

Colt was watching her strangely. Clearly he hadn't guessed where this was heading. Maybe he trusted her more than she realized.

"IUDs expire," she said. "I'd had mine for seven years. My doctor kept sending me reminders to have it changed, but I kept forgetting to make an appointment."

"For how long?"

She didn't flinch from his gaze. "A year."

Colt's expression was like granite. "Are you saying you got pregnant on purpose?"

Kate wanted to cry. "I don't know. Not consciously. But unconsciously maybe. I was fighting to hold on to our marriage. I thought that once you saw the baby—our baby—you would experience that kind of unconditional love and then . . ."

Her voice dropped off.

"Then what?" His voice was as tight and steely as she'd ever heard it.

She looked up at him. "Then you would know how to love me like that, too."

He flinched almost imperceptibly. Knowing how ridiculous and pathetic it sounded, she hurried to explain. "It's a horrible reason to bring a child into the world. So what kind of person does that make me? To try to hold on to her husband with a child he never wanted. And now . . ." Her eyes were burning with unshed tears as her hands twisted in her lap. "You were right about karma." Her voice was practically a whisper.

But he heard her. He took her by the arm and hauled her up to face him. He looked as fierce and angry as she'd ever seen him. But it wasn't with her. "I was lashing out, Kate, trying to hurt you because I thought you didn't want me anymore. I didn't mean it. What happened was an accident. It didn't have anything to do with what you did—consciously or unconsciously. You are not being punished because you wanted a baby, okay?"

She nodded, and he let her go. They stood facing each other for a long, painful heartbeat. It was as if neither of them trusted themselves to say anything for fear that the chasm between them would only grow wider.

As if that was possible. But now, he knew he wasn't the only one to blame.

"Why is a baby so important to you?"

Kate was taken aback by the question. "I don't know." She just knew that it was.

His voice was as grim as his expression when he finally spoke. "I think we both need time to think. We can talk more in the morning."

Kate nodded, but she knew there was nothing more to talk about. They'd said everything that needed to be said.

Nothing had changed. Colt was her past, not her future. Except now she knew the full tragedy of that future in trying to get over a man who would always hold her heart.

Seventeen

After making his call, Scott didn't seem to be in any rush to eat so they took their time. He practically forced her to have dessert. "It says Annie's apple pie is 'famous.' How can you skip it?"

He'd apparently never stepped on a scale and seen it three pounds heavier at the end of the day than when he'd woken up.

She sat back in the front seat and put her hands over her very full stomach, trying not to be resentful of Mr. Washboard no matter what he ate. She'd probably gained *five* pounds after that monstrosity of pie, ice cream, whipped cream, and caramel—with a cherry on top, of course. And that was after the chicken-fried steak.

If she'd been hoping for one of the hipster-version country kitchens that had popped up in some parts of the country, she was to be disappointed. Annie's Country Kitchen was good ol' country-fried everything with not a grain of quinoa or leaf of kale to be seen.

It had been delicious.

But now they were back in the car heading . . . south. Back to DC, Natalie assumed. She'd known she

wouldn't be able to delay him taking her in forever—
even with the baby—and the attempt on their lives had
only hastened the inevitable. She didn't have any reason
to be upset. He'd protected her family, which is more
than she should have asked from him. She knew what
helping her could cost him.

And even though Scott might be helping her, she did
not delude herself that he was ready to forgive and forget.
He obviously thought she was still hiding something.

Besides, with a man like Scott, she wasn't even sure
"forgive and forget" was possible. Her betrayal had hit
him in the place that was the most important to him. Not
just his pride, but the pride he took in his job. She knew
how much being a SEAL officer meant to him. With his
background he could have done anything. He could have
been making millions as an investment banker somewhere and hanging out on golf courses and in private
clubs.

But he'd chosen a different path. A path that was all
his own. He'd told her the story of the family friend
who'd recognized his strengths in high school and had
encouraged him to think about the military. She knew
how his parents had been surprised but supportive. And
she also knew how proud Scott was of all he'd accomplished on his own—without his family's influence or
money.

He had a right to be proud of all he'd achieved and the
bright future that he seemed destined for.

Destined for until she'd entered his life, that is. He'd
never talked about what came next—he was too focused
and happy being a SEAL—but once or twice he'd mentioned something (usually in frustration) about needing
people who actually understood how wars were fought
and how to use the military effectively being in position
to make policy decisions. She knew he wanted to be one
of those people.

He had the right stuff, and she wasn't the only one to see it. Once after a meeting, she'd overhead the secretary of defense and her boss talking about Scott and that command was expecting "big things" from him.

By helping her, he was putting that future even more in jeopardy. And if things went wrong . . . Her heart squeezed. He would have every right to blame her.

He'd seemed relaxed at their late-night dinner, but now that they'd been driving for a while, she could tell he was anxious about something. He kept tapping his thumbs on the steering wheel and glancing at the phone in the console between them.

"Are you expecting a call?" she asked.

He frowned. "Yes, from Kate. I got ahold of Colt, and he was supposed to have her call me. I hope nothing is wrong."

It was clear he had a very particular kind of wrong in mind.

"From what you told me about their divorce, I'm surprised they can stand to be in the same room together."

"Yeah, it hasn't been easy on her the past month having to spend time with him again, while trying to figure out what happened with my blown op."

She heard what he wasn't saying. He was blaming himself for getting her involved. "It's not your fault, Scott. From what you've told me of your sister, she would have never forgiven you if you hadn't gone to her for help. That's what people who love each other do."

The irony of her words was not lost on her. That was what she should have done. But she hadn't trusted that he'd returned that love. He'd never told her that he loved her, but looking back she thought he had. *Had* in the past tense.

The enormity of what she'd lost hit her hard. It was too late for regrets, but that didn't mean she didn't still feel them.

She covered up the sudden awkwardness that had sprung up between them by picking up the phone and handing it to him. "You should call her."

Normally she wouldn't encourage someone to use a cell phone while driving, but the two-lane highway they were on was deserted—and breaking cell phone laws was the least of their problems.

"It's after midnight."

"She won't care."

He must have agreed because he made the call. Natalie tried to keep up with his half of the conversation, but it was clear that Colt hadn't passed on Scott's message. It was also clear that Kate wouldn't say why, and Scott's "What the hell did he do to you?" summed up what he assumed happened.

It was also clear that Kate wasn't talking. She shut down his protective-brother instincts so fast Natalie wished she could have heard how she'd done it. With guys like Scott who were used to giving orders and having them followed, that was a useful tool to have in the toolbox.

Natalie wasn't exactly pretending not to listen to his conversation, but her ears really perked up when—after explaining what had happened and assuring Kate that he was fine (no, his shoulder hadn't opened up again)—he told her that he needed a place to hole up for a while.

Hole up? Startled, Natalie's gaze shot over to him. But he didn't notice. He was concentrating on the road and on his sister. Whatever Kate's response was to his request, it was clear he didn't like it. His expression got that stony look that Natalie hated, and his flexed jaw was about as yielding as El Capitan.

"I was thinking more along the lines of a safe house," he said.

Safe house? He wasn't taking her in?

There was a long silence on his end. Kate obviously had a lot to say. It must have been effective. By the end of the conversation, Scott had agreed to whatever she'd suggested even though he didn't look happy about it. Swallowing nails about summed up his expression.

Natalie hoped she had a chance to meet Kate at some point; she could obviously teach Natalie a few things.

"Fine," he said. "You win, but it won't change anything."

Another long silence while Kate talked.

"Yeah, I know." He glanced over at Natalie, who was pretending not to be hanging on every word. "I've heard it before. But for the record so are you." Natalie suspected he was talking about being stubborn—which she agreed with. "Fix this thing with Colt or don't, but don't let him hurt you again. I have enough problems right now without a homicide charge—even if it is justifiable."

Natalie waited a few minutes after he hung up to ask if Kate was all right.

"I don't know," he said. "She sounded pretty wrung out."

"Are she and her ex trying to patch things up?"

Scott shrugged. "Some things are beyond patching."

Natalie sucked in her breath. Was he talking about them?

As there were no pointed looks, he didn't seem to be. She relaxed—a little. "I thought you were taking me in."

He shot her a chastising look as if she should know better. "I won't risk it until we figure out what is going on."

Natalie couldn't believe he would do this for her. She tried to breathe evenly, but the sudden swelling in her chest had created a logjam for air. "Where are we going?"

His mouth tightened again, and she almost regretted asking. "Fort Knox until Kate can find someplace else."

From his tone, she knew that was all he was going to say on the subject. "Get some sleep, Nat."

"I'm not tired."

But a few minutes later, her eyes closed.

Natalie woke as Scott was pulling out of the drive through and back onto the highway. She was surprised that it was light out, and after a quick glance at the clock, even more surprised to see that it was almost eight in the morning. So much for not being tired.

But it was the smell emanating from the fast-food bag that was her biggest surprise.

"Doughnuts?" she said with only slightly exaggerated shock. "Surely fried rings of dough dipped in sugar aren't part of the Scott Taylor dietary regime. What were you saying about filling your body with poison?"

He gave her a forbidding SEAL-officer frown. "They have surprisingly good coffee." She let out a sound that showed how much she believed that. "And I got them for you."

"Perfect," she said, taking the bag and digging in. "These are delicious."

He held out about a minute, which was pretty good given that they smelled like ambrosia (they tasted even better) and that she'd already eaten two in quick succession.

"Mostly for you." He grabbed the bag from her before she could take another. "But I wouldn't want you to get sick eating all that crap."

"How thoughtful of you," she said wryly, as he practically inhaled the last two.

He had sugar on the edge of his top lip when he smiled back at her. For a moment all she could think about was leaning over and kissing—licking—it off. She might have made a movement toward him before she collected herself.

She tried to cover her embarrassment. "It's nice to

know you aren't perfect and that Mr. Discipline has a few weaknesses."

His mouth quirked. "Maybe one or two," he conceded with a suggestive look at her that hinted at what the second might be. "But I'm pretty perfect otherwise."

She laughed and slugged him in the arm. It was like punching steel. She was the one who said "ow." "You are horrible," she added, rubbing her sore hand. "And arrogant."

He grinned and for a moment Natalie forgot where they were and that what had happened had changed everything between them.

It felt like old times, and it was . . . wonderful.

She finished off the last doughnut and sipped the coffee he'd ordered for her.

"I'm afraid no almond milk," he apologized teasingly; he thought any order other than black was ridiculous for coffee. "With the baby, I wasn't sure whether caffeine was all right so I got decaf."

She felt her cheeks heat. It felt strange talking about the baby with him. Strange, but also nice. "That was thoughtful. Thanks. This is perfect."

She had been avoiding caffeine.

He nodded.

Figuring the subject might be strange for him, too, she asked, "How much longer before we arrive?"

"A few hours. We should be there by lunchtime. It wouldn't have taken this long, but I wanted to avoid the interstates."

Wherever "there" was, it was clear he still wasn't going to tell her.

"You must be exhausted," she said.

She knew he didn't sleep much, but driving all night like that couldn't have been easy.

"I'm fine. I'm used to it."

She bit her lip. She should have stayed awake to keep him company. "I didn't mean to sleep so long."

"You needed it," he said firmly. "And if I was in any danger of falling asleep I would have woken you up."

"Really?"

"Really. Besides, I was able to listen to some good music."

Her eyes narrowed. "Are you maligning my taste in music?"

He didn't hesitate. "Yes."

"Scott!"

He grinned unrepentantly. "The angry-chick music isn't so bad though."

She lifted one brow with a smirk. "I'm glad you like it as I'm sure you hear it a lot. And 'angry-chick music' is demeaning."

He just laughed.

The next few hours flew by so quickly that when Scott pulled off the highway, she was shocked to realize that it was almost noon and they must be near their destination.

They'd entered Virginia a while back and had been on the highway headed toward Fredericksburg. But he'd exited before that in a town called Warrenton.

"Is this it?" she asked. It seemed to be a charming old small town, which summed up a lot of this part of the country. The Old World, colonial American quaint town surrounded by lush, verdant countryside. It was hard to believe DC was only an hour or two away, depending on traffic.

They drove through town—which didn't take long— and turned onto a single-lane country road that had a scattering of houses along with trees and grassy fields on each side.

As the countryside became more rural, fencing and short stone walls became the boundaries, and the space between houses started to spread out and increase in distance from the road. The houses also started to become more impressive in stature.

Eventually Scott turned left into what looked like the drive of a private estate. There was an iron gate, a gatehouse, and a stone wall with square pillars and flower beds. She wouldn't have been surprised to see a signpost with WELCOME TO SOMETHINGBURG, HOME OF INSERT-SOME-IMPORTANT-HISTORICAL/POLITICAL-FIGURE."

The gate was opened by an older man who'd come out of the house. Natalie assumed they would pull into the gravel courtyard, but Scott drove past the gatehouse and continued on what must have been the longest driveway she'd ever been on.

If something almost a mile long could be considered a driveway.

They drove under an enormous and very Southern-looking canopy of trees before the house came into view.

Oh my God! Her mouth dropped. "House" didn't cover it by half. The two-story gray stone building sitting atop a rise seemed to be the width of a football field. It reminded her of the English country estates that she'd seen in the movies.

She looked around for a lake just in case Mr. Darcy, wearing a wet shirt, decided to come walking out of it.

Darcy. Suddenly she gasped and looked at her romantic fantasy man. "This isn't yours, is it? I thought the compound was in upstate New York?"

He waited until he pulled the car up to another stone gate, this a good ten feet tall that seemed to encircle the property—she understood the "Fort Knox" reference now—before turning to her. "No, it's not mine, and I told you it's a country house."

"What's this?" she teased. "Just so I can get the verbiage right."

He threw her a not-amused look. "An estate."

"I'd say," she murmured as he pushed the button on the intercom.

An instant later the gate opened. Whoever's "estate" this was, they were obviously expecting them.

Natalie had been so blown away by the house she hadn't noticed the guy in a suit with an earpiece patrolling the vast parkland that surrounded the main house.

The car rolled up the flagstone circular driveway and stopped before the entrance. She wasn't familiar enough with architecture to identify the style, but it looked old, big, and English. Flat stone front, lots of windows, and a triangular-shaped white wooden pediment entry with columns. Maybe Regency?

She was back to Darcy again.

Scott parked and Natalie noticed another secret service–looking guy on the opposite side of the house as she pulled her bag out of the trunk. Whoever lived here was obviously concerned with security. "Do you have mob ties I don't know about?"

Scott gave her a glare. "Very funny."

She probably shouldn't have teased him when he was so obviously tense, but this place was out of control. Who lived like this? Did Scott? It was awe-inspiring and off-putting at the same time. It was one thing to know the man you'd been dating was wealthy and another to realize you might have no concept of what that kind of wealth might mean.

She let Scott lead her up the handful of stairs. Before he had a chance to knock the door was opened.

At first she thought the distinguished older man who stood there would be the butler. Surely a place of this size had one? But if it did, he wasn't the one to open the door.

She was barely able to control her gasp. She turned to Scott in disbelief, but he was too busy staring at the man before them.

The men were staring at each other, actually, and

Natalie felt as if she'd disappeared. Scott had that swallowed-nails expression on his face while the other man's gaze was with something more like desperation. He was trying to hide it, but it was there in the glassy shine of his weary, sagging eyes.

The silence went on a few moments too long. Seeming to recall his duties, the older man said, "Lieutenant Commander Taylor, I'm glad you called." Natalie knew what an understatement that must be. He turned to her and held out his hand—something he hadn't done with Scott. Probably because he sensed it would be rejected. "I'm Tom Greythorn."

Introductions weren't necessary, and not just because she recognized him from the news. Though he was clearly very ill, there was also enough of a resemblance for her to realize that he must be Kate's father and Scott's biological father.

She would have shot Scott another look—he'd been holding out on her big-time—but his father was watching. "Natalie Andersson," she said, taking his hand. "It's nice to meet you, Senator."

Senator Tom Greythorn had had a long and distinguished political career in Congress. She also recalled that he'd also had some kind of connection to the CIA, which perhaps explained the security and Kate's chosen profession. Scott had always referred to Kate by her married name so Natalie had never made the connection.

The older man shook his head. "I'm retired from all that. Please just call me Tom."

She nodded. As it seemed Scott was just going to stand there and stew silently, she took it upon herself to say, "Thank you so much for, uh, having us."

House party it was not, but she didn't know what else to say.

She was about to elbow Scott, but he mumbled something like "yeah, thanks."

Natalie understood his reticence—if not outright rudeness—but it didn't make the situation any more comfortable.

What did you say to the man who she'd wager Scott had no intention of ever meeting but whom he must now be indebted to?

It took a moment for Natalie to process that. Scott had done this for her. The fact that he'd been willing to put aside his anger and resentment toward his biological father to keep her safe had to mean something.

Could he possibly be—she almost didn't want to put it into words—starting to forgive her?

The former senator was trying to hide his disappointment at Scott's continued stoniness, and something about the longing in his expression broke her heart.

For both their sakes, Scott needed to talk to him before they left. It was clear they might not have another chance. Though the senator stood tall and was dressed impeccably, he was barely recognizable from the powerful, distinguished man she remembered from TV.

With forced lightheartedness, the former senator said, "I will have Dalton show you to your room." The butler she'd expected suddenly appeared out of nowhere behind her. "You must be tired. Dinner is at six, or if you would prefer, food can be sent up. Just let Dalton know."

Natalie didn't need to turn to feel his eyes on them as Dalton—who was about fifty and not, to her disappointment, wearing tails but khakis and a tailored button-down—led them up the grand flight of stairs.

It was clear Scott didn't want to talk and she knew this would not be the time to push him. She'd let him rest first.

After a long walk down the hall, she was shown into the first of two connecting rooms. From the pink tones of the room, she suspected it was the female half of a master suite. It was enormous and beautiful, furnished comfortably but tastefully with a mix of antiques and modern pieces that somehow all went together. The large windows looked out on the back of the house, which she could see contained an enormous pool and guest quarters.

She would explore more later, but for now she didn't know what she was more excited to see: the big fluffy bed or the enormous white marble wading pool–sized tub in the bathroom.

When she slipped under the warm bubbly water about fifteen minutes later, she knew. The tub. She sighed and closed her eyes. Definitely the tub.

Scott wasn't just edgy, he was downright agitated. The long, hot shower had helped, but as soon as he'd lain down on the bed to try to sleep his mind had raced in all kinds of directions.

He shouldn't have come here. He didn't want to feel sorry for the bastard who'd cuckolded his father.

Seeing the senator face-to-face had been a shock. Not because Scott could see the resemblance. He'd seen that from photos—it was one of the reasons he'd been pretty sure he and Kate were related even before the test results came back.

No, the shock had come from realizing that Kate hadn't been exaggerating about the old man's health. Thomas Greythorn III was a shadow of the imposing figure Scott had seen for so many years on the news and in the papers. It was as if all the lifeblood and vitality had been sucked out of him.

Greythorn had once been Scott's size and build, but he had to be three inches shorter and forty pounds lighter now. "Emaciated" was putting it lightly. More alarming than the shrunken appearance, however, was his skin tone, which was so sallow it looked almost green. His once-thick head of white hair was now thin and military buzz-cut short—probably due to his treatments. Scott knew he was in his early sixties, but he looked decades older.

The former senator had been diagnosed with prostate cancer two years ago. He was now in the late stages of the disease, which had metastasized to the bones. He'd been through the gamut of treatment from surgery to immunotherapy, to hormone therapy and chemo, but nothing had worked. Now the cancer was impacting his spinal cord, confining him to bed most of the time. Kate mentioned that he'd been trying a new drug that was supposed to be promising, but it just seemed to be making him weaker and more ill.

It was one thing to confront an older, healthier version of yourself like Scott, with anger and resentment, had seen on TV, and another to confront a man with one foot in the grave who'd obviously used a good portion of his remaining strength to get out of bed to greet the son who'd refused to meet him for over three years.

Overabundance of pride was obviously in the DNA.

But recognizing any similarities only made Scott more furious. It felt like a betrayal of the father who'd raised him and the man he'd looked up to more than anyone else on this planet. Knowing that he looked like his biological father was bad enough; he didn't need any more connections.

That was why he hadn't wanted to come here. Scott had one father; he didn't want another.

But lying in bed, trying to force the sleep that wouldn't come, he could feel the relentless prickle of emotions he wanted to ignore. Guilt and, worse, compassion.

The bastard was *dying*.

Scott twisted around a few minutes longer before tossing the covers back and getting out of bed. He wasn't going to get any sleep like this.

Not for the first time, his gaze shifted to the closed door that was another reason for his edginess. The thin piece of wood that separated him from what he really wanted seemed to be taunting him.

There were a lot of reasons he shouldn't give in to that temptation, but he couldn't think of any of them right now.

He crossed the room and opened the door. If she'd been sleeping, he might have turned back around. But she wasn't. She was lying in bed, reading a book that she must have picked up from one of the shelves.

She glanced up, obviously surprised to see him.

"I couldn't sleep," he said, as if him showing up in her room in nothing more than his boxer briefs was the most natural thing in the world.

Maybe it was.

There was nothing in his voice to give him away, but she heard it anyway. She looked at him with such compassion and understanding that he knew he didn't have to explain.

It was like the night when he'd gone to her after Mark had died. Mark Fallon had been a fellow officer, the OIC of Neptune Platoon (the other platoon in Team Nine), and one of his closest friends in the navy. While on a joint mission, Scott had sent him and half his platoon into a building on overwatch. The building that was supposed to have been deserted for some time had been wired to explode. Mark had gone in first and had died instantly. He was the only casualty, although a few of the guys had been badly injured.

Scott had gone to Natalie's after the funeral at Arlington. She'd opened the door, took one look at him, and didn't say anything. She knew exactly what he needed. Someone to be there for him. Someone to turn to. Someone not to ask questions.

She did the same thing now. Wordlessly, she lifted the covers and opened her arms.

He didn't hesitate.

Scott crossed the room in a few strides and slid in next to her. The next moment her arms were around him, their bodies were pressed together, and his mouth was on hers.

The edginess was gone, and all he could feel was warmth. Warmth that penetrated to the bones. Warmth that made everything else around them disappear.

This was all that was important.

This was the answer.

He groaned at the taste of her. She was like sugar, melting under his lips. He couldn't seem to get enough of that sweetness before it was dissolving away from him, so he kissed her deeper and deeper.

Their tongues twisted and twined, circled and stroked, until the soft moans and pants urging him on became more than he could take.

He couldn't wait. She was giving herself to him, opening her body and her heart with no questions asked.

With no conditions.

No promises.

Maybe it was wrong. Maybe she deserved something more in return. But this was all he could give her right now. His body. His desire. His need.

And God, how he needed her. He wanted to feel her under him. Feel her silky skin sliding against his. Feel her body squeezing him like a glove as he pushed inside. Feel her hips lifting and circling as he thrust. And most of all he wanted to feel the cries of pleasure reverberating through him as he forced her over the edge.

He tore away with a groan long enough to get rid of the limited clothing that was in his way.

She was reaching for him even before he finished, and he moved over her, pausing just long enough to look into her eyes. He might be out of his mind with need for her, and they might have made love a hundred times before, but he needed to hear her say it. She might have been able to get beyond what had happened to her, but it was new to him, damn it.

"I need you to tell me you want this."

His voice sounded as tight as the rigid muscles of his neck and arms.

"What?"

He could see the confusion in her half-lidded gaze. "I need you to say it."

Suddenly she seemed to understand. Her eyes grew suspiciously shiny. She reached up and cupped his grizzled jaw, with a look of tenderness in her eyes that melted what little ice he had left around his heart.

"I want you to make love to me, Scott." He would have groaned with relief if she hadn't stopped him. "It's just . . ." Her voice dropped off.

He frowned. "Just what?"

A slow smile spread over her face as she took advantage of his position looming over her to let her hands slide over the muscles of his flexed arms and stomach. He sucked in his breath at the bolt of pleasure that surged through his veins from the delicate touch.

When she reached the thick column of his erection, she took him by the balls—literally—squeezed as if she owned him, and then circled her hand around his cock, gripping him with a long hard stroke. She leaned up and whispered in his ear, "Just hurry."

Scott groaned and thrust deeper into her hand. There weren't many things he could do with her hand working him like this, but hurry . . . *that* he could do.

He bent down and kissed her again. But the milking torture of her hand made it harsher. More demanding. More carnal. And maybe even a little raunchy.

He licked, he sucked, he coaxed her with his mouth to stroke him harder.

He could feel the pleasure pulsing. Feel her thumb swirl the heavy head with the drop that seeped out.

The pounding of his blood, the beating of his heart, the pressure building at the base of his spine started to overwhelm his control. He was close. Too damned close.

She knew it too and guided him between her legs. He wanted to push inside so badly, his raging body started to sweat. But he let her tease herself, as he was incapable. He let her dampen herself with the sensitive tip, let her circle and nudge. But the feeling of that soft warm flesh was too much.

"Enough," he bit out. "I can't . . ."

This wasn't going to be pretty; he needed to be inside her too badly, and it had been too long.

She released her grip, moved her hands around to his ass, and he started to push. He let out a deep, primal groan of pleasure as he sank deeper and deeper, as her body squeezed and clenched, as everything slipped into place.

He reached the end, and with one final nudge that made her cry out and their bodies lock into position.

He stilled. Their eyes met. He would die and never be tired of that look of surprise—of wonder—on her face. It happened every time. Which given how many times he'd made love to her didn't make any sense. Except that he understood because he felt it, too.

He'd always felt it. He was just surprised to feel it now. He'd thought being with her again after all that had happened—after what he'd learned about her—that it would be different.

But it wasn't. *She* wasn't. The connection between them was real. Whatever else had happened between them he could trust that.

He could trust this.

He started to move. Slowly at first, trying to make it last as long as it could when every instinct—every primitive impulse—was crying out to take and plunder. To unleash the powerful emotions that were raging inside.

Emotions that he couldn't talk about but that she understood.

She wouldn't let him go slow. She met his thrust with a circle and lift of her hips that increased the pace—and the frenzy.

She started to moan. To urge him on with her naughty words. She told him all the things he hadn't known how much he needed to hear. How much she'd missed this. How good he felt. How he was going to make her come.

And then, when he couldn't hold on any longer, when he heard her cries, and his body let go of the freight train of need that had been crushing him . . .

She told him how much she loved him.

Eighteen

Natalie had forgotten. . . .

No, that wasn't true. She could never have forgotten; she just hadn't let herself remember because she was scared she would never have this kind of feeling again. The feeling of closeness and absolute contentment.

She wasn't surprised when Scott fell almost instantly asleep after they'd collapsed in a hot, sated heap. He'd rolled off her onto his back, tucked her in against his chest, and held her tightly as their bodies tried to recover from . . .

It was hard to put a name to something that incredible, that overwhelming, and that extraordinary. Touching heaven was too poetic for something so fierce and intense. Exploding? Shattering? Except that those were destructive and what had just happened was the opposite. It was forging, joining, and connecting.

It was special. It had always been special, but this time it seemed even more so as there was nothing between them anymore. There were no more veils, no matter how thin, to hide how she felt about him. How much she loved him.

She wasn't even disappointed that he hadn't said it back. She loved him unconditionally and wanted him to know that.

But he must have already known; he wouldn't have come to her otherwise. Men like Scott didn't need anyone—or at least they thought they weren't supposed to. But everyone needed someone that they could turn to when things got rough, someone they could count on for comfort and understanding. Someone who could be the tether when everything else around them was spinning out of control.

Scott had been that way for her. He still was. And though she knew he'd never admit he needed a little stability, she wanted to be that for him.

He was hurting right now. Meeting the man who'd fathered him had forced him to face his identity. No matter how much he wanted Stephen Taylor's blood running through his veins, it wasn't going to happen, and Scott couldn't ignore or pretend differently anymore. He had two fathers—the one who'd raised him and the one who'd given him his DNA—and today he'd had to accept that. What Scott was going to do when it came to Tom Greythorn, she didn't know. Just as she didn't know what his and her future held.

But right now he'd needed her, and that was enough.

It touched her that even in his pain and need he'd stopped to think of her. It hadn't been necessary. God knew they'd made love enough times for her to know that what she had with Scott was in no way reminiscent of Mick. There was no confusion about that. But it was sweet and considerate. It also spoke of the kind of guy Scott was.

It was surprising that with everything she'd been through that sex had played such a big part in her relationship with Scott—and that she could be so free and uninhibited with him. She'd refused to let Mick take physical pleasure from her. But when she was with Todd, it had been a conscious "I'm going to enjoy this." With Scott she never even got that far. She never had to think about finding pleasure; it was just there.

Neither of them had said anything. There was nothing to say that hadn't just been said.

She'd rested her cheek against his heated chest as she always did and listened as the heavy pounding of his heart as it slowed and the deep breaths turned softer and more even.

That was how she knew he'd fallen asleep.

Scott sleeping while she wasn't was such a rarity, she unfurled herself a little so that she could just watch him.

Her heart tugged with love and longing. She missed her clean-cut, golden-haired naval officer, although she had to admit the dark, dangerous, stubbly Scott definitely had that sexy thing going. Either way he was one of the most handsome men she'd ever seen. He was almost *too* perfect. She'd joked about it earlier, but it was true—and sometimes a little intimidating. But he seemed much less imposing and serious with his eyes closed and expression relaxed—younger and more boyish. It was as if only in sleep could the weight of his job—his duty—be lifted from his shoulders.

She admired what he'd accomplished and was fiercely proud of his role in Team Nine. But the constant pressure and responsibility took its toll. He might not be leading his platoon into missions right now, but trying to keep them alive while finding out what had happened to them was no less responsibility. Maybe it was more so. There wasn't a chain of command to run up the flagpole for approval. Scott was the one calling all the shots. All of them.

She wished she could carry some of the load for him, but she couldn't. All she could do was be there for him when he needed her.

She smiled, thinking if the kind of passion they'd just

experienced was the result, she wouldn't mind him needing her a lot.

Suddenly she sobered as the truth hit. She wasn't going to "be there" for long. That was the reality. It was the elephant in the room. It was also one of the reasons she wouldn't let herself wonder what this meant. What could it mean?

Even if Scott forgave her, even if he could find a way to love her again, it wasn't going to give them a future. It would probably actually be better for him if he kept his distance from her.

No matter what kind of pretty bow they put on the package, nothing could change the fact that she'd been a spy. Her future was probably in a cell somewhere facing charges of treason. The best she could hope for was that they could figure out who was trying to kill her before she went to prison.

Scott's future—until he'd met her, at least—had been lots of stars and ribbons on his chest and probably a seat at a table in the Pentagon one day. She knew how much he loved being a SEAL and how important it was to him. Could she really take any of that from him?

She watched the even fall of his breath and felt her own lungs tighten. The hope and happiness she'd felt a few minutes ago felt as if it had turned to ash in her chest.

She knew the answer.

Her life was ruined. She wasn't going to ruin Scott's as well. He'd stuck his neck out for her enough already by not taking her in right away and by helping her family. She couldn't—wouldn't—ask him to do more. She loved him too much to do that.

She probably should have let him drag her back to DC like he wanted to when he showed up at the farm. But she'd been so scared. She was still scared. But maybe there were worse things than being scared. Like seeing the man you loved destroyed for trying to help you.

But what about the baby?

She guessed that she did have to ask one more thing of him.

Scott woke with the kind of lazy grogginess that he hadn't felt in a long time. His body and limbs were heavy, as if he were sinking into quicksand.

Instinctively, he reached for the warm, soft body next to him. When his hands met only air and cool sheets, however, his eyes snapped open with instant alertness. His pulse, which had jumped as well, stalled and then sank along with his heart.

Natalie wasn't there.

He sat up and looked around the large bedroom that was pooled in the late-afternoon sunlight. His gaze immediately shot to the bathroom. But the door was open and the room empty.

Where the hell was she?

The speed with which he jumped out of bed and threw on his briefs—noticing the clothes he'd torn off her were gone—pointed in the direction where his mind was headed. He told himself she wouldn't try to slip away again—not *now*—but his heart was pounding and every nerve ending was buzzing.

He cursed and tore open the door to his adjoining room.

He stopped so suddenly that he almost stumbled. Natalie was sitting in one of the wingback leather reading chairs, with her bare feet tucked up under the missing T-shirt and underwear that he'd tossed on the floor earlier.

She was on the phone—his burner—and glanced up at him questioningly when he stormed in. Like an idiot. That's how he felt when he realized his mistake. She hadn't tried to flee; she was only making a call. A call to her family, he realized when she spoke.

"I can't wait to see it, Lanie. I'm sorry I missed your birthday. But maybe you can show me the next time I see you." Pause. She looked over at him where he'd taken a seat on the edge of the bed. "I'm not sure. I hope soon." He could hear the false optimism in her voice, and it made something pinch between his ribs. "I miss you, too," she finished quietly.

The pinch turned into a stab. He swore to himself that he would do whatever he could to see that Natalie saw her sister sooner rather than later. And it wasn't just because he was feeling guilty about showing up in her room earlier for sex without promises—which he was—or jumping to the wrong conclusion right now. After what had happened, Scott could no longer pretend that he didn't still care about her, even if he wasn't quite ready to put a label on it. Scott wanted to make her happy, and he was going to do everything in his power to get her out of this. She had put her trust in him, and he wasn't going to let her down. Which meant he had to start trusting her.

But it wasn't easy. He was used to relying on his perception and judgment, but he was keenly aware that it had a blind spot when it came to Natalie. He felt like he was going on blind faith—which didn't sit well for someone like him.

"Let me talk to Dad," she said. A few minutes later, Scott felt that agony all over again. He hated hearing her so upset. "I don't know, Dad. I hope not long. I know it's hard having them there, but it's necessary."

It was clear her dad had had time to process that she was alive and had moved on to the "I want answers" part.

"I'll tell you everything as soon as I can," she said.

Her eyes widened a little at what her father said next. "Uh, he's sleeping."

She eyed Scott apologetically, and he guessed her dad wasn't taking that for an excuse.

"It's fine," Scott said, holding out his hand. "I don't mind talking to him."

Natalie dragged her teeth on her lip a long time before handing the phone to him.

"This is Scott," he said.

From what Natalie had told him about her father, Scott expected the voice on the other end to sound weak and sickly. But the deep baritone laden with steel sounded more like a two-hundred-pound linebacker who was coming at him headfirst and didn't care about a targeting penalty.

"I don't know who you are and what's going on, but if anything happens to my daughter, I'm holding you responsible."

Make that two-hundred-*and-fifty*-pound linebacker. Natalie's dad didn't need to explain how he'd do that—the gist was implicit in his tone.

"Yes, sir," Scott said. "I understand." He looked at Natalie—who was clearly embarrassed—and held her gaze solely. "I'll protect her with my life."

"See that you do," her father said. "Or you will wish that you had."

That was explicit enough. "Understood."

Scott handed the phone back to Natalie and waited for her to finish her conversation. It didn't take long.

"I'm sorry about that," she said with an apologetic wince, as she disconnected and handed Scott back the phone. "My father is a little overprotective, and he is like a mama bear when Lana and I are in trouble or threatened. Which I guess we are."

"You don't need to apologize for anything. I'd feel the same in his shoes." He paused for a minute. "Your dad didn't happen to play football, did he?"

It was kind of a joke.

Her brows shot up. "How did you guess? He was an offensive lineman in high school and was recruited by the University of Minnesota, but his father wouldn't let him go. He needed help on the farm."

Scott tried not to groan. Offensive lineman? "He must be a big guy."

She nodded. "He's heavier now after the heart attack, but he's six-six and about two-eighty." She smiled, wistfully. "My friends were always scared of him because he looks so mean, but he's a teddy bear once you get to know him."

Right. A six-six, two-eighty, mean-looking teddy bear. Those totally went together.

"I hope I didn't wake you when I got out of bed," she said. "But I wanted to try to get ahold of Lana before they sat down to eat dinner." She frowned and tilted her head to look at him. "Was something wrong? You looked upset when you came in here."

"No," he said, not wanting to confess to his moment of doubt. "I was just wondering who you were talking to."

"I hope you don't mind that I used your phone, but I thought it better than using your . . ." She stopped and he guessed she was about to say the F-word. In this case, "father." "The senator's landline."

"It's fine," Scott said. "Is everything okay with your sister?"

She sighed. "I think so. But it's always hard to tell with Lana. With her cognitive issues, she seems to take good news and bad news in stride." Her mouth quirked. "She didn't understand why I missed her birthday party if I wasn't at the cemetery, but she mostly wanted to talk about the computer games and YouTube videos she's been watching. It was good to hear her voice and nice to talk to someone who didn't want explanations."

"How old is she?"

"Twenty-six. We're two and a half years apart."

"What happened to her? You mentioned something in the orphanage?"

He hadn't wanted to ask before, fearing it would make him too sympathetic toward her. But clearly that cat was already out of the bag. Besides, it could be helpful. He knew Kate was still looking into the adoption agency, but she hadn't come up with much beyond the link with Mick.

Natalie stiffened and her gaze dropped. She brought her knees up to her chest and wrapped her arms around them as if she were cold. He wasn't sure she was going to respond, but then she said, "It was a long time ago. We were both so young. I was three when we went into the orphanage and Lana was only six months old. Just a baby." She smiled wistfully. "She was so beautiful. My mom called her Kukolka, which is something akin to baby doll. It's one of the only memories I have of her— and one of the few Russian words I remember."

"What happened to them? Your parents?"

"They were ballet dancers. They tried to defect during a performance but were delayed in waiting for Lana and me to be brought to them after the show. One of their watchers found out and reported them. They were imprisoned and shortly after I was told by one of the supervisors at the orphanage they'd died. The irony, of course, was that the Wall came down, and the USSR dissolved not long after they were arrested. If they'd waited a few months maybe . . ." Her voice fell off, and he knew she was thinking of all the things that would have been different. "It's funny. I have so few memories of them—bits and pieces or flashes here and there—but I remember being happy and loved. Maybe that's why what happened afterward stands out so sharply in comparison."

Scott found himself tensing—as if bracing himself. "They were cruel to you at the orphanage?"

After seeing what the Russians had called a prison at the gulag, he didn't imagine a late Cold War orphanage was much better.

She thought for a moment and shook her head. "No. That's the thing. They weren't cruel, just indifferent. Although in retrospect maybe it amounted to the same thing. But if you are envisioning Dickensian characters or Nurse Ratched, the women who took care of us weren't like that. They were just cold and efficient—sterile like the orphanage itself. I remember thinking when I got there that the world had suddenly gone gray. The orphanage was colorless and joyless. In that respect I guess it was like you picture in the movies—some kind of asylum but with kids."

"Sounds pretty bleak."

"It was. But when I read about it later, I realized that at the time they thought they were doing the right thing. The doctors and child specialists thought it would be easier for us to form attachments once we left the orphanage if we didn't form them while we were there."

Scott remembered seeing something about this in the papers when there were some problems with Russian adoptions. Maybe the caretakers at the orphanage hadn't been intentionally cruel, but it had led to some kids with severe emotional-attachment issues.

"I'm sorry," he said, not knowing what else to say. "That must have been horrible."

She shrugged. "We were only there a little over two years. And Lana and I had each other." He suspected there was a lot behind that statement. "We were lucky the Anderssons were patient. Actually we were lucky in more ways than one. At first they wanted only one child. They picked me, but I went crazy when they tried to take me away from Lana. Instead of throwing me back like most people would have done with a hysterical child, they agreed to take both of us." Tears were shimmering in her eyes when she looked up at him. "I loved them with everything I had from that moment on. To take any child from an orphanage requires a generous heart, but to take a toddler with special needs . . . that requires generosity of an entirely different kind."

Scott had never met her parents, and her father had just threatened him on the phone, but from that moment they'd earned his gratitude, respect, and loyalty, too. He'd do his best to make damned sure nothing happened to them. Natalie had put her trust in him, and he wouldn't let her down.

He waited for her to continue, aware that she'd circled away from his original question. But she came back to it. "The women who looked after us at the orphanage were for the most part fine as long as we were quiet and behaved. Which was okay for me, but not for Lana. She was colicky when we arrived and cried all the time—especially that first year. I did my best to keep her quiet, and spent most nights curled up on the ground beside her crib holding her hand and rubbing her back."

Scott looked at her. "Jeez, Nat. What were you, three?"

"I was four when it happened." She shrugged as if it didn't matter. "I was caught up in a game of jump rope. We weren't allowed outside to play very often, but this was a special occasion since someone high up in the new government was coming to 'observe.' Lana hadn't been crying as much lately, and I somehow lost track of time. I raced back but it was too late."

Tears were slipping down her cheeks. He couldn't keep his distance any longer. He stood from the bed, walked over to the chair, and lifted her up long enough to sit and deposit her on his lap. She snuggled into him like a child, drawing comfort from his warmth and strength. It made him feel strangely powerful and his chest expanded until he could barely breathe.

He stroked her hair. "What happened?"

"She must have awoken early from her nap and started crying because I wasn't there. When I came in, one of the new nurses was holding her limp body away from her in her hands. I thought Lanie was dead and started screaming. I remember one of the head ladies coming in and the new one saying over and over that she hadn't done anything; she'd just shaken her a little to try to get her to stop crying."

Scott let out a low curse. "Shaken baby syndrome?"

Natalie nodded. "I didn't know what it was called then. I just knew that when Lana came back from the hospital she was different. She didn't act the way she used to. She was quiet and laconic. She didn't cry as much, but neither did she smile. She improved a lot when we came to America, but she's blind in one eye, has some cognitive delays, and occasionally has seizures."

"You were practically a toddler yourself, Natalie. It wasn't your fault."

"I know," she said, as if it was something she'd said many times because it was easier than disagreeing. But she clearly didn't believe it.

He intended to see that she did.

It was also clear where her protectiveness toward her sister—and her family for that matter—came from.

"Is there anything else you remember about your time at the orphanage? I wouldn't ask but it could be important."

She shook her head. "Not much more than I already told you. Because my parents were Soviet 'traitors' Mick told me I was put into a secret sleeper spy program to pay for their crimes."

"The program continued after the fall of the Soviet Union?"

"From what Mick said the people who set up the program were former Department S—the secret section of the KGB—who found new positions with the SVR."

Russia's current intelligence agency. "What crime was Mick paying for?"

"He never told me. All I know is that he'd been put in

an orphanage because of something his father had done. Like me, he was in America for years before he was 'recruited.'" Anticipating his question, she added, "He never told me by whom. He never told me any names of the people he reported to. I don't know what hook they had in him, but Mick was an opportunist. Whatever it was, you can be sure he made the best of it."

The hatred in her voice when she spoke of Mick hadn't lessened any with the news of his death. Scott couldn't blame her. His had only intensified since he learned what Mick had done.

"Kate is looking into it to see what kind of connections she can find. Anything else you can think of could be helpful."

"I wish I knew something, but I suspect Mick feared I'd spill my guts at some point. He told me just enough to believe him." She shook her head. "It still sounds crazy. Who would think that there was a Russian spy program involving orphanages operating since the Cold War? It sounds more like a bad TV show."

"Actually it's a good one."

She looked at him, confused.

"*The Americans*," he said. "The show was loosely based on a Russian spy sleeper program called the 'illegals' that was uncovered in 2010. If you want illogical, you should read about that one. It was embarrassingly bumbling and unsophisticated."

She turned in his lap to look up at him, obviously surprised. "I had no idea. I thought that show was fiction."

"It was some crazy shit. This whole thing is crazy."

"Believe me, I've told myself that almost every day for four years. I used to think my life was so boring. But I'd give anything to go back to boring. Boring is good. Boring is normal. Boring doesn't have hit men trying to kill you." She sighed heavily. "But that's never going to happen."

It wasn't a question, and she wasn't looking for any

reassurance, but he tried to give it anyway. "You don't know that. Once we get all this figured out—"

"*If* we get this all figured out, it isn't going to change my role in it. I'm still going to go to prison."

Every bone in his body rebelled at the idea, even if it was probably—likely—true. He squeezed her a little tighter as if he could infuse her with his certainty. "I'm not going to let that happen, Nat."

She didn't argue, but it was clear she didn't believe him.

"I'm not," he insisted, although he didn't want to think about what he might have to do to keep that promise.

"You've already done enough, Scott. More than I had a right to expect. I swear I won't ask anything more of you, except . . . I need you to promise me one thing."

"What?"

"That if I go to prison, you'll make sure the baby is taken care of. My parents will help, but they are getting older and—"

He cut her off, forcibly taking her by the shoulders to look her in the eyes angrily. "No. That isn't going to happen."

Her face fell. "I know that we weren't able to wait around for the test, but you have to know the baby is yours."

She'd obviously misinterpreted his anger. "I don't give a shit about the test. I know it's mine. But I'm not letting you go to prison, okay. I'll think of something. You just have to trust me."

"I do," she said, and then repeated, "I do. But just promise me, okay?"

"Christ, Nat. Of course, I'll take care of the baby. You shouldn't even need to ask."

"I know, but thank you." The relief in her voice bothered him. It was almost as if she'd given up. She put her head on his chest, and he swore he wouldn't let her down.

Nineteen

Natalie was rarely late. But tonight she made an exception. She purposefully took her time in getting ready for dinner, and it was closer to six fifteen when she finally left the room.

Dinner had been her idea. Scott had wanted to take the senator up on his offer to have food sent to their room, but Natalie had dragged herself off Scott's lap—and him off the chair—insisting that they go down.

"It would be rude," she'd told him. "The senator has opened up his house to us without asking any questions; the least we can do is join him for dinner."

Scott guessed what she was trying to do. A steel curtain dropped down over his face.

"You can't force this, Natalie."

"I know. And you don't have to talk to him if you don't want to. But you can't hide up in the room the whole time, either."

She tossed him the duffel bag he'd brought that included his clothes. Not that Scott standing around in his boxer briefs was a bad thing. Normally. But looking at that big, muscular body was making her feel all warm and tingly again, and she didn't want him distracting her. Which they both knew wouldn't take much effort.

He caught the bag and quirked a brow. "Hiding? He offered to send up food, not me."

"He was being polite. And so are we. So get dressed."

LC Taylor wasn't the only one who could issue orders around here.

"You know, you're kind of sexy when you are bossy."

He started coming toward her with an expression on his face that she knew too well—and usually resulted in her naked and on her back—but she held him back with her hand. Unfortunately it came up against bare chest, which made her stern-schoolmarm voice a little shaky. "Nice try. But you aren't going to distract me with that right now."

Later he could distract her all he wanted. But even thinking about later was kind of distracting, and she felt her body rev up with anticipation.

"I'm not?" he said, gazing down at her with a heated look that would have melted her socks off if she'd been wearing any. "You sure about that?"

Knowing he was right made her just annoyed enough to purse her lips together with determination and push him back. "Get dressed, Commander."

It wasn't until she'd marched into her room that she realized her mistake. She had no idea what to wear. Did rich people dress for dinner?

A quick riffling through the clothes she'd brought told her that if they did, she was out of luck. Not one fancy cocktail dress had magically appeared among the mostly shorts and jeans that she'd grabbed in the two minutes Scott had given her to pack.

The best she could do was black linen capris that were rolled at the leg and a long-sleeve white linen blouse that she wore over a white cotton tank top. As the choice was tennis shoes or black flip-flops, she went with the flip-flops.

Maybe this was a bad idea.

She was thinking about changing her mind and taking Scott up on his distracting tactics when he came into her room. "You almost ready? It's just about six." He came to a sudden halt when she turned around. "Wow! You look incredible."

Relieved as much by his reaction as by the fact that he was wearing a polo and shorts, she shook her head. "I still have to put on my makeup. You go ahead, and I'll be down in a few minutes."

He gave her a sharp frown, as if suspecting she was trying to manipulate him into something—which she wasn't. Really.

"You look gorgeous the way you are. I don't know why you women wear that crap."

"Because we women like it. And believe it or not, Scott, not everything we do is to make ourselves more attractive to men."

He grinned. "It's not? Then who are you trying to impress?"

She thought about it a minute. "Other women."

He laughed. "All right, but don't take too long."

There might have been a little bit of a plea in there.

This time she was the one to lift a brow speculatively. "Don't tell me the big bad SEAL is scared?"

He didn't miss a beat. "Out of my mind," he said as he left the room.

That he admitted it so readily made her heart go out to him. She wished there was some way to make this easier on him. But other than be there for him, this was something he had to work out on his own.

Natalie knew it was going to be awkward, but when she was shown into the dining room by the ever-ready Dalton, who'd been waiting for her at the bottom of the stairs, the silence was cringeworthy. Scott, holding a cut-crystal lowball glass that appeared to have been drained, was standing by a huge window overlooking the side garden, and the senator, clearly struggling with what to say, was seated in a chair next to the unlit fireplace.

Small talk had obviously been exhausted.

Natalie spent most of the evening serving as a bridge between the two men, who barely said anything to each other directly. Although the senator was charming and easy to talk to, Scott wasn't. He'd clammed up. Every time she tried to lure him into the conversation, it stopped, and she'd have to think of something else to say.

It was exhausting. And frustrating.

By the time they went to bed, she was angry enough at Scott for being so stubborn that she told him to get some rest and she would see him at breakfast.

He was angry enough not to protest.

She knew it wasn't at her, but she was still stewing when he crawled into the bed next to her. He didn't say anything, but just pulled her into his arms and fell asleep. It wasn't exactly an apology, but she took it as one.

She slept later than she intended, and Scott had already gone down when she woke. The senator had told them breakfast was served buffet style after eight on the patio—they could of course order hot food whenever they liked (of course)—but it was closer to nine by the time Natalie made her way outside. It was like a fancy county club, with a glass-topped wrought-iron table, chairs with thick cushions in a floral pattern, umbrellas, silver, china, and fresh flowers everywhere.

Scott was already halfway through an omelet when she walked outside.

"Where's the senator?" she asked.

"Done." The way he said it made it clear that departure had been welcome. "He left a few minutes ago."

Natalie didn't say anything until her egg order had

been taken by Dalton, and she'd sat down at the table
with the fresh fruit, croissant, and coffee that had been
set up for them on the side table buffet.

"What happened?" she asked.

Scott looked up from the paper he'd been reading
intently—or appeared to be reading intently. "Nothing
He finished eating and left. He said if we needed anything to let him know, and that I could use his office if I
wanted. He has a secure telephone in there that I can use
to call Kate."

From his tense, pained expression, Natalie knew there
was more to it than that. "Scott . . ."

He looked up at her with a fierceness on his face that
made her heart break for him. "What?"

"You have to try to talk to him."

"I don't have to do anything, and it isn't your place to
interfere."

Ouch. Natalie flushed with a sharp pang of hurt.
Nothing like the harsh truth. If she'd ever had a place in
his life to interfere, it was clear she didn't now.

She was obviously putting too much store in him
climbing into her bed. Twice. For different kinds of comfort.

Seeing her reaction, Scott swore and grabbed her
hand across the table. "Shit. I didn't mean it like that
You have every right to interfere." The sting began to ebb
when she realized he'd been lashing out, and she'd just
stepped in the way. "I know what you want, but we aren't
going to be one big happy family, okay? Whether I talk
to him or not."

"If that's true, then what's stopping you from talking
to him?" She paused, looking at the tight, shuttered expression that couldn't quite hide the pain. "I just don't
want you to regret anything. You need closure, and he's
not going to be around long for you to get it."

He held her gaze just long enough for her to know that

her words had penetrated. Whether he agreed, she didn't know as he changed the subject.

"There are other, more important things we need to talk about right now."

"Like what?"

"Like figuring out what the hell is going on and why someone wants you dead so badly. I want you to tell me everything again. Slowly, and from the beginning."

For the next hour, while she ate and savored a few cups of the delicious (even decaffeinated and without almond milk) coffee, Natalie did as he asked. Going over every inch of what had happened with the proverbial fine-toothed comb.

He asked her dozens of questions, particularly about the program she'd installed on the deputy secretary's computer, the password change, and the e-mail she'd sent to her boss afterward in an attempt to call off the mission.

"Too bad we don't have access to the deputy secretary's laptop." He paused thoughtfully. "Where did you send your e-mail to him from?"

She thought back. She'd been at home hanging out with Jennifer when Mick had called to tell her that thanks to her, her boyfriend was going to have a nice surprise waiting for him in Russia.

Natalie hadn't had any idea what he meant. But when he explained, she realized that not only had something gone wrong with her plan to sabotage the program on her boss's computer, but Scott and Team Nine were in the middle of it.

She'd been shocked and horrified. Jennifer had thought she was going to faint.

But it had taken Natalie only a few minutes to realize what she had to do. Even if it blew her cover, she had to try to get the mission called off. She'd sent the e-mail to her boss from her laptop immediately.

"What time was that?" Scott asked.

"I don't know. Evening. It was before dinner. Maybe five o'clock."

He nodded. "We were already on our way. When did you leave the text on my sat phone?"

She flushed, thinking he might be mad at her for that. She wasn't supposed to contact him on that phone. "I knew it was a risk to text you like that—which is why I didn't do it right away—but when I didn't hear back from my boss and no one showed up to arrest me, I tried calling him but wasn't able to get ahold of him. I didn't know the timing of the mission, but I didn't want to risk that you didn't get the message in time. It was probably only a couple hours later."

"Good thing," Scott said. "We couldn't get a signal so I turned on my phone and your text was waiting for me."

She nodded. "I should have realized that Mick would be monitoring my computer and e-mail. He told me later when he called to tell me you'd been killed, that he intercepted the message to my boss before it reached him."

"Where is your laptop now? It will help if we can prove that you sent that message."

She sighed. "I have no idea. It was in my apartment when I left after Jennifer was killed. I didn't want to take it with me and draw suspicion."

Scott nodded. "That was the right thing to do, but it sucks for us. It's probably a dead end—especially if Mick had a chance to get to the apartment before the police. But I'll have Kate look into it."

Scott took the senator up on his offer, and after he and Natalie finished their coffee, he went into the office to make his call.

It was already hot outside so Natalie said she was

going to grab a book and go down by the pool. He told her he'd meet her when he was done. The prospect of seeing Natalie in a bathing suit made him eager to join her.

The call with Kate didn't take long. He filled her in on what he'd learned about the adoption agency and the two laptops.

Kate couldn't quite hide her skepticism when he told her about Natalie erasing the program and changing the Wi-Fi password.

"Maybe she thought she erased the program, and the deputy secretary just reentered his password."

It was hard to argue as he had pretty much said the same thing to Natalie. "I know, but she was pretty adamant."

Kate paused. "All right. Let me run it by someone and see what they think. Maybe there's some way to track it without the laptop."

"I thought you were the computer expert."

"I am, but this person is better."

He realized who she meant. "Brittany Blake's friend?"

The specialist—or, more accurately, hacker—named Mac had helped John Donovan find Brittany Blake when Mick abducted her.

"Yes," Kate said. "She helped me track down the camera feeds from around the bar where Travis was killed for Colt. It wasn't easy. They'd been erased. Or more accurately someone tried to erase them."

Scott swore. "The Russians have reach that widespread?"

"Looks like it."

Although she was trying to hide it, there was a weary edge to Kate's voice that told him something was wrong. He suspected the source. "Do you want to tell me what's going on with Colt?"

The long pause that followed told him he'd hit the nail on the head. "No. Do you want to fill me in on what is going on with Natalie?"

He responded with his own moment of dead air before saying, "No."

"Are you sure you can trust her, Scott? There's a lot at stake here."

Maybe he shouldn't, but he realized that he did. He wouldn't have gone to her yesterday otherwise. "Yes, I'm sure. Natalie has made some pretty bad mistakes, but she's telling the truth about her involvement in leaking the information about the mission. There is more going on here than there seems."

"What are you thinking?"

"I'm not sure yet. But there was something that Natalie said about Mick a while back that bothers me. How did he stay one step ahead of her all the time when she was the one who was supposed to be giving him information?"

"You think someone else on the inside is involved?"

"I don't know. But I only talked to Mick for a few minutes, and it was long enough to know that the guy was a smug asshole but not a leader. And why did they keep Natalie around for so long?"

"What do you mean?"

"She never gave them anything useful, and yet they kept her around."

"Maybe they needed someone around to take the fall."

"Maybe."

Kate paused. "Are you sure this isn't wishful thinking on your part, Scott? Are you sure you aren't looking for something that isn't there?"

He wasn't sure of anything. Was he so desperate to hold on to her that he was trying to see something bigger?

He hoped not because he was waging his career on it. But Travis's murder and the fact that Scott's men were still being hunted told him that there was more to this than they were seeing.

He hung up the call with Kate and decided to clear his head with a run before joining Natalie down by the pool. He'd been out of commission for almost a week, and the lack of exercise was getting to him.

Maybe he'd hit the weights, too. He was sure this place would have a gym.

It did, and an hour later—after a forty-minute hill run on the treadmill and a few sets of weights—he was feeling considerably better. From a body standpoint, at least. His head, however, was still in second-guessing mode.

Scott had always prided himself on his clear judgment, on his ability to make the right call, and on his confidence in his decisions. Uncertainty was new for him, and realizing that his emotional involvement with Natalie was the source made him uneasy.

She was clearly a blind spot. How could he be sure he was doing his duty to the job and his men when his feelings for her were affecting his decisions?

He couldn't. Which left him in this no-man's-land of impaired judgment, being unsure of himself, and not knowing how to proceed, which pretty much sucked.

None of which put him in the best frame of mind when his sperm donor cornered him in the gym as he was leaving.

Scott stopped suddenly. He thought about walking around him, but the old guy looked so frail Scott was scared he'd touch him and accidentally knock him over.

"I'm glad to see you found the gym. It hasn't been getting much use lately."

It wasn't hard to guess why. The former senator was barely strong enough to stand let alone lift a barbell.

Scott clenched his jaw, refusing to let himself feel sorry for him. Lots of people had cancer. People far less deserving than a man who'd cheated on his wife and foisted a bastard off on another man.

But did the guy have to look so pathetic? Scott was

already hot from the workout, but he felt his temperature rising even hotter with the reflexive anger that seemed to rush through him whenever they were in the same room.

He never should have let Kate talk him into this. He'd known that it would be a disaster.

But he couldn't deny that they were probably safer here than just about anyplace else. "Fort Knox" was putting it mildly. Greythorn had started his career in the CIA and continued his intelligence work in the Senate Intelligence Committee as chairman. He'd made a lot of enemies along the way with his hard-line, pro-military positions and had been the focus of a number of threats from extremist groups that had obviously been taken seriously. His security system was extensive; no one was getting within a couple of miles of the estate without someone knowing.

Not that inside was any less monitored. Scott had noticed the security cameras following him to the gym. He knew this was no accidental meeting. "Yeah, I was just leaving to meet Natalie at the pool for a swim."

"I'm sure you do a lot of that."

Scott didn't crack a smile at the SEAL reference. "If you'll excuse me."

He started to brush by, but the senator's words stopped him in his tracks again.

"Is she pregnant?"

Scott turned toward him very slowly, his hands clenched tightly at his side. "What?"

If the old guy had more blood in his body, he probably would have flushed. Instead his sickly colored skin turned faintly less pallid. "I couldn't help notice that Natalie didn't have wine last night and Dalton mentioned that she'd asked for decaf this morning. When I was down at the pool earlier, I noticed a little . . . I thought . . ." He stopped uncomfortably. "It probably isn't my place to say anything, but I just want to make sure she has everything she needs."

"Damned right it isn't your place to say anything."

It wasn't any of his business. Scott fought the blast of temper that was threatening to take hold. This wasn't about Natalie's comfort—or that wasn't all of it anyway. The old man was practically salivating at the idea of a baby to carry on his foul bloodline.

The bloodline Scott didn't want.

Thomas Greythorn the fucking third wasn't getting anywhere near Scott's progeny. When he thought of how happy his *real* father would have been—the father he would give anything to have back, even if he were on death's door—it made him even angrier.

Scott came right up to his "father" and looked him square in the face. "Stay away from Natalie. I don't want you anywhere near her. We wouldn't be here if there was anywhere else I could have gone. I needed a safe place to hide out for a few days. I didn't come here to get to know you or be some big happy family, so if that doesn't work for you just say the word and we'll go. I had a father, and I sure as hell don't need one who cheated on his wife and tricked someone else into raising his bastard."

The senator showed the first glimpse of his former hard-assed reputation. "Sit down, Scott. Now."

Scott was so shocked by the steely tone, he snapped back. "What?"

"I said sit down. I can't stand for long periods of time, and you are going to listen to what I have to say whether you like it or not." His mouth was pulled so tight, white lines had appeared around his lips. The expression wasn't one that was unfamiliar to Scott; it was like looking in a damned mirror. "When I'm done you can decide whether you want to leave."

The senator sat on one of the weight benches and Scott sat opposite him on one of the machines.

"I regret a lot of things," the senator said, "but tricking another man into raising my son isn't one of them. Your father knew you were my biological child."

He might as well have smacked Scott across the forehead with a two-by-four. The effect was the same. Scott had been leveled. His head was ringing with shock and disbelief.

The senator read his reaction. "Yes, he knew you weren't his. He knew about the affair. Although 'affair' is probably putting too strong a word on it. Your mother and I were two old friends who were having problems in their marriages and had a drunken lapse one night that could have destroyed a lot of lives. It was stupid, selfish, and unforgivable, but I cannot regret it. How can I when you were the result?"

Scott was glad he was sitting. He felt as if the rug had literally been pulled out from beneath his feet, leaving him with nothing to stand on. Words stuck in his throat. "What happened?"

"The usual dumb excuses. A party without our spouses. Too much drinking and reminiscing. Me feeling ignored by my wife whose focus was on our new daughter. Your mom vulnerable from the difficulties she and your father had been having in conceiving a child— something they both wanted very much."

Jesus. Scott didn't know what to say. "I didn't realize."

"Of course you didn't," the senator said sternly. "You weren't supposed to. You were a child."

"When did my father learn the truth?"

"As soon as your mom realized she was pregnant she went right to him—before she told me, as a matter of fact. By that time I'd gotten my head out of my ass and realized how much I loved my wife and what an arrogant, selfish fool I'd been."

"Did your wife know?" Kate had seemed to think she hadn't.

He shook his head. The stern facade softened in shame. "I never told her. Maybe I should have, but I was too scared she would never forgive me or be able to look at me the same way again. And there was Katherine to consider. But your dad forgave your mom for her moment of stupidity. He did more than forgive. He considered it a gift."

Scott was incredulous. "What? For cheating on him?"

"No, maybe not for that. But for you. He'd just found out that he couldn't have a child. Not knowing how to tell your mom was one of the reasons they'd been fighting."

Scott couldn't believe it. "So he knew? This whole time he knew?"

The senator nodded. "But he never wanted you to. He made your mom and me promise never to tell you. It was a promise I came to regret. At the time, I'm ashamed to admit that I was worried about my wife and the election I was about to run. I didn't think about all that I would be giving up."

"But you kept your word?"

"Reluctantly. I felt I owed it to him. And I would have gone on keeping it if Kate hadn't come to me with what you both had found out. I'd kept up with you. Followed your progress. I wasn't surprised that you'd gone into the service. It's in your blood. I was the first in the family not to go into the military. My father was an air force pilot in Korea, and my grandfather was an admiral in the Pacific during the Second World War."

Shit. Scott didn't know what to say. Kate had never said anything. Although he supposed he'd never asked. He'd made it clear the subject was off-limits.

But it was what else he'd learned that was harder to process. He was both overcome and humbled by what he'd just heard. His father had known and loved him anyway. He hadn't been deceived.

The senator stood, obviously intending to leave him with his thoughts. "You were Stephen Taylor's son from day one. I'm not trying to change that. But I'd like to get to know the man he raised in the little time I have left."

Scott watched him go, feeling as if the world—his world—had just shifted all over again.

Twenty

Natalie felt the shadow fall over her and opened her eyes. She blinked. Scott loomed over her, his body—his big, half-naked body—blocking most of the sunlight.

For all that he was a SEAL and spent a good part of his life in the water, she'd actually never seen him in a bathing suit before—in this case, board shorts that hung nice and low on his hips, emphasizing the washboard stomach and eight-pack abs. The print was green camo with some kind of flag on the tag. Jamaica maybe?

"You carry board shorts with you on all your missions?" she asked with a laziness she wasn't really feeling anymore. Her pulse was racing a little too fast for that.

He smiled and scooted her feet over to sit down on the end of her lounge chair. "Never know when surf will be up. Gotta be prepared." He lifted a brow, taking in her white shorts and T-shirt. "I was hoping you'd tossed in a nice teeny-weeny bikini."

"Sorry. Even if I could squeeze into one right now, a bathing suit didn't make your two-minute packing cut."

He frowned, letting his gaze roam over her again. There was something hot and possessive about it that made her think he wouldn't mind a little squeezing into in certain places. Namely the chest area where he couldn't seem to take his eyes off her tight scoop-neck T-shirt.

"You look incredible. You are barely showing."

Her hand went self-consciously to the slight round bump on her stomach. The one problem with the T-shirt was that it fit snugly against her stomach, too.

His gaze followed and Natalie felt her cheeks flush. When he lifted his eyes to hers, the look that passed between them made her chest squeeze with the kind of happiness she never thought would be hers.

They were going to have a baby together and sharing that with him filled her with a new kind of joy. A special kind. Her secret wasn't just hers anymore. Knowing Scott would be there for the baby was such a relief; for the first time she actually felt truly happy about her pregnancy.

"The senator guessed," Scott said.

"He did?"

"He noticed you weren't drinking wine last night and only decaf this morning."

She crossed her arms and glared at him a little. "And not any barely there bumps?"

Scott grinned. "He might have mentioned something."

She socked him playfully, doing more damage to her knuckles than the rock-hard muscle of his arm.

But then all of the sudden, she realized what he was saying. "You talked to him?"

He nodded. "You were right."

"I was?"

He stood and dragged her to her feet. "I'll tell you all about it if you swim with me."

"But I don't have a . . ."

She didn't get to finish. He picked her up and tossed her into the water fully clothed. When she came up sputtering—and cursing—he had already dived in and swum half the length of the pool underwater.

She didn't bother trying to catch him. She knew when she was out of her league. Instead she swam over to the entry stairs and sat in the water, which actually felt refreshing, waiting for him to come up for air.

He had to come up sometime, right?

As her watch was now a doorstop, she'd guess it was a good two minutes—and four lengths of the twenty-five-meter pool—before he did.

He stopped and stood a good ten feet away from her at the bottom edge of the stairs, breathing heavily. The water was only about three feet deep there, which gave her plenty of wet chest and abs to view. But it was a big, Cheshire cat grin that was getting to her right now. He was obviously proud of himself.

"You're buying me a new watch," she said, holding up her wrist. It hadn't been expensive, but the one he'd be buying her would be. "And I've suddenly taken a fancy to little gold crowns on my watches."

He laughed at the reference to a Rolex. "Whatever it costs me it was worth it. The expression on your face was priceless."

"What if I hadn't known how to swim?"

"You would have learned fast or realized you could stand—it's only five feet there. And we'd be having mandatory lessons before anyone found out. Christ, that would be embarrassing."

He might have shivered.

"Lucky for you then that I was pollywog champ in the seven-to-eight-year division at my local swim club." Indoor swim club—it was Minnesota after all—but she left that out.

"Pollywog?"

"It's a tadpole."

"I know what it is. I was just impressed."

She harrumphed. "You should be."

He inched closer, eyeing her carefully. "You still mad?"

She gave him a long look, trying not to be distracted by how sexy he looked and failing miserably. "I don't get mad, I get even." She gave him a smile of pure evil. "When you least expect it . . . expect it."

"Now you're just turning me on," he said in a husky voice continuing his walk-wade toward her.

She shook her head and laughed. "You're weird."

"And you're hot. Especially in that white T-shirt."

She looked down and seeing everything—*everything*—screeched and jumped out of the pool. She ran over to the lounge chair to get her towel to wrap it around her.

He was laughing as he came up next to her and grabbed another towel to dry off.

"You're horrible," she said. "How could you just let me sit there practically naked? What if someone had come up?"

"They would have been jealous as hell," he said matter-of-factly. "Then I would have had to kill them for looking."

She rolled her eyes. "Don't be such a Neanderthal."

He pulled her into his arms. "My eyes only, sweetheart." He leaned down. "And unless you want to put that pool house to use, we should probably head back to the room."

She didn't need to ask why. She could feel exactly what he had in mind pounding hard against her stomach.

Maybe the wet T-shirt thing wasn't bad after all.

I t was a long time before Natalie came up for air. Scott barely got the bedroom door shut before he was sliding those big, strong hands of his under her wet T-shirt and lifting it off.

Her shorts came next.

Then he just stood there and looked at her standing in her see-through lace bra and underwear for a while. She might have been self-conscious, but she could see from the board shorts that he liked what he saw. Liked it a lot.

He reached out with the back of his finger to caress a nipple that was hard not just from the cold.

"You are so fucking hot," he said in a soft, husky voice. "I'm going to send a thank-you note to whatever company made that underwear."

She flushed, more with pleasure than with embarrassment. She might dress modestly most of the time, but she did like her sexy underwear.

The bra had gotten a little tight, but if the look on Scott's face was any indication—or the fact that his gaze was pretty much pinned to her chest—he didn't seem to mind the spillover factor.

"It's just Target," she said. "But I'm glad you approve."

"Approve." He added a second hand to his admiration, rubbing both tips with his thumbs while cupping her breasts with his hands. "I'm in fucking teenage heaven. You look like you just stepped out of a magazine."

She didn't need to guess what kind of magazine he meant. His hungry expression said it all. "Hmm. I'll take that as a compliment."

"Definitely a compliment," he said, his voice even huskier, as he bent over and took one of the tips he'd been playing with in his hands into his mouth—lace and all.

She moaned as the warmth enfolded her. As he sucked and nipped. As his hand dipped between her legs under the other tiny piece of lace.

She was already wet when his finger found her. The smooth, deft stroking nearly brought her to her knees.

Which gave her an idea.

She reached out and started to do a little playing of

her own. Molding her hand around the hard column through the damp fabric of his shorts.

When she circled him and tugged, he lifted his head from her breast and started to push her back on the bed.

She stopped him. "Not so fast. I'm going to add to a few of those teenage fantasies of yours."

He didn't need to ask what she had in mind. She'd already dropped to her knees and was loosening the ties of his shorts, which wasn't easy with the wet laces.

The side benefit was the delicious torture of making him wait and anticipate. It was easy to tell how much he was anticipating from the groans, the increasing pressure of the fingers running through her hair and holding her head, and by the size of the erection that finally bobbed free.

He was big and hard; he looked like a polished slab of red marble. She used her thumb to spread the tiny drop at the tip around the plump head. "Naughty boy," she said, bringing her mouth closer. She loved how tight his stomach muscles got as her mouth neared. "You are supposed to wait for me."

She looked up. His expression was every bit as tight as his stomach muscles as he gazed down at her with something resembling torture on his face. The fingers in her hair clenched a little harder. She knew how badly he wanted to pull her mouth toward him.

But Lieutenant Commander Scott Taylor was too controlled—and too much of a gentleman—to exert any kind of force. It was one of the things she loved most about him. Sex for him was about giving. And she knew he would give every bit and then some more than he received.

It made her warm and tingly just thinking about what he'd do to her for teasing him like this.

But right now was all about him. She ended his torture and took that big, beautiful erection into her mouth.

It wasn't easy.

Her lips stretched around the fat head, sucking a little the way he liked as she drew him deeper and deeper into her mouth. As her tongue circled and her teeth lightly raked. As she milked him with her lips and hand. Sucking, stroking, moving her mouth up and down with long deep pulls. Slow at first, and then faster as he started to lose control. As his ass clenched, as his body stiffened, as she heard him groan with pleasure and tell her how good it felt. How much she was turning him on. How he was going to come.

She loved it when he talked to her like that. When the polished, always-put-together officer got a little raunchy. But he didn't need to say anything. She knew his body too well. She could feel the clenching, the stiffening, the pulsing of the long vein as the pressure became too much. As he thrust deep into her mouth and cried out his release.

That he was still standing when the last drop had ebbed was an impressive feat. But it wasn't long before he had her back on the bed, her lacy underwear gone, her legs wrapped over his shoulders, and his head between her legs. He brought her to the slow, delicious heights of pleasure.

Twice.

But he still wasn't done with her. As she discovered when he moved over her, lifted her legs around his hips, and started to push inside.

She lifted her gaze to his, her heart warming at the tender look on his face. "Pretty impressive for a thirty-three-year-old man past his prime, LC. That's quite a twenty-minute turnaround."

He just shook his head as if he felt sorry for her. "You should know better than to toss down a gauntlet like that to a SEAL."

She quirked a single brow. "What, do all SEALs have fragile male egos?"

He answered with a hard push that made her gasp and left him fully seated inside her. He let her feel him like that for a moment—filling her completely—before responding. "No, we are all born competitors. And you, sweetheart, just gave me a challenge." He smiled wickedly. "I'll show you past my prime."

And he did. Very thoroughly, and very exhaustingly.

By the end, when he finally let her come, she was the one begging for quarter.

Scott couldn't remember the last time he took a nap in the afternoon. But after making Natalie regret her "past your prime" comment, he collapsed alongside her, feeling every one of those thirty-three years.

He fell asleep with her still half under him. But by time he woke, they'd switched positions and she had her head propped up on her chin, watching him.

"Twice in two days that I get to watch you sleep," she said with a smile. "That must be some kind of record."

He stretched a little, letting his hand slide over her bare bottom. Hey, he was a guy. He'd cop a feel whenever he could.

He patted her lightly on the ass and smiled. "I guess you just put me to sleep."

Her eyes narrowed. "Now who is issuing challenges?"

He laughed and tucked her under his arm. "Not me. I know better. You'll kill me." Realizing the duvet was still at the bottom of the bed where they'd kicked it, he asked, "You cold?"

She looked at him incredulously. "You're kidding, right? Lying next to you is like being wrapped in an electric blanket. It's practically a fire hazard!"

He laughed and grinned. "Lying next to you makes me hot." His eyes scanned her body and all the teasing left his voice. "You're so incredible. I don't know how I got so lucky."

Her expression grew serious and kind of sad. "I'd hardly call it lucky, Scott. Your connection with me hasn't exactly made your life easy—and it's only going to get worse. It would have been a lot better for you if I'd never bumped into you in that bar."

He pushed back a little to look at her, but she was drawing circles on his chest with the kind of intensity that made him think she was avoiding his gaze.

He took her chin and forced her gaze to his. "How can you say that?"

"Easy. All I've brought is deception and destruction into your life."

"Did you forget about this?" His hand found the soft curve of her stomach. "We're having a baby, Nat. And I think that's pretty incredible. Not to mention that if it weren't for you I probably wouldn't be here, and I also wouldn't have found out the truth about my own father."

She frowned. "What do you mean?"

He'd meant to fill her in on his conversation with the senator earlier, but he'd been distracted by that T-shirt. "I talked to the senator. He told me that my dad knew the whole time that I wasn't his biologically. He knew and loved me anyway."

She smiled so broadly it lit up her whole face; the warmth was contagious. "That's wonderful, Scott. I'm so happy for you. I know how much it bothered you to think he'd been deceived. What happened?"

He filled her in on what the senator had told him.

"You are lucky to have not one but two fathers who loved you," she said. "But I'm not surprised. You are eminently lovable."

So was she, and maybe it was time he told her so. "We were both lucky," he said.

Her brows drew together with confusion.

"You had two sets of parents who loved you, too. But I'm not surprised, either. You are eminently lovable yourself."

She sucked in her breath with surprise, her eyes raking his face as she took in his meaning as if searching to see whether he was in earnest.

He was. "I love you, Natalie."

"You do?"

She looked so incredulous he had to smile along with the nod. "I should have told you a long time ago, but I wasn't sure you felt the same way, and I was too much of a coward. But I'd finally worked up the courage to tell you when I got back."

"Is that what you said you wanted to talk to me about?"

"Mostly." He paused. "I'd also planned to ask you to marry me. I carried the ring around with me for weeks. I even had it with me on the mission."

He wasn't sure whether the tears that filled her eyes were happiness or sadness. Maybe both. "I'm so sorry."

"Why are you apologizing?"

"Because what I did ruined everything."

It hadn't. But he'd tell her that when they were out of this, and he had the ring back in his pocket again. "You didn't ruin anything, but we're going to need to figure out a way to prove that, okay?"

She looked up at him, her eyes full of so much trust it made his heart squeeze. When she nodded, he knew there wasn't anything he wouldn't do to keep that promise.

Twenty-one

Kate had just hung up the phone with Mac, Brittany Blake's friend whose skill with cyberespionage and subversion of cybersecurity could best anyone she knew in the CIA's elite hacking team—including herself—when the doorbell rang.

She glanced at the security system monitor and stiffened, seeing Colt standing there. Her heart started to race. It was anxiousness about a possible confrontation, she told herself. It didn't have anything to do with him or the fact that she couldn't get the other night out of her head.

He'd been so sweet. So tender. So caring. So unlike the emotionally closed-off man she'd fallen in love with.

Until she'd brought out the adoption papers.

Her heart squeezed. It was silly to still feel disappointed; she should know better. She should know better about a lot of things.

She was tempted to ignore it—to ignore him—but Colt would just find a way in. His impatient stance and the determined way he was looking into the camera left her no doubt. *Don't make me break the door down.*

She sighed, realizing she might as well get it over with. She was surprised that she'd put him off as long as she had. It had been cowardly to run, but she just couldn't face him the morning after . . .

After what? How exactly did one characterize the colossal fuck-up that had also been the single most incredible and tender sexual experience of her life? A one-night stand? Her lapse into the stupid and "how the hell could I let myself go there again?"

Whatever you called it, Kate had left the hotel at the crack of dawn and caught an earlier flight back to DC. Colt had left increasingly frustrated messages on her phone for her to call him back—that they needed to talk—but her only response had been the short, business-like e-mail to forward the camera footage from Alaska that Mac had dug up for Kate.

Kate walked from the kitchen into the foyer, going past the entry table that held the enormous bouquet of peonies. The pungent floral scent hit her senses with a burst of fragrance that was impossible to ignore, not unlike the man who'd sent them. She should have tossed them out when they'd arrived, but they were her favorite—as he knew—and she couldn't bring herself to throw away something so beautiful no matter who'd sent them.

She'd had no such tossing issues, however, with the note that had accompanied them. It had gone into the trash not long after she read it. She didn't want any more apologies. He was sorry. She got that. Maybe she could even forgive him. But ultimately it wasn't enough.

She wanted a child. She'd put that aside for him once—or tried to—but she wasn't going to do it again. And them talking about it wasn't going to change her mind.

She intended to tell him that, but as soon as she opened the door, he handed her a folder. "We have a problem."

From the grim look on his face and the fact that he wasn't reading her the riot act for not calling him back, he knew it was serious. She stepped back to let him in, while opening the folder and removing a few pieces of paper. He shut the door behind him and waited as she flipped through the printouts.

They were stills from some of the camera footage Mac had found showing from different angles the two hit men who'd killed Travis. One of the photos must have been from a street camera, two appeared to be from the bank that Kate knew was across the street from the bar—it was the camera they'd initially focused on—and the last one, which was the clearest, was at the gas station near where they'd parked.

Kate had seen them already. "What's the problem?" she asked. "These are good. We should have a better chance of identifying them. I'm running them through—"

"Don't bother," Colt said. "These guys won't be in any databases—they don't exist. But I know this guy." He pointed to the mean-looking one with the MMA fighter nose and elaborate tattoo on his neck. "The ink fooled me initially, but that's what it was supposed to do. The tattoos are fake. He's one of ours."

Kate was floored. "By 'ours' you mean . . . ?"

Colt nodded. "He works in the same group that I do. We've crossed paths once or twice."

Oh my God. The ramifications were spinning in her head: one of the men who'd killed Travis was US black ops? "Are you sure? I thought operators in your group worked alone."

"We do most of the time. But occasionally I cross paths with other operatives at the—" He stopped, obviously not wanting to tell her too much. "I've seen this guy a couple of times. His head is usually shaved but the nose is hard to forget."

Even from the not exactly high-resolution photos, Kate could see that the operative's nose was kind of pushed to the side, as if someone had hit it and it had just

stayed in that position. She'd noticed it right away her
self. It was the kind of nose that belonged on a boxe
named Lefty.

"Jesus," she said, understanding Colt's grim expres
sion. This was a disaster. It changed everything. It mean
that unless Russia had a mole deep in US black ops—
which seemed a stretch—the order to kill Travis had
come from someone in the highest echelons of the *Amer
ican* government. The very highest. Kate didn't know
much about the off-the-books group Colt worked with
but she knew they reported directly to the president
Which meant that only President Cartwright and he
closest advisors would know about or have access to op
eratives like Colt.

"Maybe Scott was right." She'd spoken her thought
aloud and Colt looked at her questioningly. She filled
him in on her last conversation with her brother. "
thought he was reaching, but what if Natalie wasn't the
source of the leak? What if she really did erase the pro
gram on the deputy secretary's laptop before he went into
that meeting?"

Colt finished her thought. "Then someone else in the
room was responsible for passing on the information
about Retiarius's mission to Mick." He cursed. "Who
was in that meeting?"

"I imagine the usual suspects," Kate said. "Aside from
the president, the vice president, secretary of state, defense
secretary, and chairman of the Joint Chiefs of Staff would
likely be involved in a high-level meeting like this about a
covert operation. We know the deputy secretary of defense
was there and I'm assuming due to Team Nine's involve
ment the head of JSOC"—Joint Special Operations
Command—"and WARCOM"—Naval Special Warfare
Command—"I'll call Scott. Natalie might know."

A few minutes later, they had confirmation of the at
tendees and one stuck out in the worst way. In a way tha

Kate had never considered, but which she couldn't ignore. Her godfather, General Thomas Murray, vice chairman of the Joint Chiefs of Staff, had been at the meeting. The man whom they'd confided in and who'd been helping them. The man who'd led them to suspect Natalie in the first place by bringing forward the information about her Russian adoption. The man whose previous position in special operations and intelligence would make him knowledgeable about operators like Colt. And, most important, the man whose son's plane had been shot down by the Russians and who had been trying to get the president to retaliate ever since.

She felt guilty even considering the possibility, but it was there.

She'd put Scott on speakerphone so she didn't need to fill in Colt. When she looked at him, she knew he was thinking the same thing—without any of the guilt. He and her godfather had never gotten along.

"Did you tell the general about Scott being in Vermont?" Colt asked.

She nodded. "He asked for an update."

Her stomach twisted at the additional "coincidence." If the general was involved, it explained how the hit team had found Natalie so quickly.

Still, no matter how much it lined up, Kate didn't want to believe her godfather—a man she'd known and cared about her whole life—could be involved with anything that could have led to the deaths of American servicemen. He was one of the most vocal voices in support of veterans and those who had given the ultimate sacrifice—especially after his son TJ had been killed in the line of duty.

Scott said what they were all thinking. "We need to see if we can get ahold of those laptops. If we can clear Natalie, it would help prove someone else was involved. I'm going to call Baylor to see if his guys can track down

Natalie's laptop at her parents' house in Minnesota. If the police got to her apartment before Mick, it would have been packed up with her other things."

"I'll go after the deputy secretary's," Colt said.

"I should do it," Scott said.

"No offense, Ace," Colt said, "but this kind of thing is more up my alley."

"Committing felonies?" Scott said, clearly ready to argue. "This is my problem. I'm not going to have you going to prison for me."

"Which is exactly why you need to leave this to me," Colt said. "So that no one goes to prison. And it isn't just your problem. Those were my guys, too, and I want to see whoever was responsible pay."

Kate wanted to argue with both of them. She didn't want either one of them getting caught. But she knew Colt was right. "Let us handle this, Scott. You have enough to worry about with keeping Natalie away from the people who are after her."

"She's as safe as she can be," Scott said. "You were right about this place being like Fort Knox." He paused. "You were right about a lot of things."

Kate took that to mean he'd talked to their father, which Scott confirmed. He told her he would fill her in on everything when he saw her. In other words, he didn't want to spill his guts—and the family dirt—with Colt listening in.

Kate couldn't hold back her happiness though that the first step, and the hardest, had been taken. She loved both her father and Scott, and being caught between them had been difficult for her.

By time they'd hung up, Scott had reluctantly agreed to let them handle the deputy secretary's laptop. But if anything went wrong, they were to let him know immediately.

Colt was watching her in a way that made her feel

self-conscious. She resisted the urge to fix her hair or look in the mirror on the wall above the flowers. Flowers that he'd, of course, noticed.

"You kept them."

She didn't want to talk about it so she ignored the half question. "We should figure out our plan for tonight."

"My plan. And the less you know the better." He gave her a hard look. "We'll hit pause on everything else for now, but we are going to talk about this when I get back." She didn't argue, knowing it wouldn't do any good. "I'll go in tonight after the deputy secretary and his wife have gone to bed. They don't have kids, right?"

She shook her head, feeling the reflexive stab in the chest at the mention of children. A stab she hid well from prying eyes; Colt always watched her carefully. But she'd grown adept at hiding her thoughts. "You aren't as good with tech as I am," she pointed out. "You might need me."

Colt was going to try to sneak in and out without taking the laptop, figuring there would be less pushback later if someone found out or they were wrong.

"It's not up for discussion, Kate. I work better alone, and having you with me would make my job harder." His eyes met hers. "I'd be too worried about something happening to you." No matter how hard she fought it, her heart still panged at that. She could hear the truth in his words. "You can give me one of those remote programs to access the computer. I should be able to manage that."

She looked at the big, imposing man who'd been her husband for almost five years and still haunted her. She'd never get used to him putting himself in danger; she'd hated when he left on ops and still did. "What if something goes wrong?"

He gave her a half smile. "Nothing is going to go wrong. Compared to some of the places I've had to get into and out of without being seen, this will be a piece of cake."

———

Famous last words, Kate thought hours later as she waited for the text from Colt to say that he'd found the laptop and inserted the thumb drive that she'd given him

She stared at the clock on her computer. Three thirteen a.m. Colt had left well over an hour ago. Richard Waters, the deputy secretary of defense, lived in Arlington, which was less than ten miles from Kate's townhouse in McLean. At this time of night, it should have taken him fifteen minutes to get there. Max.

He'd have to bypass the security—Colt had actually laughed when she asked whether he needed help with that—break inside, and then find the office where they hoped Waters would be likely to leave his computer. It shouldn't have taken this long. Had something gone wrong?

A quick social media check of Mrs. Waters's Facebook page hadn't turned up any animal pictures so hopefully there wasn't a dog to worry about. But what if the deputy secretary hadn't brought the laptop back tonight? Or worse, what if he'd gotten a new one?

Something must have happened. Every single thing that could go wrong ran through Kate's mind as she watched the slow flicker of time pass on the upper-right corner of her computer screen.

But in all the scenarios not once did she picture the squeal of a car taking the corner into her driveway too fast and then the hard screech of brakes as it came to a too-sudden stop.

She knew without looking out the window that it was Colt. Something *had* gone wrong! Oh God. The panicked hammer of her pulse skyrocketed as she raced downstairs and threw open the door.

Colt was already out of his rental car. Seeing him standing there gave her a welcome rush of relief.

But it didn't last long. He took a step toward the house and staggered.

"Colt!" she cried out, and ran toward him, realizing something was wrong with him. He almost looked drunk.

She caught him right as he collapsed. He was a big man, and his weight nearly brought them both to the ground.

"Shit!" he cursed, holding his side while trying to straighten. "Sorry."

Oh God, oh God, oh God. The helpless prayer kept running through her head. She tried to help him as best she could, but she struggled under his weight. Eventually she managed to get her shoulders positioned under him to take enough of his weight where they could walk together into the house.

They didn't make it to the living room couch. He collapsed right on the rug in the foyer, and she came down next to him.

"Colt, talk to me. Tell me what . . ." *Oh God*, she thought again when she saw the stain on his shirt. Her stomach dropped. "You're bleeding!"

Tears of fear and panic sprang to her eyes and jammed in her throat. Her heart seemed to be in there as well.

Colt gritted his teeth, clearly wanting to calm her down, but in too much pain to hide it. "Bastard shot me. He had a laptop alarm that went off as soon as I pulled the plug. I tried to leave through the window, but damn thing was jammed. By the time I got it open, he was coming through the door with a gun. He got off a lucky shot through my side as I was going out the window. Fuck," he said, clenching and rolling up against the pain.

Kate had never felt so helpless. He didn't look good. He was sweating and his skin was clammy and pale. She didn't know what to do. The blood was seeping through his fingers, forming a puddle on the rug. "I have to call an ambulance."

She started to stand but he grabbed her wrist to stop her. "And say what? That I was shot breaking into Deputy Secretary Waters's home trying to access his laptop? No. You can't. The bullet went straight through. Just get my blowout kit. It's in the car. I'll talk you through it."

Colt had been a corpsman, the navy's medic qualification, when he was a SEAL, but she'd never had any medical training. "Are you out of your mind?" she sobbed, yelling and crying at the same time. "I'm not going to let you die!"

He tried to smile, but it came out as more of a grimace. "I'm not going to die, sweetheart. You won't get rid of me that easily. But if I knew all it would take was getting shot to have you admit you cared for me again, would have done it a long time ago."

"Don't joke about this, Colt," she said hollowly. "Don't. I can't take it right now. I'm scared."

"I know you are, Kiki. I'm sorry. But no ambulance, okay?"

She looked at him helplessly. Wordlessly. The use of the old nickname (she'd played a "what's my stripper name?" game once) only made her sob harder.

"Promise me," he repeated more insistently.

She met his gaze and nodded, but she wasn't sure whether she would be able to keep that promise. She wouldn't let him die. She couldn't. She wasn't done with him yet.

She would never be done with him.

But she did as he asked and ran out to the car to retrieve his gear bag—and blowout kit—from the trunk. After getting him a bottle of vodka, which he took a couple of long drinks from to dull the pain, he was able to talk her through the harrowing procedure of disinfecting the wounds—the smaller entry wound in his back and the larger exit wound in his front—and patching him up with the military clotting gauze that had a hemostatic gent on it to help stop bleeding, something he called Israeli bandages, and more gauze to wrap around him tightly to hold everything in place.

He talked her through the whole thing, helping to calm her when her hands were shaking.

But as soon as she'd finished, he was out cold. She curled up next to him with her head on his chest, too scared and tired to move. She needed to hear the beat of his heart against her ear.

She couldn't stop the shivering. She'd never been so scared in her life. She couldn't delude herself anymore. Colt mattered just as much to her as he ever had; that was never going to change.

But something would have to.

"Why is a baby so important to you?"

His question came back to her. But suddenly it clicked, and she realized what he was really asking: "Why am I not enough?" It wasn't about the baby; maybe it never had been. Colt thought she wanted a child because loving him wasn't enough. Somehow she had to make him see that he was.

If she had a chance.

Her heart squeezed with fear, trepidation, and uncertainty. After everything that had happened, how could she let him back in her life?

She lifted her head long enough to look at the gray features of the man who still looked half-dead and knew that was a stupid question. It was too late. He was already in. He'd never really left.

I can't lose him.

She had to do something.

She got up to get her phone. She'd promised not to call the ambulance, but she hadn't promised not to call Scott. He would know what to do to keep her stubborn, mean, tender, cruel, sweet, wounded, and scarred ex-husband alive.

Twenty-two

After the dead end with Baylor at Natalie's parents' house, Scott had been up much of the night waiting for news from Kate.

Initially they'd been optimistic that Baylor's guys—or more accurately, Baylor's future father-in-law's private contractors (i.e., private army)—would find something. Natalie's parents thought they remembered seeing a laptop when they'd packed up her things from the apartment. But the guys had been through the boxes a dozen times and hadn't been able to find anything.

Scott had thought it was strange that Mick wouldn't have sanitized the apartment, but he'd had them check again and the laptop was there on the inventory list of the things in her apartment. Tellingly, however, when Natalie asked them about her journals—journals Scott didn't even know she kept—they weren't on the list.

Someone had sanitized the apartment before the police arrived.

Mick had been an asshole, but he hadn't been a stupid one. Would he have been sloppy enough to leave the laptop or was there another reason?

When Scott voiced his suspicion to Natalie, she didn't disagree. "It wouldn't surprise me at all if Mick left some kind of insurance plan to cover his ass. You think it could be on my laptop?"

"Maybe. I can't think of another reason why he would leave it there. It could be just the proof we are looking for if it leads to the person he was working for."

To say that the news that someone on the inside had been involved—and that that person could be General Thomas Murray—had thrown Scott for a loop was putting it mildly. It seemed inconceivable that someone of the general's stature and reputation could be involved. A hard-liner against Russia suddenly passing on top-secret information to them? What kind of warped thinking could justify that?

But if the leak wasn't Natalie—and Scott was convinced it wasn't—someone else in that room had passed on information. And any way they looked at it, the general made the most sense, especially given how fast Scott had been tracked to Natalie.

"I wish I knew what happened to it," Natalie said.

Scott did, too. The nine men who'd died deserved an answer, and he owed it to them to find out.

After dinner with the senator, a much less awkward one than the night before, Scott and Natalie returned to the suite and tried to get some sleep. But Scott had been restless—even for him—and slipped out of Natalie's bedroom and returned to his own so as not to disturb her.

The deputy secretary's computer would help exonerate Natalie and help prove that someone else in the room had passed on the information to Mick. But if they were going to accuse the general, they would need more than that. They would need proof.

Proof could be on Natalie's laptop, but what if they couldn't find it?

Scott had been going over every angle and he had a

hunch that there might be another connection. He sent an
e-mail to Donovan, asking him to have Brittany forward
it to her friend Mac to have her look into it. He would
have gone through Kate, but he didn't want to bother her
while she and Colt were working on the deputy secretary's computer.

He hoped to hell nothing went wrong.

He had just slipped back into bed beside Natalie to try
to get some sleep when the phone he'd put down on the
bedside table buzzed.

Natalie had been sleeping with Scott long enough to
be used to his restlessness. It wasn't the first time
he'd gotten up multiple times in the night to deal with
something that was on his mind. How he survived on so
little sleep, she had no idea, but he seemed to not need
more than four or five hours a night.

Natalie would be comatose during the day if she did
that.

But when the phone rang at a little after five in the
morning, Scott wasn't the only one wide-awake. If it was
Kate reporting back with news of Deputy Secretary Waters's computer, Natalie wanted to hear it. She followed
Scott into his room, where he'd gone presumably not to
wake her, and sat on the edge of the bed while he stood
in front of the window to take the call.

He glanced toward her and she could tell from his
expression, even in the predawn shadowed light, that
whatever the person on the other side of the conversation
was saying, it wasn't good.

Her impression was solidified when he swore. "Fuck.
Tell me exactly what happened." He was quiet for a couple of minutes as the person on the other end filled him
in. "Did Waters see him?"

Uh-oh. Definitely not good.

Scott's expression grew even more intense. "Where did the bullet hit?" Natalie gasped and Scott's gaze met hers. She could see how worried he was. "You are sure it went through?" He waited. "Okay, good. He was lucky, as usual." Another pause. "No, no, you did the right thing. I'll be there as soon as I can." From his tone, Natalie could tell he was obviously trying to calm her down. "Colt would know if it hit something vital, Kate. If he needed a hospital, he would have told you. But I'll be there soon to make sure. He's not going to die, okay? You have to calm down."

He had to repeat himself a few more times, but eventually Kate must have relaxed enough for Scott to hang up. Natalie already had an inkling of what had happened, but it was still a shock to hear that Deputy Secretary Waters had shot Colt.

"I didn't even think that Rich *liked* guns," Natalie said, referring to her mild-mannered former boss. "Let alone knew how to use one. He never said a word." She looked up at Scott apologetically. "I'm sorry. I had no idea."

"You have nothing to apologize for. A home weapon is something Colt would have anticipated. But you can't control for everything. Apparently the laptop had an alarm and the humidity this summer made the office window difficult to open." He took a few steps toward her. "I hate to leave you here like this, but Kate is freaking out, and I told her I would come check on Colt. I guess she's not as over him as she wanted me to think."

"Of course you have to go," Natalie said. "I'll be fine here."

Scott looked at her, clearly uneasy with the idea and seemingly debating with himself. "I'd rather take you with me, but I don't know what we are dealing with yet, and it's safer for you here with all the senator's security."

"Scott, go!" she said with not a little exasperation. "It's Fort Knox, remember? I'll be fine."

He held her gaze for a moment longer and nodded. After retrieving his bag, he pulled out some clothes and went into the bathroom to throw some water on his face, brush his teeth, and use the toilet.

Even though she'd seen it before, she was amazed at how quickly and precisely he operated. In a matter of minutes, he was dressed and geared up, ready to go. She knew he was already in mission mode, but he surprised her by pulling her into his arms for a long and very thorough kiss before he left the room.

She held on a little long—not wanting to let him go.

"I'll be back as soon as I can," he said. "You can hang out by the pool but try to stay close to the house otherwise."

"Take as long as you need. I'm not going anywhere. I'm sure the senator will take good care of me."

"He'd better," Scott said fiercely. "I'm trusting him with what matters most to me in the world."

And then, before the swell of happiness could rise from her heart to her eyes, he was gone.

The room seemed so empty with him gone and the sudden sense of loss told her how quickly she'd come to depend on his steady presence again.

Natalie sat on the window seat, her knees tucked in her arms, and watched the sun come up, praying that this would all be over soon without anyone else getting hurt.

Scott hated leaving Natalie behind, but if he had to go, he knew he could do a lot worse than the senator's fortress. The place was wired up tight and monitored by a well-trained security force.

Nothing was going to happen to her. At least that was what he kept telling himself as he made the forty-five-mile drive to Kate's town house in McLean. His sister must have been watching for him. The door was thrown open before he pulled up.

One look at her tear-ravaged face, and he was glad he'd come right away. He held her in his arms in the doorway as she sobbed out her fear on his T-shirt. "Where is he?" Scott asked. "Let me see him."

Kate turned and pointed behind her. "He collapsed right after he got inside. I couldn't move him."

Scott closed the door behind him a little too hard, and Colt's body tensed at the sound. His eyes opened and shut a few times before settling on open.

A gruff curse was the first thing Scott's former chief managed to say before his hand went to his injured side with another, "Fuck, that hurts. What the hell—" He stopped, as if suddenly remembering. But just in case he didn't, Kate had come down on her knees beside him. "You were shot!" she yelled accusingly, and then repeating in soft tremble, "Shot."

She looked like she might fall apart all over again, but before Scott had put a steadying hand on her, Colt had done it. "It's okay, sweetheart. I told you I'd be okay. You did a great job."

Scott had never heard Colt talk to anyone in that tone of voice. Even when they were married, he'd never talked to Kate so gently. Scott looked back and forth between the exes, wondering what the hell was going on. He'd obviously missed something, and it was equally obvious that he doubted he'd like what it was. There was an intimacy between them that he hadn't seen in a long time.

"You could have died!" she accused again through tear-filled eyes.

Colt shook his head. "It would have had to be a few inches over to have any chance of that."

She looked like she could have shot him herself. "Is that supposed to make me feel better?"

Colt tried to smile, but from the tightness of his expression he was obviously in a lot of pain, and it came out as more of a wince. "I thought you'd appreciate the truth."

"God, are all men idiots or just you?"

Colt looked at him, but Scott had no idea how he was supposed to answer that.

"Let me see how close he is to death's door," Scott said. He gave Kate a few instructions of stuff to get him, mostly to keep her out of the way while he pulled back the bandages and talked to Colt, but she'd actually done a pretty good job. Better than she'd done on his shoulder. Apparently, Colt was a better instructor than YouTube. "The exit wound may need to be stitched or stapled closed. Do you want me to do it?"

"Fuck no," Colt said. "I saw your handiwork when you had to patch up Ruiz once. I'll do it myself if I have to. Just help me up."

Scott half carried him into the living room. He laid down a blanket that was hanging over the back of the sofa, although he doubted under the circumstances that Kate would mind if the upholstery got blood on it. Colt sat rather than lay down. Scott assumed the clenched jaw was him fighting against the urge to throw up.

"How do you feel?" Scott asked.

Colt shot him a glare that said *asshole*. Scott just grinned.

"I've felt better."

"I think you were off a couple inches in your estimation," Scott said, watching the door in case Kate appeared. "That bullet barely missed a few vital organs. From the amount of blood on the rug out there, you're lucky you didn't bleed out."

Kate's sudden appearance cut off Colt's reply, which from his expression Scott was going to assume would have been angry.

"What did you say?" Kate asked.

"Nothing," Colt said before Scott could reply. "Except that I'm going to owe you a new rug. I hope to hell it wasn't one of the ones from your grandmother's house. As I recall those were worth more than I make in a year."

Apparently Scott wasn't the only one who got shit for his bank account.

Kate ignored the bait; she wouldn't be so easily distracted. "Shouldn't you be lying down? You look pale."

"I'll be fine," Colt said. "I just need a few minutes."

"You sure about that?" Scott interjected, deciding to help Colt out. "I think you might be getting a little too old for the job if you let a fifty-year-old politician get the jump on you."

"Fuck you, Ace. And anytime you want to go head-to-head in a workout just let me know. The bastard got off a lucky shot, but I still finished the mission."

Scott looked at Kate. But she was surprised, too.

"You did?" she said. "I thought you weren't able to put in the thumb drive."

"I wasn't. I had to improvise. Since the jig was up, I went ahead and grabbed the laptop. It should be in the car on the front seat."

"I got the bag from the trunk," she said by way of explanation. "I didn't even look in the front."

Scott went to retrieve the laptop and handed it to Kate when he came back in. She sat down in one of the living room chairs and started to tap. She was instantly in the zone, and Scott and Colt went over the specifics of what happened while she worked.

Scott was glad to hear that Waters hadn't gotten a good look at Colt.

"I was out the window on the roof when he fired," Colt said.

Scott didn't need to ask whether Waters had seen him get away. Colt was too good for that. He would have

parked somewhere where no one could see him and out
of the eyes of any security cameras.

After a few more minutes, Kate looked up. "I don't
see anything. I want to run it through a program I have,
and I'll let Mac have a look at it, too, but if Natalie down-
loaded a spyware program on here, I'm not seeing it."

"Are you sure?" Scott asked.

"Not yet. Give me a couple hours." She disappeared
into her office with the laptop. Colt gave up the tough act
and lay down on the couch and asked for painkillers. Scott
passed the time by getting him some toast and chicken
broth that Colt could eat to take with the pills he had in his
bag so that he could sew up the wound. Colt was one of
the toughest sons of bitches Scott knew and watching him
stitch up his own bullet hole was nothing all that new.

Apparently Kate's former fiancé hadn't moved out all
of his belongings as Scott was able to locate a fresh
T-shirt to replace the ruined one he'd helped pull off
Colt. He thought Colt might object, but other than the
fact that his mouth was a tight line, he accepted the
loaner without a word.

Having exhausted his nursing skills, Scott let Colt rest
while he went into the kitchen to get some food and fill
the other guys in on what was going on. The calls took a
while, and it was after nine by the time he went back into
the living room to check on Colt, who had just woken and
was looking a little less close to death's door.

Kate came in a few minutes later. She jellied a little at
the T-shirt but collected herself quickly. "I found a few
bits of code that may have been left over from what Natalie originally loaded, but it's nothing that would have
bypassed security or enabled anyone to listen in on a
conversation in the Tank. Mick must have learned the
information from someone else who wanted to make it
look as if Natalie had done it." She paused and looked at
Scott. "I think Natalie was telling the truth."

Scott didn't need confirmation, but it was nice to get. He decided to check in on Natalie and fill her in. He'd left her his burner phone in case she needed to reach him, and he'd taken one of the backups he had in his bag.

He wasn't alarmed right away when she didn't answer, figuring she might be sleeping after the long night. But it seemed strange that she would have turned off the phone.

He felt the first prickle of unease and decided to call the senator. Dalton answered and it took a minute for Greythorn to get to the phone. He started to apologize for the delay, but Scott cut him off. "I just called Natalie, and she didn't pick up."

"She came down a little while ago and said she wasn't feeling well," the senator explained. "I assumed it was morning sickness. She said she was going back upstairs to rest and asked not to be disturbed. Do you want me to check on her?"

Scott hesitated. He didn't want to wake her if she wasn't feeling well, but she'd never complained of illness before. Of course, he didn't know squat about pregnancy. "That's all right." It was nothing that couldn't wait. "Just have her call me when she wakes up."

When the phone rang a couple of hours later, Scott assumed it was Natalie. He was wrong.

"She's gone," the senator said. He started apologizing, saying that he knew Scott had trusted him and he didn't know how it happened, but Scott cut him off.

His heart seemed to have stopped beating. "What do you mean, 'gone'?"

"The night nurse went to leave and her car was missing. The guards said she'd driven out a while ago. But it wasn't her; it was Natalie. I'm so sorry. I didn't think. . . ."

Scott didn't say anything. He couldn't. It felt as if he'd taken another knife in the gut. It was the same feeling he'd had when he'd discovered Natalie was a spy.

He couldn't believe it. She'd left him. She'd waited until he was gone, and she'd run at the first opportunity

He'd thought she trusted him.

Blind spot.

He was a damned fool.

Twenty-three

Natalie told herself she was doing the right thing. She didn't have any choice.

She'd been waiting to hear from Scott so she was surprised to see her parents' phone number when the phone buzzed at a little after seven. Her parents woke up early, but they usually waited to call until after nine.

It wasn't her parents. The voice on the other end of the line told her he was in her parents' kitchen right now, and he was going to kill her family if she didn't bring him the laptop.

She'd told him she didn't have it and didn't know where it was—which was the truth. He'd replied that she better find it soon. She had twenty-four hours to get it to her parents' house.

"But that isn't enough time," she protested, looking at the clock. Getting on a plane would be too risky. "It's at least an eighteen-hour drive from here."

"Then you'd better hurry up and find it. And if I were you, I'd figure out a way to ditch that SEAL boyfriend of yours and keep him out of this. I wouldn't want him to

get in the way. Do anything, call anyone and they'll al
be dead."

And just in case she didn't believe him, he handed t(
the phone to her sister.

"I'm making pancakes with the policeman."

Natalie's blood went cold at the sound of her sister':
voice; he wasn't bluffing. The past few days fell away a:
if a dream. Without Scott around to fill her head witl
unrealistic fantasies, the truth of her situation came bacl
to her full force.

She'd made a mess of her life, but she wasn't going t(
make a mess of his. And she wasn't going to let anyon(
die for her mistakes. Not her parents, not her sister, an(
sure as hell not Scott.

She'd figure a way out of this or suffer the conse
quences on her own.

It ripped her heart out to leave him like this, but it wa
better than the alternative. They'd never had a chance
The reluctant Russian spy and the officer in America':
most elite SEAL team were hardly a match made i
heaven. This had only hastened the inevitable.

She knew that Scott would see her leaving as a be
trayal, but that was better than him getting even mor(
wrapped up in her problems or, worse, having him ge
killed in the cross fire.

He'd put himself out enough for her already. She neve
should have involved him in any of this.

But apparently he'd been right about the laptop bein;
important. Not that that was going to help her save he
family when she had no idea where it was.

Of the many problems facing her, however, the mos
pressing had been how to get out of Fort Knox, as Scot
had called it. She wasn't going to be able to sneak pas
all the security, and she needed a car.

She'd have to borrow one.

While getting ready, she came up with a plan. The first part was to make sure no one noticed her gone right away. She wanted as much of a head start as possible.

She hated to deceive the senator when he'd done so much for them, but she didn't have a choice. After coming up with the excuse that she wasn't feeling well and pretending to retire to her room for a nap, she instead made her way to the back entrance where the considerable staff came and went out of the main house.

In the cubbies where the women left their purses, she riffled through a few until she found a set of keys with an alarm fob. She also grabbed a pair of sunglasses.

After pulling her hair up and securing it in a bun, she put on the glasses and walked outside to where the cars were parked. She'd chosen her plain black pants and white blouse again, which happened to be similar to what most of the female staff wore.

She hit the disarm on the key fob and headed to the car that beeped. Her heart stopped when one of the security guards popped his head around the corner to check on the noise, but she ducked into the car with a backhand wave and started it up quickly.

It must have worked because the guard was nowhere to be seen in her rearview mirror as she backed out.

Ready with a lie that she was a new maid if the guard at the gate stopped her, she was relieved when the gate opened automatically as she approached and he just waved her through. Even with the big sunglasses, she made sure to block her face as much as she could when she waved back.

Her heart was still thumping a short while later when she got onto the highway toward the famous Route 66, which would eventually take her to the interstate heading northwest. She'd gotten past the first hurdle, but she had much higher ones ahead.

She had about twelve hundred miles to figure out wha
she was going to do. How was she going to bluff her wa
through saving her family's lives without the computer
Could she delay them? Convince them to give her tim
to find it? Offer to exchange their lives for hers?

The ring of the phone beside her made her jump. Sh
picked it up, saw the unfamiliar number, and put it down
It wasn't the guy calling from her parents' house, and i
it was Scott trying to reach her . . .

She couldn't talk to him.

She ignored the first call.

And the second and third. But when she pulled the ca
over for gas a short while later, she looked down at th
phone again. Natalie's heart sank to her stomach as sh
read the short text on the screen:

Trust me.

Those two words were like a stab to the heart all ove
again. She knew how much trust he'd put in her to hel
her, and it felt as if she were betraying him all over agai
by running. But how could she let him ruin his life an
destroy his career for her? How could she put his life i
danger for hers?

She forced her gaze away from the phone that tempte
Your mess. You have to do this alone.

But then something happened to remind her that sh
wasn't alone. She felt a flutter in her stomach. And jus
in case she didn't realize what it was the first time, th
baby moved again.

Their baby.

Natalie could go this alone and try to save her fam
ily, but without the laptop they would probably all di
Or she could do what she should have done the fir
time. She could put her faith and trust in the man sh
loved.

She did have a choice.

Natalie looked at the phone and took a deep breath.

Scott didn't have to explain what had happened. Kate and Colt could figure it out from his expression.

"She ran?" Kate asked.

Scott nodded grimly, anger and humiliation curdling in his gut. He couldn't believe he'd let Natalie convince him that he could trust her. That she wasn't lying to him again. Deceiving him. Fucking him for . . .

He couldn't even go there. And he'd bought it all, hook, line, and sinker.

He didn't want to think she'd been playing him again, but what else could he think? She'd run the first time that he'd left her alone.

He didn't know whether to put his fist through the wall or sit down on the couch and put his head in his hands. He was devastated enough to do both. Aside from the personal knife through the heart, he was keenly aware that she might have taken the answers for avenging his men with her.

But aware of his sister and his former chief watching him, Scott forced himself to calm down and think rationally. Or try to think rationally, which was damned hard when the woman he'd risked everything for had just left him.

He drew a deep breath and sat on the couch. The past week replayed in his head over and over. What had he missed? Where had he gone wrong?

She'd seemed so in earnest, so genuine. So terrified. He would have sworn she was telling the truth. Could his judgment really be that off?

He shook his head. He didn't think so. She *had* been telling the truth. He'd bet his life on it.

The fist that had been wrapped around his insides released a little. There had to be another explanation. But what could have made her leave like that?

"Where would she go?" Colt asked.

"I have no idea."

"Do you think she is still working with them?" Kate asked.

Scott didn't like what his sister was implying even if he'd just had a similar thought himself. Did Natalie know who was behind this and was she trying to protect them?

He thought back through what she'd told him over the past week. Looked at it from every angle and tried to put aside his personal feelings.

He knew what would make her leave.

"No," Scott said with sudden certainty. "Natalie was telling the truth. If she ran, it's because they got to her. They must have threatened her with something."

It wasn't hard to guess what. There was one thing that he knew would send her running. Her family.

But why hadn't she called him? The anger started to build again. He told her he would protect her and her family. He thought she trusted him. She should trust him, damn it. He'd put everything on the line for her. What more did he have to do?

"Maybe she's trying to protect you," Kate said.

That took him aback. "What are you talking about?"

Kate shrugged. "If I were her, I'd worry about you getting in trouble from helping me." Both Colt and Scott looked at her as if she were crazy. "What?" Kate said. "Are men the only ones capable of protecting the people they love?"

"Yes," Colt and Scott said at the same time.

She shook her head. "You are both cavemen. Women are perfectly capable of being stupidly overprotective, too."

Colt didn't seem to like that any better than Scott did, but wisely he didn't say anything.

Scott swore. It made a perverse kind of sense and sounded like something Natalie would do.

God damn it, hadn't she heard him when he said he

loved her? If she got herself killed to try to save him from losing his career, he'd never forgive himself. She was the most important thing in the world to him.

The unhesitating realization of that even shocked him a little. For as long as he could remember the job and his career had always come first. He'd never seen a wife and family in his future. Although he supposed he'd never seen himself falling in love with a Russian spy and going AWOL after having over half his platoon wiped out by a missile strike in Russia, either.

When the rug had been pulled out from him about his father, it had felt like he'd lost his family. But Natalie had given him that back.

He was probably still a little too much "my way or the highway," but she'd helped him see gray in situations where he'd previously only seen black-and-white. Right and wrong weren't always clear-cut. People made mistakes. He might not be all that tolerant in his professional life where mistakes got people killed, but that rigidity didn't need to extend to his personal life.

"What should I do?" he asked Kate.

"Keep calling and texting."

The suggestion worked. A few minutes after he texted Natalie to trust him, the phone rang.

Recognizing the number, his heart jumped. "Thank God," he said answering. "Are you okay?"

"I'm sorry," she said with a broken sob.

He was so glad to hear her voice he could have cried. He forced himself to be calm, not wanting to scare her off. "What happened, Nat? Where are you?"

When she told him—and what she planned to do—his heart stopped beating for a good minute. When he thought of what would have happened to her, and how close she'd come to walking into a situation where she likely wouldn't have come out alive, he had to fight to control his newly discovered temper. Instead of blurting,

What the fuck, Natalie? he managed a much less angry, "I'm glad you decided to trust me. We'll figure this out together, okay?"

"Okay," she said softly.

"I mean it, Natalie. Nothing is going to happen to them. Your family will be safe. You have my word."

He didn't care what he had to do; he would make sure of it.

"Okay," she repeated in a much stronger voice.

"Good. Now, where are you?" She told him, and he gave her directions to get to Kate's. "I'll be waiting. And Nat?"

"Yes?"

"I love you."

She paused, sounding relieved. "I love you, too."

As soon as they hung up, Scott was on the phone to Baylor. He didn't bother trying to control his anger when informing him that at least one of the men at Natalie's parents' house was dirty. "God damn it, Tex! I thought you said you could trust these guys?"

Baylor swore. "I'm sorry, LC. I don't know what to say. Marino"—Steve Marino was Baylor's fiancé's stepfather—"personally vouched for every one of them. I'll have him run the names and see what we can find."

Even though he suspected Marino's intelligence department was full of former operators and spooks and quite capable, Scott said, "Send them to Kate, too."

"Will do."

"And Tex, tell Marino to look for a connection to General Murray."

There was a dead pause on the other end of the line before the sharp curse, which told Scott that the senior chief understood the implications. "You've got to be shitting me."

"I'm afraid not," Scott said.

Baylor swore again and said he'd get back to him as soon as he could.

Scott spent the better part of the next two hours staring out the window and trying not to climb the walls.

"You're making me dizzy," Colt finally said from his position on the couch. He'd managed to get up and use the bathroom to clean up a little, and he looked at least a good few steps from death's door. "Why don't you just sit outside on the doorstep? It will be easier than going back and forth to the window."

Scott gave him colorful instructions on what he could do with that suggestion. "She should be here by now," he told him.

"Not if she doesn't want a speeding ticket. Especially considering how many times she probably had to slow down to answer your phone calls."

"I'm sure you'd be totally laid-back if you were in my position."

Colt might have smiled. It was always hard to tell with him. "No judging, man," he said, holding up his hand. "Just a friendly observation."

Colt had distracted him so when the doorbell rang, Scott jumped. He raced to the door and a moment later Natalie was in his arms.

Only then did he realize how amped up he'd been. His body seemed to calm instantly. The rapid heartbeat, the rush of blood, the on-edge nerves . . . all settled. Life was good again.

Christ, she'd scared him.

He didn't realize he'd said the last aloud until she looked up at him, her worried, big brown eyes as wide as saucers. "I'm sorry. I was terrified and didn't know what else to do. He is in their house, Scott. He was standing right next to my sister when he called."

He could hear the tears in her voice and pulled her in tight against his chest. Instead of shaking her as he wanted to for running, he stroked her hair and murmured soothing words until she calmed.

He would have kissed her, but Natalie had pulled back. "I'm sorry. You must be Kate." Apparently his sister had come up behind them. He could tell from Natalie's expression that she was uncomfortable and maybe a little anxious. "I . . . I've heard a lot about you."

Kate came forward, extending her hand. "And I've heard a lot about you." As that could be taken more than one way, Scott was glad when she added. "I'm very happy that you are here."

Natalie took Kate's extended hand and seemed to relax a little. Scott showed her into the living room to introduce her to Colt. But seeing him only made her upset again.

"I'm so sorry," she said to Colt. "I didn't have any idea that he had a gun."

"That makes two of us," Colt said wryly. "But in my line of work I should have expected it. Besides, you did me a favor."

Colt looked at Kate and something passed between them that Scott wasn't sure he liked. Not if it was going to mean his sister was hurt again.

"At ease, sailor," Colt said, guessing Scott's thoughts. "I fucked up my life once. I have no intention of doing it again."

Kate clearly didn't like the turn of conversation and brought it quickly back to the threat against Natalie's family. "I ran down the names that Dean passed on. There is one that sticks out."

Scott knew what that meant, and he could see from Kate's expression that she was finding it difficult to accept what the facts were pointing to.

"Someone connected to the general?" he asked.

Kate nodded. "One of the men employed by Marino served under my godfather when he was the head of the Army Intelligence Support Activity."

Aka "the Activity," which was a special ops intelligence unit.

At Natalie's confusion, Scott filled her in on what they suspected about General Murray. Her eyes got big really fast. "Are you serious? He has always been so kind to me—always going out of his way to say hello. And isn't there talk of him being on the ticket as vice president in the next election?"

Kate nodded. "That's the rumor. Which could explain some things." She didn't elucidate and turned back to Scott. "I talked to Dean, and Marino had come up with the same person. It's being taken care of right now."

Natalie looked back and forth between the siblings. She'd seen pictures of Kate so she knew they had similar coloring, but it was still strange to see those little nuances that a camera didn't capture. Like the way Kate's gaze leveled the same way as Scott's when she had something important to say.

"What do you mean, 'taken care of'?" Natalie asked anxiously. "Is something happening at my parents' house?"

Scott was saved from answering by the phone. It was Baylor. When he hung up, he had the news he wanted to tell her. "Your parents and sister are safe. They have the guy who called you."

Natalie was visibly relieved, although not completely relaxed. "How do you know he was working alone? What happens if I don't show up with the computer at the appointed time and someone else goes after my family?"

"Marino is on his way to their farm right now to make sure there aren't any more surprises. He is taking personal responsibility for this. And my senior chief is going with him. You can trust him, Nat. Baylor won't let anything happen to them."

———

Natalie wasn't convinced the threat to her family was over. Whoever was behind it was clearly in panic mode and trying to tie up any loose ends. She and her computer both qualified. If they could get to her family once, who was to say they couldn't get to them again?

She tried to talk Scott into going to Minnesota, but he wasn't having any of it. "I promise you will see them soon, but not until we have this thing locked down. We're close, Natalie. Just be a little more patient."

It wasn't until she'd talked to her parents and sister, however, that Natalie relaxed. They assured her they were fine and being well taken care of; her parents hadn't even realized there was a threat until it was over. Marino must have taken his private plane because he and Scott's senior chief, Dean Baylor, arrived while she was talking to her sister.

Natalie smiled, thinking how Lana had been going on about some new online computer game—

"Oh my God," Natalie said suddenly. Of course. It made perfect sense.

She was sitting in the living room with Colt watching a baseball game—Scott had gone into Kate's office with her to make a call—so he was the one who replied. "What?"

"I think I might know what happened to my laptop." Natalie fished around in her purse for Scott's burner and called her mom.

A few minutes later her mom called back. "You were right. It was under Lana's bed. What do you want me to do with it?"

"Give it to Dean and tell him not to let it out of his sight. I'm sure Scott will be in touch with him soon."

As soon as she hung up, Colt looked at her. "She found it?"

Kate's ex was a good-looking guy but kind of on the scary side. Except for the prime physical form component, he didn't look much like a SEAL. Although from what Scott said, Colt wasn't exactly a SEAL anymore and was working in some kind of black ops. Colt was the polar opposite of Scott's clean-cut officer appearance—which pretty much went for Kate as well. Scott's sister had that refined, elegant Grace Kelly look.

Natalie wouldn't have put Colt and Kate together but appearances weren't everything, and something about Colt obviously spoke to both Kate and Scott. Natalie knew how much Colt's friendship had meant to Scott and how his false accusations had stung. Colt had a lot to atone for.

Maybe she and Scott's former chief had that in common.

Natalie nodded. "My sister had it. I should have thought of it before. Lana is special needs and loves computers, but she's gotten into trouble before with games on the Internet so my parents are really careful. They have parental controls that prevent her from accessing certain sites and monitor her usage, which Lana hasn't been too happy about." Natalie smiled. "She's slow, but not unsavvy. She figured out ways around the controls so my parents had to take the computer out of her room. She must have seen my laptop in one of the boxes and taken it."

"She sounds like a teenager."

"Pretty much," Natalie agreed with a laugh. "I should tell Scott."

"Tell me what?" Scott said, coming back into the room with Kate.

Natalie filled him in on the laptop.

"That's great," he said. "I'll have Baylor bring it back and Kate can have a look at it."

Natalie was surprised by his tempered reaction. "I thought you'd be more excited," she said.

"I am," Scott assured her. "It will help prove that you tried to send a message when you found out what was going on."

"But?" Colt said, as it was clear there was one.

"But even if Mick didn't leave a trail on the laptop," Kate explained, "we have some new information that leaves little doubt that my godfather was behind the leak. We found the link."

Scott's suspicion had paid off. Brittany Blake's friend Mac had called when he and Kate were in her office.

"What link?" Natalie asked.

"Between the general and you and Mick."

She looked taken aback. "But I barely knew General Murray."

"He knew you," Scott explained. "He'd probably been watching you and the other kids brought to America in the program for some time, waiting in case you were ever activated. Remember when I mentioned the Illegals Program that was uncovered back in 2010?"

She nodded. "The one that was the basis of the TV program."

"That's right," Kate said. "Guess who was on the national security staff when that plot was uncovered?"

"Murray," Colt said flatly, not missing a beat.

Scott nodded. "The adoption program for the kids of Soviet 'traitors' was apparently connected to the Illegals Program. But as none of the kids had been activated at the time, its existence was pretty much kept under wraps and buried. Mac only uncovered a few references in the files because she knew what she was looking for."

"Jeez," Natalie said. "So I was under surveillance not only by the Russians but by the Americans, too?"

"We're not sure," Kate said. "Mac wasn't able to find out much more. The idea was that not all the kids would be turned or utilized. They'd wait and see how they grew up and be given opportunities when possible. The kids wouldn't be traditional sleepers or moles or Russian spies who are groomed in America; they would be typical Americans being forced to work as agents. They were a new brand of unaware asset, making them harder to track and uncover."

As Kate was obviously having difficulty accepting the general's involvement, Scott stepped in to continue. "My guess is that Murray kept knowledge of the program to himself and maybe a very few others. The theory being that if one of you were activated, he would have control. If you weren't, the whole program would have been forgotten about and lost in the archives. Mac said that when it was originally conceived the program was much bigger, but unlike the Illegals Program, it never really got going after the fall of the Soviet Union. It was just there lying in wait in case it was ever needed."

"I feel like a spare tire," Natalie said, taken aback by the whole capriciousness of it all. She'd been a widget in the machinations of two countries. "What about Mick?"

"I suspect Murray got to him early on and turned him," Scott said. "He was probably a double agent. My guess is that any information Mick gave the Russians, Murray knew about."

They all took a moment to process what that meant. It hadn't been a Russian plot. The bad guy had been on their side.

"It wouldn't have been hard to turn him," Natalie said, not hiding her bitterness. Scott alone knew why and instinctively put his arm around her. She might not need his comfort, but he was going to give it to her anyway. He loved how she settled in against him as if she belonged there. "Mick's allegiance was to himself. If the general gave him the right incentive, he would have sold his mother to the highest bidder."

"Sounds like a charming guy. I'm doubly glad John
Donovan had good aim," Kate said, referring to the shot
that had killed Mick and probably saved her life.

Colt's tight mouth suggested he might have something
to say on that subject, but probably wisely he refrained
from commenting.

"So what now?" Natalie said. "Is the link enough to
take to your commander to prove what happened to the
platoon?"

Scott and Colt exchanged a look. It was, but going to
Commander Mark Ryan or Captain Trevor Moore wasn't
how this was going to go down.

Twenty-four

Kate saw the look exchanged between Colt and Scott after Natalie asked her question and immediately knew what they were planning. She'd been married to Colt for long enough to know how he thought—how men like him thought. They weren't going to hand this off now without all the answers. SEALs didn't leave a mission unfinished; they would see this through to the end.

"No!" she said, glancing back and forth between them. "Whatever you are thinking, no!" She spun on her ex-husband, who looked a lot better than he had a few hours ago but was still pale from loss of blood. "You were just shot, for God's sake! You aren't going anywhere!"

Natalie had obviously been around Scott long enough to figure it out as well. "You can't be planning to confront him?"

Scott's jaw squared in a way that Kate was too familiar with. She knew when stubborn was setting in. He addressed Colt first. "Kate's right. You should stay here. Baylor will be here in a few hours with the computer anyway, and I will call Donovan for additional backup.

Spivak and Ruiz would want to be here but are too far
away for me to wait. I want to talk to the general before
midnight."

"Fuck you, Ace. There is no way I'm staying behind.
These were my guys, too. I'm good to go."

Colt was one of the toughest guys Kate had ever met.
He lived the BTF mantra—Big Tough Frogman. Kate
knew he'd be "good to go" if every bone in his body was
broken and he had ten bullets in him.

Scott had clearly expected the reaction—as had she.
Her brother shrugged, and then probably because he was
still angry at Colt and knew how much it would piss him
off added, "Just don't get in the way."

Colt's eyes narrowed, but he'd obviously realized he
was being baited. His reply was more sarcastic than angry. "I'll try not to let my hobbling around slow you
down, Ace."

Scott turned to Natalie, who was clearly agitated with
the direction the conversation was taking. "I promised
you that I would keep you and your family safe, and this
is the best way to do it. You have to trust me, Nat. I know
what I'm doing."

If Natalie's torn expression was anything, he was obviously asking a lot. Clearly she didn't like the idea of
him going into danger any more than Kate did. "But
what if you are walking into a trap?"

Scott shook his head. "He doesn't know we are on to
him. But even if he suspects, he'll want to hear what we
have to say, and we'll be ready." He smiled. "This isn'
our first rodeo."

"I'll go with you," Kate said.

The reaction from Colt and Scott was instantaneous
with differing levels of crudity in the "not a chance" response.

She waited a few minutes for the swearing and male
overprotectiveness to calm down before replying, "I

makes the most operational sense. I will call him and tell him we're on our way over and need his help. I'll say something about Natalie being in danger. That should get you in the door without any problems."

Scott gave Colt a look that Kate read easily enough: *you better do something about this.* Apparently her brother had decided that Colt had some kind of influence with her. Was it that obvious?

Ever the tactician, her ex-husband had apparently realized that anger and threats weren't going to get the job done so he decided to go with the "honey, let's be reasonable" approach.

The cajoling tone from him wasn't something she was used to, and it wasn't without effect. "That's a great idea, Kate. You should definitely call him and tell him we are coming and need his help. The direct approach will keep him off guard and sneaking into the ancestral pile to confront him wouldn't be easy with his security. But you don't need to be at Blairhaven in person to achieve the same thing. You aren't an operator and having you there will make our jobs more difficult." He paused to let that sink in. In other words, *your presence will compromise our safety.* "I know you care about him and this is difficult for you, but it will be harder on him to have you there, too."

Damn him. She could fight anger, but not reason. "But if he's guilty, he could be like a cornered animal."

She already suspected that the general was in panic mode and trying to cover his tracks.

"Which is even more reason for you not to go," Colt said evenly, looking into her eyes with an intensity she couldn't turn away from. "We're trained for things like this."

And you're not. He didn't need to say it.

"So the women need to stay back at the castle while the men go off to fight," she said, not without a little bitterness.

He gave her a grin that melted her heart and some of her anger. "In this case, yes. I'd have it that way all the time if I thought you'd agree."

"Not until you agree to the same," she said with a sugary smile.

Colt just laughed.

He might have won this time, but it wouldn't always be that way, and they both knew it.

Colt knew not to put too much hope in Kate's agreement, but it was hard not to think that it meant something. That maybe they were on the same page for the first time. That maybe they understood each other now. That maybe there was a place for thought and consideration in the volatile emotional Molotov cocktail of their relationship.

He'd been angry at her for running the morning after in the hotel, but he understood it. His reaction to the adoption papers had been reflexive and less than ideal, but she'd surprised him. He'd realized kids might be in the future, but he hadn't realized how immediate that future might be, and it had jellied him.

He'd needed time to get used to the idea.

But she'd been dodging him too long and getting shot last night had put everything in rather instant perspective. The clock was running and there was no telling when it would run out.

He'd planned to talk to her before he left, but it was Kate who cornered him as he was leaving the dining room where he, Taylor, Donovan, and the recently arrived-with-laptop-in-hand Baylor had gathered for a makeshift op brief.

This was Taylor's mission, but they all had opinions. He listened and decided on the straightforward course of action to present Murray with what they had and see what happened—in other words, light the fuse and wait for the explosion. It was what Colt would have done. Sometimes there wasn't time or room for subtlety.

He supposed that could apply to him and Kate as well.

"I want to talk to you," she said.

She turned and headed upstairs, which he took to mean that he was supposed to follow her.

She went into the master bedroom that she used to share with her former fiancé. Just the reminder made Colt's blood heat and teeth grit. He didn't like being in here. It made him feel as if he were crawling the damned walls.

"What is it?" he asked. "Did you find something on the laptop?"

"Proof that Natalie did try to send a message, but not who intercepted it. Brittany called Mac and she is on her way over. I hope she can find something while you are gone."

Even if she didn't, the general wasn't going to know that.

"All right." Colt made the mistake of looking at the nice king-sized bed and his mouth fell in a hard line. "What else?"

Kate's composure slipped. She looked as if she was about to burst into tears. "What else? What do you mean, 'what else?'! What's wrong with you? I thought you wanted to talk but you're acting like you can't wait to get away from me."

Colt swore. Crossing the distance between them, he pulled her into his arms. "It's not you; it's this damned room. I don't like thinking about you and Lord Percy in here; it's driving me nuts."

He could feel her body relax against him. A small smile crept all the way up to her eyes, which started to twinkle. "Oh. I didn't even think about it." She tilted her head to study him in a way that made him want to shift his feet and pull on the neck of his shirt. "I thought you weren't going to get jealous anymore."

"I'm not. This is me being evolved." He looked down at her upturned face and the air seemed to squeeze right out of his lungs. He let the emotion rise up inside him rather than push it back down the way he used to. But, shit, it still scared him. She held his heart in her palm, and it made him feel vulnerable in a way he never had before. "I thought I was doing a good job."

She laughed, and her eyes crinkled at the edges the way they used to a long *long* time ago. "You are. I just didn't know what to look for. Next time you have the look of someone with Icy Hot in your jock, I'll know what it means."

He grimaced at the thought. That had happened to him once when he was the FNG (fucking new guy on the team) and the memory still made him wince with re-membered pain.

"Next time?"

He knew he sounded too hopeful, but he couldn't hold it back.

She nodded. "I was coming to tell you that you better come back with just one bullet hole in you because that's all I can deal with right now." She looked up at him, the emotion he'd never thought to see again shimmering in her eyes. "I was so scared, Colt. I thought I'd lost you again."

Colt pulled her in tight, closing his eyes and letting his cheek rest on the top of her head. The feeling of over-whelming relief swept over him. She was going to give him another chance. He couldn't believe it.

But he probably shouldn't mention how much the one bullet hole hurt, and that he had no intention of adding to his pain tonight.

Finally he pushed her back to look in her eyes again. "You're sure?"

She nodded and drew away. She walked over to her purse, which was on the desk, and pulled out the same file she'd showed him before. He didn't stiffen when she handed it to him.

He gave her a wry look, assuming she wanted him to agree to the adoption. "Your terms, huh?"

She gave him a funny look and then shook her head. "No. Just look."

He opened the file and his heart jackknifed. Pretty much everything inside him flipped upside down and the blood drained out of him. He looked at her, not knowing what to say. The adoption papers that she'd filled out had been torn in half.

"I love you, Colt," she said. "And if you love me that's all I need to be happy. That's enough. You're enough." She smiled. "More than enough."

He was floored. It felt like everything inside of him had hit the ground at his feet. He knew how much having a child meant to her, and the fact that she was willing to give it up for him . . . what the hell did you say to that? "Humbled" didn't cover it by half. "Shame" covered the rest. What kind of selfish asshole made the woman he loved think she had to choose between him and a baby?

He forgot that he didn't even want to look at the bed and instead sat down on it. His legs weren't feeling very strong. "Jesus, Kate. I don't know what to say. I do love you. But I never meant for you to . . . you don't need to do this. I know how much a child means to you."

She sat down next to him. "But you mean more, and I want you to know that. Although if we are going to give this another shot, you have to agree to see a counselor with me and at least talk about the possibility of adopting in the future. But if it's really something that you don't want, I can accept that."

Colt had already figured out what he wanted, and at that moment he was certain of it. If she loved him enough to do something like this, he would love her enough to put aside some of his own fears.

The possibility of how to do that had come to him in the hospital. It might take a little work, but he would see that it happened.

She mistook his silence for resistance. "Colt? Is that okay?"

He swept her into his arms and kissed her before there could be any confusion. It was better than okay. It was fucking perfect. Kate had made him the happiest man in the world, and he would do everything in his power to see that she never regretted it.

It turned out the bed didn't bother him as much as he thought. He put it to good use for the next fifteen minutes— which was as much time as he had—and couldn't give a damn who'd slept there before. He was going to be the only one to sleep there from now on.

Twenty-five

Scott knew he wouldn't be able to relax and focus on the mission until he and Natalie came to a little understanding. Mostly about how she wasn't going to ever scare the shit out of him like that again.

After the op brief broke up, he found her in the kitchen with Kate. He told his sister that he needed to talk to Natalie in her guest room.

But talking wasn't really on the agenda. Never one to mince words—or actions—he made his point in about fifteen minutes, which was about as much time as it took to shut the door, tug down the necessary clothes, lift her up against the door, and sink in deep and hard over and over until they both felt a lot better.

It was maybe a little primitive, but it was damned effective.

"I'm sorry," she whispered in his ear when he'd collapsed against her afterward.

He didn't say anything for a moment. Scott wasn't just coming back down to earth and trying to find his breath again; he was also taking a minute to savor the connection and the soft, silky warmth of her body.

God, how he loved this woman. He intended to spend the rest of his life showing her how much.

He didn't know how this was going to all go down, but he knew they were going to be together, and he'd do everything in his power to see that she wasn't held responsible for any of this.

Finally he pulled back enough to run his thumb down the curve of her cheek. "No more Lone Ranger, Nat. We're a team. You and me, okay?"

"Roger that, sir," she said with a mock salute. She gave him a wry smile. "I got the message loud and clear."

"Good, because I don't have enough time for a repeat."

She laughed and pushed him back so they could redo their clothes, and a few minutes later he was kissing her good-bye.

It was her turn to look worried. "I don't like this," she said.

"I know." He gave her a kiss on the head before letting her go. "But I need to do this. I need to finish it."

He owed it to the nine of his men who'd been killed to find out the truth and bring who was responsible to justice.

She understood and nodded. "I love you."

"Good. Now hold that thought until I get back."

Scott said good-bye to Kate and left. He was the last one in the car. Baylor was driving the big black Navigator that he'd arrived in. Scott assumed it was armored and had been lent by Marino.

Donovan, who'd taken shotgun, turned and looked over the backseat as he slid in behind Scott. "Feel better, LC? You were looking a little edgy there for a while."

Scott usually tried to minimize the swearing, but that rule tended to fall by the wayside with Donovan. "Fuck you, Dynomite."

The big blond operator who looked like he rode in on

a surfboard just grinned. Apparently they all guessed what he'd been up to, and they were all snickering.

"Good to know you're human, Ace," Baylor said with a snide grin. "We were worried."

Scott had given him hell when Baylor had put the book aside a few times when he had met his soon-to-be wife, Annie. He supposed he had a little bit of crow to eat.

Scott turned to Colt, who was seated next to him, and noticed he was also looking relaxed and smiling. *Smiling!* His eyes narrowed. "Anything I should know about, Smitty?"

It was the first time Scott had called him by his call sign in about three years. "Smitty" came from Smith, which came from Smith & Wesson. Colt had once told him that as an infant he'd been abandoned at a police station by his birth mother. The officer who'd found him had taken to calling him Colt because he'd kept reaching for his gun. It had stuck. The director of the orphanage had come up with Wesson to go with it. Whether it was true or not, Scott didn't know. It was hard to tell with Colt.

Colt noticed the use and his smile only deepened. "You'll be the first to know, little brother."

Which Scott guessed pretty much said it all. "She forgave you already?"

Colt nodded. "Looks like. And before you think about giving me a lecture, I don't need it. I'm not going to fuck it up again, and I'll hand you the gun to shoot me if I ever hurt her again."

Scott wasn't convinced. He smiled as he thought of a way to see just whether things had changed. "Did she tell you who she's working with?"

To Scott's surprise, Colt's mouth fell in a hard white line. "Dan Gordon."

Colt knew about that and he hadn't flown off the handle? Maybe he had changed. Scott had to admit that if the former Delta operator turned CIA agent was working with Natalie, he wouldn't be looking so calm about it.

Donovan let out a slow whistle. "Gordog? I've heard about him. No one is off-limits with that guy. Supposedly he had to leave Delta because he banged his CO's wife."

Thus the nickname. Gordon dog. Gordog.

Scott took a little perverse pleasure as Colt's expression darkened with Donovan throwing oil on the fire that had to be simmering. But to Colt's credit, he didn't lose his temper. "Kate is a professional. She can handle herself."

"It's not her I'd worry about," Donovan said under his breath.

Colt was clearly not going to let it get to him, but Scott would wager big money that Colt and Dan Gordon would be having a little heart-to-heart the first chance Colt got.

Scott didn't blame him. He'd do the same thing.

They didn't talk much on the ride to the general's. The four of them had been on plenty of ops together before Colt had left the team, and they usually would have continued giving each other shit to pass the time and keep the mood light, but this one was different, and they all knew it.

There was nothing light about it.

For three months, the surviving members of Team Nine had been waiting to find out who was responsible for the deaths of their platoon brothers, and it was beginning to look like they might get their answer.

Although it was not the answer that any of them wanted.

When they arrived at the Murray estate, Scott and Colt were immediately led into the general's office by his butler. Apparently Kate's call had done the job, and the general was expecting them.

Baylor and Donovan were on overwatch and had stayed with the car to ensure that Colt and Scott weren't surprised if the general attempted to mobilize his security. But other than a man at the gate, and the guy they'd seen roaming the grounds, there didn't seem to be a surprise army lying in wait.

Both Scott and Colt had been assessing the situation every step of the way to the office, and nothing appeared out of the ordinary. But if the general was responsible for killing Travis and sending the hit team after Natalie, they knew they had to be prepared for anything.

Scott had met General Murray once or twice at meetings in the Pentagon, but the four-star general had aged in the past few months. He looked more like seventy than late fifties.

Scott's mouth tightened. Guilt? He didn't know, but if Murray was responsible for setting in motion the ambush that had taken the lives of his teammates, he hoped it ate him alive.

The general took his seat behind his desk and motioned for Scott and Colt to take the two chairs opposite him. He pulled out a decanter of dark liquid—from the smell, whiskey—and poured a glass. He offered one to them, but they declined. From the ease with which the general downed the first glass, Scott got the feeling it was a frequent occurrence. He had the bloated, flushed look of someone who'd been drinking for a long time.

"Katherine said you had something about Natalie? She's in danger?"

"You tell us," Colt snapped.

Scott shot him a look for going off script. This was his part.

"We know the truth," Scott said.

The general's glassy eyes met his without reaction. "What truth?"

"We know that you were one of the handful of people who knew about Russia's secret adoption sleeper program. That you buried it and then decided to turn Mick into a double agent when he was activated. We know that you knew Natalie was a part of it and that you used her, tried to have her killed twice, and threatened to kill her family if she didn't bring you the computer that proves your guilt. We know that you hired the men who killed Travis Hart in Alaska." He paused and dropped the bomb. "And we know that you were the traitor who gave Mick the information to pass on to the Russians about my platoon's recon mission to the gulag." In spite of his vow to stay cool, Scott's fury rose as he was talking. He found himself leaning over the desk at the man who sat there like he was telling him the weather. "A mission that saw eight of my men, eight American servicemen, killed by two missiles."

Scott didn't know how he expected the general to react. Maybe with denial? With shame? With violence? It sure as hell wasn't with anger and defiance. "It is a soldier's duty to sacrifice. Those men lost their lives for the good of their country. Just like my son. He paid the ultimate price as well. How dare you come in here and accuse me of being a traitor! I gave my son for this country; I would never betray it."

Scott was taken aback by the venom. The general's cool facade had shattered; he looked like a rabid dog, practically frothing at the mouth.

"TJ's 'sacrifice' wasn't because he was betrayed by someone on his own side," Colt said. "You set those guys up. You let a team of American SEALs walk into a fucking ambush. That isn't sacrifice; that is murder."

The general turned his bright-eyed gaze on Colt. "You better than anyone should know that national security isn't always pretty. What do you tell yourself to let yourself go to sleep every night?" He gave him a look of disgust, as if he shouldn't have to explain it to someone like Colt. "This is war, and sometimes people have to die for the greater good." He turned to Scott. "You're an officer. You know that sometimes officers have to send men in when they know they are going to be killed. Think of all those boys who got out of the first boats at Normandy. They laid down their lives so that others could follow. Do you think those officers didn't know exactly what was going to happen? That they were sending their men to the slaughter? *That* is war. *That* is the reality. Like it or not."

"But this isn't war," Scott said. "It's a personal vendetta. And Eisenhower didn't call the Germans to tell them we were coming."

The general flushed angrily. "Don't fool yourself. There is a war going on right now, acknowledged or not. And Russia is winning it. Ivanov acts with impunity and NATO and its allies are too damned scared to start World War III to do anything about it. He knows it and gets away with murder."

He'd gotten away with the general's son's murder. Scott knew that's what this was about. General Murray had always been a vocal opponent of Ivanov and a hawk when it came to war with Russia, but TJ's plane being shot down must have sent him off the deep end. He'd lost perspective and convinced himself that the ends justified any means. But it was the logic to his argument that made him so scary; even now, he clearly believed he'd done the right thing.

The general's hand tightened around his empty glass. His face was red with anger and he looked ready to explode. "If the president had a sack, none of this would have been necessary. But she left me no choice."

"So this was about starting a war?" Scott said.

"It was about forcing the president to get off her fucking ass and retaliate. She might be able to ignore one pilot, but an entire platoon of SEALs? That would have demanded retaliation."

"Except that it didn't," Colt said. "Because Ivanov

outplayed you." He laughed and the general looked in
danger of having a heart attack, his face had turned so
red. "The Russian president didn't want to be forced to
declare war as he'd promised if there was another American 'incursion' so he sent his missiles but claimed they
were a test. Ivanov didn't take credit for wiping out a
platoon of SEALs and our side had no interest in letting
it be known that we had a team illegally in Russia, so it
was a stalemate."

"That's why you involved Brittany Blake," Scott said,
continuing the narrative. "You went to the press secretly
not to get justice for our guys like you said but to get it
out in the public so someone would be forced to do something."

The general didn't say anything, but it was clear he
was furious. Ivanov had made a fool of him, and they all
knew it. "That will change," Murray said. "When I'm in
the White House those boys will have their justice."

He was out of his mind. "Those boys you sent to their
slaughter?"

"Those boys who were doing their duty," the general
said defiantly.

"And what about Travis?" Colt asked. "Was he doing
his duty, too?"

The general's defiance cracked a little. "That was unfortunate."

"No," Scott said. "That was you trying to cover your
tracks when you found out not all of us were killed." He
paused. "And what about Natalie? Was she doing her
duty, too? Or was she just another pawn in your game?"

"Natalie was a spy," the general said coldly. "I was
shocked when I realized the Russians had activated a few
of the children from the program after so many years.
But it was around the time things with Russia started to
heat up, and I assume they were looking at all the

angles—and all their assets. I just ensured that she didn't do any real damage."

"You mean you took advantage of the situation," Scott said. "You used her for your own ends and tried to make her your scapegoat. And then you tried to have her killed to protect yourself when you discovered that she tried to call off the mission."

The general's lack of response and his obvious lack of remorse infuriated Scott. Clearly, Natalie, like the rest of them, were just disposable pawns in the crazed bastard's efforts to avenge the death of his son and force the US into a war with Russia.

Colt looked at Scott. "I feel like I'm fucking watching *Dr. Strangelove.*"

SEALs on deployment watched a ton of movies, and among the long list of quotable favorites was the dark, satirical comedy by Stanley Kubrick. Scott knew exactly what Colt meant.

The general's dark fury directed at Colt suggested that he wasn't too far gone to understand the reference to the general in the movie who thought twenty million deaths were worth it to destroy the Soviets.

"I assure you, the Russian threat to the US is not a joke," Murray said. "They are far more dangerous than ISIS or a lone-wolf terrorist with a car or a bomb. Look what happened in the last election. That is only the beginning. They have the ability to destabilize not only our government with technology but our entire infrastructure with their close-to-operational antisatellite weapons. And this is in addition to the known military threat and the rumors of a secret doomsday project." So apparently Team Nine's mission hadn't been a complete ruse, Scott thought. "Someone needed to do something. What I did was for the good of the country."

Scott didn't disagree with the threat; he disagreed

with one man playing God and murdering people to achieve his ends. Murray could call it what he wanted, but slaughter wasn't sacrifice. It was betrayal, treason, and murder.

Disgusted, Scott picked up the general's phone and handed it to him. "Call them off."

"Who?"

"The men you have doing your dirty work," Colt said. "I recognized one of the CAD operatives you sent after Travis."

"Why should I do that?" Murray said, continuing his defiance.

"Because it's over, but it's up to you how it ends."

The general looked at him for a long moment, weighing his options. But it was clear he understood. Justice would be served, but whether that was in this room or in a courtroom would be his decision.

Murray picked up the phone and made the call. Whatever threat there was to Natalie, her parents, or the other survivors was over.

When Scott and Colt left the room a few minutes later, the general was slumped over the desk, a gun in his hand and a bullet through his temple. Ever the soldier, he'd fallen on his sword rather than face the public shame of what he'd done.

The end had been written and justice had been served. Nine men could finally rest in peace.

All that was left was to clear Natalie, and Scott had an idea about that.

EPILOGUE

Natalie had just finished cleaning the glass from the newly installed living room windows when she heard the car drive up.

With a cry of happiness, she tossed the rag into the bucket and ran— or waddled—down the new sturdy wooden porch stairs. The spray of bullets had torn up most of the front of the house, but thanks to help from Becky Randall and a good portion of the town selectmen (as well as an appearance or two from the sheriff), the house had been mostly repaired within a few days of Natalie's return to the farm in Vermont a few weeks ago.

As promised, Scott had taken her to Minnesota to visit her family right after the general's death. Scott hadn't been able to stay long as he'd had to return to Washington to contact command and deal with the political shit storm of five members of the Lost Platoon, as Brittany Blake had dubbed them, coming back from the dead.

As Natalie's fate for her role as an unwilling Russian agent was still uncertain, Scott thought it better that she stay in hiding until it was decided. To avoid the chance of someone recognizing Natalie Andersson, she'd stayed with her family for only a few days before returning to Vermont as Jennifer Wilson.

But her family would be coming for a visit soon, and she hoped to convince them to stay. She had a few propositions for them.

Scott had managed to get away for a few days at a time to visit her, but the debrief and damage control plan were both time-consuming and stressful. As Colt had predicted, Scott had spent a lot of time locked up in a little room going over every facet of what had happened.

But now he was here, and she was in his arms before the car door had slammed shut.

He spun her around, kissed her, and then put her down to look at her as if memorizing every inch.

She smiled a little self-consciously as he put his hand on her stomach. "You look so different."

She laughed and rolled her eyes. "You mean I look pregnant."

He looked crushed by the changes. "I've been gone too long."

It had been only about ten days since he'd been here but she'd "popped," as they called it. There was no hiding it now.

"You have," she agreed. "But you are here now, and believe me, I still have a long way to go. You have plenty of time to watch me get fat."

He frowned. "You aren't fat; you're pregnant."

Unfortunately right now it felt the same. But she was too happy to argue with him. "Why didn't you tell me you were coming?"

"I wanted it to be a surprise."

Very aware of her appearance, she made a face

"Don't you know women don't like to be surprised? Especially when they've been in the sun all day working outside."

"You look gorgeous."

He swung her up in his arms, carried her inside, and proved it on the living room couch. As she'd yet to put up the new shutters on the windows, they were fortunate that no one stopped by unexpectedly—they certainly would have gotten an eyeful.

Scott had insisted on stripping every last piece of clothing off them both before settling her on his lap and letting her sink down on him inch by inch.

He pinched her nipples and cupped her breasts as she rode him. Sliding up and down that thick slab, until she drove them both to the peak. Right when he started to come he brought her down hard and ground his body against hers until she shattered in a chorus of gasps and cries.

Still collapsed on his lap, she recovered enough to pull back and look at him. He'd shaved and cut most of the brown dye out of his hair, looking more like her clean-cut officer. But there was still an edge to him that hadn't been there before.

He'd loosened up a little. He was still by the book and held those around him to a high bar, but he wasn't quite so rigid and uncompromising as before. She didn't know whether it was her, his biological father, or that he wasn't trying as hard to prove himself worthy of the name of the man who'd raised him. Maybe it was a combination of all three as well as what he'd been through with the team. Betrayal on all its levels had fundamentally changed him.

"I didn't realize you were such an exhibitionist," she said with a glance to the window.

"I'm not," he said with a smirk. "I told Brouchard to make sure we weren't disturbed."

Her eyes narrowed. "You mean the sheriff you've been having keep an eye on me?"

He didn't bother denying it. "Yep."

"I don't understand. I thought you didn't like each other."

"We came to a little understanding."

"What kind of understanding?"

"The kind where I won't kill him, and he won't ask you to dinner again."

She rolled her eyes. "He doesn't strike me as the back-down type."

Scott smiled, caught. "He's not. I think it had more to do with your friend."

"Becky?"

He nodded. "As much as I hate to admit you were right, it was just friendly interest in you on his part. Apparently there's been something going on with him and Rebecca for a long time."

Natalie wasn't surprised. She'd have to get the whole story out of Becky the next time she saw her.

"So if you are here, does that mean . . . ?"

He nodded, lifted her chin, and planted a soft, tender kiss on her lips. "It's done. It's over."

Her eyes searched his face as if not trusting herself to believe it. "All of it?"

"All of it. For the good of the country and to avoid war, what happened in Russia is going to stay buried for now—as is the general's role in it."

Natalie had figured as much. In the press, General Murray's death by suicide had been blamed on grief over the death of his son, which she supposed in a way was true.

When the four men had returned from General Murray's house to tell her and Kate that he was dead, Natalie knew she wasn't the only one wondering whether the "suicide" was by the general's hand. But Scott said they'd given him a choice and the general had done his part.

"And . . . ?" she said anxiously, wanting to shake him for making her wait.

His eyes twinkled. "And your role has also been buried. The president agreed that you'd suffered enough, and when it came down to it, nothing would be served by putting you in prison. It helped that you had tried to call off the mission and ended up saving six men."

Natalie didn't realize how worried she'd been—despite Scott's assurances—until that moment. She burst out crying.

Scott chuckled as he repositioned her on his lap—still naked—and bundled her in his arms.

When she had exhausted her tears of relief, she looked into his amused gaze and blinked back watery eyes. "You shouldn't be laughing at me."

He was unrepentant, and the look he shot her was a little smug. "You should have trusted me more. I told you it would be all right. Looks like you might be able to have that farm and cheese business after all."

She smiled, biting her lip. Now probably wasn't the time to tell him that she had some ideas about that. He hadn't been the only one busy the past few weeks. She and Becky had come up with an idea on how to fend off the developers, and it involved Scott. Or rather, some of those millions he had put in trust when his father died. "Have you ever heard of land conservation?"

He looked momentarily confused by the non sequitur. But he caught on quickly enough. "A little, but why do I think I'm going to be hearing a lot about it, and that it's going to cost me?"

She beamed. He was no dummy. "You never did get me a new watch. Maybe we can come up with some kind of deal."

He waggled his brows, and she swatted him. *Ouch. Blasted muscles!*

"Not that kind of deal. I can't believe you are trying to negotiate with sex."

He sighed. "I have a feeling there is going to be very little negotiating involved. You already have the *take the ball and run with it* look." He glanced down at the Yankees sweatshirt that was still on the ground. "Which reminds me. I need to get you a new shirt."

Natalie just didn't get the whole Red Sox–Yankees rivalry thing. It was just a *game*. "This one is just fine. Besides, it was Jennifer's, and it reminds me of her."

He swore, apparently realizing he was going to lose that one.

Suddenly the ramifications of what he'd said earlier came to her. "What about you and the team? If this stays buried does that mean you won't be a SEAL anymore?"

She would blame herself forever if he had to stop doing what he loved.

"Not exactly. I've been offered a new position."

"You have?" *Thank God!* "That's wonderful."

He looked at her uncertainly. "I hope you still think so when you hear it. The president figured that being dead is pretty much the best deep cover you can have, and she wants Retiarius to go completely black. I would be in charge of a new SEAL squad composed initially of the survivors and a few others handpicked by me, who will only be known by a handful of senior officers. We'll report directly to the president."

Even though he was trying to hide it, she could see right away that he wanted to do it. "It sounds like an incredible opportunity. Of course you are going to accept."

He looked at her intently. "Are you sure? It's going to make things more difficult for you here. You'll have to lie—or at least not tell the complete truth—to a lot of people."

She winced a little. "Can I tell Brock and Becky?"

He smiled at her expression and kissed her on her wrinkled nose. "We'll talk about it."

"What about Colt? Will he be a part of it?"

Scott shook his head. "Not right now. Colt is taking some time off to spend some time with Kate and the baby."

"Did you say *'baby'*?"

He grinned at her expression. "Yes, baby. Apparently Colt had the idea when they visited Travis's girlfriend in the hospital. She planned to give the baby up for adoption, but Colt convinced her to do a private adoption. She liked the idea that one of Travis's friends would be raising the baby and agreed." She could tell that Scott liked the idea, too. Travis's death had been hard on him. "They brought the baby home yesterday. I would have come yesterday, but I wanted to stick around and meet my new nephew." Scott beamed, but then practically snickered. "You should see Colt with him. He's ridiculous. I've never seen someone so nervous in my life. He didn't want to put JR in the car to drive him home because he was worried some lunatic would crash into them."

Natalie laughed along with him but didn't have the heart to tell him that he'd probably be the same way. He'd figure it out soon enough. "JR? They named him after Colt?"

Scott shook his head. "James Robert. They named him after Travis."

It took her a minute to put it together. "Jim Bob?"

Scott nodded. The shadow that passed over his face wasn't quite as sad anymore. She suspected that knowing Travis's son was now in the family forever helped.

"I'm looking forward to Kate and Colt meeting their niece in a few months," she said.

"Me, too," he said, with another hand on her stomach that warmed her instantly. It took him a minute. "Wait! A niece? We're having a girl?"

She nodded, laughing at his reaction. "Yes, I found out last week at my checkup. I wanted to wait to tell you in person. The doctor also gave me this if you are curious." She handed him an envelope. "It's the test results. I don't want you to ever wonder."

He took the envelope and ripped it into shreds. "I won't. I don't. I never really did. I feel like an asshole for even suggesting it."

She traced her finger along his tight mouth, seeing how angry he was with himself. "Don't. You had every reason not to trust me at the time. I'm sorry for lying to you. I'm sorry for all of it."

Scott kissed her, and their current state of clothing made it easy to take up again where they'd just left off. This time, he made love to her slowly and sweetly. With every stroke, she felt the promise of her new life. Her new future.

She knew with Scott she might never have the "boring" life she thought she wanted, but he'd always keep her safe.

And maybe a little excitement wouldn't be so bad.

She was lying down beside him on the couch curled up in his arms when he reached down to retrieve something from the pocket of his jeans. "I almost forgot the most important thing."

"What's that?" she said lazily. In truth, she was so wonderfully exhausted she could barely lift her head to look at him.

"As far as we know the Russians still think you are dead, and if we are going to keep it that way, you are going to have to change your name to make sure no one ever connects you to Jennifer Wilson."

He sank down onto one knee next to the couch.

That brought her up quickly. She dragged the afghan that she'd pulled down on them with her as she sat up.

Her heart stopped when he held out a ring. Not just any ring, but an enormous *diamond* ring.

"How about Jennifer Taylor?" he asked huskily.

She looked back and forth between him and the ring in wonder—and not because the gorgeous monstrosity had to be at least ten carats. She was so overwhelmed, so happy, she didn't know what to say.

"Will you marry me, Natalie? I should have asked you before I left for Russia."

Her heart seemed to have stopped beating and was lodged in her throat. "Are you sure?"

"I've been sure for a long time. I carried this with me the entire time on the mission. It brought me luck. It brought me back to you."

She hurried up and nodded before he could take it back. "Yes, yes, I'll marry you!"

"Thank God," he said, dragging her into his embrace again. "I thought I might have to bring out the big guns to persuade you."

Her brows drew together in question.

"Your parents. I asked your father's permission a few weeks ago—which I'm not sure he would have been inclined to give if I hadn't mentioned the baby."

Natalie laughed. Her father had given Scott a hard time. Her father liked Scott, but he didn't seem to realize that. Natalie had been amused by the whole thing. She'd never seen Scott uncertain before.

"And I think your mom and sister have already been planning the wedding. Your mom was disappointed that she wouldn't be able to tell any of your friends—with you being dead and all—but she seemed excited to hear that the senator had offered to hold it at his estate."

Natalie suddenly understood the expression about feeling as if you'd been hit by a freight train. She couldn't believe he'd done all of that without her knowing. "Wow, you've been busy."

"I wasn't taking any chances. It pays to be a winner."

She laughed at the use of the favorite SEAL saying, looking forward to the next seventy years or so of Mr. Take Charge SEAL Commander realizing that she played to win, too.

Annie Henderson definitely wasn't in Kansas anymore. Or Louisiana, for that matter. Edge of the world was more like it.

Seated in the guest house pub (or more accurately, the pub with a few rooms above it) in the small seaport village on the Isle of Lewis—at least she thought it was the Isle of Lewis, but it could be Harris, as the two islands were apparently connected—after three flights, including a harrowing, white-knuckled forty-five-minute ride from hell in a plane not much larger than a bathtub, Annie was feeling a long way from home and distinctly out of her comfort zone.

But that was good, right? Doing something important and making a difference couldn't be done from her living room couch by getting upset with what she saw on TV. She had to get out there. *Do* something.

"It will be an adventure," her boyfriend, Julien, ha
assured her. *"Don't you want to help? Do you want t
see more dead dolphins and seabirds covered in oil?"*

The memories brought her up sharp. Of course sh
didn't. What she'd seen on the Louisiana shoreline afte
the BP oil disaster had moved her so deeply it ha
changed her life. The wide-eyed Tulane freshman wh
thought she wanted to be a veterinarian had switched he
major to environmental science, and after graduatin
pursued a PhD in marine ecology. When Annie hadn
been studying, most of her free time was devoted to th
ongoing cleanup effort and the attempt to return the loca
habitat to its natural state.

She never wanted to see anything like that happe
again. Which was why she was here. Although initiall
when Julien and his friends announced plans to go t
Scotland to join a protest against North Sea Offshor
Drilling's exploratory drilling west of the Scottish Heb
rides, Annie had refused. Activism wasn't new to her, bu
it wasn't like her to follow a man she'd known only
short time four thousand miles away from home to
place she'd never heard of before.

But after Julien had shown her pictures of the white
sand beaches of Eriskay, the rocky promontories an
seashores of Lewis, and the giant granite rock outpost
in the open waters of the North Atlantic such as Rocka
and Stac Lee near St Kilda that served as nesting place
for fulmars, gannets, and other seabirds, she knew sh
wouldn't be able to enjoy the vacation she'd planned t
visit her mother in Key West. So she'd thrown caution t
the wind and joined her new boyfriend and his friends

Just because so far her "adventure" wasn't exactl
what she'd expected didn't mean she should overreac
She hadn't made a mistake in coming. So what if she fe
a little bit like Dorothy wondering how the heck she'
gotten here? Scotland wasn't Oz and Jean Paul La Roch

wasn't the Wicked Witch of the West—even if right now they both kind of seemed that way.

She supposed she couldn't really blame the Islanders for not holding out the welcome mat to the activists who'd descended en masse to the remote island. Oil brought jobs, and the Islanders considered the drilling a local matter. The activists were outsiders—who were they to interfere? But Annie hadn't expected to feel quite so . . . *conspicuous.* Which was a nicer way of saying "pariah." Her group stuck out even in the height of the summer tourist season. The dour, unsmiling locals had turned to stare at them as they entered the bar, and although they'd eventually turned away, it still felt as if their eyes were on her.

But it wasn't just the locals. The man whom Julien had been so excited for her to meet, his mentor, and the person he spoke of with such reverence she'd half expected the pope to walk in, had been a shock. She didn't know Jean Paul well enough to dislike him, but her first impression of a weasel or a ferret hadn't improved any in the two hours since they were introduced. "Bad vibe" was an understatement.

She also didn't like how he was staring at her. It was as if he was sizing her up for something. Coldly. Mercenarily. In a way that a pimp might size up a prostitute.

It made her uneasy. *He* made her uneasy.

Julien Bernard, the French graduate student who'd swept her off her feet when she met him two months ago, seemed to have picked up on his former teacher's disapproval as well. He seemed to be trying to "sell" her to Jean Paul by singing her praises. If he mentioned her "brilliant" PhD dissertation—which was the last thing she wanted to talk about after just defending it—one more time . . .

On cue, Julien said, "Did Annie tell you about her research—"

Annie looked around for a distraction—any

distraction—and her eye caught on the headline of
newspaper left behind by the prior occupants of th
wooden booth. "Look at this," she said, holding it up an
cutting him off. "The story has made it across the pond.
Did people still say that? She started to read from th
article. "The Lost Platoon. Like Rome's famous los
Ninth Legion, the secret SEAL Team Nine has disap
peared into thin air." Annie put the paper back down o
the table. Allegedly the navy didn't have a SEAL Tear
Nine, although suspiciously they acknowledged the ex
istence of every other number from one to ten. "I wonde
what happened to them."

"Who cares?" Julien said. He gave her that charmin
and oh-so-French shrug and raising of the brows tha
made him look even more like his countryman, the acto
Olivier Martinez. She'd always thought Halle Berry's e
was incredibly sexy and could admit that that might hav
been what initially had caught her eye at the fund-raise
a couple of months ago. But it had been their shared pas
sion for the environment and horror at the devastatio
wrought on the Louisiana coastline after the disaster tha
forged the real bond between them.

"You shouldn't read that trash, *ma belle*. It's all lie
and gossip."

At least it was entertaining. Which was more than sh
could say about the independent newspapers and politi
cal publications that he and his friends devoured. Anni
did enough scholarly reading for her research; she didn'
need it for her pleasure reading, too.

Although Julien's European charm and modern-da
beatnik intellectualism were what had drawn her t
him—she'd never met anyone who seemed to know s
much about everything—he could definitely be a cultura
snob sometimes.

She couldn't help teasing him a little. "I don't know."
She flipped the paper back to the front. "The *Scottis*

Daily News looks pretty good to me. And they have lots
of pictures that make it so much easier to follow along."

Only Julien realized she wasn't serious. The others at
the table looked alternatively appalled and embarrassed—
except for Jean Paul. He looked . . . *wicked*.

"I'll get you, my pretty, and your little dog, too!"

Maybe if she tried imagining him with a green face
and a pointy hat—he already had the long nose and
beady eyes—she would stop thinking about far more ne-
farious bad guys from Mafia and cartel movies.

No luck. At least a handful of years older than the rest
of them, who were all in their mid-twenties, Jean Paul
looked like a villain right out of a mob movie, even down
to the slicked-back hair, mole, leather jacket, and gold
chains.

Men shouldn't wear bracelets. It should be a rule.

As for the others at the booth, she didn't really know
any of them that well. She'd met Marie, Claude, and Ser-
gio at Julien's apartment in New Orleans many times
before they'd all traveled to Scotland together, but they'd
never really welcomed her into their cabal. They weren't
rude or unfriendly, just not inclusive. She took it to be a
foreign thing, as they were all international graduate students like Julien, who was also a teaching fellow at the
University of New Orleans.

Despite her eight years at Tulane, she hadn't held that
against him for too long.

Julien smiled and shook his head, reaching for her
hand to bring it to his mouth. "Forgive me. I was being
a little condescending, wasn't I?"

She gave him a look that said, *You think?*

He laughed and picked up the paper. "Very well. We
will discuss these missing soldiers."

"SEALs," she corrected, and then explained at his
befuddled expression. "Soldiers are army. In the navy it's
sailor, but SEALs are their own breed."

"Well, with any luck your SEALs are at the bottom o the ocean somewhere."

Annie knew that Julien had strong feelings about th US military—some of which she shared—but it wasn like him to be so bloodthirsty. She frowned, noticing hir sharing a look with Jean Paul. Was that it? Was he tryin to impress the other man?

"Don't you think that's a little harsh?" she asked hir

Julien would have responded, but Jean Paul spok first. "Harsh? I'd say it's justice. SEALs are nothing mor than hired killers. Just because the government is the employer does not excuse what they do." He gave her pitying look—as if she were either the most naive woma in the world or the most stupid. "Do not tell me you ap prove of their methods or the shadow wars that the fight? I thought Julien said you went with him to the re cent rally to protest military action in Russia after you fighter pilots were caught spying."

Allegedly spying. Although the "accidentally strayin off course" excuse had sounded a little suspect to her a well. The incident had nearly caused war to break ou between America and Russia—the situation was sti precarious. It was a game of nuclear jeopardy with th two players ready to pounce on the button.

"She did," Julien said, immediately jumping to he defense.

Though she knew the impulse had been well intentioned, she didn't need Julien or anyone else t speak for her. She wasn't going to let his friend intim date her. As she didn't have a bucket of water—th thought made one side of her mouth curve—she looke Jean Paul right in his mobster hit man eyes. "Just becaus I do not want to see us embroiled in another war does no mean I want to see innocent men killed."

Jean Paul smiled with so much condescension she wa

mazed he wasn't choking on it. Or maybe that was just er wishful thinking.

"I assure you that if there is any truth to that reporter's tory, those men are not innocent. What do you think hey were doing when they 'disappeared'? If it was le-itimate, why would your government keep silent? Per-aps they do not acknowledge these men because doing o would expose their illegal activity?"

He had a point, but that didn't mean that American ervicemen should be the ones to pay the price for the overnment's failures. "I do not like the shadow wars be-ng fought by our Special Forces in many of the hot spots round the world any more than you do, but that's because don't want to see any more of our servicemen who think hey are doing the right thing and are only following or-ers killed or destroyed by war and a government that has urned them into highly skilled machines who can't adjust o real life when they return. The psychological toll it akes on them is horrible. War is all these men know how o do. Special Forces like SEALs only have it worse."

She didn't realize how passionately—and loudly—she vas speaking until she finished and realized that more han just the people at her booth were staring at her.

So much for avoiding the "Loud American" cliché.

She felt the heat of a blush stain her cheeks. Pushing he painful memories of her father away, she filled the ncomfortable silence with a jest. "Anyway, who knows? Iaybe Geraldo will have a TV special and get to the ottom of it."

Unfortunately she forgot that her audience was too oung and not American, and her attempt at humor was otally lost in translation.

Her ever-gallant boyfriend tried to help her out. "Ger-ldo?" He picked up the paper. "But I believe the re-orter's name is Brittany Blake."

She shook her head, deciding it wasn't worth explaining the overly hyped TV special on the "secret" vaults of Al Capone that were opened live and contained only a couple of empty bottles. Her father used to joke about it

In the days when he knew how to laugh.

"It was a bad joke about conspiracy theories," she said. "Forget it."

"Ah!" He laughed belatedly.

"You speak very passionately on the subject," Jean Paul said perceptively.

Oddly he seemed to approve. Not that she cared. Although for Julien's sake she wished she could like his friend. But she didn't. She'd felt as if a black cloud had descended over them since he arrived.

In response Annie gave a Gallic shrug that a Frenchspeaking Belgian such as Jean Paul should understand It was none of his business. "If you'll excuse me, I think I will find the ladies' room."

Making a quick escape, she heard Julien explain behind her, "WC."

She'd forgotten that Jean Paul hadn't spent much time in America. She'd learned from Julien that "bathroom" and "ladies' room" didn't translate well in Europe.

For a Tuesday night the pub was packed, and Annie had to "excuse me" her way through the crowd of men in front of the bar—there were very few women—as she made her way to the "toilet." Given the number of locals she assumed it was a favorite hangout. Although from what she'd seen of the town, the Harbour (with a *u*) Bar & Guest House probably didn't have a lot of competition

She had nearly made it past the long, glossy wooden bar lined with taps of ales and ciders, when the door that she'd been about to go through opened, and she had to step back to avoid being hit. Unfortunately she stumbled over someone's foot and knocked into—nearly onto—a man who was seated at the end of the bar.

Instinctively she reached out to catch herself before she fell on his lap. One of her hands found his leg, and the other . . .

Wasn't gripping rock-hard muscle.

"Oof." The grunt he made gave the location away. Even through the denim of his jeans, she could feel the unmistakable solid bulge of something else. She pulled her hand back as if it—he—were on fire.

Or maybe that was just her. Her cheeks flamed with mortified heat as she hurried to apologize. "I'm so sorry! I tripped and didn't see . . ."

The man looked up from his hunched position over his beer, and the cold, steely blue eyes that met hers from beneath the edge of his faded blue cap cut off her breath like a sharp icy wind.

Her first thought was how the hell had she missed him? Her second was *What did I do?*

He was a big guy. Tall—even with him seated on a stool, she still had to look up to meet his gaze—and broad-shouldered, he wore an oversized sweatshirt and puffy down vest that, had she not felt the evidence to the contrary, she might have thought hid a little extra bulk. But that bulk wasn't fat; it was all muscle.

The guy was built like a tank. Or maybe a prize-fighter. Beneath the heavy beard—what was with those anyway?—the face that met hers had the tough, pugnacious masculinity of a Tom Hardy or Channing Tatum. Sexy as hell, but maybe a little too much to handle.

She liked men a little softer. And there was nothing soft about this guy. Not just his body, but the way he was looking at her. It might be the middle of summer, but the iciness emitting from those striking blue eyes made it feel like the dark days of December.

Shiver. She managed not to do that, instead giving him a friendly smile. "I'm sorry again. I hope I didn't hurt you."

Which hardly seemed possible, as he was about twic her size.

She expected an immediate denial, a few assurance that it was nothing, and maybe even a return smile. Th was what would have happened in any bar in Americ In the South it would have been given with a lazy draw a charming twinkle, and no doubt a ma'am or darlin' c two. In New Orleans, it would be "cher" or, as it wa pronounced, "sha."

What she got was a shake of the head and a gru grunt that she assumed was meant to serve as his ac knowledgment, before he turned sharply around to hunc back over his beer.

She stood there for a moment, staring at the broa back, hunched shoulders, and straight—maybe a littl shaggy—dirty blond hair beneath the faded powder blu cap.

What in the world?

She shook her head at his rudeness. Maybe this wa Oz after all.

Ready to find
your next great read?

Let us help.

Visit prh.com/nextread